'I bend my knee be[...]
Egyptian said in a ri[...]
To learn all about yo[...]

'I am Zarah,' she [...]
means Eastern Brightness.

'Zarah!' he said easily, and nodded his head. 'A very pleasing name.' He rubbed his chin thoughtfully. 'Tell me, what is a pretty child like you doing here in the lord Ramose's camp?'

His eyes gave him away, for all his lips smiled. He was not questioning her out of courtesy; she knew that instinctively. He was some kind of spy and Ramose would not be pleased if he knew the man was here—yes, somehow she knew that, too. The need to survive was nudging at her brain. Even though this giant, god-like man half frightened her to death, she must act the part that had been set for her; she must!

She drew herself up as tall as possible and smiled, then said with quiet dignity, 'Lord, I am Zarah, Princess of Anshan.'

'I bow before you,' he said, and made the merest nod of his head. Was it the light, she wondered wildly, that was making his eyes twinkle so? Was this great rock of a man in fact laughing at her? 'Please,' he said as he took hold of her arm, 'make yourself comfortable. You may tell me all about Anshan, and of your father, the king of that land. Speak to me of all those things you love and have left. I want to know all about you. Yes, everything. . .'

Irene Roberts lives with her husband, well-known local artist, Trevor Roberts, in Malborough village, South Devon. She has two sons, one daughter, three cats and three dogs. After due consideration Irene believes that the three cats are the bosses of her home.

Irene Roberts has written over 100 novels under her own name and various pseudonyms. She has been featured on local television programmes and has often been a guest on Devon radio, BBC and Devonair. She is Founder Life President of Kingsbridge Writers and is Reviews Editor of the South Hams Newspaper group. *Kingdom of the Sun* is her second Masquerade Historical Romance.

KINGDOM OF THE SUN

BY

IRENE ROBERTS

MILLS & BOON LIMITED
15-16 BROOK'S MEWS
LONDON W1A DR

*First published in Great Britain 1987
by Mills & Boon Limited*

© Irene Roberts 1987

*Australian copyright 1987
Philippine copyright 1987
This edition 1987*

ISBN 0 263 75680 7

*Set in Monotype Times 10 on 10 pt.
04-0387-92930*

*Typeset in Great Britain by
Associated Publishing Services
Printed and bound in Great Britain by
Cox & Wyman Ltd, Reading*

PROLOGUE

Makare Hatshepsut, Great Queen of Egypt, reigned 1501-1480 BC

Hatshepsut reclined on her couch, smiling. She was good-looking and powerful, and she knew it.

'The king is dead!' she cried, 'and I am alive. Now I will reign supreme.'

'Impossible, Beloved,' her adviser warned. 'You must marry the boy.'

At this Hatshepsut laughed aloud and proceeded to go her own way. By the year 1490 the queen was still of the same mind. She had been married to her father, Thutmose I, and then to her brother Thutmose II, to safeguard the throne. She rejected her half-brother, Thutmose III. He had been born to Isis, who was not of royal blood. Contemptuous of him, the queen had herself declared Pharaoh of the Two Lands. Prince Thutmose, despite the existence of a powerful party asserting his rights, was kept waiting in the wings.

The queen surrounded herself with eminent men. Relations with Byblos flourished and once more timber from the land of Nega was stacked on the quay at Thebes. The turquoise mines of Sinai were reopened, and so it went on. Determinedly keeping to peaceful policies, Egypt became rich and ignored the enemies gathering at her borders.

One dignitary of the queen's entourage stood out: the Grand Steward, Royal Chancellor, Chief of Chiefs of Work, Senenmut. It was he who was responsible for the building of the queen's great temple, the 'Sublime of Sublimes' at Dier el-Bahri. On the walls of this mortuary building the story of Hatshepsut's 'divine' birth was recorded—and can still be seen today.

Prince Thutmose, whose reign began officially at the same time as the queen's, bore no love for her. Neither did he accept her right to reign supreme. So it was that the Theban court became the breeding-ground for treachery and intrigue. The struggle for power swept on, gathering momentum as the years went by. . .

CHAPTER ONE

A WISPY CLOUD drew a veil across the face of the dying moon. Suddenly a shriek cut the malevolent silence of Egypt's swampy lower Nile. As the night animal died a million Delta creatures set up a clamour of protest. The outcry subsided as quickly as it had been born.

There was an uneasy peace in the slave compound as the occupants slept. All except Zarah, the fourteen-year-old.

Zarah's long black hair made wings of shadow against the beauty of her face. Terrible pictures danced in her mind. Her sensitive lips trembled in an uncontrollable way. And all the agony in her soul and confusion in her heart gave way to a final, selflessly loving prayer.

'Let him die.' Her whisper choked on a sob. 'I pray that my beloved Harad has received the sweet mercy of death.'

Slowly the pink glow filtered in at the east and then, with a deep guttural resonance, the chorus from the temple priests welcomed the dawn. All around Zarah the sleeping figures began to move uneasily. Some of the dark shapes moaned. They were despairing and had no hope even in their dreams, wakefulness itself being the cruellest pain of the day. Unlike the rest, Zarah had known some affection. This even though she had been a slave for all of her years. Her young master, the only son of the magus Caiphus, had been captured while trying to save her, and Harad had suffered for his pains.

He had made his bid for freedom and failed. Again Zarah remembered the sneering cruelty on the face of Judas the slaver while the torture had been going on. But even more obscene had been the enjoyment burning on Neb the overseer's evil countenance.

'I hate them!' Zarah's mind rose high, her revulsion so great that it stung like pinpoints of fire in her brain. 'May

the gods give me strength. May they give me the power one
day to make them pay!'

She froze. Neb was approaching and shouting out orders.
The women around Zarah were awake at once, and trembling as they pulled themselves to their feet. They feared and
despised Neb, who was adept at inflicting cruelties where the
marks never showed.

He walked directly to Zarah, evil triumph on his face. Her
hate and terror made her want to scream. She remained mute
as, exquisite and fragile, she too took her place in line.

'So!' Neb said silkily. 'You are at last going to pay for your
keep. They think you are perfection. I find you obscene. How
you rate high above the rest in my master's mind I will never
know. Soon now you will be gone, and good riddance, I say.
I hope that the Egyptians give you to a lover of Bast the Cat.
Have you watched holy cats play with young rats before the
final kill? My master thinks that you are a pretty child. I think
that you belong with all the other vermin crawling about in
Egyptian grain.'

He reached out as though to touch her and she cowered
away. He laughed, softly and deep in his throat.

'You are trapped, just as the boy was trapped. Where is
the one you called Young Master now? Rotting in all the
hells, I expect, just as you will be one day. Now, pull yourself
up. Up, I say!'

He pulled her roughly into an upright position, his lips
drawn back in a smile of disgust.

'Push yourself out—hard! There are those who have a fix-
ation about breasts, and you have very little to show. There
will be a man arriving who has come expressly to look at
you. If he is not impressed, if he leaves without you and you
are left on the Lord Judas's hands, he will not be pleased.'
He paused malevolently, then added, 'And I think that by
now you will know what that means. Punishments here are
long and slow.'

The thought made Neb lick his thin lips and his saliva ran;
his small black eyes began to glow. If I live, Zarah thought
wildly, and if all the gods help me, I will return here one day.
I will kill Judas, and I will laugh as they die.

The shadows were showing that soon now the gates would
be opened and the people looking for new slaves would be

allowed in. Zarah was only dimly aware of Neb going to the next slave to take out his venom on her. She heard the silken cruelty in his voice, and the young, lovely, black girl gasp as spiteful hands reached out to her nakedness. Neb would be careful. It was more than his life was worth to damage goods owned by Judas, the merchant of slaves. But Neb was a master at the game.

Suddenly Judas's imperative command rang out from beyond the gates, which were opened by a servant who grovelled as his master walked by.

Neb's hand snapped away from between the slave girl's legs, and now his sadism was hidden behind a mask of cringing deference.

Fat, oily, dressed in fine robes, Judas ignored him. The slave merchant was openly rubbing his hands together as he walked beside a tall stately Egyptian.

The newcomer had a noble bearing. What he was thinking was hard to tell. His eyes were heavily outlined with black kohl. He wore a white linen apron over his loin-cloth and a nemset head-dress that flowed and was striped with blue. The wide round collar glittered with gold and was studded with red and blue stones. There were thick bands of gold round his wrists and arms. There were woven papyrus sandals on his feet. As they came towards Zarah, Judas was being as ingratiating as only he knew how.

'The girl is not yet a woman, my lord, but she is no longer a child. She holds a great beauty, but remains untouched.'

'And if I do not take her,' the Egyptian said with grim humour, 'and a buyer comes looking for a child wise in the ways of the sex-arts of the world, you will swear this same slave has experienced it all.'

Judas clasped his hands against his heart and exclaimed, 'Call the priests of the temple and let them examine her if you doubt my word.'

'I know you too well, Judas, to do such a thing. Besides, your faith is not mine. Priests are priests the world over, greedy to placate their gods, and greedy for gold. Take me to the girl-woman whose beauty is, according to you, beyond price.'

They had now reached Zarah, who, in spite of Neb's orders, cowered away, keeping her head low as she stared, in mortal fear, down at her small feet. The Egyptian's hand went under her chin until he was able to get a clear view of the fragile loveliness of her face. With gentle care he opened her mouth in order to look at her teeth.

'Like pearls, my lord,' Judas said quickly. 'Her teeth are like evenly matched pearls.'

The Egyptian ignored him as he continued to concentrate on the matter at hand. His hands roved over Zarah's flanks, her breasts, and ran down the length of her spine. He was dispassionate, needing to be sure that she was as perfect as the first brief inspection made her out to be.

'She will do,' he said at last, and without haggling, handed Judas a bulging leather bag which contained a collection of rubies so magnificent that they could not be bettered anywhere in the world. 'And remember, there is to be no word of this transaction. If you speak, I promise you that you will lose your life.'

'My valued, most beloved friend,' Judas gabbled. 'My word is my bond. It has to be. How else could I survive?'

'You live because you know too many secrets and men pay you to keep quiet. They are afraid of you, Judas. I am not. If you value your fat hide, you will forget all about the transaction carried out on this day.'

'My mind is blank,' Judas said earnestly, and his fat fingers clutched at the leather bag. 'May God shower many blessings upon your proud and noble head.'

'I do not need the blessing of your god,' the Egyptian said crisply. 'But I do need the good graces of a very great queen. I was told by She Whose Word is Law to search to the ends of the earth for the most beautiful child. I only hope that this girl will be considered lovely enough.'

'She is—'

'—no longer your business.' The Egyptian cut Judas short. 'Have her sent to my caravan. I want no further delay.'

'I hate them all!' The words swung wildly in Zarah's mind. 'They are all big and strong, but so shall I be one day, and when that happens I will cry out the name of Harad, and I will have my revenge.'

Zarah was relieved and strangely comforted to learn that Thickneck as well as herself, had been bought by the Egyptian. It was the giant eunuch's task to look after and guard her at all times. It was Thickneck who was told where they must go.

He led her swiftly away from the slave compound and the temple area. They reached an open space where the sun had baked the marsh ground hard. Here there were camels, oxen, asses, large tents and many people all milling about. The caravan was scheduled to leave at dawn next day, and there was a great deal to do.

Numb with shock, grief and fear, Zarah stayed as near to Thickneck as she could. All of the movement and confusion around her seemed to belong to another time, another place. The only reality was that Harad was dead and that Caiphus, whom she had looked up to as God, had been unable to bring about a miracle and come to rescue his son.

Caiphus, the great and wise, had been as ignorant of the future as she. The stars had not warned him of danger, the sacred signs had left no message saying that Harad was not safe. If Caiphus of all people had been helpless against the will of Fate, she thought fiercely, then she cared less than nothing for the great man's predictions, and all his fine words. The men who paid many weights in gold for the wisdom of Caiphus—and believed what he said—were merely gullible fools. Stupid and not worth a second thought.

'I hate Caiphus!' The agonised cry singed into her little-girl thoughts. 'I hate him because he turned out to be the most treacherous of all! He knows nothing. His gods are nothing. I live in hell everlasting and there is no such place as the Kingdom of the Sun.'

'Do not cry,' Thickneck said. His voice was a hoarse whisper, but not unkind. She looked up and found that he was staring down at her. His scar was standing out, making him look more ferocious than ever. Zarah was too numb to care. Suddenly his ugly black face creased into a grin as he swept her high in his arms. 'We are gone from Judas,' he said. 'And for that mercy at least, we must rejoice.'

'I am rejoicing,' she wept obediently. 'I am obeying. See? I—I rejoice!'

If anything, his arm tightened around her more protectively.

'You do not have to obey me, Morning Light. I have no authority over you. We are both owned by the Egyptian and we must do as we are told.'

She clung to him desperately and cried out in fear when a tall, lovely Egyptian woman came and ordered her to go to the near-by women's tent. Startled at this show of terror, thin painted eyebrows raised in consternation.

Thickneck explained. 'She has suffered too much. She is afraid. She has seen someone she loved tortured and killed.'

'There is no need for her to fear the Great Ramose. His brother Ahmose, perhaps,' the lady said carefully, 'but our lord and master has a heart that is kind.'

'We know nothing of this Ramose,' Thickneck replied. 'The ways of Egypt are unknown to us, and your lord master could be the devil from hell.'

'He is fair and he is kind. His word is law since he is the mouthpiece of our great queen. In her name, he desires this girl to be made to look even more beautiful.'

'She is too young. . .'

'To look beautiful?' The black-painted eyes widened innocently. Thickneck had no option. He had to let Zarah go.

'He will wait for you here,' the woman said to Zarah. 'Is Morning Light your name?'

'Eastern Brightness is what I am truly called. Zarah is my name.'

'I see. Well, there is no difference. No difference at all. Come, child, we are aching to make a great fuss over you.'

Still dazed and barely comprehending, Zarah followed the woman into the luxuriously appointed tent.

'Sit down, Morning Light,' the woman ordered, and indicated a beautifully woven folding stool. 'Let me see what can be done with you.' She smiled then, and pushed Zarah down. 'Do not be afraid. I am Bentresht, First Wife of Ramose. He is a wise and kind man. If you obey him, your life in his household will be exceedingly sweet. Of course, if you do not. . .'

Since Zarah was incapable of replying, Bentresht asked, 'Do you speak Egyptian? I am told that you were Persian born.'

'I—I speak Egyptian a little,' Zarah breathed. 'I know that your name means Daughter of Joy.'

Bentresht laughed, and the sound was neither musical nor warm.

'Good! Very good! And, now, let us see what we can do about you. You must look like us, and yet be different—in a Persian kind of way. Let me see. . .'

Zarah sat still while Bentresht set down a box which held many small pots. These contained kohl with which to paint the eyes, and red ochre colouring for the lips and cheeks. There were scented oil-cones to set on one's hair. These melted in the heat and sent out wave after wave of sweet perfume. There was henna, used to stain hands and nails. There were ivory combs and many jewels.

Bentresht clapped her hands, and a group of pretty young women came in, laughing and giggling. They were all friendly and alive.

'This is Zarah,' Bentresht told them. 'She is a little princess from the kingdom of Persia, and she was going to the Great House to see She Whose Word is Law. But robbers fell upon her entourage and now we must help her. She will stay with us until she has overcome her distress at such a terrible ordeal.'

There were soft cries of sympathy and eager hands reached out in friendship to the young and frightened girl.

A long time later Zarah stood mutely before Bentresht. The woman looked her over very carefully, then said, 'You are beautiful, Zarah. So beautiful indeed that you almost take my breath away. But nothing on this earth is worth the rubies my husband gave.'

'Lady, I am a. . .'

'You are Princess Zarah,' Bentresht said firmly. 'Your man will verify the fact.'

'Thickneck?'

'He is your personal manservant and he will guard you with his life. You must give him a better and rather more imposing name.'

Too weary and confused to do anything other than accept Bentresht's words, Zarah allowed herself to be led away to a small tent set apart from the rest.

'This is your place,' Bentresht explained. 'And you have only to clap your hands to call those who will obey your slightest wish. Your man will be given clothes befitting his exalted position. Later on, my lord Ramose will send for you. I promise you, he will be well pleased.'

Ramose, He of the Hawk-like Face, sat on his carved chair and wondered for the thousandth time if he had made the right choice. The oil lamps flickered against the walls of the great main shelter, sending shadows leaping over the tightly woven walls. Ramose waited and felt his unease grow.

It was an eerie, whispering night, dark and moonless. Great glistening stars hung in the sky of deep purple and blue. Fireflies flashed and sparkled in the tamarinds. Ramose's face was drawn as he gazed out. Tomorrow would be the beginning of the journey home. At the end, he would be the man that the Great Royal Wife, Queen Hatshepsut, either loved or hated. He prayed to Amun that he had used his judgment wisely and well. He had many enemies at court, perhaps the greatest of them all being his own brother Ahmose, who was loyal above all to the young prince Thutmose III.

The faint whispering music of golden bells made him stiffen. He sat still, staring at the girl-woman coming slowly towards him. Behind her, the massive figure of Thickneck, who was now resplendent in a leopardskin. He had also been given a wide gold headband which kept an ostrich feather in place against his curly black hair. As Ramose's eyes returned once more to the small figure coming so uncertainly towards him, Queen Hatshepsut's voice rang in his ears.

'Find me a beautiful child—one that will take his breath away.'

It was a floating, misty, little creature that was now drifting towards him in a cloud of blue and gold. She wore Persian dress and a gauzy veil that foamed and billowed round her like the Holy Nile, yet it barely hid the outline of her delicate limbs. Circling the slim waist and coiled round the slender body, with its gold head resting just above her heart, was a huge golden peacock. Its opened tail, studded with coloured stones, cascaded round the back and to the hem of her filmy covering. Her Persian headband was hung with tiny gold bells. There were more gold bells round her wrists and ankles. Her fingers with their red-painted nails were heavy with gold rings set with turquiose and stones of deep green.

A haunted, wistful face, with eyes that seemed too large, gleamed like a pale night lily from under the bells. As Ramose gazed at her, he had the feeling that Zarah might slip away and become lost in the mist she so resembled. He felt a keen sympathy for the man who had brought her up. A magus, so Judas said, who had sold her because in a very few years she would no longer be a child. The magus, according to Judas, was not allowed to surround himself with women, least of all with such a very beautiful little wisp of life.

Ramose knew very well that Judas had lied. The child had probably been stolen, and so there must be a demented wise man wandering alone in the world. But the magus's loss was his gain. Amun had been merciful and this girl-woman was beautiful indeed.

'You are to be taken to my house, Zarah,' he told her. 'And there you will rest and be prepared in order to be presented to Egypt's greatest queen.'

She continued to stand obediently before him, her gaze now on the ground. Her slim form was trembling and sent a fresh wave of whispering from the small bells.

'You must know,' Ramose went on, 'that from this day you belong to no less a person than Hatshepsut, Queen of the Nile. It is her plan to give you to a young prince. Once in his house you will look listen and learn. At the time of each full moon, you will return to the Great House and answer to Hatshepsut, the One Whose Word is Law. Do I make myself clear?'

Zarah stared down at her feet, silent still.

'The prince has a great friend whom he loves as a brother,' Ramose continued. 'Per Ibsen is his name. You will become dear to Per Ibsen should Prince Thutmose not look your way. Perhaps it will be through the friend that you will reach the prince's heart. Either way, you must be like a finely tuned harp, ready to make divine music whenever you are played. Do you know what a man expects of you? Have you been entered by a man, or is your body still whole?'

'My master, Harad, he. . .'

'Just so! Remember all that he taught you, whether he gave you pleasure or not.' The deep voice became less authoritative and more understanding. 'You are young to have been taken by your master, and it must have been worse to go through Judas's hands. His treatment must have left scars on your soul. However, that is over, done with. From this day you are Zarah of Anshan, a Persian princess.'

He clapped his hands, and a servant wearing a short white skirt and a heavy gold necklace appeared.

'Go to the beloved First Wife of my House with this message,' he said. 'Tell her that Ramose is well pleased.'

He turned back to Zarah and his dark eyes, so heavily outlined with black paint, were twinkling a little now.

'Child,' he said, 'if you are careful and clever you can go far. There is a great deal of jostling for power and position in Pharaoh's Great House, but you are essential to My Majesty's plan.' A thought struck him, and the twinkling grew more pronounced. 'I am told that you were brought up by one of the magi. Is this so?'

'Yes,' she whispered. 'Caiphus is his name. He is. . .'

'Then try and remember all the tricks of his trade. My Majesty is a one for magic, predictions and messages from the stars. Above all, she is religious and gives gold in abundance to please our god Amun.' He laughed softly at a joke known only to himself, then he looked at Zarah again. 'Go now and remember all that I have told you. Do well, and your future is assured. Disobey or displease and back to Judas you will go.'

Terrified of the threat, Zarah all but melted away, then almost sobbed with relief to see that Thickneck was still patiently waiting for her.

'Come,' he said. 'We are now of some importance, it seems.'

As they neared her tent, she saw what he meant. Soldiers guarded her tent area, some of them holding reed torches high. Her heart sank. So she was still a prisoner, for all their fine words. Not a princess, a slave! She glanced sideways to see the expression on Thickneck's face. It looked wary, even cruel. He was like a giant bear looking for a way of escape.

But he was as much a slave as she and there was nothing that they could do.

A group of guards were laughing and joking together and making great play of passing a gourd full of wine to and fro. They were blocking the view of Zarah's tent and so it came as a sense of shock, when she had passed them, to see yet another Egyptian nobleman waiting there. He was a young man and stood proud and tall. His muscles rippled under his oiled skin. He was good-looking. His hair was shoulder length, natural and not a wig. It was cut in a fringe above strong geometrically arched brows. His dark eyes were very dramatic and outlined with malachite. He was clearly very rich, for his wide golden collar was studded with precious stones, as was the belt he wore tight round the waist of his knee-length white cloth. He wore thick bands of gold on his wrists and arms, and sandals of plaited leather. He was the most handsome and the most awe-inspiring man that Zarah had ever seen.

His eyes opened wide with surprise at Zarah's timid approach, then he bowed before her, a sweeping most courteous gesture spoiled because the ghost of a smile was twitching at the corners of his mouth.

'I bend my knee before your gracious beauty, Lady,' he said in a rich, deep voice. 'Am I to know you? To learn all about you? What is your name?'

'I am Zarah,' she whispered, 'which in your language means Eastern Brightness. My—My man prefers to call me Morning Light.' She was speaking without thinking, too breathlessly, too quickly. But everything that had happened to her made her feel drained. She was feeling strangely empty and numb.

'Zarah!' he said easily, and nodded his head. 'A very pleasing name.' He rubbed his chin thoughtfully. 'Tell me, what is a pretty child like you doing here in the lord Ramose's camp?'

His eyes gave him away, for all his lips smiled. He was not questioning her out of courtesy; she knew that instinctively. He was some kind of spy and Ramose would not be pleased if he knew the man was here—yes, somehow she knew that, too. The need to survive was nudging at her brain. Even

though this giant, god-like man half frightened her to death,
she must act the part that had been set for her; she must! She
took in a deep breath and tried to smile bravely up into the
face that looked almost golden in the glow from the flames.
But suddenly it was all too much to bear.

'I can't do it any more,' she heard herself whispering desperately. 'I can't! I can't!'

The Egyptian seemed lost in thought. If he noted the tear-
stained face and saw how one small hand clutching at the
filmy blue robe trembled, he said nothing. His silence was
awful, Zarah thought; truly terrible. The big man was like
one of those great statues hewn out of stone. Tall, grim-
looking things that had, in lamplight, a ghastly kind of still
life of their own. She could hear her heart beating and sensed
that the bustle of the camp was being muffled somehow by
strange and uncanny night noises. The man standing so
authoritatively before her was part of the night too, as cold
and as bleak, and as indomitable.

A tear coursed down Zarah's face and fell on her hand.
This small happening helped her to pull herself together, and
she straightened. Her face, so distraught before, now
assumed a placating expression.

'Forgive me,' she said breathlessly. 'I am ashamed. I was
feeling sorry for myself.' She smiled sadly. 'It is hard to be
sent away from one's home, even though there is great honour to be chosen to be my father's ambassador and be
presented at a great queen's court.'

'Oh?' His black eyes snapped sharply.

Zarah's hesitation vanished. She could almost sense
Thickneck's relief. She was doing well and playing the game
the way it should be. For Thickneck's sake as well as her own,
she must act out the charade. She drew herself up as tall as
possible and smiled, then said with quiet dignity, 'Lord, I am
Zarah, Princess of Anshan.'

'I bow before you,' the stranger said, and made the merest
nod of his head. Was it the light, she wondered wildly, that
was making his eyes twinkle so? Was this great rock of a man
in fact laughing at her?

'You must be tired,' he was saying. 'And yes, also very
sad.' He turned to Thickneck. 'Fetch a rug. A large and

beautiful one befitting the daughter of a king.'

Thickneck turned on his heel and vanished and Zarah wanted to cry out to him not to leave her. That without him near her she felt too vulnerable and terribly alone. In a matter of moments he had returned, bearing a magnificent Persian carpet of traditional design in red and blue. It was laid, with great ceremony, on the ground.

'Please,' the Egyptian said as he took hold of her arm, 'make yourself comfortable.' He sat her down and took his place beside her. 'I will have some honey wine brought for us to drink, and perhaps some fruit and bread. We will eat and drink together, you and I. You may tell me all about Anshan, and of your father, the king of that land. Speak to me of all those things you love and have left. I want to know all about you. Yes, everything.'

He was setting a trap for her, and she had to get out of it. There had been no time to mull over the story, to learn the part she must play. What to do? The panic that was never very far away these days rose to the fore. She sat there, pale and trembling, lost for words, her mind blank. A gourd full of honey wine was brought forward. A small amount was poured into a silver cup and the Egyptian took it and handed it to her. She began to cry in earnest and turned her face away from the wine.

'Forgive me,' she wept, 'but I cannot speak of—of my father or my home. I—I am just too sad. Tears have tightened up my throat.'

'If you drink this,' he said sternly, 'you will feel better. Come along, drink!'

He looked so firm and so determined that she obediently took one sip. She did not like the taste and had a sudden terror that the concoction was poisoned. She made a wry face and put the cup down.

'I cannot drink this, thank you. I—I do not often have wine. I don't very much like it. I always choose to drink sweet water. Your honey wine burns my tongue.'

'Impossible,' he told her firmly, and the look in his eyes was so intent that she began to shiver. Who was he? she wondered wildly. Why had he made it his business to come here and question her? She frowned, realising that the men

gathered round, being so merry and still making a great deal
of noise as they continued to drink, had somehow made a
quite effective screen. The stranger would not be in sight of
the lord Ramose's tents, and she knew instinctively that that
was exactly how it had been planned.

How could she escape? If things went wrong and the lord
Ramose finished with her, she would be sent back to Judas
and Neb. Anything was better than that, even death.

Just then a night bird called harsh and clear. Not once,
not twice, but three times it called.

With casual ease for a man of so great a size, the Egyptian
got to his feet.

'We will meet again, Zarah of Anshan,' he said smoothly.
'But now the time has come for me to leave.' One large hand
reached out to cup her chin and lift it so that she was looking
up directly into his face.

'Your father's grief must be deep indeed,' he said. 'You
are neither old enough nor strong enough to face all that you
will have to go through here. Take care, and remember that
little princesses are numerous at court. Like you, their main
object in life is merely to manage to survive.'

With that he and his men vanished into the darkness that
seemed more intense now the rush lamps and reed torches
had been doused.

'Sweet Light of Dawn,' Thickneck said quietly, 'now go
into your tent and stay there. Do not move. You must
promise me that. I will stay here and be on guard at all times.
Be wary, and no matter who calls your name, stay where you
are. We seem to be mixed up in a very strange game and if
it is up to me, it shall be a game that we will win. But we must
take care.'

'You'll promise not to leave me?' she asked anxiously, the
fear making her eyes almost too large in her face. Her hand
went out to touch his arm. 'I—I don't think I can go on
without you.' Her smile was slight and sad as she whispered,
'Indeed, there is little hope in my heart now. My young master, whom I loved, is now dead, and—and that great brute
of a man frightens me. Thickneck, he is like a king! A man
used to having the world kneel at his feet. No, I—I don't
honestly think that I can go on.'

'Yet you will, because you must,' Thickneck stated in his gruff matter-of-fact way. 'And remember that it is the gods that determine the winners of the day. Remember this, too: those the gods love best are the ones ready and willing to help themselves. We must never give in, sweet Morning Light. We must think of victory, never of defeat. Go in now, sleep. I will never be very far away.'

Zarah obediently went into her tent and was grateful for the rug that Thickneck had set down for her in such a way that she could roll up like a little cocoon. The camp was still now, and the air was chill. Night breezes were moaning and seemed to hold blustery messages from the gods. Zarah closed her eyes, but she could still visualise the striking face of the Egyptian who had made her feel such fear and awe.

She slept at last, and her dreams took her back in time, to the happy days when she belonged to the magus and his son, the sweet and handsome Harad who had been her young master.

The real and bitter world had slipped away and she was laughing and shouting and jumping in the rock pool and daring Harad, her beloved breast-brother, to catch her if he could. And Harad had smiled, his eyes as large and as lustrous as black grapes.

'If I catch you I shall beat you,' he had cried. 'And running to my father will not help you. He knows the trouble and trial you are.'

Zarah's lips curved upwards as she smiled in her sleep, dreaming of those fine days, those wonderful days when she had been a child of the wilderness.

It had been good to be owned by Caiphus, the wise man with nomadic ways. He was an interpreter of dreams and could also read the messages of stars. He was tall and old, his beard white. His was a gentle soul. He travelled the world, a much sought-after sage since his predictions were usually right.

Zarah's parents, so the jolly black nursing woman, Nadia, told her, had been killed while journeying across the salt deserts to the west. Their entourage had been slaughtered or else taken as slaves. Zarah had been thrown to the ground.

A female baby was not worthy even of the mercy of death.

Caiphus had come upon her at dawn when the morning sky was glowing pink and gold.

'We will call her Eastern Brightness,' he had pronounced. 'Zarah she shall be from this day, for that is the meaning of her name.'

He had called for Nadia, who had suckled Harad since his own mother had died at his birth just over one year before.

'Nadia,' Caiphus had said. 'You have large well-filled breasts, for all you have suckled one child for so long. Is there enough in you to give to this pathetic young soul?'

From that day Nadia had loved and cared for them both and treated them the same. This even though Harad was the Young Master and Zarah's sole duty in life was to be his slave.

The years had gone by, warm and gentle, with Zarah attending the handsome young boy, and obeying him at all times. She sat behind him, ready to serve, and herself listened attentively as Harad learned the wisdoms at his father's knee. Besides attaining knowledge and understanding of the Aramaic cuneiform writing, he needed an understanding of Egyptian writing.

In time, Zarah, slave of Harad, adopted daughter of the wise Caiphus, tent-dweller, came to know and understand many of the habits and customs of the different peoples they met as they travelled from place to place.

Harad's boyish contempt for all women and girls was greater only than his scorn of learning. Given the choice, he would have been a warrior or a hunter. But this was not to be. However he tried to wriggle and evade, it was always the same. He was brought to his father by a grinning servant, and made to concentrate on the sacred symbols Caiphus had written on tablets of clay.

Zarah, quietly obedient, and attentive at all times, had a mind that sucked up facts and figures as readily as a sponge. She memorised magical signs and the symbols made by the careless patterns of the stars. Neither the Lord Master nor the Young Master realised how much Zarah had absorbed. Nothing but blind obedience was expected of a female slave. This, no matter how greatly beloved.

Zarah remembered the Lord Master saying to Harad, 'Read the signs, my son, then take careful note of the thoughts that flash unbidden into your mind. These thoughts are the true messages from the gods. Put sign-readings and your own instincts together and let them make sense.'

'And if they do not?'

Caiphus had looked at Harad with quiet certainty. 'They will! Remember that it is a clever wise man who can convince those who have given him gold. But it is a brilliant man who leaves his listeners happy and confident with a future looking bright. Nothing is so destroying as fear. Do not be afraid of fear.'

'You speak in riddles, O Father,' Harad had said, and pulled a face.

Caiphus had shaken his head slowly and looked very wise. 'One fears what is to come, and does not realise that worrying about the future effectively kills the present. Always maintain your own sense of pride and dignity, and fight fear.'

'O Father, I have to admit that I am sometimes afraid.' Harad had forgotten his arrogant façade. 'I hate bad dreams.'

'My son, make no mistake about it, there will be times in your life when you will feel afraid. This is no sin. The sin is to show your fear. Never show what you feel. A truly brave man is usually unimaginative, or else such a great actor that he is able to delude even himself. This is good! I say again, we must always endeavour to hide the fact that we feel fear. So, remember, make others accept that things will be good for them, that there is nothing to worry about. And always hide it if you become afraid yourself.'

Somehow, to Zarah, child that she was, the last two lessons seemed to be the most important of all.

One evening, when the stars were like a host of thorn-fires burning in the sky, Nadia went to Zarah, her expression concerned.

'Go quickly to the Lord Master's tent. He has something important that he wishes to say.'

Because Nadia had looked so concerned, Zarah ran, but on reaching the main tent she relaxed. Caiphus, leaning back against bright cushions, seemed happy enough. Near him, on a lower level, Harad was munching dried figs. With the sweetmeats set before them there was also a skinful of sweet wine. At her entrance Caiphus looked up and beckoned her forward. She approached him and made her obeisance, then waited in humbleness and love.

'Zarah,' he said solemnly, 'from this day forward you must hide your form and your face.'

She had looked at him blankly, thinking how fine and noble he was, and how elegantly he leaned against the hard cushions, his staff at his side. Gradually a sick fear entered her soul and forgetting the lesson, she fell to her knees, her hands clasped in a supplication.

'Lord. . .' she began, but he silenced her with a wave of his hand.

'It is my command that you wear the robe and the veil. I will not tolerate disobedience in this.'

'My Master—am I to be given to the desert people?'

He had smiled faintly at that.

'My child, would I give away my oxen, my camels, my ass?'

'I—I would die with the desert people,' she had stammered, and turned wildly to Harad for support. He stared over her head. Not even the Lord Master's son ventured to speak when Caiphus used that tone. The old man was puzzled as he asked, 'My child, what do you know of the ways of desert people? Nothing at all! You cannot judge.'

She had not dared to reply. Over the years, Nadia had told her a great deal. Desert females were always covered from head to toe, because it was their tribal law. They were silent and secretive behind their face-covers—some having only slits for their eyes. Even so, it was common knowledge that they became wildly, fiercely alive when ordered to the master's couch. They knew many ways to satiate man's desires and used them all with frantic urgency, so it was said. It would be death to them otherwise.

'I beg of you, Lord Master,' she had wept. 'Please do not send me away.'

Caiphus relented. His voice became gentleness itself.

'Do not worry, my child. You belong to my house, and to Harad, my son. You are safe in our hands. However, you are nearing womanhood, and you are lovely. Indeed, you are too beautiful for your own good.'

'Zarah is ugly,' Harad teased, his confidence returned. His dark eyes twinkled as he tweaked her long flowing hair. 'And also she screams.'

She had remained obstinately silent, too much in awe of Caiphus to cry out as Harad so obviously desired.

'She may well scream if she is taken from us by Judas's kind,' Caiphus observed. 'It is against such a happening that we must guard. We are nearing bad territory.' He turned to Zarah once again. 'Now perhaps you understand, child, since you have already met Judas and must have an inkling of what he has in mind.'

Zarah remembered the fat slave merchant very well. He and his retinue had joined Caiphus's camp for a while, and the way he had stared at her had made her flesh crawl. Later that night Judas's slave foreman, Neb, personally visited the women's tent, this while Caiphus was telling the future to Judas himself. Thin, sharp featured and with spiteful black eyes, Neb had imperiously sent Nadia away. Then he ordered Zarah to approach. Trembling, she had obeyed.

The man had looked her over. His hands cupped her newly forming breasts. He pulled open her mouth to look at her teeth, then his hands slid downwards, over her thighs. Having made up his mind, he turned abruptly and walked away.

A short while later, Nadia crept back to the tent.

'Flower,' she whispered. 'That evil man has returned to his master Judas and given his report. The outcome is that even now Judas is offering two heavy gold bands for the one he calls the virgin slave. You, my flower! The slave merchant wants you for an Egyptian nobleman!'

Caiphus had politely refused the two gold bands, then four, then eight. At length he became angry and threatened Judas with the evil eye. This scared the slaver, who finally went away.

'You are not being punished, my child,' Caiphus told her. 'You are dear to me. All men have an eye for beauty and, it seems, the Egyptians have a special liking for pretty virgin slaves.'

Comforted, but frightened still, she had crept away, not to the women's tent, but to the Young Master's. Harad, now eleven, was all but a man and she was his slave. It was her place to sleep on the ground at the foot of his blanket, ready to serve him at all times.

Later, when the moon was like a large and beautiful full-blown rose, Harad came to her. He stared at her oddly and she, very aware of how distant he had been since Judas had crossed their path, made as if to rise.

'Be still,' he said, his voice cold. 'Why do you disobey?'

'Forgive me, Young Master,' she whispered, not understanding his change of mood. 'I was not aware that I had disobeyed.'

'Did Nadia not give you a robe and a veil?'

Startled, she looked at the things she had placed so carefully to one side. Neatly folded, they seemed heavy and frightening to her. She wore the straight linen garment falling from her armpits, which was held up by straps over her shoulders, when it was necessary to dress. At night, when it was cold, she wrapped up in a cloak. Often she wore few or no clothes at all.

'I—I believed that I was allowed to go uncovered while away from all eyes but yours, Young Master.'

His sensitive face was still distant as he said, 'You are at liberty to call me Brother while we are alone, Zarah. As to the rest, you must obey.'

'You—you are very angry. What have I done?' she whispered urgently. 'Forgive me! Oh, please, forgive me!'

'The slaver wanted you,' Harad said angrily. 'He was prepared to pay a fortune. He has a rich client, he said, who would buy you for a price. An Egyptian, I understand.'

'I did not know.'

'Egyptians are all the same, so they say.' Harad's dark eyes flashed fire. 'I have no doubt that Judas the slaver would have let you go to a man who would ravage you even though you are not yet fully grown.'

'I—I am sorry.'

'Egyptians are like the scarab beetles they so admire,' Harad said fiercely. 'They are always scrabbling behind balls of dung!'

'Egyptians and slavers make me afraid,' she had whispered plaintively. 'And if I have to be ravaged, it must be by you. I have always belonged wholly to you!'

'That is true, Zarah,' he replied earnestly, and his handsome young face leaned closer to hers. 'And I may do with you as I will.'

'Young Master, I. . .'

'Take off your shift.'

Her heart was beating, her mouth went dry. There was fear and excitement running in her veins. It was as if she had been awaiting this moment all the days of her life. Harad, the beloved, was looking at her as he never had before. Even though she was not yet a woman, she was now sure that Harad was a man. Her lips curved in a childishly mischievous smile as she slowly rose to her feet in order to step out of the fine white flax linen she wore. Then, with eyes downcast, she stood before him as naked as the day she had been born. She waited anxiously, wishing that her new-formed breasts were larger, that there was more flesh covering her supple young bones.

'You have changed,' he said at last. 'You have altered in ways that I like. I can understand why that man wished to pay such a high price for you. I can understand him, but I want to kill him just the same. Come here!'

She had taken the one small step necessary, gasping as his hands began moving over her in a careful, tentative way. He explored every inch of her, sliding inexpert hands over her thighs, then stroking, cupping her tiny breasts in his hands.

'They are like lotus-buds,' he said roughly. 'And your body is like a sapling, perfect, pliant and ready to bend. I want you to lean backwards, arch against me. Do as I say!'

Joyfully she obeyed, daring to look into his face as she did so. The expression in his eyes told her all that she needed to know.

'You belong to me,' he said, and the words were deep in his throat. 'Do you understand?'

He pushed her down and began to fumble between her legs. Then, with a grunt of satisfaction, he took her. There was no love, no tenderness, but all the triumph in the world. He used her with a rough, boyish enthusiasm and with no thought apart from his own need. She knew this, accepted it, and cried out in pain and joy. He thrashed into her and against her, his hands brutal in their grasp. Harad was a young animal, experimenting completely for the first time. She was his slave, his vassal. He exulted in his moment of power. It was over very quickly, but he was well pleased.

From that time, Harad changed. He became a turkey-cock, strutting and proud. He was possessive and jealous, and insisted on the veil and the dark robe with a fiery passion that Zarah had never encountered before. She became a virtual prisoner in his tent. Only Nadia was allowed near.

'You have fulfilled the Young Master,' Nadia told her. 'But to keep him attentive, you must learn many ways.' She threw back her head and laughed so hard that her chins wobbled. 'And I will tell you how to delight him. Many such things old Nadia knows!'

'You have known many men?'

'How else do you think this woman has survived all these years? A man must burn and woman must slake his thirst—though she must be like the great salty green. Let him drink his fill, but in such a way that he is always thirsting for more.'

Laughing and teasing, then whispering low, Nadia told Zarah of many ways that would delight the Young Master, finishing by saying firmly, 'And remember, Flower, that apart from that which lies between her legs, a woman's next best asset is her tongue! She must use it in many ways—and in many places!'

She laughed again, her black shiny face mischievous and alive, and Zarah smiled, and felt wise and shy, and more worldly than the Young Master by far. It would be good, she thought, to delight her beloved in all the ways that Nadia described.

But happiness was a transient thing. One night, when the moon made a black and silver mosaic of the world, while Zarah waited alone in the tent, life as she had known it came to an end.

A huge black eunuch had burst in. Like an enormous vulture he had appeared, and before she could cry out, his hand covered her mouth. She was lifted and carried away as effortlessly as the Wind God lifted a single straw.

Judas had swift camels waiting and an eye for much gold. He had dared even the danger of thwarting a man capable of turning upon him the evil eye.

How far and how long she had been borne away, rolled in a blanket and slung over a camel's back, Zarah never knew. She was almost suffocating at times, but her situation was not nearly so desperate as that of the other slaves. They were made to walk, tied one to another around their necks, in a single line.

Some died. It was of little account. Human life was as disposable as chaff. Cruelty was so much the order of the day that the victims took it for granted. Cruel masters were commonplace. But Zarah was allowed to drink blackish water from the goatskin supplied to Neb. She was also allotted half of the handful of dried figs that were the slave foreman's ration. Neb's cruel black eyes told her what he thought about this state of affairs, but he kept a still tongue in his head.

Judas was never far away, and there were also a great many spies. The slave merchant thought Zarah a great prize and valued her as such. Even so, Neb was cunning as well as cruel, and she was in a bad way by the time the slave compound was reached.

Two mornings later, Harad was dragged into the male slave compound that was divided from the women by a fence of woven reeds. This, and the giant eunuchs always on guard, was sufficient to keep them apart.

How Harad had known where to find her, Zarah never knew. All she was sure of was that he had been caught trying to save her, and her moment of fierce joy at the thought was soon banished by an immense fear. Her brave and noble Young Master was now himself a slave.

The most evil-looking eunuch was the gentlest by far. He was a black man, called Thickneck. He had a vicious-looking scar that gave an evil leer to his face. It was Thickneck who turned a blind eye when the two young ones crouched, one on either side of the fence, to whisper together.

'Young Master,' Zarah breathed, 'why are you here? How did you find me?'

'My father was reading a man's fortune and so I left him to come to you. I saw you being taken. I followed on the swiftest camel, but did not dare approach until now.'

'Perhaps the Lord Master will come after you,' Zarah whispered hopefully. 'He will come to save you, I am quite sure, my lord Harad. You came after me. 'I—I am glad.'

'You are my property,' Harad whispered fiercely. 'Common slave merchants cannot take what is mine!'

'The lord Caiphus will move sun and moon to come for his beloved, most precious, son!'

'My father will not have missed me before dawn, Zarah. The night winds will have destroyed any tracks I made.'

'The camel,' she murmured desperately. 'What of your camel, Harad?'

'I fear it is stolen by now, but we must not give up hope.'

It was Neb who had put an end to hope and replaced it with despair. He had come upon Zarah, heard her whispering, and in a voice loud enough to be heard by both, told them the truth.

'Your Young Master is to become someone's beautiful boy, and I have no doubt that he will be emasculated to this end. You will be an Egyptian's slave.'

In spite of her terror of Neb, Zarah cried out, 'No! This must not be. He is my Young Master. He is the son of Caiphus the wise!'

'It has been agreed. He is old for the knife, but Judas will take a chance on whether he lives or dies. He is strong. I believe he will live. As a beautiful boy, he will bring in many standard-weight rings of copper or gold.'

'No!'

'Why not?' Neb sneered. 'What other uses can be found for such as he? He is not built powerfully enough to be put to hard labour. Masters do not like paying good gold for slaves who quickly die. As he is now, he would be too good-looking to serve in a house—since women are what they are.'

That same night Harad had been caught trying to escape. He had been whipped, but his terrible torture had not truly begun until it had been carried out before them all, as a warning, the next day.

Zarah bit her lips until they bled. She knew that she would never forget the sound of Harad's screams. She would always remember the love and fear on his boyish face on that last fatal day.

'You belong to me, my Morning Light, but you are to go to the Egyptian. Judas has already sent a message to him, according to Neb. I must try to get us away. I must escape first, then find a way to set you free. I must find my father. He will know what to do.'

'Do not go,' she had whispered urgently. 'You are my heart and soul. Do not leave me alone in this place. The Lord Master is too far away.'

'I must try. I must!'

'No, I beg of you! You are my breast-brother. Without you, I shall die!'

He had made his bid for freedom, and had failed. He had been made to pay the price.

CHAPTER TWO

THE STARS WERE only pale shadows in the sky when Thickneck scratched at the sleeping girl's ear to wake her. His touch was gentle, and Zarah looked up into his face and was unafraid.

'It is time,' he said.

The journey at dawn began with a great deal of commotion. Men cursed, beasts jostled, protesting, camels grunting bad-temperedly as they rose from their knees, their side baskets heavy with loads. The caravan of Ramose was large, and since there was safety in numbers, spirits were light. The Egyptian nobleman was happy and so were the people who served him. It became clear, even to Zarah, young as she was, that Ramose was a kindly man, one whom guards, servants and slaves would follow to the death.

The caravan carried all household goods, large and small. There were vast tents and folded Persian rugs, anything and everything necessary to give comfort to the man who travelled in the name of the queen. Great containers full of grain and jars of oil were carried by camels and pack animals of other kinds. There were dried fruits, spices, onions, honey and sweetmeats. Goatskins were bloated with drinking-water and there were great jars of wine.

Bemused, Zarah was continuing the journey in a carrying-chair borne by four strong men. Thickneck, her guard, strode importantly by her side.

'You are a princess,' he said in his hoarse whisper, 'and must travel as such. You will be a great lady when you grow up.'

Her eyes widened in fear. 'You will never leave me? Promise that you will never leave me!'

'You have my word, Morning Light. How can it be otherwise? I am now owned by you.'

'And—And you are not angry?' she asked anxiously.

He threw back his head and laughed aloud.

'Angry? When I walk tall and am as good as my own man? When I wear a leopardskin, a feather, and a band of gold? I am so angry that my heart sings!'

When the sun was high, Ramose's caravan met that of a Persian prince, a handsome Aryan of medium height. He had a high forehead, a straight nose, and his hair was fashionably frizzed in front and gathered in a bunch at the back. He wore a crown, a thick gold band studded with jewels and rosettes. His drooping moustache twirled at the tips and his square beard hung in four rows of curls, as was the Persian fashion of the day. His robe was purple, with wrist-length sleeves, and it covered most of his body. Even so, it was possible to catch a glimpse of white trousers above his low-laced shoes. His name was Gimillu.

Ramose went, with much pomp and ceremony, to drink and eat with Prince Gimillu, when they stopped for the night. A herdsman, whose duty was to care for the animals that would provide meat and milk for the journey, sent for the woman who milked the ewes. Later the milk would be made into cheese, butter and *mahst*. Zarah watched the woman, and waited for the call that she had been told would come. Thickneck stayed near, his eyes vigilant. He was determined that no harm would come to the young and fragile Morning Light. Zarah was conscious of his presence and comforted by it.

She saw the world about her now as a mysterious place of great cliffs, black clefts and deep ravines. Fires of thorn bushes crackled and blazed. The Persian guards on duty wore round felt caps with neck-flaps, tight long-sleeved leather tunics, and laced shoes with projecting tips. They were tough wiry men with hard faces, whose journey to the Nile from Persia had taken a great deal of effort. To cross the waterless desert involved a march of no less than three days. A treaty with the king of Arabia had made the route possible to travel, because he had agreed to place out sufficient water in skins on the backs of camels all along the way. This ingenuity had made the king a very rich man.

Bentresht came to Zarah, and she was smiling.

'You are to go to Prince Gimillu now. It is a great privilege to visit a son of the Shah, the King of Kings, in the royal tent. He will not speak to you, but he will look you over very carefully. Do not be afraid. My lord Ramose will be there, and your man will be on guard at your back.'

Zarah followed Bentresht to the great tent, where a guard allowed her, Brentresht and Thickneck to pass.

Inside, all was opulence. Hard cushions were everywhere, covered with coloured cloth, and magnificent Persian carpets on the ground. There were many servants and slaves in attendance. Decorated dishes contained exotic foods, and jars held a great deal of wine.

Musicians began to play, and dancing-girls in veils and trousers gathered in at the ankles and wearing jangling ornaments began to weave intricate measures to the music of flutes, one-stringed harps and tight little leather drums. At the far end of the tent, on a throne-like seat set on a specially made wooden dais, was Prince Gimillu. Near him, in the place of honour, Ramose, Nobleman of Thebes.

At an order from the prince, Zarah was nudged forward. She began to tremble. The Persian was greedily eyeing her from head to toe.

'What is your name?' he asked, and there was oil in his voice.

She tried to appear calm and unafraid. 'I am Zarah, Princess of Anshan, O Lord.'

'Ah!' His narrowed black eyes were suddenly speculative. 'And you are bound for Egypt?'

'I am, Lord.'

'And what would you say if I told you that the plan has been changed,' his voice became heavy with meaning. 'That you are not Egypt bound after all?'

Zarah sensed rather than saw Ramose stiffen in his seat. She also knew, though she could not see, that Bentresht now had a hunting-cat look in her eyes. Gimillu persisted. 'What if I told you that you now belong to me?' He licked his lips in a slow, calculatingly obscene way, and his eyes were wicked with intent. 'How would that please you, eh?'

Please, God, help me to say the right thing, Zarah prayed silently as she made a deep and graceful obeisance before the two noblemen.

'Great lord Gimillu,' she said quietly. 'Personally, I would be honoured to find myself chosen by such a noble and handsome lord. But one part of me, the honourable part, would be at great variance with my joy.'

'How so?' Gimillu asked, amazed.

'The grace and favour of choice is not mine, Lord. I belong to Egypt by express order of my father, the king.'

Gimillu threw back his head and laughed, and lifted his goblet towards Ramose, spilling wine as he did so.

'O yes, my friend, yes! I recognise her. I will swear to it, should I be asked. I will swear on my heart that she is indeed princess of Anshan.' He began to embroider the lie with relish, laughing and drinking and slurping over his wine. 'I know her father very well, Ramose. Her father the king, did you hear?'

'That is good.' Ramose's face remained calm as he replied.

'Hai!' Gimillu warmed to his theme. 'I will even go so far as to mention her sisters by name! But, tell me, what if the new mistress disdains the wares? I presume the girl is destined to work for She Who Must Be Obeyed? That she will be summoned to your Royal's court? What if the girl is not, after all, welcomed there?'

'Then Zarah of Anshan will take safe shelter under my roof.'

'Ha! And, I must presume, also in your bed? I tell you, if the deal falls through, I will take the girl off your hands. I know ways to get the greatest of pleasure from the bodies of little princesses, who, I may add, are not so rare as you seem to believe.'

Ramose, distinctive and rather sphinx-like at that moment as he saw through Gimillu's bluff, smiled faintly.

'I paid rubies for this girl. Rubies that can never be matched in size or value anywhere in the world. That is how decidedly I stand by my own good judgment. So—should Zarah be unacceptable to the Great One Most High, I will personally take and greatly enjoy that for which I paid so high a price.'

'And',—Gimillu almost choked in his wine which was his derision—'you will truly try to delude yourself that a good bargain was made? She is worth that much?'

Zarah found herself praying that her knees would not fail her and give way, that her lips would not tremble. That her eyes did not betray her fear. Gimillu's mood was changing. His eyes now had a baleful glare.

Ramose remained unmoved. He smiled and raised his painted brows as he asked, 'My dear Gimillu, how can you give breath to such an unnecessary question. You only have to take one look at the beauty of this girl!'

Instead of feeling relieved, Zarah felt a swift uprush of unease. By saying what he had, because of the undisguised look of admiration he had given her, the Egyptian had made an implacable enemy for her—his wife! She knew it because she had heard just one harsh, vicious intake of breath coming from the First Wife Bentresht.

Suddenly the Persian prince laughed. 'I would bargain with the devil for the amount of gold you have offered me. Enough of business. Now it's time for pleasure. Choose a girl, any number of girls. They're all artistic in dancing. As for couching, I do not know; they are new, and to be replaced when our destination is reached. The price they bring will serve to purchase more of their kind. Variety is the spice of life, and boredom is a curse.'

He called for one of the dancers to be unveiled and brought forward. Small and fragile, her skin was bronze, her eyes like almonds in her small painted face. She was clearly terrified.

'She will do,' Gimillu said, and licked his lips. 'She will wait by my couch. Now, my friend, your choice?'

'I have my wife with me on this journey,' Ramose said easily. 'High-born women have equality of rule in the Egyptian home.'

'Which shows how backward you Egyptians really are,' Gimillu boasted. 'And how soft! My ladies of high and noble birth are with me also, but they are out of sight and for my eyes alone. They know their duty, to bear me sons. Slave girls, dancing-girls, serving-girls, they are for the moment. To be used mightily, to be enjoyed, and then to be set aside. My First Wife and the others of the harem accept this, and obey.'

'Women have always been adaptable, no matter how highly or lowly born,' Ramose agreed. 'But with me it is different. I greatly care for and love Bentresht, my wife.'

'Who will grow old and wrinkled all too soon, Ramose.'

'So will you and I.'

'Then let us drink to the present.' Gimillu laughed again, and called for more wine.

At Ramose's signal, Zarah was led away. She cowered in her tent, sick and trembling, grateful to see Thickneck's dark shadow outside. After a while she crept to the tent opening and whispered fearfully, 'Thickneck, what will happen to the dancing-girl the Persian prince uses this night?'

'If she pleases him, she will be placed in the royal harem, I expect.'

'And if she does not?'

'He will give her to pleasure his men.'

'And will they be kind to her?'

'Men in the service of Gimillu will probably not be kind. They are a rough lot who have few pleasures, by the look of it. They will be enthusiastic, greedy and in great haste. Kindness will not enter into it. But you are too young to concern yourself with such things.'

'When—When they unveiled her and I saw her face, I could see that she was no older than me and—and she was very afraid, Thickneck.' Her voice hesitated. 'A short while ago I thought I heard a scream.'

'Then perhaps she is a virgin, little Morning Light. If that is the case, and if she pleases the Persian, she will be raised above all others—for a while.'

Early next morning there was a great deal of commotion. Dogs were barking frenziedly, camels were grunting and baring their teeth. Men and women were bustling about, preparing to break camp.

Keeping well out of sight, Zarah watched the scene. She saw the despicable Gimillu getting ready to leave. Shortly afterwards, the wild dogs that always skulked round a caravan set up a fierce and frantic cacophony of noise outside the Persian soldiers' quarters. She gasped with shock and grief as a brutish-looking man threw the mutilated body of the dancing-girl to them, and hid her burning face in her hands, unaware of Thickneck's approach.

He said flatly, 'Just be thankful that it did not happen to you.'

'Oh, Thickneck,' she said brokenly. 'How cold and hard you sound.'

'I am hard and I am strong. It is the weak who go to the wall. Now get ready. We are to leave quite soon.'

Gimillu and Ramose bade their farewells and went their separate ways. Angry and afraid, Zarah sat obediently in her fine carrying-chair. Thickneck strode easily alongside.

After a while she asked fiercely, 'Why did they kill her? Why?'

'The girl belonged to a far distant race. Her body was considered to be sacred by her people, since she was a priestess. Not even her own king would have been allowed to touch her. That is what I heard.'

'But—But Gimillu. . .'

'To Gimillu she was a slave—nothing more; nothing less. They say that the girl dared to fight him, even going so far as to scratch his face.'

'Oh!' Zarah's eyes opened wide at such courage. 'My master Caiphus would have admired her greatly. She was so brave!'

'She was stupid,' Thickneck retorted. 'She had the skin whipped off her back for her pains. Then she was given over to Gimillu's men. They enjoyed her, one after the other. It would have gone on, but, fortunately for her, she died.'

'I will remember Gimillu,' Zarah whispered, and her throat felt tight. 'I will never forget that her eyes bore the same expression as Harad's when he realised the time had come for his ordeal. Oh yes, I will most certainly remember Judas and Neb and Gimillu.'

'That is right,' Thickneck observed. 'Make certain that you remember very well. Whenever you have a doubt about doing as you are told, remember what happens to those who dare to disobey. Being obedient will allow you to survive.'

She remained quiet, not daring to tell Thickneck that she had not been thinking of survival, but of revenge.

By evening, the men had ceased their joking. The animals' heads sank lower. The mules and asses dragged their feet and the camels moved on, unmindful of everything except their own bad tempers. The guards of Ramose looked more forbidding, their firm dark limbs powerful under their short white loin-cloths. The wide handkerchief head-dresses flowed out behind their ears, their weapons tucked into their belts.

The world seemed empty of people other than those loyal to Ramose. There were not even nomads to be seen: the tall, hawk-faced and silent black-cloaked women who spent their lives drifting from place to place. Zarah was ready to weep, she was so tired of the endless journey. She wanted to walk, to stretch her limbs, but it was not to be.

'You are a princess,' Thickneck told her. 'Princesses must be carried everywhere.'

'I hate it! I am used to walking. My master Caiphus. . .'

'Hush!' Thickneck's hoarse voice held urgency now. 'Remember, if you value your life—and mine—that you are Princess Zarah of Anshan, and that was how you were born.'

'Why could they not have chosen a real princess?'

'Because, Morning Light, princesses belong to great families. Princesses have fathers who wield power. You are a child, and are alone except for me. Ramose is the man with the strength and position here. We can only wait and see what plan he has for you. We can only tremble in the terrible knowledge that we are merely pawns in a game about to be played by a great queen.'

Later, half hidden in a fold of orange-brown hills, buildings appeared, mud-brick houses, flat and homely, hugging an area fringed by palms. As the caravan drew near, the headman, his elders and sons, left the community and came out to meet Ramose. They were a fierce-looking people, tall, who held their heads as high and arrogantly as the camels did. The headman raised his hand in greeting, to which Ramose courteously replied. A ram was brought forward and slaughtered.

Zarah's weariness was banished. A great feast followed, and then music began. Warriors drank strong beer, many men linked arms and, with rapt expressions and fierce black eyes, began to dance.

Zarah's head began to ache because of the billowing smoke from the thorn fires, so she walked with Thickneck back to the privacy of her own tent. It had been set where a line of black oxen were tethered as a windbreak against the open side. Wearily she crawled in and closed her eyes. She knew no more until she was awakened by the clatter of the women whose duty it was to rise early and make the bread. Her cheeks were wet with tears, and though she could not remember, she believed that she had dreamed of Harad.

After an early start, within a short time they had reached the vast river. A great ship with one sail, many oarsmen and a luxuriously fringed deck-house for the passengers, was waiting at the quay, and a plank sloped down from its side to the ground. Safe in her carrying-chair, Zarah was lifted aboard. As soon as she was able, she stepped timidly out of the chair and went to join Thickneck. They stood close together, wide-eyed, at the edge of the boarding plank, watching the busy scene on shore.

Suddenly there came a great commotion, and a band of soldiers headed by the stranger that Zarah could never forget came into view. The soldiers scattered the people before them like so many flies. Her heart was beating hard against her side because she felt sure that the nobleman had seen and recognised her at a glance. But his compelling dark eyes looked away.

He called his men to a halt, and his clear, firm voice rang out over the water. 'Hail, Ramose! It is I, Per Ibsen. May I join you aboard?'

'You are welcome,' Ramose replied. 'I greet you in the name of the queen.'

'To the queen and to all of those of her blood,' came the calm reply.

Zarah watched as Per Ibsen walked up the plank, to be greeted by Ramose. They made an impressive pair and, outwardly at least, seemed the greatest of friends.

Bentresht came to stand at Zarah's side. 'So,' she said coldly, 'he is spying on us again, girl. Be warned, and remember that the Great Royal House is divided in two. Take special note of that young man. He is very close to Prince Thutmose—who hopes one day to take the place of the queen. But My Majesty is a fine match for him and all of his kind. May the great Queen Hatshepsut rule for ever, I say.'

Bentresht's expression was such that Zarah felt terror. She began praying desperately that the man did not remember her, that he did not tell the lord Ramose of his visit to her tent.

Almost as though he felt her large frightened eyes on him, Per Ibsen turned and stared down at the small figure that barely reached up to his heart. His face was expressionless, and all Zarah knew at that moment was that she felt ill. That the great Per Ibsen still made her afraid.

When the sun was sinking like a bloody ball in the west and the sky became a banner of saffron and gold, Zarah crept out of the place set aside for her and went to join Thickneck, who was squatting on his haunches in the prow of the ship. It was the night of High Nile and, replete, the holy river was rested and calm, lying quietly until the deep purple sky became burnished by a large full-blown moon. The river changed into a pathway of living silver.

'I have been listening to the talk,' Thickneck said. 'This is a special time set aside for the ladies of the land. They believe in the god of the river, Morning Light, and they also believe in magic. Soon you will hear what I mean. Be quiet and listen.'

From the shining yet shadowed river bank rose the sound of prayers that were as old as humanity itself. As the soft yet urgent voices mounted, Zarah stood up, wishing to see. But her moment of curiosity died almost at birth and lethargy replaced it. She made as if to take her place again, close against Thickneck's side. She felt him watching her, but was too numb to care. Swiftly he jumped cat-like to his feet, sweeping her high in his arms as he did so. She gasped, then one small arm went tentatively round his neck and hung on.

'They will drink nine times, and they will sprinkle their young nine times,' Thickneck told her. 'Apparently it has always been so.'

Wide-eyed, cradled safely against the giant eunuch, Zarah watched. Clearly visible in the moonlight, the women entered the river, their wet garments clinging to their bodies. Those who had children set them gently in the shimmering water, then, cupping the water in their hands, they poured it over the heads of their young. This they did nine times.

Women with no children religiously took nine sips of the holy water, and their prayers were an entreaty wafting through the air.

'O God of the River, bless my son.'

'Oris, Great God, let my belly stretch with the weight of a child.'

Then, high and mournful above all the rest, a woman cried out in despair, 'O please, Sweet God, let this little one live! He is fading fast and my other children are all dead. I am old, O God, and this baby is the last.'

The sad words soared, cutting wedges of pain in the air. They hung, suspended in the moonlight, until they echoed into silence against the far river bank. There, shrouded, and in their last resting-place, lay long-gone pharaohs in the Valley of Kings.

'The world is terrible,' Sarah whispered against Thickneck's ear. 'And I feel too sad and too old for my years. I am afraid, and I feel cut in two.'

'I know,' he said hoarsely. 'I know.'

'I—I keep remembering my young master,' she wept. 'How beautiful he was in life, and how monstrously he died. I want to scream, my terror is so great, but I am afraid of being sent back. I—I want to die!'

'Sometimes dying is best,' Thickneck agreed. 'Life is for the living, not for the living dead.'

He turned and set her down with infinite care. Once she was comfortable, he curled his great body round her, shielding her as best he could. She lay still and mute. Until Judas had captured her, she had never known grief. Her life had been one of sunlight and laughter, affection and love. With Harad, she had been a child of freedom while they were alone. But with Caiphus she had almost quivered with her adulation. Now Thickneck seemed almost as wise as the old man had been.

She found herself eyeing him with child-like curiosity. Something in her own frozen heart reached out even further to him. Somehow she sensed that he was as lost and as alone as she. In a sure and certain way she knew that with Thickneck guarding her, she need never be afraid. Leaning near to him, Zarah cautiously ran her small fingers over the scar on his face.

'Does it still hurt?' she whispered anxiously.

'No,' he replied.

'Was it Judas who cut you?'

'It was Neb. It happened many years ago, on the day they emasculated me. Young as I was, I fought them. I snapped the bonds round my body, but was unable to break the leather band tied about my neck. Even so, I struggled, and the band cut into my throat. This you can tell by the sound of my voice.'

'Neb is the devil himself!'

'Judas made Neb into the thing that he is—and, cruel though he is, Neb is also afraid. He could tell that if it took me until eternity, I would wait on him and get my revenge. It would have suited him better had I bled to death under the weight of the knife. But I have survived, as you can see, very well.'

'I thank the gods for that mercy,' Zarah breathed. 'With you at my side, Thickneck, I am not so afraid. You are so large and strong, and you look very fierce.'

He seemed not to hear her, and was now almost speaking to himself. 'I became merely a thing on that day instead of a man. I am large. I am ugly, and I am also very strong. I owe my life to the great thickness of my neck. That is how I came to be named. By Set and all the devils, I pray that one day I will give them good cause to remember me.'

'What did they call you—before?'

He looked at her, surprised. 'My parents called me Napata. I was born in the kingdom of Kush.'

'Did Judas kill your parents and then carry you off?'

'My parents were hungry, so they sold me to Judas,' Thickneck said, and his hoarse whispering voice was quite calm. 'Now here I am, bodyguard to a child no higher than my knee. So! I am considered to be fit only to be a nurse-maid. I do not know whether to laugh or to cry.'

'I am higher than your knee—Napata.'

'Not very much.' He smiled. 'I am Thickneck, remember? I no longer wish to be called by the name given to me by parents who sold me. I am no longer that innocent child.'

'But Bentresht said. . .'

'You must be quiet in case they discover that you are not sleeping in the grand shelter they prepared. It would not go well for either of us if the lord Ramose found you so familiar with a slave. Yes, Morning Light, for all my fine leopard-skin, feather, and gold band, I am still just a slave. You, on the other hand, are now a princess who comes from the Persian city of Anshan.'

'You will not leave me, Thickneck?'

'Not while I breathe. Now go to sleep. I will wake you in time for you to go back to your place.'

She closed her eyes obediently, but her small hand reached out and closed trustingly round his giant black fist. As she began to drift away, the fist unclenched and dark fingers enclosed her own.

'Harad,' she murmured, and moonlight glinted against her cheeks and made living crystals of her tears. Then a fierce message of warning brought her sharply into wakefulness again. She froze against Thickneck and stared up with large frightened eyes. Catlike, Per Ibsen had come upon them. He now stood, legs astride, looking down at her. His silence was almost too terrible to bear. Terror made her mind race. She knew what he would ask.

'What do I find here?' he queried mildly. 'A princess refusing a fine couch and preferring the company of a slave?'

'Forgive me,' Zarah said, and she looked up at the stern figure like an innocently trusting child. 'But Napata is the only face I know from my own land—where my father is a king. Napata is my man, and as soon as I know the laws of Egypt, I will set him free.'

'To return to Persia?'

'No!' she whispered, and then her terror could be hidden no longer as her small frame was racked by sobs. 'I want—Napata—to stay with me.'

'Then tell the lord Ramose how you feel. I am sure that your wish will be his command. Now it is best that you go back to your own place, Princess. Ramose rates you very highly, and he will be angry if he finds you like this.'

She thought he must hear the tempestuous beating of her heart as she struggled to her feet. Thickneck stood tall, and Per Ibsen stared at him thoughtfully for a second or two, then said, 'Go with her, Napata, and guard her well. If you are asked why you are too near the women's part of the ship, tell him that you followed my orders.' Then, before he dismissed them both, Per Ibsen added carefully, 'The princess is fortunate to have found herself so loyal a man. Do you not realise that your punishment for this outrage could have meant death?'

'I know, Master,' Thickneck replied, and Zarah wanted to scream out, she was so shaken. She had not known!

Per Ibsen looked at her, then said in a disparaging way, 'Your self-willed action could have brought about terrible retribution for your man, Princess. Perhaps in the future you will think more of him than of yourself.'

They were dismissed. Trembling, and almost too faint to move, Zarah went towards her allotted place.

'You have done well, Morning Light,' Thickneck whispered. 'From now on, play your part and play it with all your heart and soul. They are all out to play some kind of game of their own. With the gods on our side, we will be able to beat them all.'

'I am so afraid,' she gasped, and nervously brushed a long strand of hair away from her face. 'It is all too much.'

'You are alive, Morning Light.' His tone was matter-of-fact. 'And you must learn to be quick-witted enough to stay that way.'

'Per Ibsen—'

'—is curious, even suspicious, I think, but we will play the game their way. We will watch and wait and I promise you we will survive.'

Zarah wished that she could feel as certain as Thickneck sounded. She thought of Per Ibsen, of how magnificent but sharp-eyed and horrible he was. She would not put it past him to follow them even now. He was suspicious of a princess who was so totally terrified of everyone except her slave. He would wait his time, she knew it, and catch them in the act—talking about Judas and the horror of the slave compound. He would learn the truth; and if he did, it would be

in his power to have her stoned, and Thickneck killed slowly,
and the noble Ramose and all those in his house shown up
for the tricksters they were.

Thickneck stopped a few paces away from the shelter, and
Zarah crept through the opening. She was filled with dread
as she curled herself in a tight little ball in the place that had
been set apart for her. Although she closed her eyes, the figure of Per Ibsen was there, planted firmly in her brain. With
all her heart and soul she found herself wishing that the giant
Egyptian was on her side. With him as well as Thickneck to
look after her, she thought, she would have all the strength
in the world.

'Per Ibsen,' she whispered his name aloud. 'Per Ibsen, my
lord!'

If only she were as lovely as the lord Ramose had said. She
wondered how it would be to have a man such as Per Ibsen
look at her as Harad did once he had become a man. Her
cheeks burned and she tried to push her thoughts away. But
strangely, on this fear-filled, moon-drenched, river-rippling
night, she felt more woman than child. She had been looked
on as a woman and used as such, and had taken it all,
accepting her place in the scheme of things, and seeing what
had happened to her as the natural course of events. Her own
needs and desires were of no account. She was a chattel, a
plaything, a slave.

Now she had to accept what had been on her mind from
the first moment she had come face to face with the Egyptian, the large, good-looking stranger who had such dark and
piercing eyes. She remembered again how he had held her
arm as he had helped her to take her place on the Persian
rug. And the curious terrifying, thing was that she had never
felt so unnerved and taken aback at the feel of a man's hands.
Tentatively she rubbed her fingers over the place on her arm
where he had grasped her. She had thrilled at his touch in a
half-frightened yet very exciting way. Then fear returned as
she whispered to herself, 'By all the gods, Per Ibsen is a devil.
He must be to have such strange powers. I must do as Thickneck says: think as he does, trust no one, be wary at all times
and, above all, I must put Per Ibsen out of my mind.'

But she could not.   *   *   *

Per Ibsen drank from his fine metal cup that was decorated with gold. It was filled to the brim with sweet Nile water. He was frowning, and his eyes returned again to the women's part of the ship. He kept thinking of the wounded expression in the little princess's eyes. He was increasingly bewildered at the bits and pieces of a very strange story that was only beginning to come together; a story almost too incredible to be true. Yet he was sure he was not mistaken. But for the presence of Bentresht, the whole thing would not have seemed feasible. But, wild as it seemed, his instinct told him that Ramose was attempting to carry out a scheme dreamed up by no less a personage than the queen. The whole affair was bizarre, and yet there was nothing to which Hatshepsut would not stoop to keep her stranglehold on the throne.

For this one small scrap of life to be picked up and carried towards an uncertain fate, as a sacrifice in the game of power, was not unusual. Foreign kings gave young and pretty daughters away as a matter of course. Daughters were merely links to be used as beneficially as possible in the patriachal chain. Persian princesses, or Lebanese, it made little difference. They were taken from one royal court to another and moved like ivory statues in a board game. It had always been so.

'By Set and all devils!' Per Ibsen swore. 'I am sickening for something. A fever, perhaps. Why else should it annoy me that she went off with that large ugly Kushite with all the love and trust in the world, yet looked at me as though I belonged in hell?'

A strange restlessness seized him. Zarah! What a ridiculous little creature she was. How vulnerable and afraid. She was also stupid, for she had risked her man's life. She needed to be taken hold of and shaken hard. She needed to be taught a lesson, to be told that, princess or pauper, there should always be dignity and pride.

Per Ibsen put his cup down with care and at last admitted to himself that he was angry, not because she was as young and ethereally lovely as the blue evening moth, but simply because he himself felt so cut off and lonely. He wanted to get on with his work, the creating and moulding of great works in granite and stone. He disliked the journeys allotted to him on a duty as tasteless as this. He was a tough, open man who enjoyed the hunt, hard work, and all down-to-earth things. He did his duty as loyally as the next man, and would have laid down his life for his beloved Thutmose, but girl-baiting—for this was surely turning out to be nothing less—was not for him.

Through the years, he had known many women and girls. A man was expected to prove himself at court, and prove himself he had—mightily. However, females were there for relaxation and ease, to be petted and played with and put away at the end of the game like the toys they were. One did not think about toys; they were merely there to be picked up, put down, forgotten. Yet now a fragile, beatuiful girl had looked up into his face with all the fear and dread in the world—and he could not get her out of his mind.

CHAPTER THREE

UNABLE TO SLEEP, feeling claustrophobic in the sheltered place set aside for her, Zarah was relieved when the people around her began to wake up. There was a pearly sheen to the sky and the moon was a faraway smudge against the backcloth of oncoming dawn. Because she sensed that she was being watched, dimly aware that it meant death if she forgot for one single moment the part she had to play, she called out imperiously, 'Napata, I wish to eat.'

Thickneck made his obeisances, then turned uncertainly. He was plainly relieved when, at that moment, Bentresht's serving-girl came. She silently handed over unleavened bread, dried dates and figs. There was grape juice to drink. Thickneck took the fare and with exaggerated care tested everything before proffering it to Zarah himself.

'I do not think there will be poisoned food offered to us,' Zarah said gravely. Then she turned to the serving-girl. 'My man will also eat and drink. My father, the king, ordered that, at all times, Napata must be treated well. Napata is one of my father's most trusted men.'

To Zarah's astonishment the girl obeyed at once by hurrying to the part of the ship where the early meal was being apportioned. Zarah experienced a thrill of power, fear and delight. She, a slave, had actually given an order, and it was startling and most awe-inspiring that her order was in the process of being carried out. Then she forgot that the girl had hurried back to hand the eunuch a good helping of drink and food because the tall and handsome young Per Ibsen was leaning against some large earthenware jars. He was watching her closely. Her mouth went dry. A pulse beat like a frantic hammer in her throat. Did he know that she was a slave girl who was less than the dirt under his feet? She had to convince him. She must!

'Napata,' she said angrily. 'I do not like the juice of the grape; it is time that you remembered the fact. I have always enjoyed the sweet coolness of God's water. Always, Napata. Forget again, make this mistake once more, and I will have you whipped. Perhaps you will condescend to remember that. How lightly you seem to regard your lowly black skin.'

Per Ibsen looked carefully into the lovely face of Zarah, Princess of Anshan. It puzzled him because the timid little thing of a mere few hours ago had changed suddenly into a cheeky, saucy young bird, one that the big fellow now serving her could crush with a blow of his hand. He found himself wanting to snare the small person who, for all her fine show of arrogance now, was still unable to hide the wealth of pain and fear gleaming in the back of her eyes. He felt that to catch and hold such a silent, vulnerable creature, to feel its young heart fluttering against his lips, would be like holding the sweet breath of all Egypt in his arms. But such an embrace could mean death, not to him but to her. Per Ibsen knew this without being told. And since it was suddenly very important to have this exquisite girl-woman alive, he clenched his hands. For once in his life, he was not at all sure what to do.

Suddenly he grew cold with hate. He loathed Ramose, whereas he had thought him not at all bad before. But Ramose had snared a fragile bird of paradise and, at the very least, its feathers would get ruffled at court. At the worst, the little thing would get broken and torn.

Then Per Ibsen saw Ramose striding towards the girl, and he knew that he was dealing with no ordinary rogue. He felt he had met his match this time and that Prince Thutmose had, too. The knowledge made him grit his teeth. What was the nobleman planning in his dark mind for the little princess? How was she going to be used—in what was quite clearly going to be yet another intrigue at court?

'By Set and all devils,' Per Ibsen said to himself, 'I will kill Ramose if the girl comes to harm.' It was then that he had his first lesson in fear. It was not for himself, but for the fate of Zarah that the cold sweat beaded his brow.

Zarah looked up, and again caught Per Ibsen's fixed gaze. I am a princess, she thought desperately, and I am that man's equal at least. She took in a deep nervous breath and smiled across at him. A shy smile full of innocence and trust.

Per Ibsen gave her one long straight look, then turned his back and walked away. Zarah was unable to hide her relief from the watching Thickneck. She saw the conspiratorial gleam in the giant's eyes and felt aburdly pleased. But fear returned with the coming of Ramose. He spoke to Thickneck.

'Set her on top of a large grain-bin so that she can see more clearly.'

The eunuch obeyed, then stepped back, once again in a guarding position. Ramose stood next to the bin, his face almost level with the girl's. He was quietly proud of all that he saw. He was a fervently nationalistic man. 'Now you can see the full magnitude of our famous harbour, and the full glory of the valley of Thebes,' Ramose told her.

In spite of her awe and fear of him, Zarah gasped at the magnificence of the scene. The sky was now a glory of rose, violet, saffron and blues. The air was thick with noise. Men were greeting each other, calling out good wishes for the day. Others shouted orders to servants, or raised their whips over the backs of heaving, grunting slaves.

Beyond the harbour, as well as flanking it on either side, there were towering monuments. From the great houses of the rich, steps led down directly to the water's edge where small family craft of all kinds were merrily bobbing. Ramose began to speak, and his words showed how greatly he loved his land.

'You will see,' he said in his proud refined way. 'Egypt is literally glowing under her great and beneficent god Amun. She is at the height of her power and glory, and nothing—and no person, no matter how great—must stop her from going on. We are at peace with the world and that is how we must remain. A long time ago, in our queen's father's time, a savage battle with the Sudanese was won. The rebellious chieftain was crushed, his army destroyed. His body was hung by the heels from the bow of the first God-King Thutmose's ship. The people who saw it fell flat on their faces in fear and awe.'

He was silent then as he saw it all in his mind. His head was held high. Really he was an exceptionally noble-looking man. He went on, speaking to himself rather than to Zarah.

'When the old king left this earth to become God, he left his power to his daughter Hatshepsut, who is sometimes called Makare. She married Thutmose, her brother, who was a weak and ineffectual man. Even so, our forces were strong and able to uphold Egypt's might. Nubia and Kush are settled and happy to be ruled by viceroys. Do you understand what I am telling you?'

'Oh yes, Lord,' she breathed politely, but she was not listening to his words. She was remembering those other, long-ago dawns that she and the beloved Harad had shared.

'We are a truly rich and mighty land.' Ramose was all but gloating now. 'African trade flows northward by both caravan and boat. It is a never-ending flow. Thebes groans under the weight of ostrich feathers, giraffe tails, leopard-skins, ivory, gold and baboons. And that is not all! There are exotic woods, heavy with perfume, and odd little men. Dwarfs, they are called. They have comically wrinkled faces and make wonderful pets. And of course we must not forget the legions of slaves. What would we do without them? The loyal and obedient ones, I mean. The others. . .' He shrugged, and his voice took on a new meaning and an unspoken threat.

Zarah stood by him, immature and vulnerable, perched on the bin. There was a hard knot of nerves tightening in her stomach, and she felt sick. She had never felt less interested in a land, or view, than she did now, but she dared not look away. Through eyes now hazed with the pain and memory of what happened to slaves trying to break free, she stared at the towering monuments that stood in the middle distance. Many of them were glittering brilliantly in the morning sunlight, for they had been painted and layered with gold.

On shore, she could see small and large whirlpools of people. They wore the clothes of foreign races, but they seemed to be at ease as they walked along the pathway near the river's edge, heading for the harbour itself. Travellers, traders, merchants, followed by their servants and slaves. There were occasional carrying-chairs, their occupants hidden by flax curtains, all heading towards ships that would take them on journeys up or down the great Nile.

Above all, there were the Egyptians themselves. Rich, smooth-skinned, with black fringed hair and painted eyes, they stood out from the rest. Zarah's eyes burned with unshed tears. How greatly Harad would have enjoyed the scene! How he would have envied the group of Egyptian soldiers now walking along the path in double file. They were fine, strong men, their tanned skins burnished with oil. How proudly they carried themselves, their spears, axes and bows. They were a peaceful army led by a pacifist queen, yet they walked tall, their chins high.

Ramose's eyes were not on the shore. He began speaking about the different vessels crowding the river. She wanted to scream, wanted to cry. Above all, to run away. But to where, to whom? She was helpless aboard a large ship where officials abounded. Officials who knew very well how to cope with a disobedient slave. Yes, slave! Princesses had no reason to run away.

Deep down a warning voice whispered to her to be cunning, to take care. She must listen, learn, memorise. Above all, she must act as if she knew nothing, understood nothing, was aware only of each day that came and the need to survive. But, one day, her mind sang, the lessons Harad and I learned at Caiphus's knee will prove how magic they are. I must be careful. I must analyse. I must watch and wait. And—I must, above all, forget the look I saw on the lord Per Ibsen's face.

'That is Phoenician ship,' Ramose told her. 'They are natives of Canaan, the Land of Purple. Their traders are the richest of all, for they deal in mauve-coloured dye. Only the highest and richest can afford such royally coloured robes. If you are clever, if you impress the queen, perhaps you will one day own a purple cloak.'

For such a colour, many murex shellfish die, Zarah thought, remembering childishly chanting the fact obediently after Harad's father a long time ago.

'Would you like such a cloak?' Ramose asked in a heavy, humorous way. He was looking at her in such a way that she bit her lip and stared ahead of her, her fear, always near the surface, flaring anew. His expression clearly belied his studiously superior attitude. His question refuted his parental tone. Zarah did not reply, so he left her, his face cold.

She stared ahead, comforted by the knowledge that Thickneck stayed near. Ramose made her heart beat too quickly, made her wary. She was glad that he had gone away.

The sun leapt fully into the day now and Thebes was transferred into a wonderland. The joyful sky was an immense and glittering blue that reflected and danced on the Holy River. Along the banks, the verdant crops were already wallowing and spreading their roots in the rich black mud. Tall, graceful palms looked like so many one-legged fuzzy-wuzzies with bushy green hair. It was a sight sufficient to make a desert traveller weep with joy. But Zarah's tears, now unchecked, were sad. She could not forget Harad. The memory of his tortured screams rang more realistically in her ears than the winching of the tall wooden cranes.

Unexpectedly, there came a new sound, one unfamiliar to her these days: men singing and laughing. She turned to see. Cheerfully contemptuous of the far larger vessels, small fishing boats were weaving in and out of the water lanes. And Zarah's heart flew out to the fishermen, and she wanted to join them and be as wild and free as they seemed to be. So intent was her interest that for a moment she forgot her grief. She was unaware of the speculations of Ramose's wife.

Bentresht's beautiful cat's eyes narrowed as she watched the girl who was to be such an important pawn in the game Queen Hatshepsut played. Let her be all that My Majesty desires, Bentresht thought, and felt fear for lord Ramose, whom she so dearly loved, but also hated at times.

She moved towards Zarah, having sent her serving companions away. They went, twittering and laughing, to enjoy amusements of their own. Bentresht looked regal in her tight-fitting sheath dress, and was proud in a quiet way. Yet she must at least seem to make friends with the pretty girl slave—if this would, in any way, serve Ramose's cause. But the rubies were another matter entirely. Her secret fury grew.

Zarah's heart lurched as she became aware of the woman. Bentresht now stood next to the grain-bin, and her heavily outlined eyes were distant and cool. Her full red lips were sweet, but set in determined lines. Her wig, long and black, was decorated with little gold rosettes that matched the elaborate collar she wore.

Zarah winced as Bentresht made to speak. This great lady is used to power, she thought wildly, and she is used to having her own way. She exacts obedience, and although she commands with a smile, those little green glints in her eyes give her away. I wonder how many slaves she has had killed? I do not trust her, and I never will.

'We are a great river country, Princess.' Bentresht's cool, distinct voice underlined Zarah's title. 'Even so, in some places, eating fish is condemned. Certain fish are sacred to local districts, you see.'

Zarah had been on the earth for only fourteen years, but her lustrous dark eyes were suddenly wary and old. She frowned into the sun and moved imperceptibly away until she reached the very edge of the grain-bin. She cared nothing for Bentresht, who was so obviously pretending to be kind, whose every word and action had been sickly sweet right from the start. Zarah shivered, feeling as though she were a lamb being lovingly caressed by hands about to deliver her up for slaughter.

'Have you ever eaten the flesh of a fish, Princess?'

Zarah had not, but she gritted her teeth and did not reply.

Benstresht went on, 'People who eat fish are very wicked, and they are most certainly unclean.' Then, surprisingly, she laughed warmly. 'But it must be admitted that peasants care little for all that. They eat their fish and they live well. To be frank, they consider a good catch to be a personal gift from the River God—and from Pharaoh's scribes, who turn a blind eye.'

Zarah was not pressed to reply because Ramose chose that moment to return. Bentresht greeted him with affection and with the air of an equal which Zarah found hard to grasp. Women in the lands she knew were very much under the lord and master's thumb. To disobey meant death, just as it meant dire punishment to show even the slightest hint of having a will of one's own.

Ramose in his turn greeted Bentresht with courtesy and warmth. He signalled to Thickneck to lift Zarah down from the bin. The Egyptian turned to Bentresht once more.

'It has all been arranged,' he said firmly. 'Princess Zarah of Anshan will journey to our home in fine style. Messengers will go before us, spreading the word that the lord Ramose has, as a guest in his house, a very young and lovely princess. The event will be the centre of gossip in every gathering-place.'

'And so it will appear completely natural that the queen, on hearing about the girl, will ask you to take her to the Royal House! How very clever, my lord.' There was admiration in Bentresht's voice. 'Surely those at court, and My Majesty herself, cannot fail to see how fine and loyal a personage you are. May God see to it that you receive all your fair and just rewards.'

Ramose smiled a little bleakly at that. 'I, too, am finding it in my heart to pray to Amun. And I pray also that the queen is still of the same mind.'

'She is surrounded by treachery,' Bentresht replied. 'But she is very wise and knows her real friends.'

'Do not be blinded to the facts, Mistress of the House. It all depends on My Majesty's mood. Life at court is very uncertain these days, particularly since the queen knows that loyalties are so divided. She could stop all the squabbling if she would agree to marry Thutmose the Third.'

Bentresht looked quickly to left and right, for they were speaking of things that were dangerous when said aloud. But only the ignorant little girl slave could hear, and perhaps the eunuch, but they were of no account.

'How can the queen take yet another relation?' she said bitterly. 'In the cause of the succession, her father took her as his Great Wife. Then she married her brother Thutmose for the same reason. Now she is being pushed to marry the son of Isis, who was one of her husband's lesser concubines! He is bloodthirsty and arrogant, and reflects the views of the warmongers at court. Hatshepsut stands for peace and plenty. Thutmose the Third, and those behind him, stand for destruction and death!'

'I know all of this, Wife.'

'But you cannot feel as a woman, Lord! The queen cares nothing that Senenmut is a commoner, and she would gladly give him the throne.'

'And all of Egypt's gold to Amun and his priests. It will never be allowed to come to that.'

'But. . .'

'Enough!' Ramose said sternly, and he strode angrily away.

'Beloved!' Benstresht called in her cool clear voice, but she was ignored. The flaring of her nostrils and the expression in her eyes gave away her very real fear. It was then that her favourite personal maid came up. She was of a good height, though not as tall as her mistress. She wore a pleated robe of fine woven flax. Her bracelets, studded with turquoises, matched her elaborate necklace that had a gold counterpoise.

'My lady?' the newcomer said, and her face showed concern.

Bentresht shrugged, and her face became hard. 'It is all right, Nebutu. There is nothing that can go wrong. We will do very well providing the girl does as she is told and keeps her wits about her. And I swear by Holy Bast that I will see that she does!'

Such was the look in Bentresht's eyes as she swore in the name of the cat goddess Bast, that Zarah's resolve never to trust Ramose's wife was fervently renewed.

At last the great ship nudged cautiously against the bank and all was noise and confusion after that. Zarah held on to Thickneck as she and other members of the Ramose retinue were taken ashore. As she was helped into the carrying-chair that was ready and waiting, she was again very conscious of Per Ibsen's watching eyes. She felt herself shiver under his gaze and she was very aware of the sense of power he had about him. She remembered Bentresht murmuring, 'So! He is spying on us again.'

Per Ibsen, for all his air of friendship towards Ramose, must be on the opposite side. Zarah knew then, with a gnawing certainty, that her safety, at this stage at least, rested with what Per Ibsen might or might not say about her to Prince Thutmose III. She made herself look away from the tall, quietly distant young nobleman, and pretend an interest in the sights around her that she did not feel.

The order came and they began to move off—following Ramose who had elected to ride ahead with his men. Benstresht, in her ornate carrying-chair, headed the procession, and the rest followed in order of rank. Peeping from behind fine flax-weave curtains, Zarah was startled to be once again looking directly into Per Ibsen's eyes. She had not realised that he would be travelling in their direction, and she shivered again and turned away. When she dared to look again, Per Ibsen had gone.

It was with a great deal of noise and rejoicing that they went through the main entrance of Ramose's house. The gatekeeper gave a great cry of welcome and threw himself down in the dust at the nobleman's feet. They went up a path that led to a family chapel which contained an altar and a stele with a carving of a king worshipping Amun. Here, everyone waited, now on foot, while Ramose and his wife gave thanks to the gods for their own safe return.

They entered the house through an inner courtyard and a porch whose doorway bore Ramose's name. A servant, openly joyful at the family's return, ran forward with a gift of a lotus flower that Ramose accepted benevolently. They walked along the pillared loggia and into the central hall.

The main living-room, Zarah saw, had massive red-painted pillars that supported the ceiling. There was a large hearth with a brazier for cool evenings, and a wide limestone slab. Here, near-naked serving-girls poured cooling water over the travellers' hands and feet.

Dazed, fearful, still unable to grasp that, in this house at least, she was a personage of rank, Zarah had her hands and feet refreshed. She then obediently followed one of the obsequious girls to a guest-room. It was square with a high ceiling, and had a bed, table, chair and a tall water-jar set in a wooden stand. It was luxury, but Zarah could not relax.

'I want my man Napata,' she told the serving-girl quietly. 'He, and he alone, must attend to my needs.'

The servant, thin-faced and plain, looked distressed. She threw herself down at Zarah's feet and whispered in a supplicating manner, 'Do not be angry, Princess. Forgive me if I have displeased you in any way. I am to be your personal maid, and your word is my command.'

Zarah sensed the girl's fear. 'What is your name?'

'I am Tyi.'

'I am glad that you are my personal maid, Tyi, and I hope
that you always will be.' She smiled gravely. 'It is just that
Napata is from my land and he knows my ways. I wish him
to be present, as well as yourself. Perhaps—Perhaps you and
Napata will become friends.'

Tyi gave Zarah an odd look. Terrified in case she had gone
too far with her overture of friendship, Zarah added imperiously, 'You will help me to bed. It has been a long journey,
and I am tired.'

It was strange how quickly Zarah learned her role after
that, and how at home she came to feel in the lord Ramose's
great walled house. It was magnificent, decorated in bright
colours, with painted beams and designs of fruits, flowers
and rosettes. There was little furniture, for the house was
given over to the feeling of space and light. But there were
sufficient stools, chests, beds, small tables and tall jars to
make everything very pleasant indeed. Used to the woven
shelter of Caiphus, Zarah wondered at all she saw. The
rooms were many and included the women's room, the master's private bedroom, his private suite. There was a
bathroom and a lavatory and, on the other side of the hall,
a door which went up to the roof.

The gardens had a central pool, trees and exotic shrubs.
There was a household well, the cattle yard, chariot and har-
ness-rooms. Along the southern walls were the servants'
quarters, the granary court with enormous corn-bins, shaped
like beehives, in which wheat and barley were stored. Grain
was very plentiful in the House of Ramose, and it was as well.
It was used not only for dough and beer, but as a means of
exchange, and also Zarah learned, to pay wages and taxes
and buy all kinds of goods.

The moon waxed and waned three times. Still the queen
did not call. A tutor was hired to teach Zarah as much as
possible about life in a rich Persian house, and these lessons
she relished. Gradually accepting that she was to continue
to be the Princess Anshan, she began to revel in it all. She
never wanted to leave the luxury of this house with its exten-
sive grounds surrounded by a nine-metre-high wall. Here,
for a while at least, she felt safe. Not so Thickneck. He had
taken an instant dislike to Tyi.

'That one is trouble,' he said in his low, strangled voice as they sat in the garden alone. 'And she spies. Then she makes her report.'

'To Ramose?'

'No. To Bentresht.'

'But—they do not mean us harm, Thickneck. I am quite sure of that. At least not actual physical harm. Lord Ramose. . .'

'Do not be deceived because you are given food and drink.'

'And beautiful clothes—and powder and paints!'

'It is all merely to make you more beautiful. To show your perfection.'

'Then. . .' she said hesitantly, 'is that so bad?'

'Does the lamb complain while it is being fattened for slaughter?'

'They—They mean to kill me, Thickneck? Is that what you are saying?' Her eyes flared with fear. 'I do not understand.'

'There are many ways of walking to death, Morning Light.'

'But—But I am to be given to a great queen. Thickneck, it was she who ordered me to be bought. She—'

'—Is going to give you, in turn, to a young prince; and you know what that means.'

'Yes,' she said defiantly. 'That I will be honoured—just as the lord Ramose and Bentresht, Mistress of the House, honour me.'

'Really?' Thickneck's black eyes were derisive. 'Apart from the daily visit of the tutor, who teaches you lessons in the high-born Persian ways? Apart from Tyi, who is as sly as they come, who else in this great house do you see—who honours you?'

'My lord Ramose.'

'Two nights ago, when he showed you off to a group of old men close to the queen's ear. Before that, you were ignored.'

'Lady Bentresht—'

'—Comes merely to see that you are learning the manners of a high-born lady, and the etiquettes of court. You are a slave, Morning Light, and your life hangs on how long you are able to live out their lies. Remember that. You are a slave playing a part. You must be aware at all times. Act like a princess, but you must think like a slave who is determined to survive.'

'Thickneck, you are being unkind. You are determined to destroy the bubble of my joy.'

'Morning Light, I am going to make sure that you and I live, and live as well as we do now. So be wary of them all. Learn to use them as they mean to use you. Do not be taken in by words of friendship, because they are the most treacherous words of all. One needed only to watch the lord Ramose and Per Ibsen as they ate and drank together last evening to recognise that.'

'Per Ibsen? He—He was here, Thickneck?'

'He haunts the place,' Thickneck said sourly. 'And all the world knows that he comes as Prince Thutmose's spy.'

Zarah bit her lip and felt the return of her fear. She had been foolish to believe that all of this could last. It had been wishful thinking on her part. After Judas's compound where food, drink and the basic niceties of life were non-existent, she had begun to glow under the weight of Egypt's benevolence. Now Thickneck had brought her back to reality, and she felt shame. She had begun to enjoy herself. To forget—not Harad. Never Harad! But she had begun to live and breathe, and thoroughly to enjoy being a princess. She reached out and clutched Thickneck's hand fearfully.

'I am afraid of being sent to the Great House to see the queen,' she said. 'Why is she waiting so long?' Hope reared.'Perhaps she has forgotten me.'

'Not while Ramose has the sweet breath of life,' Thickneck said. 'If it all turns out as he plans, you will be like a gold strand of security wrapping up the parcel of his life.'

'Because he and the queen share a secret?'

'Yes.'

'But,' she said carefully, 'it has happened sometimes, that a secret shared has brought about not security but death. The queen could have our lord and master killed.'

'Ramose is too clever to fall into a trap. Make sure that you too become too clever to be trapped. Remember, Morning Light, that your actions bring not only your safety, but also my own.'

'I will remember,' she said softly, and her eyes filled with tears. 'Don't be cross with me, please. I rely on you.'

Thickneck stared down at her long and thoughtfully. His ugly face was so stern that she wanted to cry out in despair. In all the world she had only this giant man that she could trust and love. She would not survive without him. He was wise and he was kind. He no longer belonged to her in the sight of the law of this land, but, in the truest sense of the word, she belonged to him.

Trustingly she slipped her fragile hand into his massive palm and felt weak with relief because his fingers closed comfortingly round her own. Then, because she loved him so much, she said, 'I learned a very important thing, Thickneck. In this land it is necessary only for the owner to state that a slave is free and it is so.' She looked up at him uncertainly. 'And—And it is accepted in this house that you belong to me. Is that not so?'

'Yes, Morning Light.' His face had gone very still. 'I am your slave.'

'Then it is in my power to set you free.'

'And you will let me go?'

'I—I hoped that you would wait for me. Wait until they let me go too.'

'And if I do not?'

Suddenly her face lit up with a warm slow smile. It curled the corners of her lips and sparkled like stars in her eyes.

'You could still go. You may go now. You are released.'

'He frowned, not sure that he understood. 'You have said the words, Morning Light?'

'I have! I said them before the lord Ramose, and his scribe who set down the facts. It is recorded, Thickneck, that Napata of the Kingdom of Kush was given his freedom by Zarah, Princess of Anshan. You may go where you please, and you may do what you please. You may even become a fisherman if you like, and laugh and sing. You can choose.'

She beamed up at him, her delight like pure golden sunlight. But her smile faded because Thickneck was looking so angry, so fierce. Then he turned away and he seemed to grow taller. He was suddenly proud, his head held high. He warranted his leopard loin-cloth, his ostrich feather, and the oil on his magnificent black skin. His chest expanded as he drew in a deep breath. Then he threw back his head and seemed almost to be sniffing the air.

Thickneck's naked feet seemed to be barely touching the ground as he walked rapidly away and out of the gates of Ramose's house. He did not look back at the small forlorn figure standing so still. Napata from the Kingdom of Kush was free!

Zarah walked to the garden pool that gleamed pure and beautiful under the sun, and saw her reflection in the water, her large eyes holding all the sadness in the world. Then grief and loneliness shook her so that she hid her face in her hands and gave way to despair. She did not hear Bentresht's approach, and was unaware of her until she felt the older woman's touch. She lifted her tear-stained face as Bentresht asked sternly, 'Why do you cry, child?'

'My man, Napata. He has gone.'

'Then we will have him brought back to you. If necessary in fetters and bonds.'

'No! I have given him his freedom, Lady. The letters that record the fact have been written by the scribe. I am happy for Napata, but sad that he has gone and left my own wretched self. Without him I feel so alone.'

'We will soon alter that, Zarah,' Bentresht replied, quite missing the point. 'I will give you many male attendants, if that is what you want. And as many slave girls, too. Now dry your tears and return with me. We must make you very beautiful. You are to go to the Great Royal House by order of the queen.'

As Zarah walked obediently behind Bentresht, she could feel the blank, curious stares of the servants, and wanted to run. The Egyptian people were cold, suspicious and frightening, she thought, for all their air of kindness and graciousness. They had black souls under their painted smiling faces, and she preferred the people she had seen while travelling with Caiphus: Scythians; powerful Assyrians; smug, comfortable Babylonians and migrant peoples with distance in their eyes and the basic desire for survival burning like a white heat in their veins.

Egypt, Holy Egypt, unlike the wilderness, glowed under
the beneficence of the Nile, smooth, ruthless, civilised and
powerful, with a great queen who had dark treachery in her
mind. Suddenly Zarah was remembering all the stories told
to her by the beloved Nadia about the devil women. Queen
Hatshepsut must be the queen of all devils, she thought
wildly, and I am being served up for her to eat. I wish I were
with Thickneck, wild and free. I wish I belonged to one of
the fishermen I saw.

'Remember this,' Bentresht said. 'My Majesty is swift in
her anger, but she is as swift in her delight. If you please her,
if you have remembered your part well, I think you will
become a great favourite.'

Bentresht had turned, her eyes following Zarah's every
move. This made the girl hesitate and want to draw away
from the woman who smelt like flowers because of the scent-
cone she wore on her hair. She went on, 'If you please My
Majesty, it might happen that she claps her hands together
and orders a purple cloak for your shoulders.'

And yours? Zarah thought bitterly. Bentresht, Mistress
of the House of Ramose, I am not your fool. You want a
purple cloak for yourself.

'You must please Queen Hatshepsut and then you must
delight the prince. You will be sent to live in his house. You
must learn all the secrets in his heart. Then, at the right and
proper time, you must tell those secrets to the Great Royal
Wife. Do you understand?'

Zarah was not listening. Bentresht was merely repeating
the words she had said many times before. But what did flash
into Zarah's desperate mind was something that the lord
Ramose had once said: 'Try and remember all the tricks of
the magus' trade, little girl. My Majesty is a one for predictions and for receiving messages from the stars. Above all,
she is religious and gives gold in abundance to please our
God Amun.'

I will remember and I will wait my chance, Zarah thought,
and yet she felt just too tired, too sad and too old. Then, with
all the fatalism in the world, she told herself that she would
live if it were Mithra's wish, but that perhaps after all it would
not be so sad and lonely in the Kingdom of the Sun.

Then unbelievably, she heard the hurried beating of bare feet and Thickneck's harsh wheeze. He came up to them and, having abased himself in the dust before Bentresht, rose and grinned at Zarah in his wicked way. Her heart was singing while her mind was wary. Thickneck had lost his ostrich feather. For this, Ramose could call him to account.

'Morning Light,' Thickneck said, 'I have made my first transaction as a free man. This is for you! It will bring you good fortune, so I am told.'

She took the small gold scarab that he held in his great palm, and tried not to choke. Thickneck, so proud of his prince-like feather and fine leopardskin, had let his insignia of high rank go—for her!

'Thank you, Napata,' she said gravely and was very aware of Bentresht's narrowing eyes. 'I will carry this lucky charm all the days of my life. I—I feel I will need it. I am to be made ready to visit the queen.'

'Then I am in time,' he replied.

'Without the feather that shows you are a man who is loyal, a man to trust?' Bentresht drawled. 'Without the plume that denoted you as the favourite of a far-away Persian king?'

'Perhaps—Perhaps my man could be given a new feather, Lady?' Zarah asked quickly, and felt a small sense of victory begin to wake, for clearly she had the whip hand now. The queen's plan needed her, Zarah, for it to succeed. It was too late for Bentresht to replace her. The noble Hatshepsut had ordered the presence of the Persian princess—who was not a princess at all. It was all very frightening, because the queen's word must be instantly adhered to. Not even the lady Bentresht would dare to disobey.

'Perhaps a far larger feather, Lady?' Zarah pressed home her advantage. 'Perhaps a very large and fluffy white plume?'

For a moment Bentresht stared at her through narrowed eyes. For a short moment there almost seemed to be a battle of wills between her and the slave, but her hands were tied. She had to give in.

'Very well,' she said carelessly, then clapped her hands, and a slave came running.

'Tell the Master of the Household that a better plume is needed for Napata of Kush. A fine white plume that will be worthy of a noble guard seen to be in the presence of the queen.' She sent an evil look towards Thickneck. 'Go with the slave and present your unworthy self to the Master of the Household. He will see what he can do.'

When they had gone, Bentresht turned back to Zarah. 'It is my wish that you discard the Egyptian linen you are so fond of and, from now on, wear Persian clothes. You must also make a regular habit of wearing the jewels my lord has lent you, as well as the gold ornamental bells. . .' She was unable to stop herself from adding, 'The sound of which gets on my nerves!'

'I am sorry, Noble Bentresht.'

'Rubbish! You are not sorry at all. Now, since I have no interest in the whole business of your most insignificant self, I shall place you in the care of my own top lady whose name is Nebutu. With her own hands she will paint and powder you, and colour your nails. You are a princess, and you must remember that at all times. Oh, and most important, you will hide your affection for Napata. From now on you are to treat him with the correct amount of arrogance and contempt.

'Lady,' Zarah replied quietly, 'I cannot do that. He is my friend. I owe him a great deal. I would never treat him with anything other than the greatest respect.'

'Respect?' Bentresht snapped, and her lips curled with disdain. 'He is not even a man.'

'To me, he is more than a man,' Zarah replied gravely. 'I don't mind if the whole of Egypt knows that I greatly love and trust someone who is my friend.'

She looked directly into Bentresht's face, her expression calm for all she felt as though fire-drums were beating painfully at her side.

'You will be careful how you speak to me,' Bentresht snapped, and looked as though she realised that a despised lamb had suddenly changed into a young lion. 'And you will do as you're told!'

'But Napata. . .'

'During your visit to the Great House, Napata will act the part of the Persian king's most loyal and respected man. He will appear to be far above the others in your retinue.' Her eyes grew feline and cruel. 'But, after the visit, I do assure

you, my girl, that your eunuch will be another matter. Oh
yes, I promise you that.'

Twin patches of colour now burned high on Zarah's
cheekbones. Even so, she held her position and with quiet
dignity replied, 'Lady, when we return from the queen's
Great House, I will crave audience with my lord Ramose. I
will tell him that I must have Napata with me at all times.
He is my strength. Without him. . .' She paused signifi-
cantly before adding, 'Without him I do not feel that I will
be competent to play the part that has been set for me.'

Bentresht stepped forwards furiously, her hand raised to
strike, but good sense stopped the blow. Her voice was low,
yet sibilant, as she burst out, 'You will act as you have been
told to, or else I will see to it that your body feeds the wild
dogs! You will. . .'

'Lady.' Zarah's eyes were steadfast, even though her voice
trembled a little despite all she could do. 'Lady, I have no
desire for all this. My only concern is for the safety of my
friend. I do not wish to be presented to Egypt's queen, or to
play the part of a princess. None of this has ever been my
choice.'

As she stopped speaking, Zarah realised that she was going
the wrong way about things. This tall, magnificent Egyptian
woman would never allow her hands to be tied by a sibling
slave. No, there must be another method. The one certainty
in all this, like it or not, was that she was as insignificant in
the scheme of things as they said she was. She had to go along
with the plan that had been conceived in the mind of a great
queen, no matter what it cost. But she and Thickneck must
come out of it safely. They must! I will do as I am told, Zarah
thought, and I must keep my wits about me, just as Thickneck said. If I live, I will learn to be as cunning as hey are.
I must learn to act the parts I must play—and I will start
now.

Slowly and elegantly she placed both arms, breast high,
before her. She held her palms down as custom demanded,
then bowed her head in gentle supplication. 'Lady,' she said
quietly. 'You are the daughter of gods. Who else would allow
me to speak as I have just spoken to you? Who else but a
goddess would have listened to my plea? Thank you for

allowing Napata his new ostrich plume.'

Bentresht was watching her very thoughtfully now, and there was a gleam in her dark eyes.

Zarah went on, 'I pray that the Great Queen is pleased with me. If she is—and if the opportunity comes, I will tell the Great One Most High how kind and caring all those in the House of Ramose have been to me.'

'You are over-acting,' Bentresht said in a cold voice. 'You are far from stupid, though I know that you would have me believe you to be a fool. Be warned,   by Set and all the devils. Be warned! I am here wasting my time with you only because it is my lord Husband's wish. To me, you are less than the dirt at my feet, a nothing, a slave! And one more thing, even should your master Ramose look at you favourably from time to time, never presume to raise your eyes to his face as you have just done to me. If you dare to look upon him, I swear I will blind you with my own bare hands.'

'I have never. . .'

'No?' Bentresht's face was suddenly a mask of cruelty as she towered over the pale-faced girl. 'If you value your life, remember that you were brought here with consummate ease, and that your disappearance would not cause one small ripple on the Nile. You are quite unimportant, plan or no. Do I make myself clear?'

'Lady?' Zarah whispered and her lips trembled in spite of all her trying.

The knowledge that Bentresht had seen her as a threat so far as the lord Ramose was concerned had come as a great shock. Surely Bentresht was deranged? Zarah felt then that she was as helpless as a river moth caught in a spider's web; a prisoner who had no way to fight. She had done nothing to make the lord Ramose look upon her as anything other than the slave he bought to serve the queen. She had done nothing! Suddenly she remembered how Ramose had stared when he had sent for her to show her off to his friends. Had her master really been looking at her in a different way? Then the certainty grew. Any kindness from the lord Ramose could and would mean that she would receive some certain and quite devastating cruelty from Bentresht.

'I pray to Amun,' Bentresht snapped, 'that the queen sends for you soon. I want this thing over and done with. I want you in the palace under the wing of the prince. There you can use your eyes and ears—and then that scheming little mouth can, in turn, do its tittle-tattling to the queen. My lord Ramose will be proud to have brought the whole matter to a good conclusion and I will make a sacrifice in the temple—out of gratitude that at long last I have your vile person out of my hands.'

She turned away then, her back straight and tall. Watching her made Zarah tremble with fear. She wanted to throw herself down and cry, but did not. She remembered all that beloved Caiphus had said.

It was late the next day when a message arrived that the queen was disposed to see the Persian princess. Well pleased, Ramose came to look at Zarah where she was standing, surrounded by excited serving-women. Looking at her master from under her lowered lids, Zarah felt a delicious warmth in her heart. It was true! Her master felt kindness and concern for her—and it almost seemed that he did not want her to go. He clapped his hands, and a maid came forward and handed her a magnificent purple cloak.

'This is for you to keep,' Ramose said gently. His kindly expression did not change, and he seemed quite unconcerned that Bentresht swept in and took in the situation at a glance, her eyes narrowing in fury and hate. The nobleman went on, 'When you wrap the cloak round you, child, remember that it was the lord Ramose who chose you as the most exquisite little creature in the world. And know that he wishes you well.'

He stalked away, tall, proud, regal, followed by the silently seething Bentresht. The women of the house surged round Zarah then, intent on making her even more beautiful for the queen. Her pleasure in the cloak disappeared and her fear returned.

Later Zarah sat in her litter in isolated splendour. The air became chill and she gathered the cloak about her, grateful for it, since her Persian dress was thin and fine and infinitely beautiful, but scarcely warm. Yet it was not the cold that

made her tremble, but the memory of the look on Bentresht's face as the entourage had left. Now it was getting
late in the land where twilight came and dissolved into night
in a twinkling of an eye. The coolness suited the litter-bearers and their strides were long and easy as they made their
way swiftly towards the palace.

Thebes was a city of beauty and grace. It spread away from
the Nile and was laced with broad boulevards. Villas of the
rich stretched like great white cats sleeping behind high sun-
set-drenched walls. Near the docks and in the poor quarters,
the ordinary people crowded together in tiny square hovels,
but the dying sun had turned even these poor dwelling-places
into cubes of molten gold.

Zarah tried not to be afraid, but she was. She was frantically trying to remember all that she had been told about
the life of a princess of Anshan, but her mind had gone blank.
She desperately wanted to do well, for Thickneck—who was
keeping up the pace alongside her litter with powerful ease—
and also, surprisingly, for the lord Ramose. She knew that
he loved the queen as he loved Egypt. That the two were syn-
onymous in his mind. She thought of how gentle and kind
he had seemed and, when he had presented her with the
cloak, he had reminded her somehow of Caiphus, though
she accepted now, in her innocence, that the lord Ramose
had looked at her in not quite the same paternal way as had
Caiphus. No, the noble's expression had been of a male.

They reached the palace gates and the sentries allowed
them through. Zarah's mouth went dry, her heart began to
race. They were in a vast square courtyard, where the litters
were set down and then a tall, thin palace official came to
meet them. He was shifty-eyed and pale, and his full lips were
trembling alarmingly. Drawing Ramose to one side, he
began speaking quietly and rapidly. He took no notice when
Zarah moved into her allotted position directly behind her
lord and master.

'Your brother Ahmose is present'—the long thin face of
the dignitary was working in terror—'and somehow he has
learned of the queen's plan. We do not know if he is to con-
front My Majesty before the prince, or whether he intends
to extort gold from her. There is worse. There is to be no

private audience as was first planned. The queen intends this
to be a public meeting and pretends that she has sent for the
girl out of mere curiosity. We are undone!'

There was no time for more. Suddenly a great fanfare of
trumpets sounded. Guards came forward to take up their
positions before and behind Ramose's entourage, and the
official placed himself before them all. They entered the palace and walked towards the Audience Chamber.

In spite of her awe, Zarah was conscious of tall pillars
exquisitely painted red, blue and gold. There were rich
hangings, tall chairs and long low tables covered in gilt. There
were tall jars, and statues of long-gone kings and queens and
ornate shrines wherein either sat or stood the imperturbable
figures of gods.

Tall Nubian Princes of the Guard stood at intervals in the
pillared hall, and attendant ladies, beautiful with their
painted faces, black wigs, gold collars and jewels, lined their
way like so many slim and dainty blossoms fluttering in a
breeze. With a soft shuffling of naked feet, a craning of necks,
there was much curiosity about the little princess, and yet
still the Throne Chamber was not yet full in view. Now they
came to where the most favoured courtiers waited, then the
knot of royal relatives, princes and friends and finally to the
intimidating figure sitting rigidly on her magnificent gold
throne set on a high dais.

The queen wore the plain white dress of Egypt, but her
whole person glittered with gold and jewels. The head-dress
was of golden wings wrapped round her ears, the Horus
bird's body resting on the top of her head. The ureas was
poised in the centre of her brow; emerald-eyed and ruby-
tongued, it was ready as ever to spit fire into the eyes of My
Majesty's enemies.

Stone-faced, the queen waited until the procession had
come to a halt. Her glittering eyes seemed to be the most alive
part of her. At her signal, Ramose stepped forward and made
a low obeisance. The queen looked down from her high van-
tage-point. The red paint on her cheekbones stood out
harshly, and her black-rimmed eyes had a hypnotic, almost
snake-like glare. She totally ignored the small, terrified girl,
who was trembling so violently that the subtle whispering of

the little bells she wore was the only sound. Zarah looked exquisite. Behind her the giant Thickneck, now holding her purple cloak, looked subservient, but his eyes were wary.

'We welcome you, O Ramose,' Hatshepsut said coolly. 'We have heard much of your charming foreign guest. We wished to have sight of her.'

'Your Gracious Majesty,' Ramose replied with quiet dignity. There was a knot of warning in the pit of his stomach, for he had seen the priestly figure of his brother watching, cat-like, near one of the pillars to the right of the throne. Ahmose, Priest of the Temple of Hathor, who stood solidly behind Prince Thutmose's cause.

Then, with some commotion, the prince himself entered the Audience Chamber. Marching one step behind him, Per Ibsen. The prince made a careless salutation to the queen, stared long and hard at Zarah, folded his arms and waited in a coldly imperious way. He was a fine-looking, awe-inspiring man with a broad chest, thick neck and the family prominent nose. He exuded strength, and clearly would not suffer fools gladly. At the present time he was very much master of the situation.

Zarah knew that she did not want to be owned by Thutmose. He frightened her. As his eyes had flicked over her, she had felt that she was being eaten alive. Her large sad eyes glanced in Per Ibsen's direction and in her heart and mind and soul she was praying that the young nobleman could weave some kind of magic spell that would save her. The lord Ramose was helpless, she could see that now.

'We would hear of your journeyings, Ramose,' Hatshepsut commanded.

Ramose began playing for time. He began speaking of the hazards of desert travel, of the mortality among the camels of his caravan. He told of the wreck of a proud ship he had seen and of the death of many fine men. He went on to speak of the great peninsula south of the Syrian desert he had visited and of the mountains of Sinai. In a place in the central south, bordering the Great Green where there were luxuriant forests, there flowed perennial streams down the high steep sides of the hills, to sunny meadows and verdant glades. He had journeyed east to Mount Sepher and bought frankincense for the queen. He had visited the market at Ophir and acquired ivory and peacock's feathers for My Majesty.

'Tell us of the Persian court,' Hatshepsut commanded. 'And how fares the Persian king?'

'Most High,' Ramose side-stepped the question. 'It was there that I found the perfect Persian flower. I plucked her from her setting that she might glow, in all her innocence and beauty, here at court.'

'Persian flowers are unnecessary,' the queen said blandly. 'We agree that the girl is beautiful, but Egyptian blossoms have attractions of their own. We thank you for letting us have sight of her. Now, for my interest alone, tell me of her father, the Persian king.'

Having completely dissociated herself from Zarah, and then asked about the non-existent father of a slave, the queen had put a proud and loyal man at a total disadvantage, and she knew it. Ramose, who had not gone to Anshan but to Judas's slave compound, was momentarily silenced. Hatshepsut grew angry and impatient. Her long red-painted nails were now tapping furiously against the gold arms of her throne.

'We are disappointed at your lack of grace, Ramose,' she said haughtily. 'And we have no particular interest in your presence now.'

'I am sorry, Majesty,' Ramose replied quietly. 'With your gracious permission, the princess and I will withdraw,'

'I think not,' Hatshepsut's tone became calculating. 'The girl is undoubtedly beautiful. She will stay here—just as the people of Egypt, who have heard of her, will expect. After a day or so, she will be returned to you.'

'No! I will take her,' Thutmose said crisply, and there was a greedy look in his eye. 'Her looks please me.'

'The Persian king gave his daughter into my lord Ramose's keeping,' Hatshepsut replied smoothly, then her eyes narrowed because Ahmose, the priest, who had looked so smug at the prince's swift offer, was now clearly taken aback at her firm refusal to let Zarah go. She continued, 'Thus it will be that, when her stay here is over, she will return to the House of Ramose.' She turned to the man who had so easily fallen from grace. 'You may take your leave now, Ramose, and we will have the princess returned to you at our pleasure,' She signalled to a servant. 'Take the princess to a place of rest. I will talk to her tomorrow, perhaps.'

The servant led Zarah away, and she wanted to cry out that it was terrible to stay here in this place. She had seen no mercy in Hatshepsut's cat's eyes. She was feeling ill with fear and knew that now she looked upon the House of Ramose as a sanctuary, whereas she had seen it only as a prison before.

Ramose's face was ashen, his eyes bleak, as he prostrated himself full length on the floor before the queen. She began tapping on the arm of the throne again, impatient for him to be gone. He was an embarrassment to her. Had it not been for the treasure his ships brought, and for his great popularity with the people—he was looked on as a hero by those who remembered his exploits as a young man—she would get rid of him here and now. As it was, she had to be expedient and wait her time. At her signal Ramose stood up, then, looking neither to left nor right, he stepped away. He walked with dignity, his head held high, but there was heartbreak in his eyes. Napata and the men followed him.

Per Ibsen, watching the leave-taking, found it in him to wish the nobleman well. The older man seemed to have some affection for Zarah, and in his care, he felt, the girl would do well. But now she was under the queen's roof—and Thutmose. . . Per Ibsen loved the prince and would give him the last drop of his blood should it be necessary, but he found to his own surprise that the last thing he wanted was for the great Thutmose to take an interest in Zarah.

The queen dismissed everyone from her presence, and, feeling relief, for her tempers were swift and punishments severe, the people around her melted away. Ahmose, brother of Ramose, left the chamber very quickly indeed. The queen's one look had told him all that he needed to know. She had guessed that he had learned of her secret plan, and that had it been possible for him to prove it then and there, Thutmose would have been furious enough to bring about an almost instant revolt. There would have been civil war! The queen's right to the throne would have to be proved yet again. But she had been too astute, and had foiled his attempt to bring her into disrepute. Now she would be after revenge. Ahmose knew that his only safety lay in reaching the Temple of Hathor. Within its precincts he would be safe.

Alone, Hatshepsut sat deep in thought, then called for her most trusted personal guard. He marched briskly to her presence, shot his arms forward and bowed his head in a swift formal salute. His face was empty of expression, and his eyes were those of a killing machine.

'We will have Ahmose, Priest of Hathor, disposed of, Wen-Amun,' she said coolly. 'And it must happen before he has the chance to speak with the prince. See to it that the priest steps aboard the Boat of Death tonight.'

'Ai! And the lord Ramose, O Queen?'

'He will live—for the time being. At the right and proper time there will be rumours whispered about him. His loyalty to the court will be questioned. Then his death will come as no surprise. In the meantime, he has arrived in Egypt riding on the crest of popularity. However, we will never forget that he knows too much. But, for the present, he shall continue to breathe the sweet breath of life. We are not unmerciful.'

In the early hours of the next dawn, when the Nile was turned into a river of gold by the joyously rising sun, fishermen found Ahmose, Priest of Hathor, floating face downward in the water.

'He was an enemy of My Majesty,' they muttered together. 'It is fitting that he died. We will not tell the great and all truthful brother Ramose of this death of shame. Ramose is good; Ramose is mighty. We will say nothing to shatter the delight of his return.'

'Even so,' an empty-faced, cold-eyed bystander said, 'it is rumoured that even the lord Ramose was sent away from the queen's presence in some disgrace last night.

'How could this be? they asked in amazement, and there was much speculation after that.

Zarah awoke to the sound of music and wondered where she was. Then she remembered, and tried frantically to remember all that she had been taught about Persia. She was here to be tested, she knew, and the memory of the look in Hatshepsut's eyes made her fear rise afresh. She left the beautiful carved bed and sat, naked, on a stool that had a plaited leather seat. She was not sure what she must do, but she was not left alone for very long. A group of serving-girls came in, wearing loin-cloths, necklaces of beads and flowers, and very little else. They escorted Zarah, laughing and teasing, to the bath-house, there they attended to her needs. She was helped into a straight Egyptian dress of white cotton woven so finely that it clung to her. One of the girls, pert and pretty, and laughing encouragingly, tied a band of rose-pink lotus flowers in her hair.

'What shall you eat, Princess?' they chorused.

'What shall you drink: sweet wine, cold water, honey beer?'

Laughing and speaking easily, for she found herself among friends, Zarah replied, 'I'd like to drink the sweet waters of the Nile, and I have a great fondness for sesame bread—and perhaps some fruit?'

'Grapes,' they told her. 'Fat, purple, juicy grapes from the south.'

To this she happily agreed. She enjoyed the morning meal, sitting in the spacious room that had been allotted to her.

When she had drunk from a golden goblet and eaten from golden dishes, the smiling girls led her out of the room, along corridors with carved and painted pillars, and finally outside.

'Come to the gardens,' they said. 'They are famous for their beauty, and have many foreign flowers.'

It was true. The garden was large, and infinitely beautiful for as far as the eye could see. In a pool swam coloured fish, and lotus and water-lilies grew. The whole area was landscaped and enclosed by a high wall. Shaded areas were beautiful with flowering shrubs. Poppies, flax and forget-me-nots grew. Sweet-scented lilies and clover abounded. Suddenly the girls giggled and covered their mouths with their hands, and with eyes twinkling, ran away.

Zarah found herself unable to look away from the tall, handsome man who was walking so purposefully towards her. He came to a halt at her side, and carefully pointed to a sea of blue.

'That is the most treasured flower bed of all, Princess,' he told her. 'The queen would mete out death, should anyone dare to take even one of the blooms.'

Zarah was blushing. 'She—She loves them so much, Lord?'

'They are the lord Senenmut's favourites,' he replied. 'They are not natural to these parts at all. They are called cornflowers.'

With wide, wondering eyes, Zarah looked at the mass of blue. Her heart was dancing. She felt nervous, and afraid, and it was nothing to do with being in the Queen's Great House. It was because the giant Per Ibsen had sought her out, and was seemingly content to talk to her of such innocent things as pretty flowers.

'They—They are very lovely,' she agreed. 'The whole garden is beautiful.'

'Not as beautiful as you,' he said flatly. 'You are a complete surprise to me, Zarah of Anshan. To me, you are like the fine delicate mist that floats round the new moon. You are the first peach and cream mist that blushes across the face of the morning sky. I look at you now, and see you in your rightful setting. You are as one of the flowers.'

'My—My lord Per Ibsen,' she stammered. 'You are taking my breath away with such kind words. You surprise me, and—and I do not know what to say.'

'That you look on me with some pleasure, perhaps?'

'Oh, I do!' She looked up at him, and smiled. 'You are so tall, like a pillar of God. You have a body as large and strong as a fine bull. You are. . .' Her smile faded, and she looked down sadly as she remembered. 'And—And you are Prince Thutmose's friend.'

Before he could reply, a servant came running and threw himself down at Per Ibsen's feet.

'Lord, She Who Must Be Obeyed is calling for the princess. I beg of you, allow her to make all haste.'

Per Ibsen stepped back, his face bleak. Zarah almost ran after the servant, who hurried her to a large communal family room that had a warm atmosphere very different from the austere magnificence of the Audience Chamber. Even so, there was a great air of luxury over all. The throng of people talked ate, laughed. Musicians played. In one corner of the room a group of naked children were playing with painted wooden balls. No one took any notice of Zarah.

The women's dresses were dyed in many lovely colours, the style more or less the same, straight ankle-length sheaths with wide shoulder-straps. Men chose to wear broad pleated kilts of white linen, or else straight calf-length cloths tied and belted round the waist. Men and women wore jewels, necklaces or beaded collars. They liked arm-bands and, some, ankle-bands of pure gold. Now, at leisure, the men had dispensed with their fine wigs and showed their close-cropped hair or else shiny bald pates.

Suddenly trumpets heralded the queen. Silence fell. She came into the room surrounded by courtiers, relatives and friends. A slave tugged a cord that pulled back a large blue curtain at the end of the room, and at the centre of the space behind it, stood a large and ornate golden couch. The queen walked to it and made herself comfortable, while servants fussed around her with fine cushions, or else proffered lotus flowers for her to enjoy their beautiful perfume. Hatshepsut sent them all away, then raised one brow. The signal was sufficiant for a servant to hurry to Zarah and take her to the royal presence. She made her obeisances.

'Well,' the queen said easily. 'You will find us not quite so frightening here, for we are at ease and need not concern ourselves with royal duties. I would like you to tell us about your homeland.'

'O Great One Most High,' Zarah replied, mentally thanking the gods for the grace of her tutor. 'There is nothing so fine and wondrous as all I have seen here, in the whole length and breadth of my land.'

'And your father's palace?'

'A fortress made of stone. Grim and forbidding with its back against the mountains and hills. It is a hard and often barren land. It does not have the blessing of the Holy Nile.'

Hatshepsut nodded, well pleased.

'Tell me about your father, the king.'

'He does not wear linen and fine sandals, Majesty, but a sheepskin coat and high-laced boots. He is naturally dark complexioned and his body is hard and sinewy from years in the saddle. His hands are calloused from a lifetime of grasping spear-handles and rawhide reins.'

'Tell me more about him.'

'I cannot, Majesty. I am a woman. Women do not have the freedom they enjoy here. My father rarely conversed with me, and I was in his presence only by command.'

'Tell me of your mother.'

'She is a lesser wife, Great One, and she must spend her days in the king's harem. The harem is surrounded by guardrooms full of eunuchs. They are the only persons the king can trust.

'I have seen how greatly your royal father trusts eunuchs,' Hatshepsut said drily. 'Yet, on occasion, I have found them to be rather wily. Tell me, how grandly does your mother live?'

'My mother lives with a great number of other very beautiful women, Most High. They occupy tiers of apartments. Each apartment has a small hall and a tiny narrow bedroom. But the ladies are happy, Majesty, and they are secure. And although royal wives never attend official functions, there are those who are quite powerful behind the scenes.'

'What is your mother's name?'

'Mala,' Zarah replied, and kept her face straight.

The Queen stared at her thoughtfully, then said, 'What you have said does not impress me at all.'

'Oh, Majesty,' Zarah replied earnestly, 'Your great and wonderful land impresses me a very great deal. The people of my country do not sing and dance. They do not have the rich pleasures they do here. Their lives are hard, and they live close to nature because they must. Their pastime is listening to story-tellers. They are interested in the reading of dreams, and interpreting magical signs.'

Black eyes were staring into Zarah's face.

'Can you read signs and interpret dreams?'

'I—I looked up at the stars last night,' Zarah's heart was racing now, but she remembered Caiphus's words: 'Tell all that is good, make them believe!' 'Great One, I thought—I thought I saw you looking up at the moon.'

'Ah!' Hatshesput said, and leaned forward. 'What else?'

'As—As you stared in solitary contemplation of the moon, ten thousand thoughts of ten thousand nights rushed like violet shadows through my mind, and I heard a voice. A

golden voice, Majesty, and it said, "The Great One, whose
given birth name is that of Makare, is, first and foremost,
Great Daughter of Amun." '

'My birth name is Makare,' Hatshepsut agreed. 'And, yes,
my father is God. What else did this golden voice say?'

'That over hundreds of years, and then even more
hundreds of years, future peoples will speak your name. The
golden voice said, "To speak your name is to make you live
again." Thus, Great One, peoples of the future days, as well
as of the here and now, will breathe your name aloud. Majesty, the golden voice said that it is written, "Hatshepsut,
Great Queen of the Two Lands, will live for ever!" '

'And my throne?' Hatshepsut asked urgently. 'Who shares
my throne?'

Believing the queen wished to hear of her everlasting
supremacy over Prince Thutmose, Zarah replied, 'There will
be none to share your throne, Great One, not now or ever.'

'What of Senenmut?' The queen was coldly angry now,
and her eyes were hard. 'Tell me!'

'Great One.' Zarah faltered. 'The golden voice said nothing of Senenmut.'

Hatshepsut's eyes glittered. She half raised her flail as
though to whip Zarah across her naked shoulders, but con-
trolled her desire. She was unable to control her voice as she
cried out, 'You are a false prophet! You have told me nothing but lies. I will have you cut in two and your tongue torn
out. I will. . .'

Suddenly a deep, calm voice asked quietly, 'My Queen,
my beloved, have you no eyes for me? Must you give all your
attention to this poor, unworthy girl?'

The queen gasped, then smiled through her tears and
seemed to become young.

'She has spoken falsely to me, Senenmut. She made me
angry. But it does not matter now that you are here.'

'Then send her back whence she came, Beloved. Forget
her. Think only of me. See, I have brought you scented oils
and a necklace of fine stones. You are my heart, my soul,
my flower.'

And though no order was given, Zarah found herself
rushed away from the queen's presence. She was placed in a

carrying-chair and taken back to the House of Ramose in deep disgrace.

There was worse to come. Bentresht was at the gate, and it was she who heard the truth of it. There was cold triumph in her eyes.

'I will give her fitting punishment!' she told the perspiring court official. 'A punishment as great as the disgrace that this unlovely creature has brought upon my noble husband's house.'

At that, Zarah began to pray to the God of Caiphus, to all the gods of Egypt she knew, even to Amun the Unseen. But the look in Bentresht's eyes told her that her pathetically frantic prayers would be of no use. No use at all.

CHAPTER FOUR

IT WAS EVENING and quiet in the secluded garden. Ramose, distinguished in his fine black wig, his white linen and collar of gold, walked alone. His sense of grief and bewilderment was slowly being replaced with the desire to rise into favour again.

His bewilderment at the vagaries of the gods had grown rather than lessened. He had tried desperately to understand the reasoning of the deities. Why had they chosen him to be the one the queen cast down? What had he done wrong? He had always been devout, had always paid more than his due to the temple. He had been as loyal and as courageous as his way of life demanded. His allegiance to the royal house had never wavered. Over the years he had travelled the earth to bring back rich and rare cargoes for the glory of Egypt and for Hatshepsut the queen, now proclaimed Pharaoh of the Two Lands.

Ramose's vessels were the finest conceived by the ship-builders of the day, their sweeping sails proudly adorned with the symbols of his god and also his own name. He, the second son, had carried on his father's merchant business in honour and pride. It had been left to the first-born, Ahmose, to enter the priesthood, and to this end their father had paid a fortune in gold. But the younger brother had been deeply loved also. He had enjoyed a life as full and as golden as the holy orb. He had known adoration and plenty from the day he had been born, and felt no envy of his brother's very high and prestigious position in life. There were many ways of being good in the sight of the gods, Ramose reasoned. He had always tried to do the right thing and was kind even to the lowliest of slaves. Yet now, just when he had believed he would be at the height of his fame and in the greatest favour, he had been cast down and was a broken man. The gods had seen fit to desert him. Hatshepsut had seen fit to put him to one side—and she had given the evil eye to the girl.

Ramose's thoughts darted away from what the future might hold for Zarah. He frowned. He had seen nothing of her from the time of the return from the palace. Tired and disillusioned, he had gone to his private place to think and brood, and to wonder why the gods had decided to let his own brother wield such a weighty club against him.

He thought of Ahmose, his somewhat fanatical elder brother, who had always stood firmly on the side of the prince. Ahmose, the priest who had chosen to turn against his own kin simply because they had continued the tradition of loyalty to the crown. He had pointed out to them over and over again that Hatshepsut was a usurper, that the divine ruler was Thutmose III. Ramose had chosen to listen to Amun, and the words of the wise and most high Senenmut who was ranged solidly behind the queen.

There came the swift patter of naked feet and a servant threw himself down in supplication before his master, saying, 'Lord, a messenger from the family house in the city craves permission to speak.'

'Tell him that he may come forward,' Ramose replied. 'Tell him also that his business must be over and done with quickly. I have much on my mind.'

In a few moments the servant returned with a small, quick-eyed man in tow. Ramose recognised him at once, since he had held a privileged position in the parental home for many years. At his father's death, Ramose's uncle had taken over, and Pemu, the servant, went with the house. He was renowned for his wisdom and had never abused his position of trust.

'You are welcome, Pemu,' Ramose said politely. 'You have a message for me?'

Pemu's eyes darted towards the hovering servant.

'Lord,' he said flatly, 'Life, Health to you. I have come from your friend and cousin, and what I have to say is for your ears alone.'

The servant was banished.

'Life, Health, Pemu. Now tell me, what is on my cousin's mind?'

'I bring you a great sorrow with my news. I tell you, Lord, of the death of your brother.'

'Ahmose?' The young brother's eyes went bleak. 'How did he die?'

'He drowned. It is believed that his punishment was meted out by the gods.'

'Ah! The gods,' Ramose replied, determinedly pushing away the memory of two young boys playing happily together among the wild iris growing on the river bank. 'It seems they have deserted us these days.'

'Ai,' Pemu said flatly. 'But also it is believed that the revered Ahmose's allegiance to the prince had become too dangerous for My Majesty. The gods stepped in, on her side, to remove such obnoxiousness from her path.'

'So!' Ramose said sorrowfully. 'The way of life is very hard—death, too, it would seem.'

Pemu, with the privilege of a man who had known the lord since he had been a boy, looked him straight in the eye.

'Know that I love thee, O Ramose, but this I must say. It is also believed that the Persian princess—and her part in all of this—has become a source of embarrassment to the queen. Your friend and cousin wishes you to be careful of enemies. And also, with deep regret, he respectfully suggests that you get rid of the girl.'

'I see.' Ramose's tone was even, his face empty and cold. 'Then, Pemu, you must return to my friend and cousin and tell him this: I thank him for his concern. Tell him that his good name has never been linked with the foolishness of Ramose. That he need have no fear. Tell him also, that in the name of the gods I will deal with Zarah of Anshan in my own way. Now you may go.'

Pemu crossed his hands over his breast and bowed deeply. He was not usually dismissed so abruptly. There had not been the normal invitation to eat and drink and pass the time of day in pleasant, general conversation. He backed away from the lord Ramose, bowing and in haste, knowing very well the might of the master's anger.

Left to his own thoughts, Ramose was deeply troubled. He returned to the house, now lit by oil lamps, and summoned his wife, who came at once.

'Bentresht,' Ramose said evenly, 'I have not seen Zarah today. Have her sent to me. In the meantime I will tell you what I am planning to do to reinstate us. Something that will eventually bring us back into grace and favour. But, first, send for the girl.'

Bentresht's eyes flashed. 'I have put her to work. She has obviously displeased the gods, for it was their divine will that made Queen Hatshepsut reject her. I have seen to it that she has taken her rightful place in this house.'

'Ah! And may I know what that place is?'

'The lowliest, Lord. She is a slave. A nothing for which you gave up the most beautiful collection of rubies in the world. Jewels that should have been mine. I will never forgive or understand that.'

'So!' Ramose's face brightened as he smiled. 'That is at the bottom of it all. Coloured stones. My dearest wife, I will get you as many baubles as your heart desires.'

'Not like those.'

'Better,' he said firmly. 'And I will explain this to you only once again and then I will hear no more of your ungracious talk. So far as the stones are concerned, I did as instructed. I was told to find a beautiful virgin, one lovely enough to take the prince's breath away. It was essential that he like her sufficiently to take her into his own household. There she was to learn to spy on Thutmose, and every so often to tell all that she had learned to My Majesty. The order to obtain Zarah came direct from the throne! I was told that to achieve such an important affair of state, I must use my most valuable treasure. Had I owned such things, it was suggested that I bartered with pearls beyond price. The rubies were the next best thing. Come, now, this is surely my business. You are overstepping the mark and I will have no more of it! Now, have them send me the girl.'

'Lord. . .'

'Go!'

Bentresht left her lord's side, walked by the great pillars of the hall and clapped her hands. It was Tyi who came running. Tyi who was dog-like in her anxiety to curry favour with the First Wife.

'Fetch her, but see that she is clean,' Bentresht said quickly. 'And warn her to say nothing against me. If she does, she will die.'

Knowing only too well to whom her mistress referred, Tyi melted away.

Zarah, who had been all but worked to death through every agonising minute of the day, was once again lying exhausted in the stable. Even so, she lifted her head and felt fear at Tyi's approach. Since her fall from grace, Tyi had been cruel in many countless little ways, particularly when she had refused to fetch Zarah a drink of water. Tyi, Zarah thought sadly, was a survivor, and now that her young mistress had been relegated to a position beneath her, Tyi's suddenly puffed-up self was quite openly on the side of the lady Bentresht. How quickly she had lost her cowering, placating ways. And how she was enjoying seeing her previous young mistress demoted to a slave.

'Come!' Tyi said hurriedly. 'You must be made presentable. The lord master has sent for you. There is talk among the servants that our lord has been asked to get rid of you. Even so, the lady Bentresht has ordered that you hold your tongue about your affairs. Speak only when you are spoken to, and do not darken the character of my mistress with the airing of complaints. If you do, you will die.'

Zarah was taken to the female quarters, where women and girls worked on her with rapid, expert fingers. Nebutu, the most powerful of them all, was there. Zarah saw compassion in the older woman's eyes, and many of them showed sympathy towards the young girl. None dared speak.

For all the anointing of sweet-scented oils, the quick powdering and painting, Zarah looked frail and tired in her straight white linen dress. There were bruises on her, dark and angry-looking, that could not be disguised. All too soon she found herself almost running behind Tyi, who was heading towards the Great Room in haste. Bentresht would be furious that the signs of the cruel beating remained visible. Bentresht's anger would most probably be directed at Tyi herself. Yet it had been the First Wife who had ordered Zarah's punishment. Tyi had openly rejoiced at the newcomer's downfall, but had played no actual part in the game.

Trembling, fatigued, Zarah threw herself to the ground in supplication before Ramose. There then followed such a long and terrible silence that she became completely unnerved. She did not see the look of cold fury that crossed Ramose's face or the way Bentresht shrank away from him. All Zarah felt was utter relief, for when he spoke at last, his voice was kind.

'You have been accused and have suffered over a fault that was mine. For that I am ashamed. From this moment on you will take your rightful place in this house. You are to remember that it is I, Ramose, who now state even more firmly that you are, and always will be, Princess of Anshan. You will be treated as such.'

Zarah felt dazed and could hardly believe her ears. She was not allowed to look up into her lord master's face, but stared humbly at his feet.

'You have nothing to say to me, Zarah?' he asked. 'Look at me!'

It was an order, and there was nothing she could do but obey. Mindful of the fearsome Bentresht, unable to do anything about it, she slowly lifted her tear-stained face.

'Have you nothing to tell me?' he asked sternly. 'No story about what has been happening to you?'

'Great Master,' she whispered sadly. 'Napata has been sent away. Without him, I am bereft.'

'He shall be recalled. Now, return to your room. I will send for you again—when the marks on you have faded. Looking at them sends anger and bitterness to my soul. Indeed. . .'

There was a commotion in the hall and a servant came all but tumbling into the room. He barely had time to announce Per Ibsen before the man himself walked in to join them. His dark eyes took in the scene at a glance. He saw Zarah in an attitude of great servility, stretched before her master. He saw the marks of her beating, and a muscle twitched angrily at the side of his cheek.

'Life, Health, Ramose,' he said. 'I have come on official business.'

'Life, Health, Per Ibsen. I thank you for your visit. However, I have been told already about my brother's death. I grieve for him and pray that his soul weighs lightly before the feather of truth.'

'You are of his blood, Ramose. It is your duty to make the arrangements for the funeral rites.'

'Ai, that is so.'

'But his Royal Majesty, Prince Thutmose, has decided that he would prefer to carry out the funeral arrangements. It is accepted that your brother believed my master to be the living Horus and that the queen is the usurper. Therefore he asks, I repeat, asks—does not order—to see the Priest Ahmose off, and to do him honour in a right royal manner.'

'I feel nothing but gratitude towards the prince,' Ramose replied suavely. 'I am sure that my brother would choose it to be that way. I will pay the priests and the mummifiers, I will provide. . .'

'No,' Per Ibsen said bluntly. 'It is Prince Thutmose's will that it be done by those he chooses. As for myself. . .' He hesitated, for this was nothing to do with the official matter.

'Yes?' Ramose enquired.

'As for myself, I would take the princess into my home.'

'The princess of Anshan is my concern,' Ramose said quickly.

'Oh?' For the first time Per Ibsen looked down directly at Zarah, who was almost rigid with shock. 'Your concern wields heavy hands, it would seem.'

'That was not my doing,' Ramose said coldly. 'And already this sorry business is being put to rights. Zarah will be safe and well looked after in my house. It might not be so in the domicile of those who have sworn to be my enemies.'

'I will personally see to it that the princess. . .'

'I am sorry,' Ramose said flatly. 'The princess is mine, and she will not be leaving this house.'

Per Ibsen crossed his hands over his chest, bowed briefly and turned away. As he walked his spine was stiff, his legs almost rigid, his head held high. He looked larger than ever and every step he took, every taut muscle in his body showed how furiously angry he was.

'You may now leave,' Ramose told Zarah crisply. She bowed and allowed Tyi to lift her to her feet and lead her away.

Ramose turned to Bentresht.

'Wife,' he said distantly, 'I have loved you well, I love you still, but love and dislike are different matters entirely. I greatly dislike what has happened to Zarah, and I know that her punishment was inflicted by your command. All this for a handful of gems? With my own eyes I saw bruises, large and small, that amounted to more nights than there are in the full journey of the moon. Your greed and spite will therefore cost you the same number of stones. Have your jewel-box brought to me.'

'No!' Her voice held anguish. 'My lord husband, no!'

He had his way, and Bentresht's store of treasures was brought to him and set at his feet. With cold deliberation he counted out twenty-eight pieces of great value. Two of them he knew were her favourites.

'The princess shall have them,' he told Bentresht. 'And let us hope that in this way we will have allayed the anger and fury of the gods. Let this be a lesson to you, wife. Remember my words. If you ever harm a hair of the princess's head, you will receive not only punishment, but banishment for ever from my house. You deserve greater punishment than the loss of your valuables, for you have brought dishonour to my name. Leave my presence now. Do not dare to approach me again. You will wait for my call.'

Frightened and too furious for words, Bentresht bowed low before her husband and backed away as humbly as any slave. The lord Ramose, slow to anger, had never spoken to her thus before. Her hatred of the cause of this grew. Zarah! The name glittered like letters of fire in her brain.

Tyi, leading Zarah back to her room, was also afraid. She was remembering her insolences, her open triumph when the princess had fallen from grace. Should Zarah choose to, she could now have Tyi killed for her actions. Tyi knew that this would not happen, for Zarah was a sweet and gentle soul. This only served to increase Tyi's hatred. Zarah was an outsider, a foreigner, once destined for the palace. There she would have been well out of the way. But fate had decreed that the girl come here, to the House of Ramose, and it was infuriating that the lord master was already beginning to have that certain look in his eyes whenever he saw the young princess.

It is not fair, Tyi fumed. If only the lord master had looked my way instead. For him I would turn myself into the goddess of delights. I would have him eating out of my hands, given half the chance. O Amun, Great Invisible One, it could have been, might have been, had Zarah not got in the way. The only hope now is that the lady Bentresht conceives a plan to rid the house of the newcomer for ever.

As the days passed, Ramose found himself watching and waiting for the little princess, as he determinedly called her. He no longer looked on her as a child but as a frail, very lovely young woman, and comforted himself with the knowledge that Zarah had already experienced coupling with her young master. It puzzled him that Per Ibsen had made a bid for her. Perhaps the nobleman had formed some kind of devious plan of his own, but this was not to be. He, Ramose, would take care of Zarah all the days of his life. It would be his pleasure and joy to do so. He thought of his First Wife. He knew, loved and understood her very well. He had made her work hard for forgiveness and dared her to mistreat Zarah ever again.

'You must always be kind and gentle with her,' he ordered Bentresht sternly. 'Zarah has become dear to me now.'

Bentresht smiled, and turned her head away so that he could not see the expression in her eyes.

Thickneck was offered an official position, and he was to act at all times as Zarah's guard. He was allowed to use his own discretion. He had the run of the house and could come and go as he chose. Zarah clung to him, loving him and knowing that he was the only one in the world she could really trust.

It became a regular habit for her and Thickneck to walk to the river bank some little way away. It pleased her to be free from the confines of walls, for all her youth had been spent walking from place to place. Also there was hate in the air: she felt it focused on her from every nook and cranny of the lord master's home. Indeed, the pall of loathing emanating from Bentresht dissolved only when Ramose was near.

It was during these lazy relaxing walks that Zarah remembered again her beloved Harad, and her eyes would fill with tears. And, too, she thought of Caiphus, the man who had been like a father to her. She knew that she would give her soul to find him again. How alone he must feel without his son; how empty. Zarah began to pray that the lovely warmhearted Nadia lived in good health and that she would stay close to the wise man's side.

Then a great plan came to her. She would try to find Caiphus herself. She would become a wandering story-teller. This would be easy, since the fables of Egypt were so rich and wonderful, and she knew that, in the telling, she could make them come alive.

It was on one golden afternoon when the Nile glittered and sparkled as though encrusted with gems that Zarah watched a large boat being rowed up river. Beyond the green belt of crops, palms, flax and grass stretched the sands, the endless wilderness that she and the lord Caiphus knew so well. One day she would go and look, really look for the old man. One day, but not now. She must be secure enough to know that Caiphus and Nadia would be welcomed to the house. She made as if to rise, to go and tell Thickneck of her plan. In times of joy or grief, Zarah always ran to him, sure of his understanding and love. But he was leaning against a tree, contentedly carving. He liked doing this and had much sensitivity in his enormous hands. He always sat a little way away.

'Princesses do not sit side by side with such as I,' he told her firmly. 'Princesses are high-born, and they must remain remote.'

'But we are near enough to touch when we sit in the garden,' she had objected. 'Thickneck, are you disowning me?'

His ugly face became incredibly gentle. 'You are my life, Morning Light. That is why we must always remember that you have a role to play. We must not make people suspicious of us. Once they are, it could mean the end of us, as you very well know.'

Zarah frowned. She liked the idea of one day making definite plans to find her own people. She wanted to tell

Thickneck about it here and now!

Just as she was going to cast caution to the winds, she saw
the dear, familiar, quite breathtaking man coming her way.
Per Ibsen! Her heart leapt. Half of her wanted to melt against
him, the other half wanted to run. Per Ibsen had a very
strange effect on her. She remembered her sense of shock
when he had tried to buy her and have her sent to his house.
It had been the same then. She had wanted to leave Ramose
and the security of his home! But Per Ibsen was a nobleman
not on their side. The superior manner of him made her
afraid. It did not matter either way. She had no choice. She
was, beneath all the fine façade, still only a slave. She
remained still, staring at the glittering water, her hands
nervously twisting the stem of a flower she had picked. Even
the birds were quiet. She became aware of Thickneck's
watchful attitude. Per Ibsen seemed as though he were going
to walk right by her, and her heart sank. Then he changed
his mind. He looked down at her, his face grave and kind.

'Life, Health, Princess,' he said in his deep, calm voice.
'You are looking much better today.'

'And I feel much better, Per Ibsen,' she replied breathlessly, and felt her face go hot as she remembered how he
had seen her bruised and beaten before. He knelt down,
drawing her hair away from her hot cheeks with a tenderness she had not known since the days of Harad. He sat at
her side, and instinctively she moved nearer to him and so
positioned herself that her head rested upon his chest. His
heart thumped under her head with great beats like hammer
strokes. Surely, she thought, Per Ibsen has the heart of a lion.

'I would have fought the might of all gods,' he told her
carefully, 'to have you safe in my house. You are too young
a child, too fragile to be caught up in a spiteful home. There
are none in my establishment that would dare do you harm.

'O Per Ibsen,' she breathed, feeling warm and wanted, and
almost too happy to be true, 'your kindness makes my heart
fly. But you need not burden yourself over me. The lord
Ramose is my protector; my beloved Thickneck is my friend.
And there is one particular woman where I live who is specially caring. She is called Nebutu, and I have quite often
thanked the gods for her.'

'I see! You are fond of the river? You come here quite often, I know.'

'I am content here,' she began, and than added hastily, 'I led a very outdoor existence in my Anshan home. The river is quiet today, dreamy.' She stopped and smiled up at him. 'I like to sit and think and dream of—of happier days.'

'Dreaming is important,' he said. 'What we see in our dreams becomes set patterns in our thoughts. Some dreams vanish, like the white morning mists that hover above the river at dawn. Others stay. Good or bad, they stay! We have no control over our dreams. Thinking is something we all ought to do, and yet we rarely find the time. I have done a great deal of thinking and wondering lately—about you.'

'My lord flatters me,' Zarah murmured. 'I cannot begin to imagine what your thoughts have been about.'

'Where you came from—where in Anshan. Where, and in which district, can your father the king be found. What of all those who should be searching for you—to find out whether you lived or died. News travels slowly, but there has been time now for the story of your retinue being held up by robbers, your belongings and guards destroyed, to have reached them. Shouldn't your man be sent on the journey back to your parents to let them know that after all you are safe?'

Startled, forlorn, she looked away, at a heron who was watching with frozen patience for his prey. That was how Per Ibsen had been—watching and waiting for her. To find her weakness, and to catch her out!

'I would not part with Napata, Lord,' she said. 'He is the only link that I have. I am—am honoured that you have been thinking of me, but I am quite sure that the lord Ramose has done, or will do, all that he can. The lord Ramose is my guardian, and I look upon him as my friend.'

'I would like you to look on me in the same way.' Per Ibsen's face was now very close to her own. 'One that you can sit with by the river and talk, feeling secure. The outer world is often cruel. I do not want it to be cruel to you, Princess.'

'You are very kind, Lord,' she whispered, and wanted to cry because she felt her heart and soul reaching out to the large quiet man. Yet he was being cunning, trying to trap her with his sweet talk and his innocent-sounding questions. She could not keep the yearning out of her eyes even so, as she went on, 'I—I am often sad, thinking of those I loved and lost before I came to this land. It is good to know that I have—friends—on my side, and Napata is almost part of me.'

'Ah!' Again she saw the nobleman's proud smile as he looked over towards Thickneck. A Thickneck who made no attempt to hide the fact that he did not like what was going on. That he was wishing the big Egyptian further away. 'There are times when I envy your man. He is always so close.'

His words took her breath away. He was, she knew, merely playing a game with one he still believed to be a child. For one wild moment she wondered how it would feel to be held by him. She looked at his hands, how large, strong and capable they were. Yet there could be a wealth of care and gentleness in them, she knew, and oh! how she yearned for love and gentleness. To be truly loved by a man such as Per Ibsen would make her heart dance high in the clouds. To see adoration on such a man's face would keep her balanced on a shaft of air. Her soul would be like a humming-bird remaining aloft, motionless while her feathers turned golden in the glint of the sun.

'I thank you for your kindness to me, Per Ibsen,' she murmured. 'And I thank you for your concern. It—It would be nice—to be able to call you friend.'

Again his smile transformed his face. With the strength of a lion he stretched mightily, then jumped to his feet. Then he looked down from his great height and said, 'Until next time then, Princess.'

She smiled and watched him as he walked away. . .

Thickneck went to Zarah, and he was so angry that the scar on his face stood out. He had just seen Per Ibsen leaving.

'Morning Light,' he growled. 'Be warned! Per Ibsen comes here too often; he is a spy. He is out to learn all that he can about the comings and goings of the lord Ramose. Don't you realise, even yet, that our master is walking on a very thin line?'

'Beloved,' she said gravely, and her small hand curled trustingly round his giant fist. 'He was being nice to me.'

'All the more reason to keep him at arm's length. Don't you understand? Per Ibsen owes allegiance to only one person, and that is a fiery, young, war-mongering prince.'

'You—You make me feel sad,' she whispered. 'So very, very sad.'

'And you make me angry and afraid.'

'It is a terrible world when there is no one to trust.'

'No one, Morning Light?' he asked fiercely. 'Do you mean that?'

'I love and trust you,' she said anxiously, 'and I always will, so please do not act as angry and afraid on my behalf.'

'Then listen to my words. Do not trust him, and beware also of the girl Tyi. I cannot stand the thought of her being close to you at all times. I see wickedness in her eyes.'

'No, Beloved,' Zarah said sweetly. 'You see mortal terror on her face. She is what my lady Bentresht has made her, nothing more nor less.'

Defeated, Thickneck said no more. But late that night when the household slept, he sat and watched with utmost care. And so it was that he saw Tyi sneaking away from the House of Ramose, past the snoring gateman and silently moving through the secondary door. Thickneck followed her. She went to the temple of Buto, the snake goddess. Thickneck's eyes narrowed into slits. So, he thought, I was right all along. What manner of servant is it that sneaks out of her mistress's bedchamber to visit the priest whose duty it is to care for holy snakes? It was only too clear to him just what Tyi meant to do, given half a chance.

Hatshepsut paced about, her eyes glittering as wickedly as her jewels. She felt insecure and extremely angry. She saw nothing of the red and gold hall, the statues of the gods, the carved furniture and the murals. She took no notice of the colourfully dressed, jewel-encrusted courtiers—all of whom were keeping well out of her way.

With her own hands, the queen swept a favourite ornament, a bronze cat with gold eyes, from its niche. It fell, with a dull thud, to the ground. There was a frightened gasp from the people who saw this. An insult to Bast! My Majesty had just dealt a blow to the Cat Goddess and she would surely take her revenge.

The thin, balding messenger dogging her footsteps felt ill with terror. He had accomplished his task, but the news he had brought back to My Majesty had filled her with fury. He might not live to see another dawn. Mentally the man said goodbye to his sons, his daughter and the sweet Mistress of the House. He froze as the queen swung round to face him.

'So!' she snapped. 'Per Ibsen, friend of Thutmose, visits the House of Ramose yet again.' She threw her hands above her head in frustration. 'We do not forget where the loyalties of the brother of Ramose lay. Now this! We ask ourselves just what are the plots and plans being conceived behind those walls?'

'Great One,' the messenger pleaded, 'I do not think that Per Ibsen visits the house for any other purpose than that of seeing the princess.'

'Ha!' the queen sneered. 'The girl who can tell tall tales. The girl who will spread lies about me, just as Ramose may! Leave me. Let me consider what it is best to do.'

Still seething, Hatshepsut walked past the connected halls and chambers which housed the government—the palace had complete authority, both secular and religious, over the land. The officials in the queen's house were not the docile instruments of Hatshepsut's will, but were themselves important cogs in the administrative wheel. Had this not been the case, the beloved Senenmut would have been on the throne beside My Majesty long ago. The thought made Hatshepsut's fury grow.

Shaven-headed priests of Amun, high dignitaries, an army of officers and scribes came and went about on matters of domestic, foreign and religious concern. They made her nervous, the whole lot of them! She could trust no one. They were all plotting against her, she knew it. They were all on Thutmose's side, even Ramose now. And such was the man's arrogance, he was even allowing Per Ibsen openly to visit his house.

'O Ramose,' she spat. 'You had better keep a still tongue in your head. You and the girl both know too much. What a pity it is that your popularity with the people is taking such a long time to die. But make no mistake about it. I swear by Set and all devils, my time will come, and you will have to go!'

'Did you speak, Majesty?' Ranofru, the queen's daughter asked quietly as she reached her mother's side.

Hatshepsut smiled, but the grimace was not attractive by far. 'So! They are all afraid, and have sent for the only one—apart from my beloved Senenmut—who can calm me. What honeyed words are you about to spill into my ear, Ranofru? What sweet lies are you dreaming up to tell me now?'

'O dearest Mother of all that is Good, I have come with no sweet talk. Merely to tell you that the bronze cat with golden eyes is safe back in his niche once more. With Bast on our side, we will be blessed until Everlasting.'

Hatsheput's expression softened a little.

'O Ranofru, how besotted with Bast you are!'

'To me, the goddess is real, Great One. I see her smiling at me during my dreams.'

'This is no place for dreams.' Hatshepsut replied, and her lips curved and her eyes glinted in a good-humoured, but very feline, way. 'Come with me to choose what I shall wear for tribute day. As for loving Bast?' The queen threw back her head and laughed. 'Perhaps, one day, you will learn, my Ranofru, that you are daughter to the biggest cat of all!'

Zarah had been sleeping, her dreams of Harad and Caiphus all mixed up with Per Ibsen and Ramose. She was in the desert and the great eye of God was staring at her. She could not get away. The all-seeing eye was there, above her head, watching and waiting—for what? Far away, a noise shattered the pall of silence. The all-seeing eye faded as the fingers of her consciousness nudged her awake. She lay very still, alert, just looking at the man leaning over her bed.

He saw that her eyes were open, and said quietly, 'You are not afraid, Princess?'

'I—I am not afraid, lord Ramose,' she said quietly, but knew that she was.

'You will come with me? To my bed?'

She felt a great sense of despair, then came shock. The lord master was asking her, not ordering her as was his right. So, it had happened at last, just as deep at the back of her mind she had known it would. But the world was a wearisome place, a sad, sad place where slaves were slaves and had no choice. Tears glinted against her lids. She remained silent and flinched only slightly when his hand reached out to roam over her body. He stroked her, his touch firm but gentle. He was good and kind, Zarah thought tiredly, and she belonged to him body and soul. With him, perhaps it would not be so bad. She bit her lip hard as his fingers ran over her thighs and down towards that part of her that all men desired.

Ramose was feeling mad with desire for her, but he sensed the tension in the slight body quivering beneath his probing hand. He stopped what he was doing and stood there, watching her for a while, then said, 'You belong to me, Zarah of Anshan, and I am pleased at the bargain the gods made on my behalf. What they have given, I will allow no man to take away. I intend to ensure your safety from now to the Everlasting. When the moon is proclaimed right, and the sky-gazers equate the correct position of the stars, I will take you to wife. We will go to the temple. Our names will be written side by side in the holy bok. We will smash the jar, and thus the transaction will be sealed. You will live in my house for ever.'

Her face was wet with tears.

'Lord,' she faltered. 'You do me great honour.'

'The honour is mine,' he replied politely, and went away.

Zarah lay there, bewildered and not a little afraid at the turn of events. She knew that Bentresht would hate her even more now, as would all of those ladies on the mistress's side, even though she had never once worn the First Wife's jewels. Nebutu, the cool, distant favourite of the Mistress of the House, had at times shown compassion, and had occasionally been friendly. But even she would probably turn her back on Zarah now that she was to be chosen above the long-established women in the house. How blind men are, Zarah thought frantically. The lord Ramose sought to keep her safe from harm. He could have no idea of the hell on earth that was often the lot of a lesser wife.

She closed her eyes and tried to pray to the sun god, Mithra, as Caiphus had said she must. But she had no faith. How could she, when Mithra had not been strong enough to outwit Egyptian gods? Prayers, she thought, are really like broken blossoms shrivelling and withering in the dust.

How to survive, she wondered. There was one certain thing that she must do. She must please her lord and master mightily. She must make him unwilling to allow her out of his sight. She must be at his side at all times, twining round him like the star-lilies wound themselves round any large stems they could cling to. Once away from Ramose, she would be in Bentresht's unmerciful hands.

Zarah lay still, looking very small and alone. She hid her face behind her hands and wished she were dead.

The great Theban temple was glorious, as it should be because it was God's palace. God resided in his temple, and only Pharaoh, the king whom he called 'son', had the right to go to the inner sanctum and appear in his presence. But high priests were delegated to other sanctuaries to perform, on behalf of Pharaoh, the ceremonies necessary to the smooth running of the world. Holy pictures adorned the massive pillars and columns, and fables of the gods were told in brilliantly coloured murals. There were obelisks tipped with pure gold, and avenues of stone rams led to the vast arcaded courtyards. Huge statues of gods guarded the temple entrance, their wide blank eyes for ever towards the sun.

Queen Hatshepsut was carried towards the temple at dawn. Ranofru walked one pace behind her, at the head of the officials. She looked like a pale shadow of her mother.

Above, the clouds resembled pink and lavender puffballs. The sun was as yet only a half-rim of gilt edging the far eastern sky. It was time for divine service, which was performed daily. The queen revelled in this, for it was regular proof that God and the priests were on her side.

The drums beat and reedy music played as the monarch and her large entourage moved forwards towards the Avenue of Rams. The queen sat in splendour in her gilded

carrying-chair. She looked neither left nor right. She was
going to the temple to see her 'father' Osiris, and to receive
from the god the measure of divine life-essence without
which she could not perform her royal duties to the satisfaction of the High Priest.

Now the people swelled in number and worshippers began
to hum choruses that rose and fell, and held the sounds of
the wild night winds, then the sibilance of shifting desert
sands, then the rising of the Holy Nile. The hymn turned into
a roar of hundreds of throats as Hatshepsut arrived and was
then carried out of their sight. She went into the sanctuary
alone.

The was a clash of cymbals and flutes, and harps played
divine music. Two of the sun-gods and their counterparts
received the Queen-Pharaoh and placed her royal crowns,
the white and the red, upon her head.

The chief god of the temple, his tall mask covering his
human face, received the queen and stood up and embraced
her. She then slowly turned round so that her back faced him,
and the god-priest made magical passes down Hatshepsut's
back. By these passes the magical life-essence was transferred to the body of the queen. Before she moved, a god-
priest whispered in her ear. 'O Great One Most High, it might
be of interest if you decreed an interest in the happenings in
the temple this day. It is your royal duty to note that everything in thy name and the name of God is done well.'

'As always,' the queen's cut-glass voice replied, 'I bow to
the wisdom of God. It shall be as you say.'

Sure of herself, her might and power freshly established,
Hatshepsut, whose Vulture-Cobra name meant 'Fresh in
Years', turned to face the supplication of her people. Her
painted cheeks glowed and her dark outlined eyes gleamed
with joy in her power. She was at one with God, and no one
dare deny her.

She walked up a flight of granite steps so that she could
see the Hall of Proclamation the better. There were many
people there, all serious now and quiet. Then she saw Per
Ibsen at the back of the crowd. He was too large a man to
mistake. Alert at once, for it was her enemy she saw, she
waited. The priest began calling out the business of the day.

There was news from the fields: the harvest was good. Ships filled with cargo were due in Thebes soon. O great is Egypt's might. All is well in the land.

'Amun!' the crowd breathed in awe of the invisible one. 'Amun is praised.'

'Now for the linking of names.'

Hatshepsut frowned. There was no reason for her to stay. Such mundane business was beneath her notice. The god-priest must be mad. She, Hatshepsut, was the Power and the Might. She was wasting her time. But then she heard the names of Ramose and Zarah, princess of Anshan linked, and she caught the bleak look on Per Ibsen's face.

Her eyes became cruel and a small malicious smile played round her painted lips. So! Per Ibsen would have to report to Thutmose that once again she held full power, that there was none to sway her. He would also have to report that Ramose had taken the girl as a wife. What better proof could there be that My Majesty had no hand in some vile kind of plot? Clearly Ramose had brought the girl to Egypt for himself, definitely not as a pawn in some underhand game.

That night a feast had been prepared in the House of Ramose, and the whole place was full. Music was played and there was much to eat and drink, and cries of appreciation at the antics of nude dancing-girls. Honey beer and the juice of the grape flowed freely, and soon young men and women began making eyes at each other. Some couples disappeared into the garden; some preferred the roof of the house. It was all the same. The outcome would be the making of love. Wild and fierce and passion-filled, under the smiling face of the moon.

Zarah, sitting beside her husband, resplendent in gold and jewels, seemed even smaller than usual. Her face was sweet and fine as the field lily, her eyes wide and dark and incredibly sad. She had seen the taut anger on Per Ibsen's face, and it had felt as though an arrow had pierced her heart. Surely he understood that she, princess or not, had to do as the lord and master decreed? She longed for the moment when she could slip away to the privacy of her own box-like room. There she could rest and have Tyi wash her feet and help her to change into a gown of thin linen that she would wear to her husband's bed.

And such a bed! Large and wide, with legs shaped like those of a lion, ending in great golden paws, it had been taken up to the roof with great difficulty, at Ramose's command.

'I want to see the reflection of the stars in your eyes,' he had said. 'I want you up there under the sky. I shall take you, and you will accept me, and the moon will bathe us both in cloth of gold. Princess, I swear to you that I will make this a memorable night.'

'I—I still cannot believe that such a great and powerful man has—has actually taken me to wife,' she whispered. 'I—I pray to the gods that I do not disappoint you, Lord.'

Ramose had smiled at that, a gentle, almost paternal, smile and softly patted her cheek.

The nuptial feast was still at its height. Thickneck had left the hall while Zarah and her husband were sitting side by side, now watching acrobats giving a spectacular display. He was skulking in the shadows near Zarah's private room, waiting for the person he was sure would come. Then he heard Tyi's quick steps, and shrank behind a pillar. He saw that Tyi carried a tightly woven reed basket, and his lips went down, his eyes were cruel. He knew that quite soon his little Morning Light would be returning to prepare herself, with Tyi's help, to go to her lord husband's bed. Oh yes, Tyi should be there, armed with a polished bronze mirror, paints, brushes and cones of sweet scent. There should be no reed basket at all, rather a fine beauty-box with ivory carving and inlays of gold.

Tyi disappeared into Zarah's room. Thickneck gave her time. By now he was wearing the hide hand-covering that he had acquired for the price of a gold bracelet from one of the priests of Buto the snake goddess. He went silently into Zarah's room, and saw that the basket was empty. Zarah's night clothes had been laid in readiness on her bed. Tyi gasped, and shrank away from him.

'Napata!' she said. 'What are you doing here?'

'Where is it?' He answered the question with one of his own.

'I do not know what you are speaking about,' she panted. 'You have no business here.'

'Where is it?' he growled, his anger making his ugliness show.

'Who are you?' Tyi began blustering. 'Or rather, what are you? Neither man nor woman. You are a thing! As such, you have no place here on the princess's nuptial night.'

'Where have you set the viper?' Thickneck growled. 'What manner of woman are you? Your mistress is sweet and kind and would not harm a hair of your head, yet you wish to watch her agony throes. What a black and treacherous soul you have!'

'How dare you speak so?' Tyi shrieked, her face working in fury and hate. 'You are mad—and for your accusations you could be skinned alive. But Set and all devils, I wish you in hell!'

'And beat you to it, I have no doubt. In the meantime, where is the snake that you have released? I will catch it and put it back in its basket and take it far from here.'

Out of the corner of his eye he saw the living thing making writhing S-shapes as it moved about under the fine white cotton that Zarah would wear. His hand shot out, and in no time at all the reptile was caught fast and held behind its head so that it could do no harm.

In a fury Tyi leapt at him and began scratching and kicking, her face vixenish, her eyes wild. She began screaming obscenities and blackening Zarah's name.

'Stop that!' Thickneck threatened. 'You have gone too far.'

'Not far enough!' she screamed, and leapt towards a shelf for a long tortoiseshell-handled knife. She aimed a blow at Thickneck's heart. He sidestepped and caught hold of her quite easily with one hand. With one swift movement he pushed the snake's head right inside Tyi's opened screeching mouth.

Her eyes distended in horror, then terror. She shuddered and died swiftly, and Thickneck felt nausea as he watched, for he knew that such a death had been meant for the only person in the world who would ever call him 'Beloved'.

Thickneck replaced the snake in the basket. Then, with great rapidity for a man of such size, he took up the body of

Tyi and, unnoticed by the crowds still revelling and stupid with wine, he left the house. He disposed of snake and slave in the river, and returned to sit and talk easily with Harkhuf, the old majordomo. The two had become friends, and enjoyed board games and a gamble or two.

Zarah lay on her lord's bed and looked up at the stars. The air was heavy with the scent of spices and flowers. She felt strangely unreal. Ramose was beside her and his voice was soothing and kind. His hands were feeling, touching, teasing her expertly. He began whispering lyrical things, likening her beauty to that of the moon. As his ardour grew, her eyes swam with tears. How kind he was. Surely she had been blessed by the gods! With this man she was safe. He was her shield against the world.

'Dearest Lord,' she whispered, 'love me with all your might. Love me as fiercely and as wonderfully as I love and adore you.'

'My sweet one,' he said quietly. 'I feel as if the gods are all smiling upon me this night. You are a flower, a small gentle blossom.'

'No, Lord,' she whispered urgently. 'I am your wife, and above all I need you to treat me as such. I ache to give you a son.'

'My. . .'

'Wife!' she insisted. 'And in time, if the gods will it, mother to my sweet lord's child.'

He rested his face against hers, and she felt the tears.

'I have no child,' he groaned. 'Hathor has not bestowed such joy upon me.'

'I will bestow it!' she whispered against his lips. 'That I promise you, Lord.'

Then they came to her, all the lessons she had learned at Nadia's knee. And if she teased and coaxed her lord, working him into passion such as he had never known before, it was out of a sense of survival as well as the very real love and affection she bore him. With Ramose on her side, she could bear the weight of Bentresht's hate.

When the moment of taking was over, Zarah leaned her cheek against Ramose's smooth chest. 'He is my master, my husband, my father, my lord,' she thought, and tears of gratitude slipped silently down her cheeks. 'And I will be safe in his shadow all the days of my life.'

For one moment she thought of Per Ibsen, of how it might have been, but she pushed the wistful longing to one side.

Thickneck was right. The Theban had been there by the river in order to learn all that he could. To spy for his master, Thutmose the Prince. She must never forget that, never!

'Ramose, Beloved,' she whispered to the man sleeping at her side. 'I give you my life, my loyalty, and my eternal love.'

She fell asleep, lying peacefully cradled in her husband's arms.

From that day, Zarah became Ramose's little princess whom he could not bear out of his sight. He made much of her, and was so sweet and kind that her adoration of him grew in return. Bentresht remained closed in the women's quarter, and for the moment at least the lord Ramose allowed her to stay where she chose. But she was still First Wife, and when important guests arrived it was Bentresht who became hostess, her face beautiful, her lips smiling, her thoughts never shown. Tyi's disappearance caused Zarah some concern, but she forgot the girl in her own confidence and contentment.

The time of the inundation returned, and there was much rejoicing in the land. The people raised their voices to give praises to the queen, for it was the god-power in her that had given plenty in the land. The River God has responded to her call and called up the waters of the Nile. The gods be praised! Zarah's prayers of thankfulness were, as ever, in the name of Ramose. It had been he and he alone who had made all the difference in the world to her and Thickneck's way of life. The one thing that would bring complete and utter perfection, she thought, was to find Caiphus. She wanted to share her joy and comfort with him and also with Nadia, her breast-mother. She often thought, too, of the beloved Harad, but he was like a dream to her: a soft-eyed, smiling spirit that lived in another world. Her tears for her breast-brother held no bitterness now, only love. Something strange seemed to be happening in her mind. Often Harad's face was replaced by Per Ibsen's, and she would hastily brush it away and try to bring back Harad. She remembered his laughing eyes, the sound of his voice as he had teased her. How swiftly he could run, how high he could jump. He was only a boy, she thought, and felt a pain in her heart. Just a fine and wonderful boy.

Now Ramose began to speak of the plan he had made to make an expedition to the kingdom of Punt. It was a long and dangerous journey, but worth it for the fortune he would bring home. He was a fine trader and merchantman. He knew how to strike a good bargain. He would be bringing back much bounty for Egypt and the queen. It would be worth the two years or so that he would be away. Worth the time it would take out of his life.

'Take me with you,' Zarah pleaded. 'I cannot stay here without you, Lord.'

'This is a journey for men, Princess,' he had replied. 'You must stay safe in the heart of my home. I shall wish the days and nights away until my return.'

When his ship sailed away at last, Zarah watched and felt a very real grief. Ramose had become dear to her. But the following dawn brought a new and terrifying knowledge. Bentresht had now come into her own. She was mistress of the House, and her word was law. How will I survive until my lord's return? Zarah wondered wildly. Will I see the next rising of the Nile? Am I to live or die?

She flinched as Bentresht came forward, for she saw death in the older woman's eyes. Zarah felt sick. It was no use, she thought wildly, she could never fight and win against First Wife. The odds were too great. Bentresht was all-powerful and she, Zarah, too insignificant and small.

Just then there came the heavy sound of recognisable footsteps. Thickneck, she thought, and wanted to weep with relief. The giant touched his left breast with his right hand, bowed, and said, 'Life, Health, O She Who is Above Us. I thought I would accompany the young mistress to the river today. Is this permitted?'

The older woman's expression was evil. 'The young mistress will have no time for river walks from now on. Neither will she have time for such a pathetic, incomplete man as yourself. The Lord Ramose has put the reins of this house in my hands. From this day, you will not be allowed through the gates. Do I make myself clear?'

'No!' Zarah cried out in anguish. 'You cannot do this. He is my friend.'

'Most noble lady,' Thickneck began, 'I. . .'

'Go!' Bentresht snapped. 'Accept that from now on it shall be as I say. Should I wish it, I could have you cut down where you stand.'

Napata squared his great shoulders, but Zarah's fear for him knew no bounds and she cried out again, 'Go, Napata. Go now!'

With a silence that was almost too terrible, Thickneck swung on his heel and left the trembling girl.

Bentresht's smile was malevolent. 'He has shown some good sense at last. Now, my girl, we will see to it that you will learn your true place in the scheme of things. You will go to the animals, the cattle and the kitchen birds. You will clean and care for them as though they were fashioned from gold. My lord's horses will have coats that gleam like the Nile under the sun. You will gather all dung. Hard work will never harm such as you. You will eat food befitting your true status. When I wish to go into the matter of your venomous self in more detail, I shall send for you. Then we shall see what we shall see.'

'Lady,' Zarah began in distress. 'I will do all that you wish, and more. But please, I beg of you, see that no harm comes to Napata.'

'His sort are not worth a single roll of the dung-ball the holy scarabs so love,' Bentresht sneered. 'Forget him, and go about your chores. The servants and ladies of the house all see you for the outsider you are. There is and never has been a place for you here. No one will speak to you, no one will go near you. Disobedience means death. One more thing. . .' Zarah half turned, but was unable to dodge the spiteful hand that whipped out to catch her full in the face. 'Let it be known that, on this day, I swear before all the gods that you will never have a place in my Lord Ramose's bed again.'

After that, life became drudgery of the most harsh and lowly kind. As for the nourishment befitting her place, there

were days in a row when Zarah received no food at all and
was forced to chew on goose-grain when the overseer was
not near.

For all the hardship and hunger of her long, heat-heavy
days, Zarah chose them above the torture she received when
she was ordered to Bentresht's private sanctum. It became
the woman's pleasure to question Zarah closely and beat her
with a whip until she replied. The questions were always the
same.

'Tell me about the slave compound. Who ran the slaves?'

'Neb,' Zarah would whisper through ashen lips.

'And was he liked?'

'He was hated and feared by all.'

'Why?'

'He was—was so cruel.'

'He could not have been so harsh. It is not good policy to
injure slaves.'

'He was adept at hurting where it did not show,' Zarah
had to admit in a tight whisper, and felt herself cringing
inside, and wanting to scream out again the falseness and
treachery of the world, the bestiality of all men, of the venom
of the woman before her now. She could only remain mute,
fearing and half knowing what was to come.

'How could this be?' Bentresht asked silkily. Then, because
Zarah remained mute, she dealt the girl a stinging blow.
'Answer me!'

Bentresht's eyes opened and glared like a tigress about to
leap on its prey, and devour. In fear and trembling, heart-
sick, old memories and horrors now wickedly alive, Zarah
whispered about Neb's spiteful hands—of where he put
those long-nailed dirty fingers to pinch and scratch and tear.
And all the while Zarah relived the misery, the torture and
loneliness of those days and heard again the high, long-
drawn-out screaming of the beloved Harad.

When Zarah was completely broken, the physical torment began and while it was going on, Bentresht would drink
a certain wine, to which a strange kind of narcotic had been
added. Then she would scream at Zarah and force her to
bend down, naked, and crawl on all fours like the animal she
was. And while she was in this vulnerable position, Ben-

tresht would inflict indecencies upon the girl's small, shrinking form. Zarah would begin to pray then even more earnestly to die, for it was peace she needed now. Just to be left alone to lie in gentleness and peace everlasting. But Bentresht flew at her, and was screaming profanities against Amun, Isis and Ra—also the queen who was the living Horus. They had all let her down. She hated them all! As she began to flog Zarah, she was in her mind flogging to death all her enemies in the world.

Not even Nebutu, Bentresht's life-long companion, knew all that was going on. Even so, of them all, it was she who tried to help Zarah in small ways. She also once had the chance to whisper, 'Do not despair. Napata is never very far away. He is the friend of Harkhuf our majordomo. Do you remember him?'

In spite of all that Bentresht could do, Zarah survived. Meek, wretched, half dead, she continued to survive. Little titbits of food were smuggled to her, and messages of courage from Thickneck. If she fell asleep at her wearisome tasks, Nebutu ordered the overseers of the animals to look the other way.

The Nile dwindled to become a mere stream struggling towards the sea that the Egyptians called the Great Green. But the people were sure of the inundation, and new crops were sown and harvested in quick succession. Such was the beneficence of the gods, there were always two harvests a year. The queen continued to reign supreme.

After the second inundation, Bentresht's distended eyes became furtive, then wary. Two years, Ramose had said. Two years! If Amun was on her husband's side, Bentresht knew that he might be returning before the end of the year. One look at Zarah, at the state she was in, and all would be lost. In spite of all she had done, the girl had not died from what could be explained as natural causes while at her daily tasks. There was nothing else to be done, but to have the princess killed. But who, and how? No one must connect her demise with the lady Bentresht, for this would mean the end of her reign in the House of Ramose. Perhaps even the end of her own life.

Then she had an idea, and called for a servant. She
ordered, 'Take this message to Per Ibsen from me. And
hurry. Tell him. . .' Hurriedly, furtively, she spoke, quite
unaware that Nebutu had overheard.

It was the ever-watchful Thickneck who took it upon
himself to confiscate Per Ibsen's reply. What Nebutu the
favourite of Bentresht thought was hard to tell. As for the
wizened Harkhuf, he was Ramose's man and wholly on
Thickneck and Zarah's side.

In a while Bentresht came to realise that it was up to her
to bring about the death of the little princess. Her eyes
became slits of evil. Her mouth was tight. Awful figures were
dancing and gibbering in her mind. She thought she saw an
image of Zarah choking to death on fruit that had turned
into large rubies, and began to laugh. Then she screamed out
her hatred and defiance of the gods, but she was most vind-
ictive towards Amun, the invisible one.

Zarah, huddled in with the milking cows, felt weak, tears
scalding her cheeks. She wanted to give in, wanted above all
to join her beloved Harad. The world of Everlasting must
be kinder than this. She was too humilated and sick to want
to keep up the struggle for survival, but she had to, for
Thickneck's sake. She tried to think, to remember exactly
what the message whispered by an old gardener had been.
'Thickneck says you are to eat with the mistress tonight. You
must exchange your dish of fruit for hers. This is important.
Let the lady Bentresht eat your fruit. On no account eat of
it yourself.'

A weary hand fluttered to push a stray strand of hair away
from her thin face. Eat with Bentresht? Exchange fruit? Was
the whole world going mad? But there was no mistake. A
house servant brought the message.

'You are to go to the women's room to be dressed and
cleaned. It is the First Wife's desire that you eat with her this
night.'

In fear and trembling, Zarah went to the house. She was
washed and anointed with scented oil and dressed in fine
white linen. All this by women who now, as from the first,
still continued to look on her as the outsider who had caused

the weight of their mistress's displeasure to fall upon their own miserable heads. There was not one who dared to give the frightened girl even a kind look. At last she was taken to Bentresht.

Bentresht sat at a small table, with an empty stool opposite her. Her eyes were cold and empty as she looked at Zarah, whose beauty had grown rather than lessened because of her frailty.

'I have decided that you have been punished enough,' Bentresht said in a brittle, unfeeling voice. 'So, as lesser wife to my lord husband, you shall sit with me and eat. From this day we shall be sisters under the skin. Sit down.'

'Thank you,' Zarah whispered, and tried to look from the dish of fruit set nearest to her hand.

She had never felt less hungry, but picked at the dishes set before her because she knew that she must. And all the while Bentresht's eyes became more strange. Her voice held excitement, and the woman seemed to have grown larger. She began tormenting the naked serving-girls, whose skins all clearly showed signs of the First Wife's wrath. They were all like wax in her hands, Zarah thought, and realised then that she was far from being the only one consistently suffering Bentresht's cruelty.

The meal was ending, and as Bentresht turned to rail at a girl who had seemingly deliberately spilled wine on the mistress's dress, Zarah swiftly exchanged the golden dishes that were full of fruit, so that hers was now nearest to Bentresht's beautiful hands. There then fell a silence so terrible that Zarah thought the pounding of her heart could be heard for miles. Bentresht smiled coldly.

'Come, eat the fruit of your adopted land, Zarah. Try those delicious purple grapes.'

Zarah froze. She sat there, wide-eyed, helplessly staring at the woman whose hatred of her own small self had grown to the point that all discretion had been thrown to the winds.

'Eat!' Bentresht said again. 'Eat to please me, if not yourself. See? I will myself show you how good they are.'

She reached forward in a terrible way, began pulling grapes from their stalks and putting the fruit into her over-painted mouth. The girl who had spilled the wine was transfixed, as were the other servants. Harkhuf appeared as if from nowhere, but Bentresht was unaware of this. Her expression changed to hate, then to horror. She opened her mouth to cry out, but no sound came. To Zarah, it all seemed to be happening in a terrible kind of slow motion. She could not move, could not think. Waves of darkness overcame her, and then, as if by magic, great arms closed round her and Thickneck was carrying her, unresisting, away. He took Zarah back to the room that had been hers when she had been Ramose's dearest and most favourite wife.

There were many willing to help make things fall into shape after that. It was given out that Bentresht had died through a kind of fit brought upon by over-indulgence of some vile drug. Many stepped forward to swear by the gods that Bentresht had become steadily more unstable from the moment of Ramose's departure. The head of the family house in Thebes took over. Bentresht was laid to rest in her tomb, with the most perfunctory services and proceedings. There had been whispers, put about by the majordomo and others, that Bentresht had taken lovers, that she had brought shame to the family name. The whole affair was hushed up, over and done with by the time the great lord Ramose returned.

He came to his house and saw that things were as he had left them, that the slaves and servants sang as they worked. They were happy and relaxed as they laboured for the pleasure of the gentle young wife. But Ramose's eyes held grief when he heard of Bentresht's death, and he seemed to age. He went at once to the family temple and begun to pray that her soul might weigh lightly before the feather of truth. He shaved off his eyebrows and every hair on his body as the mark of his sorrow. He called Zarah to him.

'You have done well,' he told her. 'I will take my seclusion for the required amount of time. I do not wish to be disturbed at my prayers for my beloved First Wife. I desire you to ensure my privacy at all times.'

'Yes, Lord,' she whispered, loving him with her eyes. 'And—And when the time of mourning is over, you will send for me?'

'As sure as the sun rises and sets, I will send for you, Princess,' he replied.

'Lord?'

'Yes, what is it?'

'I require a great favour, for a friend.'

'Tell me.'

'It has come to my knowledge that Nebutu, First Wife's favourite, has longed to serve in the temple of Bast for a very long time. Will you sign the papers and put on your seal?'

'I will see to it,' Ramose said tiredly. 'Now, please, Princess, leave me to my thoughts. I leave everything to do with the house in your hands.'

Because she was left to herself a great deal while Ramose grieved, Zarah had the freedom necessary to begin her life as a story-teller. She made her plans and began her journeyings with only Thickneck in her confidence. Deep in her heart and soul was the need to find the beloved Caiphus again. The magus who had been her father, her mother, her life and her world. And there were times when Caiphus's face changed and became that of Ramose. She would reach out to them in child-like faith and love.

Her dreams still held terror. Again and again she saw Bentresht's eyes as she died of the poison that she had herself sprayed on Zarah's dish of fruit. Then Bentresht changed into Neb, Neb to Judas and Judas to Gimillu. Then there was the great queen reaching out to kill her. But Thickneck always saved her in time. Beloved Thickneck, who, in an inexplicable way, changed into Per Ibsen. Per Ibsen, the quiet man who was always standing there, waiting, in the secret regions of her heart. And at times both Per Ibsen and Thickneck smiled down gently. At these moments, Zarah would waken with tears in her eyes.

News of the happenings at court began to filter through. It seemed that the stranglehold of Thutmose III had reached out and claimed even the soul of Hatshepsut's child. The whispers grew, and Zarah, who saw the great queen as a terrible and vengeful god, knew that danger was near. For the rumour was that the queen's daughter was about to seek the shelter of the temple of Bast. Zarah's fear for her friend increased.

Unaware of all this, Ramose left his grieving. Then, in the evening, when the stars looked like a host of fireflies dancing around the tamarinds, the great lord sent for his wife. Zarah went to him, trembling in gratitude, joy and love. She felt safe in his arms, secure. He made love to her in a slow and careful way. She clung to him and knew the gods to be kind.

The next day Ramose returned to his business affairs. The strain of grief had gone from his face. He was happy to let Zarah do what she would. She was the light of his life, and he let it be known.

In love and happiness, Zarah began to get on with her plans.

CHAPTER FIVE

THE GREAT HOLY temple gleamed dark and mysterious under the moon. It was tall and its pillars seemed large and strong enough to hold back Time. The land around the temple lay shadowed and still. The people, now asleep in their houses of sun-dried brick, were assured of their safety. The temple shadow was their shadow. They lived under the beneficence of the cat-goddess Bast. She was the expression of joy and love.

'Ai! Ai! Ai!'

It seemed as though the ghosts of those happy cries still whispered on the night winds and echoed up to the lazily blinking stars as a slim, mysterious story-teller left her carrying-chair and walked swiftly towards the causeway that led to the temple itself. She was dressed as a desert woman and her robes reached to the ground. The ends of a head shawl covered her face. Only large, exceptionally beautiful dark eyes showed, and they held in them all the mystery in the world, all the knowledge and all the grief.

Zarah had survived in Egypt for six years already, and Thickneck had too. Bentresht had not, neither had Tyi, but the great and noble Ramose grew even more besotted with his sweet young wife, a Persian princess. It was said that Ramose was like wax in her hands.

The desert woman entered the temple and went through the massive main hall to the shrine. There, sphinxlike, inscrutable on her golden throne, sat the woman-figured, cat-headed goddess Bast. All around, pampered and adored, were the holy cats. The death penalty was the reward for anyone daring even to attempt to harm one of the magic, most psychic, deeply revered feline friends of Bast.

The desert woman slipped behind the shrine and there took off her robe to reveal her Egyptian dress. She then went into the sanctuary. Here a lady with a fine strong face and a firm nose sat on a carved chair. On her lap, she held a large cat. It purred loudly as she gently stroked its bronze-coloured head, and its large twitching ears were upright even though it slept. It woke at Zarah's entrance, and looked at her out of wide, almond-shaped, brilliantly yellow eyes.

'Beautiful Mau,' Zarah said. 'How peaceful he is, and how tranquil it feels in here.'

'Life, Health, Strength be to you, Zarah of Anshan,' Nebutu said, and she smiled with her lips, but her eyes were cold. 'You are still that to me. Why have you come here?'

'What is wrong?' Zarah asked as she sat on a stool at the neophyte's feet. 'You are cross, yet I felt sure that I would find you quiet and crying. I thought to find you in grief, not angry with me.'

'Me? Why should I grieve?'

'I thought you would be very sad because your lord father died today.'

'My lord father was a mean and greedy man. He resented the gold he was asked to give to the temple. He had no soul. I cannot pretend a grief that I do not feel.' Her expression altered and held open contempt and distaste as she asked caustically, 'Tell me, would you grieve if Ramose died?'

Zarah's face glowed, her eyes became soft. 'He must never die. Never! He is my rod and my staff. He is wise, kind and a gently paternal man. He treats me with love. Yet in some way I was the cause of his fall from grace.'

'He adored Lady Bentresht. He grieved when she died.'

'And so did I.' Zarah gave a queer little smile that belied her words. 'As did I, Nebutu.'

'I would have thought the opposite,' Nebutu said meaningfully. 'After all, it could have been you who ate the poisoned fruit. You were with her that evening, were you not?'

'Amun was on my side,' Zarah said gravely. 'And my beloved Napata too. Do not be angry with me because your mistress is dead and I am alive.'

'I detest treachery,' Nebutu said, 'and you were the viper at my lady's heart. I will never forgive you for taking her place, even though I know it was you who told my lord

Ramose how I desired to finish my days here.'

Zarah smiled and held out her hand to Nebutu, but the older woman frowned and looked away. Zarah's expression became pleading.

'You were kind to me, Nebutu. Don't you understand, even now?   have not been many who have treated me as gently as you did in your time. You were understanding and humane, and you shielded me from the spite of Bentresht when you could. She grew to hate God when the plan went wrong; did you know that? She blamed Amun, the lord Ramose and, most of all, me.'

'Do not pretend to be simple-minded.' Nebutu's strong face went hard. 'How can this be when you are such a remarkably clever child? Bentresht despised you because her lord husband looked at you with greed in his eyes. And you saw, too. I did not know then how determined you were to take my mistress's place.'

At that, Zarah's expression changed. She shook her head so fiercely that her hair swirled about her shoulders like a cape of dark silk. Her dark eyes, so thickly fringed with lashes and so beautifully painted with kohl, flashed with defiance. She almost spat out the words.

'Do you want the real truth, Nebutu? If I open my heart to you, will you be my true and loving friend? I want you to like and trust me. Have I not acted in your favour all this time? Is safety, luxury and loving care still not enough?'

'I cannot trust someone who seeks to bribe.'

'I do not mean to bribe you, I ask only that you look on me as a friend.'

'How can a Persian princess need the friendship of such as I?' Nebutu's tone was openly cynical now.

'I was never a princess. I was a slave. I was brought here to spy for My Majesty. See? Now I have spoken the truth, I have placed my life in your hands.'

'Which is no new thing, Zarah. I have known for quite a long time.' Nebutu looked smug. 'Quite a long time, my child.'

Zarah stared at her, startled into silence for a moment or two, then said, 'Did the lady Bentresht confide in you?'

'No. Napata, who you chose to call Thickneck, did. Much as I loved my lady, I could not stand by and see you walk into the trap she had set for you where Per Ibsen was concerned.'

'I—I do not understand.' Zarah looked afraid.

'Per Ibsen is untrustworthy in My Majesty's eyes. You would have been banished, perhaps much worse, had you been discovered on Per Ibsen's couch. Do not forget how vulnerable we all are where the queen is concerned.'

'Per Ibsen?' Zarah frowned, remembering the tall, handsome man, and thinking again how quietly hypnotic he was. 'He has not come near me for a very long time. Yet he watches me. I feel his eyes. He reminds me. . .'

'Yes?'

'He makes me shiver. He reminds me of a great mountain lion that licks his paws and seems at peace, and yet all of the time he is watching and waiting for his prey. I am puzzled. How could I have been discovered on Per Ibsen's couch?'

'Before lord Ramose made you his wife, Bentresht told Per Ibsen that you loved him. He sent you a lotus flower and a jade carving that said how he adored you. Napata stopped these gifts. He sent them back—as though from you— together with a message of contempt. Per Ibsen said nothing. He seldom does. He is a strong man. Perhaps too quiet for his own good.'

'But Thickneck. . .'

'Because I had warned him, he bowed in gratitude before me. It was then that he told me the truth. How it came about that you are both so loyal to each other. Of what you have been through together and why you are both so determined just to survive. He also said that he trusted me above all others.'

'He—He told you why I am so full of hate?'

'In your place, I, too, would want to see Judas the slaver and his foreman Neb die slowly. I can understand your hatred of the vile and cunning Persian, the prince Gimillu, but I did not want, ever, to see my beloved Bentresht die. I am grateful to you for your kindness to me, but we can never be friends. You poisoned my mistress.'

'I watched her take what would kill her.'

'Yet she spoke kindly to you. Acted fairly towards you—this, knowing that you were a slave.' Nebutu's voice held utmost contempt.

Shocked, Zarah spun round, holding her head high. Her face was now taut with anger, her hands clenched into balls at her sides.

'Before my lord Ramose returned from Punt, I knew more about Bentresht's *kindnesses* than you ever will!' she said. 'I know what it is like to have to grovel to stay alive. What it is like to have to tell what Neb used to do to me, with his long spiteful fingers inside me, over and over again. I know what it is like to be put to work for all the hours of the day and half of the night too, and then have to go on all fours at the feet of my lady, naked as the lowliest slave, to await her pleasure.'

'You were a slave. It was your duty to wait.'

'I would be so hungry that I would eat what not one of lady Bentresht's pets would touch. But she intended me to starve. What do you know about starving, Nebutu? You have always had a house, and food in your stomach. You have always had a place where you really belonged, where the lady of the establishment cared about you. But I was naked, hungry and grovelling, yet still she was not through.' Zarah began to sob quietly, and she wrapped her thin arms round her body and rocked to and fro. 'She would begin to taunt me and call me "Princess". She would make me go on my knees, in the position of a dog. I had to kiss the dirt at her feet and then I had to ask. . .'

'Yes?'

'I had to ask, literally beg—beg to be touched by her in the way Neb used to do.'

'I did not know.' Nebutu frowned, then said again, 'Truly, I did not know.'

'Of course you did not,' Zarah wept. 'This went on in her private sanctum, where she was supposedly praying to the Invisible One, Amun. In truth, she hated God for deserting her. She hated God for making the Great Queen change her mind.'

'You think she blamed Amun?' Nebutu's expression was one of horror and disbelief.

'She screamed out her condemnation of God,' Zarah said firmly. 'It was the Invisible One's fault that the queen decided to pretend that the plan for spying and treachery was nothing to do with her. It was the fault of God that the queen ordered Bentresht to care for me like a daughter, and yet paid nothing towards my keep. She gave no thought to all that lord Ramose paid in order to acquire my pitiful self, and gave him nothing in return for all his hard work. It was Amun who made the queen swear, in the hearing of Per Ibsen, how dearly she loved Thutmose the Third.'

'She did not blame God, Zarah. This cannot be.'

'She was cold and cruel in her hate of God and because it was the queen's wish that Bentresht should care for me, she turned her face and would not. She did not want my presence to remind her of the mistake her lord husband had made. She wanted me to die.'

Nebutu's lips curled. 'But quite clearly you did not.'

'Because my beloved Thickneck managed to get food to me from time to time. Just enough to keep me alive.'

'But my lady Bentresht died while you and she sat together enjoying a sumptuous meal. How did you acquire the poison? Did Napata get it for you? I am not so stupid that I cannot see the truth.'

'How little you knew her,' Zarah said bitterly. 'Were you really so unaware of her wickedness? Were you really so blinded by her sudden sweet bouts of teasing and gay laughter? Were you so honestly fooled by her beautiful but treacherously smiling face? Do you not understand? I did not starve. I did not die! Bentresht then decided to try another way. She pretended to repent and asked my forgiveness. She invited me to eat at her table. The poison was for me, Nebutu. Yes, for me. Thickneck knew. He has watchful eyes and a great instinct for these things. He warned me in time, and all I had to do was change my dish for hers. I watched her die—I was glad.'

'It was the loss of Ramose's love that must have sent her mad.' Nebutu was still trying to find an excuse for her mistress.

'She did not lose my lord's love. My lord cherishes and cares for all of his women, and he always will. What she did lose were the rubies that Ramose gave to Judas in order to acquire me for the queen. Bentresht never forgave that.'

The silence about them was broken only by the loud and pleasurable purring of Mau. Nebutu stroked his bronze coat that was so magnificently spotted dark brown. The markings round Mau's eyes were distinct, just like those the Egyptians painted round their own orbs. His tail was long and tapering with silky brown bands, and his legs were exceptionally long. He was a beautifully aristocratic creature, fine and fitting to live at the feet of the beloved goddess Bast.

Zarah, her face wet, her tongue salty with the taste of tears, found herself wondering bleakly how it was that cats and the cat goddess were so venerated in this land. They all seemed powerless to help her where Nebutu was concerned.

Bast, the famous symbol of fecundity and beauty, was depicted with the head of a cat and a mysterious bewitching glance. Enigmatic and lover of the night, Bast was also the symbol of the moon.

'Why do you worship Bast?' she asked plaintively. 'What do you find so special about her?'

'She controls the fertility of man and beast. She cures illnesses, and'—here Nebutu faltered—'and watches over the spirits of the dead. She watches over my lover's soul.'

'Oh!'

'We were cousins. He said goodbye to our home and joined a great ship that left the river and went far out to the Great Green. There have been many brave and fine sailors who have never returned from the Great Green. It all happened a long time ago. But I am fortunate, because his father was a priest of Bast, and the worship and care for her wellbeing was scrupulously passed on to the eldest son. It was because of my beloved's memory that I am allowed to be here. My father did not help me. My eldest cousin did.'

Zarah looked at Nebutu, who remained so remote, so calm and serene.

'You are like the holy cats you so greatly adore,' she murmured. 'You are beautiful, refined and clean! Had you wished it, I am sure that the lord Ramose would have decided to keep you in his house—and honoured you above all others.'

'No!' Nebutu said firmly. 'I want only to journey through this life in a right and correct manner. I want the gods to allow me to join my beloved's Ka in the new existence. I have a place waiting for my body, in his tomb. I am prepared for, and look forward to my death.' She gave Zarah a long, cool look and realised that she was staring at a full-blown young woman. A woman with charm and bright honest eyes. A small person who had always had a fight on her hands merely to survive.

'Zarah,' she said. 'I believe you. Now tell me, why did you really come here?'

'To tell you that there is great panic in the land. The queen's daughter, Princess Ranofru, has run away. It is rumoured that she has sympathy with Thutmose, and that My Majesty knows!'

'But why did you come here to me?'

'To warn you that it is whispered that Ranofru's intention is to get to this temple to throw herself on the mercy of Bast. Now I must go. You know what may happen next. What you choose to do about it is up to you, but. . .'

'Yes?'

'But, O sweet Nebutu, I know very well what it is to be alone and afraid. I hope that you find it in your heart to help Ranofru. Life, Health, Strength be to you.'

'Life, Health and Strength to you also,' Nebutu replied and there was a strange expression on her face as she watched Zarah go. Then, with infinite tenderness, she sat Mau down. He stretched, yawned, then arrogantly stalked away. Nebutu hurried across the dark and secretive courtyard that was surrounded with small cells. She scratched on the door of the first, and whispered, 'O Princess, it is I, Nebutu.'

The door opened cautiously and the reed-like figure of Ranofru gleamed under the light of the burning rushes she held. Her face was pinched and colourless. There was a world of anxiety in her voice as she asked softly, 'Was there a reply to my message, Nebutu? Do you bring me a word?'

'O Princess, I have this to say. The message is "Per Ibsen will come." '

'May Amun-ra watch over us all,' Princess Ranofru sobbed. 'I am deathly afraid.'

'Do not be frightened.' Nebutu tried to give comfort. 'If Per Ibsen is to come for you, you have some very powerful friends. Per Ibsen is Thutmose's shadow, is that not so?'

'My mother the queen also has powerful friends and advisers,' the princess said bitterly. 'And she listens to them all in turn. The only living soul whom she will always believe in is Senenmut. He is the one she confides in, too. I hope and pray that Senenmut loves me, as I love him. I hope he remembers how it was when he taught me all those years ago.'

'Do not worry,' Nebutu said quietly. 'Per Ibsen will come soon and he will take you safely away, and the prince himself has given his pledge.'

Zarah walked to her carrying-chair and ordered the men to hurry. When they reached the House of Ramose, she paid them two rings of silver, saying, 'I am late. I took too long at my prayers. I shall be whipped for being too long preparing the lord Ramose's evening food.'

One of the men laughed raucously. 'O Mistress, it is rumoured that the lord Ramose's wife is Persian born. Do Persians eat the same food as we?'

'The very same,' Zarah replied and, hiding in the shadows, Thickneck relaxed when he heard her laugh. She was undiscovered still. He allowed no servants to see her pass.

Zarah hurried into the house, changed out of her desert robes and into her most seductive dress, then she went breathless and joyful to her master's bedroom where he was waiting for her, as she knew he would.

He looked noble, proud, even without his black wig. He turned and smiled at her, then lifted his head from the wooden headrest and said, 'So, you kept your promise. You were not too long at your prayers.'

She gave him her slow smile. 'I must confess, lord husband, that I go to see Taueret the Great One: Goddess of childbirth, and stay there so long praying to delight your soul with a son! But, Beloved, I am always so anxious to return. Perhaps my happy leave-taking offends the Holy Standing Hippopotamus. I am still not with child.'

'You are my daughter, my sister, my wife. I don't need a son.' Ramose's eyes were wet with tears. 'I feel warm and loving every time I see you.'

'And I feel warm and loving every time I see you,' she said gently. 'I dread it when you leave the house without me. I look for you when I am alone, and I keep imagining that I see your likeness living in my heart.'

'You love me?'

'Yes. I do love you,' Zarah replied, and she spoke the truth.

'Then you will take off your dress and allow me to do as I will?'

'Gladly,' she replied humbly. 'It gives me great pleasure to be one with my lord.'

She was quivering as she stepped out of her white flax linen, smiling as he told her that he would have preferred her to wear the filmy veil and little gold bells. She knew that he loved her best when she wore nothing at all.

'Dance for me, Zarah,' he commanded. 'Dance as they do in old Persia. Tempt me with every move. Be my princess!'

'I am merely a slave,' she reminded him. 'You bought me from Judas, remember? I dance as Egyptian girls taught me. I know nothing of Persian ways. But, for you, my lord husband, I will try.'

She began to move, slowly and gracefully, her small body wonderful to his eyes. He watched as her pace grew faster, her movements teasing. Her hands were like doves in the air, fluttering, swooping, then resting on her breasts. Ramose left the bed and walked towards her. She bent towards him, weaving slowly now, her hips gyrating, her eyes smiling invitingly into his.

He sank to his knees before her, his arms went round her waist. His lips closed over her flesh. He began to take gentle little nips and bites. A fiery agony went to the pit of her stomach. She becamefilive as she never had before.

'Lord,' she moaned, and wild longing seared through her as his hands began to massage and tease.

'You are beautiful.' His voice was almost guttural, and now he was pushing her backwards. He took her savagely, greedily, and it was over too soon.

In a very short time she was lovingly sent back to her room. Ramose would sleep, she thought wildly: dear, sweet beloved, he would rest until dawn. But she was awake, burning, needing. She was being consumed by a terrible fire. She bit her lip until it bled. She drank strong wine. She paced the floor. Over above everything else, she was hearing Nebutu saying: 'Per Ibsen sent you a lotus flower and a jade carving that showed how he adored you.'

It was dawn before she fell asleep, to dream of the huge, quiet man who featured in all her fantasies. Per Ibsen. She whispered his name again. Per Ibsen!

The Nile receded, then returned and Egypt flourished. Another new year had come and the land was assured of its grain. Then one scarlet and gold evening, when the air was full of the scent of flowers and the birdsong was soft and sweet, Zarah went in search of Ramose. There was joy in her heart and love in every fibre of her being. The whole world, she thought, is wearing a diadem of silvery delight. She found him in his favourite place in the garden. His eyes were closed and he seemed to have aged. She could not wait. She had to wake him. She touched his face gently and he opened his eyes, smiling when he saw who it was.

'Ramose, my life,' she said tenderly. 'I may speak?'

'To hear your voice is to hear the cooing of doves. What is it, my dear?'

'O Beloved,' she said, and her voice was a song. 'Hapi, god of the Nile and bringer of fertility, has heard my prayers. All the gods of the world have, and they have smiled on me at last. Ramose, I am with child!'

Ramose was wide awake now and looking at her, almost unable to believe what he had heard. Then he smiled, a wide all-embracing smile that almost split his face in two. There was exultation in his voice as he took her in his arms and, hoarse with emotion, said, 'O Princess of my heart, Amun has been merciful at last. I thought all was evil against me. You have been the one ray of comfort in my life. Did you know that when My Majesty, who is God, looked at me with loathing in her eyes, I thought that death would be preferable to life?'

'Lord!'

'Hush, my sweet precious. It was only a momentary thing. You have been like scented oils healing my burning wounds. You have made my heart alive, and my body spring with youth again. And now'—his voice lowered and held awe—'now I will actually live to see my child take its sweet breath of life.'

'And through him, Lord, you will exist to the Everlasting. You will live in the soul of your son and after that, through his sons, for ever.'

'You are right,' he agreed with tears in his eyes. 'And I feel a great humbleness and joy. O Mistress of the House, I feel such a great river of love for you, that I am like a man drowned.'

'Do not drown,' she whispered swiftly, and held him tight. 'Never go away from me. You are the light of my life.'

She looked lovingly into his eyes that were so dramatically outlined with green malachite. Her heart was filled to overflowing because, at last, she had found a way to thank him for his adoration and care. She had longed for this child as ardently as he, and she, too, had prayed for a son. Her plans for the baby were full of sunlit visions, of happiness, and love.

Zarah and Ramose stayed close together in the garden. They were both silent, their eyes tender and full of dreams. . .

The queen was puzzled, and her mouth went thin in an ominous way. She tapped her foot impatiently and stared at the man who was sprawled before her, in complete obeisance, on the floor.

'Only the impious would dare to oppose me,' she said in her clear, high voice. 'I am My Majesty! The chosen one of the gods. Why do you concern me with idle talk? I have surrounded myself with eminent men, and entrusted them with the most important functions in the state. You, who hold the position of Chief of Scribes, should know better.'

Semna, tall, thin, with a brilliant mind, lifted his cadaverous face and tried to explain that he was not alone. The queen's eyes began to glitter, but the scribe, committed to the truth, had to go on.

'Majesty, though he has voiced it not, I believe even Senenmut.'

'Not Senenmut. I will kill you for saying that!'

'Then, if my death is delivered by your own dearest hand, I will be content.'

A deep voice said from behind one of the pillars, 'Life, Health, Strength to you, Majesty.' Senenmut, large, plain, with the strength of an ox, came forward, and with dignified grace lowered himself in order to lie face downwards on the floor.

'Beloved!' The queen's voice became gentle. 'You must rise. So, too, must you, Semna, my friend. Be patient with me. I just do not understand. I cannot believe that the number of nobles wishing for war is growing as fast as the flight of the locust swarm. It does not make sense. Egypt has become rich under my reign. I stand for trade. I stand for peace.'

'That is the problem, Majesty,' Senenmut said quietly. 'Because you are so set on keeping the peace, petty princes of Palestine and Syria see an opportunity to throw off the yoke imposed upon them by your lord father. We cannot allow that to happen. Palestine serves as a bridge between the rivers Nile and Euphrates.'

'This I know, Senenmut.'

'Majesty, the caravans of the world trade-routes pass that way. Palestine is like a jewel in your crown. It is situated in the Fertile Crescent. We cannot let it go.'

'It will stay in the arms of Egypt, Senenmut. I cannot believe that you have been listening to such wild and foolish talk. I expected it from Thutmose and his kind, but not from my own dignitaries.'

'Majesty,' Senenmut insisted, taking his life in his hands. 'The prince of Kadesh. . .'

'Kadesh now, Senenmut?'

'Majesty, the great city of Kadesh, which is situated on the River Orontes, is important to us. We need to crush the prince of Kadesh here and now. He seeks to crush us!'

'We need to find out who it is that is spreading such slanderous lies,' Hatshepsut said sibilantly. 'We need to think about who will best be served by all this talk of aggression.

I find myself contemptuous of my advisers. They are quaking fools. Leave now, else I will strike out blindly with my tongue and flail. I will call the guards and have them cut you down.'

Semna began crawling backwards, his fear almost visible. The bear-like Senenmut stayed perfectly still. But on this day the Great Queen was not disposed to give in.

'Will you suffer the indignity of having my guards drag you out of my sight?' she said, and there was cold venom in her voice. 'And do you not think that you, above all people, should have had your mind on matters rather nearer to home? What of Ranofru? A year has gone, and she is still not found.'

'By my life, health and strength, Pharaoh,' Senenmut said slowly, 'am I to believe that the One Chosen by Gods is saying that she is also a mother? I thought only Egypt was her child. That she dismissed the daughter who was so openly on the side of Thutmose the Third.'

At that Hatshepsut stood up and in cold fury struck Senenmut across the face with her ceremonial flail. He did not flinch, but just stood, towering over her, and she hit him again, then again. When blood began to flow, Hatshepsut's eyes widened, and she cried out in anguish at what she had done. For she knew that he had merely quoted her own words.

Senenmut stood there, silent, his eyes showing no expression at all. Then, with cold deliberation, without asking permission, he turned and walked away.

'Come back!' the queen ordered. 'I command you to return!'

She was helpless. Angry tears sped down her cheeks and made deep pools of heartbreak in her eyes.

'Senenmut,' she cried out, unmindful of her frightened servants and stoical guards. 'Beloved, come here!'

The large quiet man continued his walk. He did not falter. He did not look back.

Thebes throbbed with life in all its contrasts. Great houses belonging to the rich were dazzling in colour, imposing in design. The mud hovels of the poor, set in lines, were mere boxes of dried brick. The temple of Amun was the most splendid, in its red and gold, yellow and blue, with holy hieroglyphics covering the pillars. Even Pharaoh had to kneel in supplication before Amun.

The people were milling about, seeing to their daily affairs. Children played contentedly on the flat roofs of their houses, their companions tame quails or sleek well-fed cats. Oxen, camels and asses made their way along the road from the temple to the harbour, where men from all lands haggled with traders on the quay.

Senenmut did not look at these things. His brow was furrowed as he wondered how he could best serve his queen. But disquiet was growing among those who loved Egypt enough to look beyond the current prosperity. And there could be no mistaking the fact that Prince Thutmose was one of the band that wanted to stand up and fight.

The favourite of My Majesty frowned as he continued his journey. He was remembering how, many years before, a religious procession had left its original route. The statue of Amun-ra went to where Isis, mother of Thutmose III, stood with her son. The statue had seemingly pointed direct to the boy. To the watching people, the message was clear. God had, in this manner, chosen the successor to the throne. Thutmose was given the Horus name, Valiant Bull of Thebes. The people of Egypt began counting the years of the young king's reign. The Royal Wife, Hatshepsut, had other ideas.

'He is merely a prince, and he cannot become a king unless I marry him,' she proclaimed. 'And this I will not do. Take him away!'

She swiftly seized power and jealously held on to it. So the young man with a determined face and the dominant family nose was kept safely in the background. But the years were quickly passing. Prince Thutmose, with his short neck and powerful chest, had grown into a formidable man. He bore no love for the queen, and he was fiercely nationalistic. He would kill her if he could. She had not dared to kill him.

Senenmut sighed and made his choice. He liked Isis and found her to be a timid and gentle soul. He was fond of young Thutmose, and had looked on him as a bright pupil in the

matter of religion and law. On the other hand, he loved Hatshepsut the queen. Thus his course was set. He would stand
by the delight of his soul, and he understood her well. She
would expect him to return to her at dusk, but for once she
must wait.

The queen must learn, and learn quickly, that she must
never again hit out at the lord Senenmut. She was the ruler
of Upper and Lower Egypt and of other conquered lands.
But she was a woman. She must accept that, although he
was her willing subject, he was also a man. Above all, a man!
Relaxed now that he had made his decision, even though it
might well mean his death, Senenmut began to walk. He
watched the people who were bartering their wares by the
banks of the river. There were pets for sale, animals for food,
beasts of burden, all to be bartered, and the learned scribes,
sitting with their papers before them, were ready to record
all transactions with their long reed pens.

The heat of the day began to become unbearable, and he
went to the house of his eldest brother Senmen. He was made
very welcome, and given meat and wine once the near-naked
maiden had washed his hands and feet and anointed his face
with sweet-smelling ointments.

Senmen was old and wise, his eyes kind. He knew how it
was.

'You have suffered a great deal, for you adore a queen who
is as high above you as the stars,' he said. 'It is bad for a man
always to stand beneath a woman and be in second place. It
rejuvenates him to become, for a while at least, the one on
top. To be first! Here, in this place, you are a man. You are
the High Lord in the eyes of the women in this house. Take
your pick of the beauties here, enjoy them, have your fill.'

Senenmut thought grimly of his beloved and of the stinging weight of the flail. He chose two young and willing
women and took them to a private part of the house.

'I am a man,' he told them. 'Amuse me. Tempt me. Pleasure me until I can press out no more seed.'

And with soft sighs and endearments they loved his body
and caressed it all over with their hands and their tongues.
They sang sweet songs that held all of the seduction in the
world, then from sweetness they changed to voluptuous-

ness, and Senenmut's tiredness and bitterness fell away. There was no haste, no urgency in the loveplay, just a fluid sensuousness overriding his will. He was ready now, and the more experienced of the two lowered herself, taking him into her in a slow and melting way. Gradually the rhythmic urgency of her hips, as she tried to take him in even further, invited his own savagery. He lunged hard and fiercely, now aware of the raw explosion of naked desire.

He rolled over, taking the girl with him until it was he on top. The second girl was moaning and kissing his back, biting him with her small pointed teeth. He grunted deep in his throat and rammed into the girl beneath him. He felt power, he felt agony, above all, he felt hate. He beat in and pulled out, beat in again and again, thrashing her violently, seeing the frozen grimace on her face, hearing her faint cry for mercy, but he had gone too far. He assaulted, drove in, retreated, fiercely invaded again.

And it was not his brother's serving-girl he felt helpless under him: it was the great queen. The screwed-up face and opened mouth were not those of an ignorant woman, but Hatshepsut's. And the keening and begging for her turn, for her body to be so used, came not from the madly kissing, biting servant clinging to his back, but from She Whose Word is Law.

They worked on him, both of them, until he could take no more. Tired, tight-lipped and still angry, he took two gold bangles from his arms and gave them to the girls. They snatched them covetously, their eyes sparkling with greed, and left, with their lawful perquisites.

Senenmut slept, but on waking he was still on edge and unable to relax. He left his brother's house and again began to walk. He left the river bank with its date and dom palms and flowering plants. He went by the corn that had by now grown to nine cubits high and went on to a ruined temple that had been built by the ancients. Now the old ruin had become a meeting-place for the people, living quarters for the homeless, and a resting-place for travellers. Its tall pillars, towering above granite rams and fallen stones, seemed to hold up the sky.

Here the one with ears to hear would learn the gossip of all Egypt and beyond. Senenmut went on, barely noticing what was happening round him until one particular figure stood out from the rest. Per Ibsen! What was his interest here?

He was standing a little apart from the crowd, and out of the view of the woman who was the centre of all eyes.

'Who is she?' Senenmut asked a skinny old man.

'Life, Health, Strength, Lord,' the old man replied and his wrinkled face held awe. 'She has the power of words. One can see the events she speaks of, may the light of Re strike my eyes! It is said that she can read the stars and tell fortunes. It is believed that she holds nothing less than the mysteries in her hands.'

'Then she is most unusual,' Senenmut replied politely, but he had come across cunning tricksters before. Many pretended to unravel fortunes, providing they received payment in gold. Such people might fool My Majesty, but they would have to get up early to fool him.

'In truth, she is one on her own,' the old man said. 'For she asks nothing. She is here often and holds no begging bowl. She is loved for the help and advice she gives. But, most of all, she is loved for the way she tells tales.'

Soothsayers and story-tellers were not of great interest to Senenmut. Per Ibsen, the young man close to Thutmose, was! Anxious to see the person who had seemingly captured the interest of the young nobleman, Senenmut edged near. He was disappointed. The story-teller was robed as a desert woman, and a fine linen scarf covered her face. Even though the small figure was standing quiet and still, she had an air about her that held attention. The crowd around her grew greater, and an impatient labourer, with dried brick-mud staining his loin-cloth, cried out, 'Begin a story for us, O teller of tales. Your sweet voice makes us forget the misery of the day.'

'Ai! Ai!' The rest took up the cry. 'Speak to us of magical things. But, first, tell us your name.'

It was then that Senenmut heard a young crystal-clear voice coming from beneath the enveloping scarf, and it was a melodious sound.

'My name is Zarah, and I must for ever hide my face, as is the way of my land. I say Life, Health, Strength to you all.'

'Life, Health, Strength,' came the reply.

'I will begin,' the small figure said, and she sat down, very gracefully, on a fallen stone. 'I have a story to tell, and a question to ask.'

Intrigued, Senenmut decided to stay, to listen, to watch—and, above all, to learn.

CHAPTER SIX

THE SURROUNDINGS WERE eerie, and the slight figure who was so cleverly hidden by her flowing robes had an air of mystery. Senenmut was careful to keep out of the way of Per Ibsen. He noted that, in his turn, the young nobleman had taken great pains to hide himself from the desert girl's view. It had to be a girl. One knew by her voice. The listeners were openly entranced.

The tale Zarah told was as old as Egypt itself. It was of King Setna and his magician son's visit to the Land of the Dead.

'And so,' the sweet voice held all the expression in the world, 'Setna's soul, which looked like a great golden bird with the king's human face, flew into the west, following the glittering soul of his son. They sped into the First Region of Night and saw beneath them the Mesektet Boat in which Ra began his journey along the ghostly River of Death at the end of each day.'

'Tell us about the boat,' a listener cried. 'Tell us what you saw, for clearly you visualised it all, and your words are true.'

'I can tell you that the boat was royal and its trappings were so magnificent that they would make mere mortals gasp. It was alive with colours of emeralds, turquoises, jasper, amethyst, lapis lazuli and the rich shimmer of gold. The towing-ropes were also made of gold, and great gods pulled at the ropes until the boat entered the First Region of Night. Six giant serpents curled round the pillars on either side, and they hissed and writhed and threatened all of the Doubles who journeyed in the boat. And all the Doubles were of those who had died that day. And many were afraid, for they were being taken to the final Judgment Hall.'

'And did the boat stop at the First Region?' someone called.

Zarah slowly moved her head in negation.

'It was not allowed. It moved on its way through the thick darkness until it came to the Second Region, and the portals swung open so that the boat could journey through the kingdom of Ra.'

'Ai!' The listeners were enthralled. 'Tell us about the kingdom of Ra.'

They fell silent as the young story-teller continued.

'The kingdom of Ra was full of happiness and peace. It was guarded by the Spirits of Corn, who make the wheat and barley grow. And these same spirits caused the fruits of the earth to increase. Ra was a place in which there lived the spirits of gods and heroes of old. All is beautiful in the kingdom of Ra, but the boat did not stop. It journeyed on into the Third Region, where stood the Judgment Hall.'

'Ai! Ai! The Judgment Hall,' breathed the crowd, for they knew the story well. 'And it was there that the dead disembarked?'

'That is the truth,' Zarah agreed. 'But the boat continued on its way through the nine other Regions of the Night. . .' The high, expressive voice carried on, but Senenmut was no longer interested. It concerned him that Per Ibsen, the young bull, the strong, the rich friend of Thutmose III, was all but hiding and yet listening with such an attentive air.

At last the story came to an end. Everyone had learned the lesson, once again, that evil-doers were dragged down, and that the good flew high, to live in the land of plenty and peace.

'And there, O friends,' Zarah told them, 'they waited until God returned to earth, taking with him all those who had proved worthy, to live as his subjects for ever.'

'Amun!' the listeners whispered, and their eyes grew wet with joy. 'Amun!'

'Now, story-teller,' someone called, 'your question. Ask us your question now.'

It was then that Zarah's throat grew dry. She felt all of the yearning and grief rise up and threaten to choke her. She remembered Harad, her love, as a young and smiling boy, not as she had seen him last. But above all she remembered the sweet and kindly old patriarch she had so dearly adored.

Her need of him, her desir to look up into his face once more and to quiver with joy at the beauty of his words, had not lessened with the years.

Her voice trembled with emotion as she said, 'My question is simple. I wish to know if anyone here has either seen or heard of Caiphus the Wise, Caiphus the Great?'

'Who is this wise man?' a beggar asked.

'He is my master. He is the interpreter of dreams and he can tell from the stars what Fate has in store.'

'Why is he great?' an old woman enquired.

'He gives bread to the hungry, water to the thirsty, clothing to the naked, and tenderness and care to those who are unwanted and unloved.'

'Then he is truly great,' the beggar cried out, and those about him murmured in agreement.

'He is a kindly, wondrous man,' Zarah said yearningly, 'and he belongs here in the kingdom of the Nile.'

The question and answers were not as exciting as the story, and the people melted away into the shadows. Zarah stood still, vulnerable and sad, unaware of the three who had stayed hidden in the background to watch and wait.

Then the third, a giant black man, went to her. He was without his ostrich plume and fine leopardskin, and wore a simple loin-cloth so that no one would know who he was. He began coaxing her away.

'You must not continue to do this, Morning Light,' Thickneck said hoarsely. 'You torture yourself. Your old master must be dead by now.'

'He was the father of my young lord, and the master I loved,' Zarah wept. 'I want to find him. I am living a lie, and only he can tell me what I must do.'

'Are you really unhappy? Does not Ramose adore you so greatly that he gives in to your every whim?'

'He would not allow me to come here, Thickneck. He would not want me to ask the questions I do. If the truth about how I came to be here came out, and for what purpose I was bought, the queen would deny it all. Just as she did before, remember? But she would use stronger words now that Thutmose's followers grow in number. She would say that the idea of spying was my lord husband's! That would most surely mean his death.'

'Yet, knowing this, you still want Caiphus to come?'

'In answer to a desert story-teller's plea, not that of the First Wife of Ramose's house!'

'I still think,' Thickneck's voice held reprimand, 'that you put your adoration of this Caiphus above the love you bear for Ramose, your lord.'

'They are two different loves,' Zarah whispered urgently. 'Love of the present and love of the past. O my sweet and faithful friend, I am so greedy for love.'

'Which you will, in time, give to your child.'

She looked up at him, her eyes glowing like dark crystals in the light of the moon.

White teeth flashed as Thickneck's wide grin all but split his face in two. 'My every breath is devoted to you,' he told her. 'You are with me in spirit every moment of the night and day. The child will be as the one that Fate has decreed that I can never have. I will cherish and guard it as my own.'

'It was not Fate,' she said, and her face grew white and cold. 'It was Judas and Neb! Do not think that I have forgotten our vow, Beloved. Neither our vow nor our hate.'

'And that, above all, shows what a good and gentle soul you are,' Thickneck said. 'You seek for your love before you exact your revenge. Leave the evil-doing to me. Let me be the sin-eater for us both. Morning Light, you must be the white and shining side of our partnership, and I will be the black.'

'No,' she whispered fiercely. 'We will be exactly the same. Now I am tired. Please take me home.'

They walked away together, side by side as friends.

'So!' Per Ibsen muttered, 'It is a man called Caiphus she seeks. Caiphus the Wise. I will remember that name.'

Senenmut watched as Per Ibsen hurried away from the ruined temple. The large man then turned, deciding to follow the desert story-teller and her man. But they had vanished in the shadows, almost as magic in their disappearance as those of the gods in flight. God's boat continued its slow silent journey along the never-ending black river of the Underworld.

The boat completed its journey several more times, and still Zarah was unable to find the whereabouts of her old master. She needed him as she needed a father. Her love for Ramose grew. She continued to wear her all-enveloping robes and journey to the ruins whenever the coast was clear. Her fame as a story-teller grew. A special stone seat was kept for her, and it came to be known as Story-teller Place. No one but Zarah was allowed to rest there.

Gradually the people came to respect her and the ways she answered their questions. She seemed to understand them and their problems, and to be able to find answers in an uncanny way. She was able to make true predictions and see how events would work out. And the people revered her, believing her to be half magic and infinitely wise.

Zarah found that she liked speaking to the people, helping where she could. She remembered all Caiphus's teachings, but knew best the most clever words he had said: 'Take note of the thoughts that flash unbidden into your mind. Put those and the signs you have been given together and let them make sense. Above all, remember to send those who come to you away happy and confident, in faith that their future is good!'

Ramose suddenly became older and very sick. In spite of his joy, he became more interested in his own funeral. The leg doctor and back doctor could do nothing. He stayed in his house a great deal now complaining of his pains.

Zarah immersed herself in her wise-woman role. She left her home secretly, and ensured that her lord husband did not know of the strange double life she led. She had to remember at all times that the First Wife of Ramose was a Persian princess of Anshan, a princess whose past was a mystery, since it all belonged to a land far away. And, above all, she had to remember that her lord husband was innocent and had taken no part in a proposed royal intrigue.

Zarah's thirst for knowledge became almost feverish, it was so unquenchable. She began journeying to temples to read the stories so beautifully depicted in bright coloured pictures on the walls, and gradually she became conscious of someone other than Thickneck who watched her at all times. Everywhere she turned, it seemed, she would see him somewhere near. Per Ibsen! Thutmose's man, loyal to the side opposite that where Ramose, her lord husband, stood. She did not know why she felt such fascination for the prince's spy.

One evening, when she was sitting on the river bank, enjoying the ceaseless music of the waves, he came to her. His muscles were large and rippling, gleaming under the tanned skin that was smoothed with oil. His wide collar was thick with red and blue stones. His muscular arms heavy with gold bands. On his broad chest there rested a pectoral of a large emerald scarab, with behind it the large, full spreading gold wings of a soul. Clearly Per Ibsen was a very rich man. His fine linen cloth proclaimed it, as did his magnificent purple cloak.

Zarah looked up at him, as he came to a halt before her, with a marked coldness in her eyes. But her cheeks were flushed and there was a fluttering in her throat. With quiet deliberation he leaned against a palm tree and folded his arms. He seemed powerful, god-like and a man among men. She did not greet him in politeness as she knew she should. He waited. In cold superiority he waited, but she kept a still tongue. At last he said coldly, 'Life, Health, Strength, lady Ramose.'

'And to you, Lord.'

'It seems a long time since we met.'

Her eyes narrowed at that. 'O Per Ibsen,' she said courteously, 'I have seen you often and only too recently. I have noticed your figure in the background—many times, in fact.'

'That is because I cannot tear myself away from your beauty,' he told her evenly. 'You should be flattered by that.'

'Your tone suggests that there are reasons other than my looks that have brought you here, Per Ibsen,' she said and her face held open suspicion and contempt. 'I believe that you are spying on me for reasons rather less frivolous.'

He raised his brows sardonically and continued to stare into her eyes.

'It is dangerous for you to wander about alone. There are many thieves and murderers who would kill you and take the jewels you wear.'

She smiled faintly, and he found himself thinking that she grew more beautiful with every passing day. She had a glow about her, and it suited her to be with child. She was like the goddess of maternity, yet there was also about her an air of childishness that made a man fiercely protective.

'I am never alone,' she told him. 'My beloved Napata. . .'

'Whom you choose to call Thickneck when no one else is near?'

She was greatly surprised and pretended a casualness she did not feel. The man knew too much already, she thought, and felt a renewed tinge of fear.

'You have learned much, Per Ibsen.'

'I know that your giant Thickneck is a man that I would choose to have on my side,' he agreed smoothly. 'And I have seen him, and know how ferocious he can be in your defence. But he is only one man. Even more disastrous, you insist on his keeping in the distance with your serving-girls while you sit about, thinking and learning, quite alone.'

'Nevertheless,' Zarah replied, and now there was open warning in her eyes, 'he can run like the wind. He can read my mind. I would not even need to call, he watches me so.'

'Mistress,' Thickneck said from behind them, 'may I attend to your needs?'

'I am thirsty.' she told him, and saw the tight expression darken on Per Ibsen's face and knew that she had made him angry. The ghost of a dimple lurked in the corner of her mouth, but there was still an anxious look at the back of her eyes.

'Do not worry about me, Per Ibsen. I have never felt more healthy or more safe in my life.' Her defiant laugh rang out very shakily. 'And, with the great Ramose as my lord husband, I do very well.'

He smiled bleakly. She did not even have the sense to change her name as the story-teller, and relied, as did that black shadow of hers, merely on a change of clothes. Because he remained so silent, she grew even more ill at ease.

'Thickneck,' she called. 'Wait! I will come with you. Wait for me!'

Per Ibsen watched them, but his expression had now changed in a subtle way. He appeared to notice nothing except the small, beautiful girl-woman. She who was being so carefully shielded by the massive Kushite as they went to join the waiting group of servants and slaves. Yet Per Ibsen's gaze had not missed the two men who had been watching their encounter. Two men who had tried to stay hidden in the shadows a small distance away.

The Egyptian was puzzled. He had recognised the men at once. The tall, thin man, wearing a sharp knife in his belt and a long woollen robe, was a cunning rogue who had been at the bottom of many devious deals. He came from desert stock. His companion was a Persian with deep-set eyes and a shifty look. There was an air of self-indulgence about him, and dissipation.

'Gimillu's men,' Per Ibsen said thoughtfully. 'That means that Gimillu himself must be near. What can he want, and why is he having Zarah, First Wife of Ramose, watched?'

He stood very still, waiting until the disreputable pair went away. They did not attempt to follow the girl, and he stayed where he was. The evening was beautiful, the river still and calm with the silhouettes of dhows on the surface looking like so many giant black moths. Far in the west the sun had all but reached the horizon. For a moment it was poised like a gigantic ball of molten gold and then took a sudden plunge into the depths of the underworld.

A cloud rose as it disappeared covering the great river with a misty veil of mingling blood and gold. A soft breeze came moaning over the water, whispering and sighing among the fronds of the palms. Per Ibsen was not superstitious, but in spite of himself he shivered. A ghastly trail of blood seemed to be flowing in the river, and it was all somehow tied in with Zarah. For some time he could not throw off the uncanny feeling that assailed him. He felt that he had been sent a warning by the gods.

The sun poured down like a slow golden river. Days came and went. Time passed by in joy, peace and plenty. Egypt continued to prosper. But on her borders there was growing unrest.

Hatshepsut, She Whose Word is Law, was sitting idly fanning herself with an enormous fan of dyed ostrich feath-

ers. Two slaves stood behind her, immobile, expressionless.
At a sign from the Queen, they moved trembling peacock
fans to and fro, for the air was sultry, and scarcely a suspicion of a breeze blew across the waters of the Nile.

'I would drink a cup of wine,' she said, and the words fell
from her lips like so many sighs.

'By your command, Majesty,' said the old seneschal. He
left the royal presence backwards, his eyes on the floor.

Kneeling at the queen's feet was a young nobleman of a
great family of the hills. Bek had grown up in the atmosphere of the great house. His father had sent him to do
homage to the queen in his name many years before, and the
boy remained joyfully. He was now a man, slim, slight and
beautiful, and a great favourite of the queen.

She sat on her throne, her strong face sad and remote.
Bek's fingers strummed against the stringed lute, as he played
the soft notes of the love song he had written to his most
august, beloved, queen. The music held passion. It was warm
and languid, as sultry as the scent of jasmine on hot summer
night air. The last nervous notes from the lute strings faded,
whispered, then died.

'I am not in the mood for your music,' said the queen.

Crushed, Bek silently spread himself on the ground before
her, both arms outstretched, palms downwards. The steward appeared with the wine-bearer, and the two men moved
swiftly across the floor strewn with the skins of wild beasts.
Hatshepsut drank deeply from a cup of gold, then dismissed
Bek, her painted face hard as she watched him leaving her
presence backwards. His dark eyes were lowered in reverence.

Suddenly Hatshepsut's expression changed. She had a
wicked look on her face. 'Send for my nephew,' she said
coldly. 'I will speak to him. And fill my cup again.'

The seneschal obeyed, then melted away.

Later there came the sound of footsteps and Thutmose
III, Lord of Two Lands, marched into the Great Hall. The
prince had a determined face and a strong nose very much
the same as the queen's. He was a rather formidable man,
strong-faced but with deceptively full lips. His eyes were
direct and heavily outlined with green paint. He stood firmly

astride as he came to a halt before the queen. He did not debase himself, but he did bend low in a gesture of courtesy and respect. Behind him stood Thuti, a general in the army, and Per Ibsen. They both prostrated themselves and did not rise until she signified that they might.

'Life, Health, Strength to you, Great Mother, Great Wife,' Thutmose said. 'You are well?'

'I am well and strong,' Hatshepsut replied smoothly. 'And the gods are on my side.'

'Amun be praised!'

She smiled and indicated that they might sit on the low stools at her feet. She had known all of them as children, and was fond of them in her way.

'O Thutmose,' she said softly. 'Why will you not see things as I do?'

'And why do you still refuse to marry me?' he replied.

'Because I do not choose to give up my throne,' she told him. 'And because I prefer to see my soldiers idle and happy to be alive. Come, let us speak of more pleasant things. Have you visited my temple at Deir el-Bahri?'

'Ai. It is a splendid, quite remarkable sight. Senenmut is a great and gifted man. The temple he has designed will stand throughout the centuries. Future peoples will learn of Hatshepsut through the great temple that will be known as Sublime of Sublimes. And this because of Senenmut! I am surprised that you can bear to send him away.'

The queen's eyes began to glint. She tapped her feet angrily on the step of her throne. She knew that Thutmose was taunting her, for it was common knowledge that Senenmut and she had quarrelled again. He refused to return to the palace, and ignored all the messages she had sent, but explained his work. He wrote:

Great One Most High,
    I am doing important and splendid works in your name. All the world knows that in response to an oracle of the god Amun, which enjoined that the routes to Punt should be explored, you sent five great ships away in the ninth year of your reign. In your wisdom, you ordered that

trade with the ports of the Red Sea—which were
interrupted during the Hyksos wars—should be
resumed.

O Majesty, it is being recorded that your fleet
sailed from the Nile, along the canal in the eastern Delta, into the Red Sea, and arrived safely
in Punt. Egyptian produce was bartered for
myrrh trees, ebony, ivory and other exotic
goods.

Great was the pride and wonder of the people
of Thebes when they saw how successful the
venture had been. And this wondrous event
occurred because of the faith and insight of
Egypt's Great Queen. Now all of these momen-
tous happenings are being portrayed on the walls
of the temple, so that they will live for ever.
Those that come after, in times beyond the
imagination of this life, will see the living pictures and they will gasp with wonder, stand in
awe and admire.

Hatshepsut knew, just as all those who heard of it knew,
that this was merely an excuse on Senenmut's part. Even so,
it was given out that Senenmut stayed away to oversee very
important work. But those near the queen knew how it really
was, and smiled behind their hands.

Senenmut would not return to the palace under orders.
He had no intention of letting her get away with her bouts
of bad temper, her arrogance. Senenmut would not bow the
knee and be brow-beaten. He would return to a woman, but
never to a queen.

And the queen, for her part, reiterated that she would
never give in to a mere man! It was stalemate, and the queen
was in turn both angry and sad.

She became cold and impatient now, because her nephew
knew exactly how things were. His remark had been a gibe.
She would remember that.

'You radiate a certain consciousness of power, Thutmose,' she said icily. 'It surrounds you like an aura. I feel
that I am faced with a man who is certain to make his own

success through sheer force of will. However'—her tone became almost sibilant, '—you will not make your way through your Great Queen's bedroom door.'

Thutmose half smiled and looked down his nose in a manner very reminiscent of the queen.

'Forgive me, Great One,' he drawled. 'I presumed too much. It is unusual for you to send for me. I believed. . .'

'That I was lonely?' She smiled grimly. 'I would as soon take Bek! I sent for you to ask where you have hidden Ranofru. Is my daughter in fact dead?'

'I do not know, Majesty.'

'You lie! It is common knowledge that my daughter loved you. That she believed everything you said. You took her to your bed, Thutmose. Have you disposed of her now that you have had your fill?'

'It is true that Ranofru loved me, Majesty,' Thutmose replied. 'And she looked to me for the companionship that her own Great Mother could not give. I knew that it was her intention to go away. She could not bear being in the middle of two opposing sides. But all that happened a long time ago.'

'How dare you speak such sacrilege! I am the living Horus!' Hatshepsut was chillingly angry now. 'I am the mouthpiece of God. My life is devoted to Egypt and to keep the peace.'

'And to amass wealth,' Thutmose said quickly. 'To fill the bins with grain. To make offerings of extravagance to Amun, to have great obelisks covered with gold. O Great Majesty, you are like the ostrich whose feathers you hold. You bury your head in the sand! Our enemies are already beating at the door, and you, with all your talk of peace, might just as well let them in.'

Everyone held their breath. The guards stared straight ahead. Slaves pretended that they had not heard. The Great One Most High would most certainly cut off their ears if she suspected they had.

'You go too far!' Hatshepsut's face was almost evil in her hate. 'It is in my power to have you put to death where you stand.'

'This I know, Majesty.' Thutmose's eyes glittered into the queen's. 'But the repercussions of such a deed would be more than the court could stand. Can you not accept that your policy of peace is ruining this great and glorious country of ours?'

'I can only accept that you are a fool. You have dared too far. I will not forget your treachery—for there is falseness and hypocrisy in your heart and mind. You speak treason, no less!'

'I have only a great love for Egypt in my aching soul,' Thutmose replied. 'Not falseness. Love!'

'Really? And for Ranofru?'

'I adored her as a sister.'

'As she delighted in you. She would have told you where she was determined to go. O Thutmose, at least you can tell me where my daughter intended to stay.'

'She had a wish to take sanctuary in the temple of Bast,' Thutmose said blandly, knowing that the queen's daughter was no longer there. 'She had a friend, a postulant, whose name is Nebutu, who is in turn first cousin of the priest.'

The queen's eyes narrowed and her painted fingernails made rapid tapping sounds on the arms of her chair.

'The name Nebutu is familiar to me.'

'She was once the personal maid to the wife of Ramose,' Thutmose carelessly replied, unconscious of how still and watchful Per Ibsen had become.

'Ramose,' the queen said coldly. 'Oh yes, Ramose.'

'You know him, Majesty?'

'Yes—Ramose! Now I remember!'

With studied carelessness, the queen picked up her spite-ful-looking ceremonial flail. 'I am not surprised that such a liar and hypocrite should be mixed up in this thing. To spite me, I am sure that he will do, or has already done, Ranofru terrible harm. Yes, Thutmose, to spite me!'

'It is to the goddess of Bast that Ranofru prayed,' Thut-mose said smoothly. 'And that is nothing to do with a rather fine and charming old man. Majesty, let us forget Ramose, and speak of how we can best protect Egypt from ravening, foreign hordes.'

But she was not listening to him. She was remembering a plan she had made a long time ago, a plan that would not go down at all well with the honest and upright Senenmut, should he ever find out. And her days would be filled with fear of the poisoned cup if her nephew Thutmose came to know how greatly she loathed and mistrusted him.

She knew that she would never feel certain of Ramose. He would not keep a still tongue in his head, should he ever get the chance for revenge. She Whose Word is Law had used and then rejected him. She had told him firmly that she had never sent him in search of a beautiful girl to blind Thutmose's eyes. That he was either mistaken or a deliberate liar. She remembered now how he had looked, how confused! For a moment or two he hardly believed the words he had heard. Then, as the implications of her about-face dawned on him, he had prostrated himself full length, arms outstretched, on the ground at her feet.

In his utter loyalty, he had accepted her decision. He had taken the blame for his actions upon himself. Her rejection automatically blackened his character to those in My Majesty's inner command. Quick to take her lead, there had been those who had openly branded the noble Ramose as a treacherous, quite despicable, man. It said a great deal for him that he was able to maintain a quiet dignity while leaving his post of great honour inside the Great House.

Once outside the palace and in his own home, he had continued his life as before—though it had been rumoured that the lady Bentresht was never the same again.

The Great Queen, in her wisdom and mercy, had been gracious and kind. She had allowed the lord Ramose to continue in his own sweet way. It had put her in a very good light at the time. Now she began to wonder whether she had been too forgiving, too lenient, too short-sighted by half.

Hatshepsut moved uneasily and watched her nephew from under her lashes. The passing years had treated him well. He had grown large and good-looking and with the strong features with which most of the royals had been blessed. He was a renowned huntsman and a champion in all masculine games. He was a great user of women and did not suffer fools ladly. He had the effrontery to consider his father's wife witless and self-centred. She became a usurper from the moment she had so deliberately donned the red and white crowns, presuming to proclaim herself Pharaoh of Upper

and Lower Egypt, no less! A position that he clearly believed
belonged to himself.

The queen knew that Thutmose III was waiting for her to
make just one mistake, and then he would pounce. The
unfortunate Ramose might well be the fatal error she had
made. Ramose, who had remained a popular figure in Egypt
in spite of all the name-blackening the court circles had done.

A warning bell rang in Hatshepsut Makare's mind. This
was no time to antagonise this strong-looking young man.
Her tone softened and became mellow. She gave a warm
smile.

'Cousin, let us drink wine and be pleasant together.'

'Brother,' he said flatly. 'My father was none other than
the Great King.'

She raised her finely-arched brows, then shrugged in an
expressive way.

'Let us forget our differences, and all about Ramose, who
has already done us quite considerable harm. I am in need
of wine, food and music, and I will have my way.'

She clapped her hands and musicians began to play.
Dancing-girls gyrated, acrobats performed. Bek was
recalled. Food and wine was served and also some especially
strong beer. Thutmose relaxed and began to eye a full-
breasted girl.

Per Ibsen was uneasy and could not relax. The people were
now beginning to speak openly of the disappearance of Hatshepsut's child. The queen had not minded the princess's
leave-taking, looking on the event as meaning that she had
one enemy less. A scapegoat was needed. Someone was
about to be blamed for the banishment of Ranofru, who had
still not returned from the journey to other lands that she—
so it had been given out—had decided to undertake. If the
queen determined to turn the evil eye on Ramose, he would
die most horribly and so, too, would every member of his
house.

Per Ibsen thought of Zarah, whose time was growing near.
Beads of sweat were glistening on his brow. He knew as if it
had been written in letters of fire that the queen needed to
have a good story to tell the people. One that would put her
in a very good light.

In truth Hatshepsut had long since lost the love and loyalty of her daughter, and now someone would have to pay dearly for that. Per Ibsen knew then that, no matter what the cost, he must warn Zarah. It would do no good to speak to Ramose himself. The man would merely accept the queen's will and her divine right to punish him for a crime that he had not committed.

It was late when Per Ibsen was shown into the gardens of the House of Ramose. He found Zarah sitting by the pool that was fringed with irises. She was the most bewitching creature he had ever seen, and he wondered how she could find it in her foolish heart to put herself in such a very shapeless robe. She was with child and he still saw her as infinitely beautiful. She turned, surprised.

'Oh!' a small voice gasped unbelievingly. 'It is you! The gods must have known that I was thinking of you just then.'

'Then may the gods be praised,' he said, and his face grew gentle. 'What were you thinking about?'

'I was remembering that we are on opposite sides, Per Ibsen,' she said gravely. 'And I find it in my heart to wish that were not so.'

'We are not on opposite sides,' he said steadily. 'Our masters are. There is a world of difference. You must accept and understand that.'

'Yes.' She watched his face with big enquiring eyes. 'But I find it hard to trust the words of noble people in Egypt, even yours, Per Ibsen. My heart pounds, for I wonder why you have come. I am happy that you have, but I am also afraid.'

'I would like you to believe that I would do nothing to harm you.'

'And I would give thanks to Amun, Mithra and all the gods in the world, if I could accept that. But, in all of Egypt, there are only two people in whose words I could believe implicitly. Two, Per Ibsen! Is that not very, very sad?'

She looked so mournful and defenceless that he wanted to take her into his arms and carry her to safety. His face grew bleak. She was like a small and vulnerable bird.

'You are fortunate to have two people in whom you can believe,' he said at last. 'Even I am uncertain about whom I can really trust.'

For a little while there was silence, and he studied his companion, examining every inch of her face that was shadowed and mysterious now as the day drew to a close. She was looking thoughtfully up at the sky, almost unaware of him, it seemed, until a small hand crept out, mouse-like, to close over his fist.

'I like watching the moonlight,' she said softly. 'It is so pure, it is so fresh and white, and—and the moon itself is like the single, most beautiful jewel of truth sailing on a dark sea. My lord Ramose is like the moon. He is high above me, yet his light shines down and surrounds me. He is my god!'

'The name of the moon god is Chon.'

'Ramose!' she insisted sweetly.

'He is your husband.'

She looked at him then, and her lips curved in a mischievous smile.

'He is my god, Per Ibsen. Husbands are mere men.'

'I am a man,' he said flatly.

'Yes,' she agreed, and her eyes were suddenly doe-like and shy. 'I know. And now, may I learn why it is that you have come to visit me here?'

'You must be careful. There may be treachery.'

'Should you not have told this to my lord Ramose?'

'He is too loyal and too trusting for his own good.'

He watched her smile die away and a careworn look take its place. Her lips trembled. He saw the glint of tears. Unable to stop himself, he held her close. A moment later an anxious face was laid against his heart.

Zarah closed her eyes and wanted to stay where she was, safe for ever, This strong man seemed so dependable, somehow. He always seemed to be near, hovering somewhere in the back of her mind. She saw him sometimes in her dreams, throwing his lion-like head back as he laughed aloud. But that was only in dreams, she thought wistfully, where she was weak and womanly and ready to forget that he was dangerous and on the side of Thutmose, whereas her beloved Ramose stood behind the queen. She pulled her weary figure away and got up, smiling tremulously into his stern face.

'Per Ibsen,' she said breathlessly. 'I thank you for coming to warn us of danger. You are very kind. But—but I must tell you that the lord Ramose has lived dangerously all the days of his life. He accepts his fate, and he will continue to do his duty as he sees it. I am of the same mind as my lord husband. He is, as I have already said, head and shoulders above all men.'

Dismissed, frustrated, Per Ibsen went away.

CHAPTER SEVEN

PER IBSEN PAUSED in his work. He was designing a new home for Hathor, the goddess that the prince most revered. Apart from Thutmose, Per Ibsen most admired Senenmut, who had taught him as a boy. Now the news was that the queen's beloved had returned to his home. Per Ibsen decided to visit him there.

Senenmut lived in a style expected of a nobleman who was architect, tutor and also High Steward of the temple of Amun. He owned a great many slaves and cattle. His corn-bins were so full that the bakers had to climb to the highest steps before they could fill their ladles with grain.

The kitchens of Senenmut's house were always full of the smells of good food. The stables held many fine horses. There were ornate chariots in the chariot house, their sides deco-rated red, blue, yellow and gold. Comfortable quarters were provided for the stewards, the women and the servants of the house. Even the lowliest of the slaves had warm accom-modation in the livestock yard. And each person in bondage was given a wooden chest in which to keep belongings, and one jar of oil. So it was that Senenmut was known far and wide as a good and just man.

Per Ibsen found Senenmut sitting in the shade of a loggia. The older man was contemplating the lotuses that bloomed in splendour, and also the water lilies that made cup-shapes the colour of dawn in the large ornate pool.

Senenmut loved his garden, where rows of sweet tamar-isk, palm trees, oleanders, poppies and palms grew, also the unusual cornflowers and flax blossom, fruit, vegetables and vines.

Senenmut smiled as Per Ibsen approached him, and bowed.

'Faith, Health, Strength, O Senenmut,' Per Ibsen said. 'I hope that I am welcome here?'

'You are welcome if you are a friend,' Senenmut replied. 'But why does Thutmose's man come openly to see the man who is loyal only to the queen? You are a man skilled in the creative arts, but above all you stand for the prince.'

'I have come,' Per Ibsen said bluntly, 'because you are the only one who can help.'

Senenmut smiled. 'If that is the case, then your reason must be something to do with our queen. No, tell me, what is My Majesty managing to do now?'

'She is looking for someone to blame for the loss of her daughter Ranofru. My Majesty has learned that Ranofru had an affinity with the temple of Bast—the temple wherein now lives a serving-woman who once worked for the noble Ramose.'

'Ah! The man who gave our great queen so much cause for distrust!'

'O Senenmut, I have searched high and low, but I can find no treacherous thing about him. Indeed, he is widely know as a fine, upstanding man.'

'He played false to the queen. I understand that he was putting cunning plans forward. Plans that could have brought about open enmity between her and Prince Thutmose. I believe that you, in particular, should be disturbed by that.'

'I feel quite sure that this man is incapable of such a thing.'

'Tell me more about Ramose,' Senenmut said thoughtfully. 'You seem determined to be on his side.'

'He is not very young now. He has a young and very beautiful wife. . .'

'Ah!' Senenmut replied. 'Now we are really getting at the truth. . .'

Senenmut called for his steward to summon the litter-bearers. The standard-bearer walked to the front and took up his position. The standard was of gold and bore an emblem of two sacred birds and also the message, 'One Who is Favoured by Two Kings'. This showed that the young

Senenmut had held high position in the Great House even in Hatshepshut's father's time.

The litter-bearers ran smoothly through the wide streets, where the people went about their business in the usual way. But the times were not usual, Senenmut thought, and Thutmose III was growing strong. It would be well to have as a friend Per Ibsen, who was so clearly on Thutmose's side. It could happen that his beloved might need such a friend if the winds of Egypt began to blow the wrong way.

It was late by the time Senenmut reached the Great House, home of the queen. He heard music and singing, but did not go that way. Instead he went to the private chamber that the queen had specially set aside for him many years before.

Slaves greeted him at his entrance, bowing low and stretching forth their hands at knee level. Beautiful negresses entered for his pleasure. They danced sensuously, their heads poised in snake-like detachment as they balanced filled water-pitchers. They washed Senenmut and anointed him with sweet-smelling oils, carrying out the orders he had already given them many times. But his anger was still a frozen coldness in his heart. He had been treated badly, and enough was enough. He would not be humiliated by a woman; no, not even by the queen! He would fight for her, work for her, die for her, for this must all good Egyptians do. But he would not be a monkey on a string, not for Hatshepsut, not even for the great god Amun.

Serving-maids came forward bearing fine clothes to replace those which were dusty after the journey of the day: a fine linen kilt that was thigh-fitting at the back, pleated at the front, and a wide gold collar that was set with turquoises, lapis lazuli, translucent chalcedony and cornelian beads. He clapped his hands once he was ready, and a steward came to take him into the presence of the queen.

Hatshepsut was reclining on a fine couch. A small black boy was fanning her with a white ostrich-feather fan. Senenmut stepped forward and made his obeisances. He then spoke the formal greetings with dignity and restraint.

'Majesty, may thy night be happy.'

'And may thine be happy and blessed.'

'You are well, Makare?'

Hatshepsut's cheeks glowed even more brightly than her paint. She could not hide her delight at seeing her love. 'Why do you speak so formally?' she asked plaintively. 'I wish to speak of soft and gentle things. I long to hear of love and loving—and forgiveness. I—I forgive you!'

Senenmut blandly ignored this. The queen had nothing to forgive him for. On the other hand, she had behaved impossibly towards him. His lips uptilted as she impatiently tapped the arm of her couch.

'Why did you return the golden harp that I sent for your delight? Did it displease you so much?'

'It neither pleased nor displeased. I merely chose to play a harp of my own. If My Majesty cares to think about it, I have always been the same. I have always been proud, remember? Even that very first time we met. Perhaps you do not recall the incident. You were very young at the time.'

She frowned, perplexed. 'I do not remember, Senenmut.'

'You were playing with your favourite wooden doll, and then you saw me and other young men at court having a competition with our throwing-sticks. I was proud of my throwing-stick; it travelled far and it travelled fast, and, more important, my father had given it to me. You offered me your wooden doll in exchange for it. I refused. You then offered an ivory gaming-board inlaid with gold, but I refused to part with my beautifully curved and swift throwing-stick; that sang its own song as it flew in the air in a great arc. You had a tantrum and threatened to have me whipped to death, young as you were. Then I was sent away, and you forgot all about me.' He smiled at the memory. 'At least, Majesty, I still have my throwing-stick, so it is good that you forgot about me so fast.'

'I did not forget. I wanted to learn all about the man who had been so rude to me, child of the king. I remember Pharaoh my father honouring you and presenting you with the Royal Seal. I watched you, Senenmut, but you did not deign to look at me.'

'You were Great Wife to Pharaoh then, so I did not dare. But I did not see your father's bride, I saw only a little girl— a very spoilt little girl who was the chosen one of the gods.'

'Senenmut,' she said imperiously, 'you are laughing at me!'

At this he looked his great queen directly in the face. Watching him closely, Hatshepsut saw the give-away twinkle lurking in the back of his eyes. Her temper began to flare. She could never be sure of him, or read his thoughts. This dismayed her, for she needed to be sure of all things and was used to having her own way. Only Senenmut could distract and puzzle her. Only he could make her feel insecure. That was why there were times when she hated him!

'Senenmut,' she said furiously, 'I do not like the look on your face. Leave me.'

He bowed very low and with exaggerated care. Then, with quiet dignity, he left the hall and its tall red pillars with designs in gilt.

The light of day was ebbing, but the palace walls were still hot with the sun-warmth of the afternoon. The clustering houses of the poor were now cubes of gold and vermilion set in the dark mystery of their own shadow. Senenmut listened to the saffron air of evening, to music, laughter and the low hum of conversation. Through the air came the lowing of cattle and the eerie calling of holy cats. But all he could think of was the witch-woman he loved. The cat-woman he adored, with her full lips and perfect body and long slender hands with nails like red painted claws. He swore softly and pushed his thoughts away. But she was like a drug to him, and he was obsessed.

Hatshepsut stared gravely at her reflection in the polished mirror. Her large, dark eyes looked the same as always: there was no outward sign of her pain. She bit her lips to stop them from trembling, and stared up at the moon god's round glowing orb.

'O god of the moon,' she said. 'Even you have the stars to play at your feet. Why is it that I am fated to be so alone?'

Her heart was throbbing with grief. Life without Senenmut was unthinkable, and yet surely it had come to that? Senenmut, whom she, Great One Most High, had chosen above all others! The man with whom she would smash the marriage jar given half a chance—and share her throne if only she were allowed. He had refused to come. Yet again he had chosen to ignore her command. She would have him stoned for his insolence!

Hatshepsut's painted nails tore at the fine linen. Her long black wig swirled away from her high cheekbones as she tossed her head. What did Senenmut expect of her? She had only to raise one brow and he would be brought to her, bound hand and foot. One word from her lips and he would be killed. She Who Ruled the World also ruled Senenmut— yet he remained remote. She had given him her command, but it had fallen on deaf ears.

Still she waited, as she always had—for Senenmut. when he came to her, it would be not to the queen, but to a woman. She had accepted that a long time ago. If he came to her, it would not be in the name of duty, for Senenmut was certainly sincere. He would come because of his deep and abiding love.

Angry, frustrated, the queen sent her serving-women away and waited alone. Then her heart lurched, for she heard the smooth deepness of his voice. He was speaking to the Nubian guards who stood on duty outside her door. A pulse began beating in her throat as the door opened and Senenmut came in. To her fevered imagination, the bronze carvings on the great door seemed to leap in the rush-lights, and smile.

Senenmut stood there proudly, and yet she was poignantly aware of a faint humbleness in him as he allowed her to recognise his need.

'Makare?' he said simply.

She stood perfectly still before him. Her mouth felt dry and, with a sick desperation, she knew that this man fascinated her and always would.

'Come here,' he said quietly. 'O Beloved, take but one step towards me.'

Although it seemed as if a great pulse was beating between them, she did not do the one thing she deemed so necessary.

'Senenmut,' she whispered, 'I—I cannot. I am as above you as the stars. I am the Pharaoh of the Two Lands. I am God and I am the queen.'

'Come here,' he said again.

She looked at him beseechingly, her soul reaching out to him, her body needing to melt aginst him. Suddenly her passion flared so fiercely that there was nothing left in the world except the raw, ravening urgency of her need.

Hatshepsut, Makare, Queen of the Nile took the one step necessary.

'You are still that child in the garden,' he told her softly. 'But now it is not your tutor telling you what you must do. It is Senenmut. Is that not so?'

His strong hands were pulling her white linen away from her shoulders until she stood naked before him. A hand then went beneath her chin and brought her head up, so that she had to stare into his eyes.

'Say Please,' he said quietly. 'I know what it is that I must do, but, Light of my Soul, you will say Please.'

She forgot her dignity and flew at him, seeking to scratch his eyes out with her long nails. He laughed deep in his throat and held her tight, so that she was helpless. He was, as always, determined to subjugate her. She was now arched helplessly backwards and fully exposed.

'Say Please!'

'Please!' she gasped, then sobbed again, 'Please!'

He was large and he was strong, and once he was inside her, she was alight. She was aware of nothing after that, only the frenzied tempest of her own need. She fought and scratched and bit. She cried out his name not once but many times. Then all that was left was the urgency to match the hot rhythmic movements of his ferocious desire. Then came the agony and ecstasy as she was lifted high on the wave of fulfilment. She gasped his name once more, like the small child he remembered, and her eyes were wet with tears.

Within a little while she slept, her head in the crook of Senenmut's arm. She was happy and content.

Before dawn he woke her, his hands seeking and kneading, until she was burning for him once more. As the sun god leapt joyfully into the day, Hatshepsut, Pharaoh, Lady Queen of the Two Lands, knew again that she was Senenmut's slave.

It was while they were enjoying milk and barley cakes with honey that they began speaking of matters other than love.

'There is a man I wish to help me to run my estate, Beloved,' Senenmut said. 'I have heard that in business matters he is very astute. Do I have your permission to approach him? Will that be all right?'

'Take whom you choose,' she replied, and smiled deep into his eyes. 'All that I have is yours.'

He ran his finger gently down the contours of her cheek. 'I do not want all that you have, Makare,' he teased. 'Merely one man. Ramose is his name.'

At that the queen gasped, and looked stricken. She could not look her lover in the eye.

'What is it?' he asked, surprised. 'Have I offended you, Great Queen? Have I upset you in some way?'

Now her eyes were glittering with suspicion. He had never needed a man to help him before.

'Ramose? Why Ramose, Beloved? I know of many far better men.'

'His ships are fast. He is rich. I believe he would be willing to use his own gold to build a fine fleet. I was thinking of another venture to Punt, my sweet lotus, to bring back more treasures in your holy name. I would use the riches of Ramose to glorify you.'

'But,' she insisted, 'why the lord Ramose, Senenmut?'

'O Beloved,' he parried. 'Why not?'

Her full red lips curled back now, to show her small white teeth as she smiled sardonically. She was thinking of Zarah, Ramose's wife. Was Senenmut, too, thinking of Zarah?

'You are too late, Senenmut,' she said. 'I heard only yesterday that Ramose is dead.'

He was now very watchful and also very direct as he asked, 'How can this be? He was not ill.'

She shrugged carelessly, trying to hide her growing unease and also the jealousy in her eyes.

'It was a robber. He knifed the gatekeeper of the house and managed to get to the garden unseen. He dispatched Ramose while he slept in his garden. The thief took all the jewellery that Ramose had on his person, but he was caught before he could make a clean getaway. Caught and killed.'

Senenmut's expression grew cold and very suspicious. He knew My Majesty only too well.

'Tell me,' he said coolly, 'how is it that you know all this? There was no mention of the nobleman's death while I was in court, and those members are usually animated only when there is new gossip to hand. And I know for a fact that Ramose was alive and well only two days ago.'

The painted brows were raised. 'You were speaking with the man and his wife, O Senenmut? You have been conniving with them?'

'I was not with him, neither have I met her, and I have not condescended to connive.' Senenmut's tone now became as hard as the expression in Hatshepsut's eyes. 'I had heard a great deal about him. I reiterate that I have met neither him nor his wife. But I do have the evidence of my own eyes and ears. He was a genius where trading is concerned, and his business prospered greatly over the years.' He paused meaningfully, then said, 'I cannot understand how it is that you know so much about all this.'

'I am the living Horus. I know it all,' she said proudly.

He shrugged, ignoring her imperious stance.

'Surely, Majesty, you have learned very quickly about an occurrence that, in its importance, could barely raise a ripple on the Nile?'

'The thief is as dead as the man he killed,' she flared. 'This I know. He was caught and punished for his sins. All the world knows that I am just and fair.'

'Hail to the queen!' Senenmut said, and bowed very low. 'The house of Ramose will tremble under the weight of such a deep loss. I, too, am sorry, for I would have liked the help of the man.'

'There are others who would be ready and willing to give gold in order to finance a further expedition to Punt,' Hatshepsut said eagerly. 'And these men are close to court—unlike Ramose, who was never especially loyal to us.'

'Had he lived to hear you say that, Majesty,' Senenmut said quietly, 'he would have a broken heart. From what I have heard, the loyalty of Ramose, his adoration of his great and powerful queen, was never in doubt. My most brilliant and renowned adherent, Per Ibsen, would also put his seal to that.'

'Per Ibsen is like a brother to Thutmose!' Hatsheput spat. 'And I will not change my mind. I have good reason to distrust everyone in Ramose's house. Does Senenmut dare to argue with me? Speak of other things. The name of Ramose hurts my ears.'

'Let us call Bek and listen to his new song,' Senenmut said smoothly. 'I believe it is about My Majesty's beautiful eyes.'

Hatshepsut relaxed, for the smile was back on her lover's face. She liked compliments, and the awkward moment had passed. Clearly, Senenmut had brushed aside his thoughts of Ramose.

Now Ramose was dead, she thought, there was only one other person who knew the truth about the whole sordid affair. That was Zarah. Hatsheput's lips curled, remembering how beautiful everyone considered the slave girl to be. Ridiculous Ramose had even taken her to wife. Well, her grief would soon be over and done. She would soon follow her lord husband to the tomb. It had been inconvenient of her, and the black giant who was her shadow, to have been away at the time Ramose had been dispatched. The orders had been to do away with all three. No matter, Hatshepsut mused, there was always the next time. . .

Zarah was inconsolable, yet her grief was too deep for tears. She felt numb and cold and very alone. The noble figure of Ramose surely could not be banished from this earth for ever? It could not be true that she would never again be able to creep into the safety of his arms. A faint moan escaped her lips, and she rocked backwards and forwards on the low stool that, as it always had been was set directly below her lord and master's tall chair.

She could see his face before her whenever she closed her eyes. She could hear his cool voice as he explained the running of his estates and introduced her to his friends, many of whom were scribes. She remembered his words of tenderness and love. She left the stool and went outside, unable to rest.

After that, she spent many hours in the garden that Ramose had so loved. She could no longer bear to stay inside, for the house seemed suspended in time, too alien and still. She imagined devils of death leering at her from every corner of every room. She was inwardly crying her hate to them, her despair, her grief, her loss. Without her beloved she was nothing at all. The ache in her was a gnawing living pain.

Shocked and increasingly tired, she, with the help of Thickneck and the old majordomo who had spent a lifetime in Ramose's employ, made the necessary plans for the funeral. Ramose's final resting-place had been erected a long time before. Even so, Zarah was prepared to give the priests a mountainful of her husband's gold to ensure that everything was carried out exactly as her lord husband had desired.

Since Ramose's spirit would inhabit his body, embalmers had to be employed to see to it that his remains were correctly preserved. As Zarah watched the boat carrying Ramose across the river to the House of Death, her tears rained down her cheeks. She would have chosen to go with her lord husband on his last journey, but, apart from the workers and the priests, the House of Death was out of bounds.

It was there that the body-workers and embalmers began their tasks. The men who worked in the House of Death each specialised in one part: so there were people with such titles as Master of the Belly; Master of the Heart; Master of the Lungs, and so on. The highest and most revered personage was Master of the Brain. It was he who detached the brain by drawing it out through the nostrils with special pincers. All was done carefully and with reverence. After this, the skull was made clean.

There was a sickly odour, and it was very eerie and still in the long dark Waiting Housew, where, in line, were large granite baths. In these the dead lay sleeping in salt, lye, spices and resins. After the correct period of time, the body would be taken to the Drying House. It was hot and close, unearthly with the awesome feel of the Afterworld everywhere. Gradually the body became shrivelled and mummified, and would then be stuffed and swathed with layers of finely woven linen. The whole process, for the rich, lasted for up to seventy days. For the poor, it took a far shorter time; even two days for one band of gold. The very poor had to take the departed to the desert themselves. There, in time, the sand produced the same condition, but the sand did not provide the ritual ceremonies of the priests. Their magical intonations were necessary to help one across the Black River.

Once mummified, Ramose would be taken to his burial chamber, in which had been placed tables, chairs, a boat, bed, musical instruments and hosts of little wooden servants and slaves; all manner of things for Ramose to use in the Afterworld. But that would not happen yet. Zarah knew that at this time Ramose was still floating in his granite bath in the Waiting House.

One evening she stood by the river and looked yearningly across to the other side. Why, she grieved, had the gods allowed such a fine and wonderful man to be so uselessly killed? Why had she and Thickneck been away when it happened? The search for Caiphus seemed so empty and meaningless now. How blind she had been, to be searching for one kind and loving man when, in the House of Ramose, she had had the whole wonder of the world!

She heard Thickneck coming to find her. Dear, kind Thickneck who could have gone his own way many years ago. Yet he stayed near. He had become a rich man in his own right, for he carved beautiful miniature cats, horses, cows and dogs. They were in great demand for the tombs. But although rich and free, he stayed at the side of his Morning Light.

'Life, Health, Strength, little one,' he said. 'You should not be standing here alone by the river. Your time grows near, and you should be resting at home.'

'I have been thinking,' she replied gravely, and her face looked like a pale daisy turning its face to the sun as she looked wistfully into Thickneck's dark eyes. 'I might lose my life while bringing forth my lord husband's son.'

'No! You are fine and healthy, and you are very young.'

'I—I want to die, Thickneck.'

'And leave me alone?'

She smiled at that. 'You have too many friends, my Napata, ever to be alone. And you are adored by the fishermen.'

'You are my heart. You must not die, Morning Light. You must never leave me.' His voice was trembling, and rasped more than usual.

She looked at him wonderingly. He was a giant. He could crush her with one hand. Yet, at the thought of losing her, his eyes had filled with tears. She put her tiny hand out to be taken into his large, firm grasp.

'Beloved,' she said carefully, 'I—I have a favour to ask. I want you to swear on your love for me to carry out one special task—should—should things not go well for me before my lord is put safely in his funeral house.'

'If it is in my power, I swear.'

'I want you to promise me, that no matter what happens you will stay here, in my place, and see to it that the lord Ramose is given all the last rites. He must have the highest priests, and he must have everything as he planned it. I promised him that it would be so. But. . .'

'Yes?'

'I could be—I may not be—able to see to it! His child will be here well before the seventy days.'

'Then I swear to stand in on your behalf.'

'No matter what happens, Beloved?' Her eyes were beseeching. At that moment he saw her as the agonised child in the compound of slaves.

'No matter what happens, Morning Light. On my love for you, I swear!'

'You have put my mind at rest,' she whispered. 'Oh, my Thickneck, how dearly I love you!'

He held her as gently as he would a fragile flower, until her storm of weeping had passed. Then, with infinite tenderness, he led her back into the house, where a personal maid took over, one that Thickneck trusted. No one was able to get near Zarah without Thickneck's vetting. He had made it his business from the time he had caught Tyi with the viper in her room.

He waited until he saw that Zarah was asleep, and then settled himself down for the night outside her room. He was on edge, wary, for he had heard a strange tale. One that did not make sense, and yet it rang true. He had heard the rumour that Ramose had been killed on the word of the queen. Now it was whispered that My Majesty was after his First Wife's blood too.

The night was early still when Thickneck heard his friend the majordomo approach.

'I have brought wine,' the old man said. 'Perhaps we will enjoy the betting board game while we pass an hour or two?'

'A good idea.' Thickneck gave his crooked grin. 'It is time for me to let you win.'

Less than one hour later, both men were senseless on the ground.

Zarah woke and, in terror, started up with a cry. Too late. A blanket was thrown over her head and the desert man whose face was covered lifted her up bodily and carried her, writhing and screaming, away and out of the house. No one could stop them, for the servants had fled.

Crazy with fear, Zarah fought to no avail. She was taken to a camel and heaved over its back. With a bad-tempered grunt it began to rise. The world seemed to be spinning in a crazy way. With an exhausted moan and tears in her eyes, she slipped into the chasm of unconsciousness.

When she came to, she realised that she had been thrown to the ground. The world around her was composed of darkness lit only by fire-thorn fires. These spat and crackled, and sent showers of sparks flying into the wilderness. The cold and spiteful night winds were making the sand sting her lips, her eyes, and it all but choked her as she tried to breathe.

Gradually, as full consciousness returned, she knew black fear. She was a prisoner, and she recognised the voice of her captor. Gimillu! Again the pictures of far memories danced like spectres in her mind. She remembered the pretty little slave who had dared to fight; who, in the name of the pagan god, had dared to scratch the Persian prince's face.

Fear was beating like a thick, dull drumbeat against her sides. She wanted to scream and run. But she was bound fast, and all she could do was to stare up at the soulless stars through her sand-gritted, watering eyes.

'O God,' she was pleading in her mind. 'Let Thickneck come after me. Let him save me. Let Thickneck come!' But then she remembered her beloved Ramose, and her fear for herself was replaced by her anguish at losing him.

She became aware of movement, and one of the men left his position by the fire and came over to stare down at her. Zarah had the impression of a cruel face and glinting eyes, then a voice called out, 'She is with us, Lord.'

'Bring her here,' Gimillu replied.

Rough hands pulled her to her feet. Her legs were
unbound. Because of her condition, she was ungainly and
staggered, but there was neither concern nor gentleness in
her captor's face and she was shoved toward Gimillu's large
black tent. The prince was sitting just inside, in the shelter
of its awning. Before him was food and drink, and by the
light of butter lamps Zarah could see that the man had
already taken far too much wine. Liquid glistened on the
three rows of curls growing on his chin, and his glittering
eyes had a feverish stare.

'So!' Gimillu said, and cruelty was running like a strand
of silk through his voice. 'Ramose managed something at
last. What a pity that we cut him down before he had the
delight of seeing his one and only child.'

Zarah did not reply, but the tears slid slowly down her
cheeks. She remembered the wide and all-embracing smile
that had almost split Ramose's face and the quiet exultation
in his voice as he had said: 'O beloved, Amun has been merciful at last.' Now she was shaking, and knew only horror
and terror of all the evil things that Gimillu could do.

'Amun-ra, Sun God of Egypt,' she was praying desperately in her mind. 'Mithra, Sun God of Persia, watch over
and bless my lord Ramose's unborn child. O gods, I beg of
you both!'

'You are still far too beautiful,' Gimillu said. 'You have
the face of a good spirit and eyes as large and as lovely as
the black grapes that grow in the south. When are you due
to bring forth your child?'

'I believe soon.'

'May it live,' he said silkily. 'May it be whole.'

'I call upon Amun-ra for that mercy,' she breathed, and
began to tremble even more.

'Ha! You pray to Egypt's God, Zarah of Anshan,' he
sneered. 'So your lord husband had his way.'

'No!' she gasped, and felt fear writhing and pulling her so
hard that she wanted to be sick. 'I call upon Amun-ra, god
of the Sun, but that is who Mithra is too. I call upon all the
gods.'

'And do they help you at all?'

The sarcasm was so evident in his voice that she wanted to sink to her knees and wring her hands in utter despair. Instead, she lifted her head and stared contemptuously into his cruel, shadow-etched face.

'O Lord,' she said quietly. 'It is evident that the gods have deserted me, since I am recently widowed and now in your filthy hands.'

'For that you will come here,' he said, and his lips curled. 'Come close.'

She did not obey, and was forced to her knees before him by the man standing behind. And then Gimillu's hands were running over her, over her breasts and moving like shadows of horror, almost caressingly over the curve of her unborn child.

'I could cut open your belly here and now,' he told her, and with an evil leer he called for a knife, and she cried out in horror and cringed, holding her stomach, cradling it as if trying to protect her baby so soon to be born. 'Has it occurred to you to wonder why I have kept you alive? Especially as your husband expired so quickly at the hands of one of my men.'

'I know only that I wish you would knife me to death this minute,' she panted. 'I want to die!'

'And so you might, had it not been better for me to keep you alive.'

'I am heavy with the unborn,' she said desperately. 'I cannot travel far before it will be my time. You need to travel quickly if you are to get safely away.'

'From whom?' He laughed softly, triumphantly. 'You will live, and I will tell you why. Ramose refused me gold, and he said that he cared nothing whether or not I held my tongue. He said that the queen had dismissed my story as a lie many years ago. So I took his advice, and I went to the queen and told her how dangerous an adversary such as Ramose was. It was Ramose's own dearly beloved queen who ordered your husband's death.'

'So! She is a living lie,' Zarah cried. 'A hypocrite and a liar, and she has no dignity. She is lower than dung.'

'She feels the same about you. You should have been dispatched alongside Ramose, and that black giant as well. You were not in the house, and Fate was kind to me. You are a living witness to the real truth. I am now in the position to ask for and receive a fortune from Egypt's great queen.'

'She is too cunning and too strong. You cannot win.'

'I have Judas and Neb as well as yourself to bear witness to a plot that owed its beginning to Hatshesut herself. To the queen who for one brief moment came out into the open and showed how desperately she wanted to blacken Thutmose in the eyes of the people he wished to lead.'

'There is no proof!' Zarah sobbed. 'And my lord husband accepted all the blame.'

'Ramose was too loyal, and he was a fool,' Gimillu sneered. 'There was proof, just as I knew there would be. And that proof was always kept hidden, inside a locket. He was given firm orders and, more to the point, they hold the queen's seal. Only a man like Ramose would have kept quiet. As I have said already, your lord husband was a great fool.'

'O Prince Gimillu, I beg of you. . .' She was openly sobbing. 'Please let me die! Allow me the sweet mercy of joining my lord husband in the Realm of the Dead.'

'I need you alive. I have told you.'

'My baby—'

'—will doubtless eventually find itself in Judas's care if you refuse to obey me.'

'You could not—not Judas!' She was screaming in her heart and mind. 'I am to be returned to Judas?'

'You are to stay in my care. You will return openly to the house of Ramose with your child and pick up the reins of your husband's estate. No, it will not be taken by the queen's men for the purposes of tax or anything else—not while I have a particular papyrus scroll bearing Hatshesut's seal.'

'No!'

'And if you do not obey, your child will be born and sent off at once for Judas to have.'

'No! Lord Gimillu, no!'

The Persian suddenly tired of his cat and mouse game. He looked Zarah over in a contemptuous manner then his expression grew hard. His voice held distaste as he snapped, 'Take her away. Keep her out of my sight. Her swollen belly is offensive to my eyes.'

Zarah's legs buckled under her and she fell. She was crying for mercy, begging for the life of her unborn child, and the terrible flickering pictures in her mind were all jumbled up. She saw the boy she had imagined that she would have. A sweet wonderful boy with Ramose's nobility and charm. But the boy of her dreams had changed, somehow, and had become Harad. A poor, helpless mutilated Harad, who had been in Judas's care.

'No!' Her cry was frenzied, high and wild.

Rough hands grabbed her round the wrists and, still screaming, she was dragged away. Her body bumped helplessly over the ground and was left near the windbreak that the kneeling camels made. Her ankles were rebound, but she was too hysterical to care. She wanted to die. Even more, she wanted her baby to die. Anything would be preferable to having the newly born infant in Judas's fat, vicious hands.

At last, sick and arched in an agony of cramp because of the manner in which she had been so brutally tied, she cried out for Gimillu.

'Tell him,' she choked, 'that it will be as he wishes. And beg him to cut me free.'

In a little while her wrists and ankles were freed. A basin containing bread and dried figs was set before her, also a skin filled with water to drink. The brutish man, a desert man, squatted near her, an evil leer on his face.

'You can wander at will,' he told her, 'but I do not think you will go very far. We are a day's journey away from Thebes, with nothing but desert between us. When the lord Gimillu is ready, we will return to your home. You will give everything to him and he will own all that Ramose owned— including you.'

She stared before her, unable to think.

'And your child, who will be born while we are here in the wilderness, will ensure that you will do as you are told.'

He threw back his head and laughed at her gasp of pain and fear. 'Truly my master is a clever man. He has a great queen in the palm of his hand, and he has you. By the gods and all devils, I can see the day coming when Gimillu rules the world. Come! Eat and drink your fill. You are too precious for us to set you free. Soon your bonds will be tied again.'

CHAPTER EIGHT

PER IBSEN STARED into Ramose's garden pool, at the water lilies, at the tiny fish that glinted like slivers of silver and gold, but he did not see them. He saw only a wistful face, a tiny figure swathed in blue, and he heard again the mystical whispering of myriads of tiny bells.

An icy hand squeezed at his heart and the tortured rasping he had heard earlier on rang and echoed in his head. Thickneck, who might not survive the night, had gasped out the whole sorry tale. And now Zarah was somewhere out there in the savage waste. He felt fear, and it sent an icy chill to the marrow of his bones. There was nothing the queen would stop at to have Zarah out of the way. He knew that now. And, may Amun forgive him for being disloyal even in thought, the young Prince Thutmose was just the same. The whole royal family were for ever jostling for power. But power was dust and ashes against the fierce immensity of love.

He thought of how he had watched Zarah. He had always been prepared to stand by and wait until she grew up. He had always known of her wide-eyed yet faint awareness of him, at first a shy and enquiring awareness that had grown into suspicion and distrust. She had become whole-heartedly on the side of Ramose, the fallen noble who had quietly but firmly set out to care for her. And Per Ibsen had to admit that Ramose was indeed a fine and just man. He came to accept that, for the time being, the little princess was safe and secure. Deep down, he was quite sure that his own time would come.

Decent or not, Ramose stood on the side of the queen. Once Hatshepsut was out of the way, and the Ramoses and Senenmuts were out of this world, he would step in and claim his own. Now, perhaps, it was too late. All he could do was to wait. Wait until the host of men he had sent out came back with answers to his questions. Without a little knowledge he was powerless. He clenched his hands, and anger and anguish were mingled in his eyes.

Finally, in despair, he walked away from the house of Ramose. It was a futile attempt to find his own procedure. He saw the great temple. The vivid light of a dying day touched the silent heights and ran in tiny red streams down the uncannily alive hieroglyphs. It was only the fantastic play of light, yet the effect was horrifying. It gave Per Ibsen the feeling that he was watching the trickling of blood.

When he made his way back to the house, a small group of his men were waiting there. They had been unsuccessful, he could tell. Suddenly there came the dull smacking of naked feet hurrying over the ground. The newcomer flung himself down and laid his face in the dirt at Per Ibsen's feet.

'Well?' Per Ibsen asked sharply.

'Lord, a small caravan with only three men. The lady was taken, struggling, to this caravan.'

'Who told you this?'

'A servant of this house saw it all, but did not dare to cry out. Everyone had heard rumours that what was about to happen was on the orders of the queen. The servant told me that the caravan set out towards the western desert.'

Per Isben took a thick gold band from his wrist and handed it to his man. Then he looked at him, and the others, and snapped, 'We will go.'

The full Egyptian moon hung like a giant ball of glowing silver in the soft indigo sky. The sands stretched away, shadowy, eerie, part of an unreal night-time world. And the silent men accompanying Per Isben were wary. Not of earthly enemies, for they could soon be dispatched, but they had a mortal dread of evil spirits. Each man in the group made sure his small pouch of salt was near to hand. Salt protected from most wicked beings, but the prowling She-devil was the one most likely to be near.

And with every forward step in that silent, moon-washed shadowy desert, the men felt the She-devil's glaring eyes. She who went about at night, searching, prowling, glaring into every mud-brick home, looking for newborn babies to

devour. The men silently prayed to Osiris, to Amun, to all
the gods, to save the one for whom their master searched
from the terrifying She-devil. But most of all they prayed for
themselves, that they did not see the Evil One. But as the
moon grew more bright, there was worse to come. They
could not escape from the *carinas,* the shadows, at their feet.

Every man following Per Ibsen was now fully aware of his
own *carina,* which travelled about with him from birth to
death. Sometimes it left its nebulous form and became a cat.
One had to be kind to cats, because they might be one's relatives or friends. No matter how hideous and maddening
their nightly noises might be, one dared not throw sticks,
sandals or stones. Cats were holy, and they were splendidly
and awesomely the living shadows of oneself! If a cat died,
it was a terrible thing. One lamented loudly and shaved off
one's eyebrow in a sign of grief and respect.

To Per Ibsen's men, on that silent march across the desert,
the *carinas* were uncomfortably real as they moved and
jerked, grew short, grew tall and always and for ever stayed
firmly attached to their feet.

Far away a jackal howled. A night creature screamed high,
then the sound wailed downwards to die in a sob and a sigh.
The winds made sand-devils whirl like dervishes, and the
watching stars on high looked like a million soulless eyes. It
was a relief, a joy to see their leader stiffen and hold up his
hand in a silent order to stop and give a gesture that meant
beware.

An orange pinpoint of light glowed in the desert, pallid
under the light of the moon, with no hiding, no subterfuge.
Per Ibsen went forward purposefully. As he neared, it was
clear that there had been no mistake. He saw Gimillu and
his two evil companions.

A thorn-branch exploded and sent up a shower of sparks
as the fire blazed into new life. Per Ibsen saw the camels, the
tent, and the three men, their faces etched black and orange
in the light. They were staring helplessly at the advancing
party headed by an Egyptian whose stern features looked as
cold and tough as stone. He held a short-handled spear, and
his followers bows and arrows, which were already unslung.

Clearly, the only road left open, Gimillu thought, was to
bluff it out. 'Who are you?' he demanded. 'And why do you

bear arms in such a menacing way? We are only three travellers, alone in the night.'

'I have come for the princess of Anshan,' Per Ibsen said flatly.

Gimillu raised his brows and shrugged. 'Look around you. There is no princess here.'

'Then perhaps you know her better as the First wife of Ramose?' Per Ibsen enquired silkily.

Gimillu knew he was trapped and his eyes were evil. 'Who are you?' he asked again.

'I am the man who is going to kill you,' Per Ibsen replied and there was ice in his voice. 'Kill you like the dog you are if you have harmed one hair of the princess's head.' He turned to his men. 'Watch them, and see that they do not move.'

As they swung round, to hurry to the tent, Gimillu sprang, in his hand a wicked-looking knife. He was agile, and his attack was unexpected, but Per Ibsen was a tower of strength, and the Persian was no match for him. With a single ferocious blow, the nobleman knocked him to the ground. Contemptuously throwing down his spear, leaving the winded and barely conscious Gimillu in the charge of his men, Per Ibsen made haste to enter the tent. Then his heart gave a great leap because Zarah was indeed there, and she was alive.

She lay there shivering, hardly conscious of what was going on, trying to keep back her broken sobs. Her hands and feet were bound, her swollen body held her where she was, contorted uncomfortably on the ground.

Per Ibsen knelt down, his sharp intake of breath making her look at him with great pain-filled eyes. He tore at her bonds and wanted to swear when he saw how cruelly they had been tied. He knew he was going to kill Gimillu slowly. He wanted to boil him in oil!

'O Per Ibsen,' Zarah gasped, as he freed her and cradled her in his arms. 'I thank you.' She began to weep openly. 'Friend or enemy, I thank you from the bottom of my heart.' She looked round her then in a puzzled way. 'Per Ibsen, I—I want and need Thickneck. Why isn't he here?'

'He will come soon,' Per Ibsen lied, and very gently helped her into a more comfortable position.

There came a great commotion, and the fierce shouting of
men, then the sound of blows and of struggling. Per Ibsen
leapt outside and was confronted by a fanatical Gimillu, who
was already bleeding from an arrow wound. He was screaming obscenities, his hand raised. He was once again armed
with a knife.

Unarmed, Per Ibsen defended himself, his men now
silently circling round the bitterly struggling pair. Gimillu's
two followers were already accounted for. They lay where
they had fallen, open-eyed, mouths agape, already stiffening
on the sand.

Per Ibsen's superiority was soon apparent. His long *carina* seemed to be executing a jerky, rather macabre, victory
dance at his feet. Suddenly the once arrogant prince was on
his knees. His eyes were distended, his expression holding no
honour in defeat, only a frozen fear. He clasped his hands
before him and bent so that his forehead touched the ground.
Debased, he gabbled, 'Mercy! I swear that she would have
to come to no harm.'

'As I have promised already. . .' Per Isben hurled at him,
but said no more, for Zarah's call came cutting painfully
through the firelight. There was a lonely pleading in her
voice.

'Per Ibsen, my lord. . .'

He swung round in quick alarm, momentarily forgetting
the craven man. His back to Gimillu, he did not see the Persian's last desperate leap. Gimillu was stopped in full flight
by an arrow fired by one of Per Ibsen's men. The missile hit
him low in his stomach, and he died screaming in agony, but
Per Ibsen neither knew or cared.

Zarah was trying to reach him; she was looking anxiously
into his face. The pain seared through her again and she bent
double and screamed. And it was for Nadia she cried: the
long-ago, far-away Nadia who had mothered her and had
loved her so. Nadia, who had cradled her against her warm
black bosom and who had sung her to sleep with soft lul-
labies.

Per Ibsen stared down at Zarah, who crouched, flushed
and feverish and bent double in pain. When the pain was
over, he studied her face. There was a wistful innocence

about it entirely out of keeping with a young woman about to give birth. It was pinched and careworn, with great sad eyes. He turned away, but a fragile hand clutched nervously at his wrist.

'Do—Do not leave me! I am afraid.'

'I will not leave you,' he promised. 'I am just going to make things as easy for you as I can.'

He turned to his men and ordered that a comfortable place should be made for her inside the black tent. When this was accomplished, Per Ibsen himself lifted her up and carried her inside. He laid her carefully on a pile of rugs and she fell back weakly, watching him with dazed eyes. He held a water-skin to her lips and she took one sip, then turned her head away. Then he sat on the leather folding chair, to wait.

The men, confident now in the normal crackling of the fire, busied themselves making things ready for the night. They ate a handful of dried fruit and chewed on raw grains of corn. They boasted loudly, trying to frighten the She-devil away with the strength of their words.

The night flowed slowly away and watered down the moon. In the east, the sky turned from deep purple to yellow and gold. Per Ibsen went to look at Zarah. Beads of perspiration stood out on the smooth young forehead, and it was drawn and shadowed with pain. When he mopped her face carefully, its heat reached him through the fine linen cloth. A strand of silken hair wound round his finger and he was loath to let it go. Then a gasping moan made the stern expression on his face relax, and he smiled into the dark eyes that were watching him now wearily. She was almost defeated by the growing thrusts of sheer pain.

'I—I cannot keep on—much longer,' she gasped. 'It is agony, and—I am on fire!'

'You are going to keep on,' he told her sternly. 'Just as all the women in this world keep on when they are in the middle of bearing a child.'

'Delivering a. . . I am delivering my baby, Lord?' She was staring at him with a strained, striving clutch at reason. 'O may Mithra be praised!'

'Why else do you think you are being bowed down?' he asked, surprised.

She did not reply, for the torment ripped through her again. But now that she was aware of what was happening to her, her terror of the drink Gimillu's man had forced on her was gone. She had believed herself to be poisoned, and that it was venom ripping out her inside.

Her eyes were luminous in the light of the lamp, and her hand fluttered out to rest on Per Ibsen's arm.

'You—You will stay with me, Lord? With you near, I—I feel more secure.'

'While you want me,' he assured her, 'I will stay. I will stay for ever if that is your wish.'

'Lord,' she gasped, 'you are—so good to me.' She was looking at him with her heart in her eyes. 'So very, very good!'

All that day Zarah lay in Gimillu's tent in travail. And she held on to the strength of Per Ibsen and was comforted by his tender care. During all those hours it seemed that they had become close. Zarah looked to the large man who had such gentle, caring eyes, and she forgot that he was not on her side; that he was Thutmose's spy.

The man who had been sent at speed, on one of the camels, to find a nursing woman had still not returned, many hours later. He and the woman arrived soon after dawn.

When the sun was high in the sky, Zarah's daughter was born. The nursing woman, tough and silent, washed the baby and bound her in swaddling clothes. And it was Per Ibsen who held her up and placed her in Zarah's greedy arms.

'She is beautiful!' Zarah wept happy tears. 'She is so beautiful that it shall be her name. Nefer!' She looked up at Per Ibsen. 'Is that a good name?'

'A very good name,' he told her, and cursed himself for forgetting who and what he was. Zarah was not his wife; Nefer not his child. With all his heart and soul he wished they both belonged to him.

Now it was over, he knew that Zarah would begin to mistrust him again. He decided to become the distant watcher she believed him to be. It would be easier for her that way, and there would be no embarrassment caused.

The following day they began a journey. To Zarah, now safe on the back of Gimillu's mount, her baby cradled in her arms, Per Ibsen seemed very far away, cold and distant. This made her feel sad. She found herself needing him at her side, wanting him to continue to share the greatest experience of her life—as the beloved Ramose never would.

'O Ramose,' she whispered softly. 'How you would have adored this wondrous child. She is so perfect, and far better than a son.'

She looked ahead at Per Ibsen again. She still needed to be close to him; though, she thought sadly, he no longer seemed to want to be close to her. But, even so, she knew for good or ill that Per Ibsen would always be a part of her life.

Since he continued to ignore her when they were camped that evening, she walked hesitantly towards him. Slight, frail, with the evening light behind her, she was ethereally beautiful to his eyes. She was, he thought, like a young goddess with her baby in her arms. She came to a halt before where he sat easily. He remained silent.

'I have come to thank you, Per Ibsen,' she said gravely. 'I will never forget what you have done for me. My gratitude knows no bounds.'

'Oh?' His expression was cold.

'For—For staying with me.' She went on quietly, 'I was afraid. I—I am ashamed of that fear.'

'You did not seem afraid.' He stared at her, and then his full lips curved in a lazy smile. 'You managed very well.'

She sounded happy, as if a weight had been lifted from her shoulders. 'I am glad. My beloved Thickneck has told me many times that I must be brave.' She was silent a moment, then added plaintively, 'I thought that he would have come by now.'

'How could he?' Per Ibsen asked reasonably. 'The seventy days necessary for the lord Ramose's preparations are not over. If you will remember, you insisted that Napata stayed to see Ramose safely in his tomb. It was Napata himself who told me this fact.'

'Yes.' She digested this, then, 'My lord husband would have been joyful to have seen our child. Thickneck will be happy also. May we return to Thebes and go to my husband's tomb and show Nefer to him? And to Thickneck, too?'

'Our journey is in the opposite direction to the Valley of the Dead,' he said flatly. 'And it is not safe for you in your husband's house.'

'Then,' she said carefully, 'may I know where I am going?'

'Not yet.'

'I am a prisoner of Thutmose the prince?'

'No. You are a prisoner of mine.'

'You are going to kill me? My child?'

'You will live, if you do as you are told and keep out of harm's way,' he said sternly.

She bit her lip and now felt afraid again of the tall, distant man. Then she dared to ask one more question.

'Per Ibsen—why did you send the nursing woman away?'

'Because it is wise that few people, outside my men, know where you are.'

'I feel that I am without friends,' she whispered sadly. Then, without warning, she began to weep. He was at her side in an instant, insisting that she sit on the blanket he had already set on the sand. Zarah sat down obediently, holding Nefer lightly in the crook of her arm. She was trying hard to keep back the tears that were slowly forcing themselves to the fore. The accumulated troubles of the last few days, coming after a lifetime of anxiety and fear, proved to have taxed her beyond her strength. The journey on the camel, so soon after her travail, had been too hard by far.

Per Ibsen put his arms round her. He felt the tearing sobs rise, but she was still trying to keep them under control. A complete breakdown was bound to come sooner or later, but he needed to get the little princess into safety. There were too many who would sell their souls for the price that must most surely now be on the girl's head. If only she would relax sufficiently to trust him, but seemingly this would never be.

'I think that by now you should be able to accept that I am your friend,' he said gravely.

'Lord,' she whispered. 'I am the lady whose husband stood for the queen. You are and always will be Thutmose's man.'

'Can't you accept, even now, that the queen is your enemy?'

She laughed shakily, unable to hide her faint derision.

'And Prince Thutmose is our friend?'

He smiled, well aware that more than a few uncomfortable days would have to be gone through before this shy person and he arrived at an understanding. A long convulsive shiver and a little moan made Per Ibsen's arms tighten involuntarily round his prisoner. He waited, fearing his action would make her pull away. Instead, Zarah unconsciously nestled closer to him, and her hand uncrumpled and gripped his tunic. It was then that Per Ibsen marvelled at his own strength of mind. The greatest temptation of his life confronted him—to hold and to keep this frail princess and her child. But he fought the temptation, knowing that the time was not right. Perhaps it would never be. One thing was certain, though: he would defy even the beloved Thutmose to keep this person safe. She would learn of his love one day, perhaps, but he would have to wait until she fully understood and accepted the fact for herself.

Zarah's heart was in her eyes as she pleaded, 'Please, Lord, take me back to my house, to Thickneck, to where I feel free.'

With wonderful self-control he turned his face from her. He knew that he would give himself away if she looked at him so pleadingly for much longer. She was desperate and scared and weak after the birth of her child. He knew very well the wild bargains women made with men when there could be no other escape.

His mouth tightened into a thin line. He wanted no such bargains where Zarah of Anshan was concerned. When she came to him, it must be out of love. He would feel only contempt should it be the other way round; contempt for the girl and for his own lack of pride.

'You are tired,' he said at last, 'and the journey has been too much for you. As for taking you back, it is out of the question. As you have said, I am Thutmose's man, and you must learn to do as you are told.'

'But, Lord. . .'

'You will return to the tent that is now set up, and you will rest.'

With noble condescension he stood in order to help her to rise. She stood before him, with a quiet dignity about her as she looked up at him, still tenderly cradling her diminutive child.

'Lady,' he said in courteous dismissal. Wordlessly she turned away.

The noise and bustle of breaking camp aroused Zarah. She woke with a sudden start and clutched Nefer against her pounding heart, calling for Per Ibsen in quick alarm. Then she remembered the conversation of the previous day and shrank back as he appeared. The look on her face effectively shattered the rosy imaginings he had been weaving throughout the night.

He said evenly, 'You must eat and drink and prepare yourself. We will continue our journey very soon now.'

As soon as he had gone, Zarah put Nefer to her breast. She was hurt and bewildered by his distant tone. He certainly did not seem to be a friend, and so she kept as far away as possible from him. Why had he been so merciful to her? Why?

Frightened, suspicious, she hugged her beautiful baby close to her heart, crying deep in her soul because Fate had decreed that Ramose would never see this longed-for child. She missed him and she missed Thickneck, too. The diminutive Nefer would never see either of them.

It was only coming to her now, how swiftly and mercilessly Gimillu and his men had perished. She forgot her fear and hatred of the Persian and his men, and saw only that Per Ibsen was a murderer. She was helpless and in his power. If he so desired he could also, and as easily, kill her.

By the next day they had journeyed to a village that was quite near the great Nile, where people could be seen. Fellahin, some not even wearing loin-cloths, were working the soil. The blindfolded oxen working the shadoofs were steadily raising the sweet water in order to irrigate the fields.

They came to a house, a large, square building, and the gatekeeper threw himself down into the dust at Per Ibsen's feet.

'Faith, Health, Strength,' he cried. 'The lord cometh, just as it was predicted he would!'

Zarah, holding back, nervously cradling the minute Nefer, was freshly afraid. She cried out in terror when a servingwoman ran out, arms outstretched, to take the baby. Then she gasped, unable to to believe the evidence of her eyes. A

large black woman was helping a tall, thin old man to walk
forward.

For a moment it seemed to Zarah that the whole world
was spinning fast. She was so filled with emotion—so afraid
that this was a dream born out of wanting—that she felt
faint. It was hardly possible to breathe. They were still
advancing, the two dearly beloveds for whom she had
searched so long.

All the wild longing, the hope, the adoration welled up
inside. All she could do—when she wanted to shout aloud
her joy—was to whisper, 'My Lord Caiphus! Nadia!' Then,
with tears streaming down her face, she went to them and
slowly sank to her knees at her lord master's feet.

And Caiphus's frail, veined hand rested gently, in blessing, upon her head and he quite unashamedly wept. Nadia
laughed aloud, and cried out, 'My child has arrived at last!
O praise be to God! The child of my heart is here and now
I'll be happy for all the days of my life.'

Then Zarah was clasped against a large, loving, bosom
and she closed her tired eyes and felt like that long-ago little
child again. As if from many miles away, she heard Caiphus's sweet old voice saying, 'My own daughter! My
Morning Light! My soul begins to sing at last.'

A feast was prepared. There was great rejoicing. Music
played. Everyone made much of Zarah and Nefer, and all
were in awe of the noble Per Ibsen. Pretty serving-girls
thronged round his brave men and plied them with beer and
meat and bread. More visitors came and greeted the great
lord who had honoured the humble village on this grand and
glorious day. And to every one Per Ibsen touched his head
and his breast in greeting, and gave his wide slow smile.

Dancing-girls and singers came in and they clapped their
hands in time with the music, just as their kind had done in
the ancient days. The wine and the beer flowed. There was
rejoicing because Caiphus the Wise had at last found one of
the children he loved. And when he asked after his son
Harad, with tears in her eyes Zarah lied. 'He had a fever,
Lord. He knew nothing! It was all over in no time at all.
Harad, your son, went to sleep and he died. It was a gentle
and merciful end.'

That night Zarah rested safe and at peace. Baby Nefer was cradled lovingly in Nadia's arms.

In her sleep, Zarah saw Per Ibsen standing on the bank of the Nile. She watched as her heart, in the shape of a little pink bird, flew out to him. He laughed joyously and caught it in his hands. Then she saw herself standing in the prow of a great ship. She was holding a lotus flower and a little jade carving of the goddess of love. In her dream she was being carried away from Per Ibsen. She wanted to jump from the ship and swim to him, to run to him, to fly! But something had happened to her legs, and she could not move.

'Per Ibsen!' she cried, and woke with a start.

The moon was smiling, a great silver circle floating in the sky. Zarah left her couch and walked outside. All was quiet, the whole world a mosaic of black and white. Then she saw Per Ibsen. He was standing very still and tall, staring ahead. Perhaps it was the alchemy of the moonlight, she thought, but he seemed sad, somehow, and very alone. And she owed him so much.

Summoning up all her courage she crept nearer to him. He heard her soft approach and swung round. Before he could order her to leave, she stepped near to him, her hands out to grasp his arms shyly.

'Lord,' she said breathlessly. 'You have brought about such magic as will make my heart happy for all the days of my life. Caiphus and Nadia are so dear to me.'

'Then I am pleased,' he told her casually. 'My part in the affair was little enough.'

'There is—something else that I wish to say—that I wish you to know,' she whispered. 'I have your permission to speak?'

'If it is important, not else.'

'I think it is. It was something I was told long after the—event—occurred.'

'Oh?'

'Lord, there was a lotus flower and a little jade statue sent to me once. It was an expression of love.'

'Really?' His face was hard now, his lips curved down.

'I never received the gifts.' she said urgently. 'O please, Per Ibsen, understand! It was all a plot to bring about my downfall. The message you received from my lady Bentresht was a ruse to make me seem an enemy of the queen. Nebutu, priestess of Bast, explained all these things to me. O Per Ibsen, please understand. I did not reject your gifts!'

'Had you received them,' his eyes were watchful now, 'what then?'

She looked up at him and felt helpless as she admitted, 'Lord, I think I would have kept them—but I do not know for sure.'

'And now?' There was still an urgency about him as he questioned her. 'What now?'

'I know that I will treasure the idea of those gifts for ever—in my heart. Just learning about them has been as precious as any real present. They are as real and as wonderful to me as the little gold scarab that Thickneck put in my hand on the day his freedom was proclaimed.'

Suddenly she was in his arms and he was looking down at her with a wondrously tender expression in his eyes. She melted against him, bewitched and bewildered because the gods of Egypt were playing such terrible tricks. Per Ibsen was as out of reach as was the earth from the stars. But she wanted—she needed. . .

Very gently he held her away, and her name on his lips sounded impossibly sweet.

'I thank you for telling me this, Zarah,' he said in his deep quiet way. 'And as for the rest. . .'

'I will owe you a debt of gratitude as large and as everlasting as the great pyramid,' she told him breathlessly. 'O Per Ibsen, I can never ever thank you enough!'

'I want nothing out of gratitude,' he said quickly, and she wondered at his rapid change of mood. Even so, on a sudden impulse, she stood on tiptoe and brushed her lips against his. Then, in panic, she turned and ran back to the tent.

The next morning Zarah went in search of Per Ibsen, only to find that he had left the house of Caiphus long before dawn. . .

As was the custom, Queen Hatshepsut went to the bank of the Nile to call upon it to rise, and in the name of Re, to give new life to all. It was hotter than usual, and the fan-bearers

worked with a will that the queen might feel the sweet breath
of air. Slaves stood by, whisks for winged pests at the ready
in their hands. There seemed to be more than the usual number of flies.

In spite of the great queen's command, the Nile did not
rise fully that year. The river deity turned deaf ears to the
gods. The people were uneasy and worked hard to irrigate
the fields. Then the locusts came and devoured what pitiful
harvest there was. After the locusts, the sun blazed down
harder than before. Then a strange fever came to the land.
Rampant, it spread.

Much of the grain in the store-bins was found to be spoiled
and had turned sour. Cattle took the fever, too. Men and
beasts sank to the ground in such numbers, and so many
children and old people died, that it was believed that Egypt
was cursed.

Fat flies multiplied and animal carcasses seemed alive and
moving under the weight of wriggling maggots. The stench
was so appalling that ships did not call in. They stretched
taut their sails and made their slaves row with a will, back
to their own pure sweet lands where there was no plague.

Senenmut, beloved of the queen, took the fever. In mortal
terror, Hatshepsut had him carried to her own private room.
The bedposts were protecting gods, and the bed itself was
supported by lions, their gilded tongues protruding from
wide-open mouths.

Hatshepsut called for the greatest physicians in the land
and offered them a mountain of gold if they would bring
about a cure.

But the queen's own man stepped away from the bed, saying, 'The lord Senenmut will climb aboard the ship of the
father the sun this night. There is nothing that we can do.'

'No!' gasped the queen, and her eyes were wild. 'It is not
my will!'

'It is the will of Amun,' the physician replied, and winced
as My Majesty dealt him a stinging blow with her flail.

'The sign of life will save him. It must and it shall!' the
queen cried, and she placed a golden, richly jewelled *ankh* in
Senenmut's fiery hot hand.

But the sign of life did not work its magic and Senenmut
died. At this, Hatshepsut screamed wildly. Her women

wailed and struck their own foreheads in mourning. It took many people to move the queen, for she rent her clothes and threw herself on the body of her love. And she fought and scratched those that had dared to try to pull her away.

Thutmose heard of the death of Senenmut, the kindly man who had been his tutor, and unashamedly wept, as did Per Ibsen and all of the members of the royal house who remembered the loving clasp of his open and friendly hand.

'He did many good things,' Prince Thutmose said. 'He was a fine and gentle man. It is sad that he was so blinded by the queen.'

'He was just and merciful,' Per Ibsen replied. 'And it was he who warned me that all would not be well for Zarah, wife of Ramose, if she stayed.'

'The great Hatshepsut has done many wicked things in our lord father's name,' Prince Thutmose observed. 'For what she wished to do, and since she sent the evil eye to all she disliked, God has punished her. She has lost her Senenmut—and Zarah of Anshan has been spared. But I do not know the story of this Zarah. Tell me more.'

But Per Ibsen feigned deafness, and did not reply.

Hatshepsut, being told of this conversation, felt hate for Zarah glittering in the centre of the grief that had made a tight band of her brain. She shut herself away in her sanctuary, and from there she climbed the steps to stand at last on the immense flat plain of the roof. For a long time she stood still, looking up into the sky. Then, with tears rolling down her cheeks, she began to whisper to Senenmut.

'O Beloved, you are with Ra and free to mingle with the stars and the moon. You live with beauty. You live free! Behold, I shall demand scented air for thy nostrils. You will take the form of a great falcon in the sky. You will sail on flood waters, as your life begins anew. But, O my soul, amid all of this wonder and splendour, do not forget me!'

She listened to the night and heard only the wind. Her eyes searched but saw not his face, only a cloud veiling the moon. With dragging steps and reddened eyes, she made her way down the stone stairway and back into her room.

The next day Hatshepsut rose from her bed, and her face was bitter and hard. She had Bek whipped cruelly because

he dared to sing a song of love. Her eyes turned evilly to those
she had once looked on as friends. Slaves trembled and bent
under her flail. A maid-servant laughed and was sent to be
stoned. She made it known that Senenmut was to be put in
a tomb on a site usually reserved for those of royal blood.
There were gasps at this, and looks of disbelief, but She
Whose Word is Law had spoken. It was enough.

After the embalming, the funeral procession formed and
Senenmut began his journey to his final resting-place. It was
near the summit of a large peak whose opening yawned like
a black gaping mouth. Reverently the mummiform coffin
was placed inside the sarcophagus, and human voices were
raised in response to the priests as they carried out the ancient
ritual for the dead.

Hatshepsut's eyes narrowed, catlike, as she stared intently
at each mourner in turn. She knew of their disapproval and
her lip curled. She saw that Thutmose was visibly moved and
all of those who had, as children, played in the royal house.
They had all run to her beloved in turn, and not one had
been refused encouragement and help. Now here they were,
hypocritically praying to the God of the Dead, asking for
joy everlasting for Senenmut's soul. But deep down they were
thinking it was sacrilege that a man not of royal blood was
to have his earthly resting-place here in the Valley of the
Kings.

'I am the living Horus,' she whispered to herself. 'And I
shall be Osiris one day. And then we shall see just where my
beloved Senenmut stands. Then, as now, my word shall be
law.'

A smile that glittered like glass gleamed in her eyes as she
looked again at Thutmose and at the men who stood near.
She saw Per Ibsen and thought again how he had visited
Senenmut, who in turn had come to her to plead for
Ramose's life. Yes, that was what it had all been about. Did
Thutmose honestly believe that he was the only one who
employed spies?

While she was a good and noble queen, her throne was
secure. She needed only to see out the end of the pestilence
and Zarah's tongue cut out of her head and the way would
be clear. There was one thing that she was determined on:

she would never take Thutmose as lawful husband of the queen. To stop that, she would again claim she was Pharaoh. She would don the false beard and wear the king's clothes. All the world would learn of the holy conception of Hatshepsut, Pharaoh-Queen of the Nile. . .

The river rose fully the following year. The plague had long ago faded and there were no more untimely deaths in the land. No more miserable funeral barges slowly crossing the holy waves.

The locusts did not return to ravage the new grain, and the fat-bellied flies had long gone. Peace reigned, and the people took heart and went the way of the queen. They, like she, believed that it was only the rumours of warmongers that kept insisting that there were even more enemies gathering at the borders. That it was all nonsense that there were at least three foreign princes awaiting their chance to break in through Egypt's back door.

Proudly, arrogantly, Hatshepsut faced her dithering advisers. 'My duty is to keep my two lands united,' she said in her clipped, superior way. 'I take the weight of the world on my shoulders. I wear the red and white crowns of the Two Kingdoms on my own aching head. I alone, as the living Horus, can bring prosperity to Upper Egypt and to Lower Egypt too. I am the Great One Most High. I am Makare.'

'Amun!' they breathed, not daring to look up into her coldly glittering eyes. 'Amun!'

'I serve the gods.' Her voice held venom. 'I am the living Horus, and in time I will be as God in the sky. I govern according to the gods' own laws.'

'Amun. O Great One. You are as the Invisible One. We bow to you—who are God. Who are as Amun.'

'I will be advised by you, my officials, ministers and scribes.' The queen pressed home her point. 'But the final word is mine, and that word is Peace. I turn my face away from war. Beware lest I turn my face away from you.'

Because the queen was determined to have her own way and needed the vast army of labourers behind her, she became graciousness itself to the people who lived out their ordinary lives. She smiled down benignly upon their bowing, bald heads. She welcomed merchants and traders. She watched the scribes at work. She took interest in the tax-collectors and praised the skill of the craftsmen. She spent a great deal of her time at the fine temple that Senenmut had designed for her alone. Feeling closest to him there, his work was all round her, holding her within granite arms.

As her lover had promised, the celebrated voyage to Punt was depicted in living colour on the walls. The full story was there. How the royal ships had brought back myrrh resin and living trees. These, replanted, were even now growing in the garden of the temple. There were pictures, too, of the very fat black queen of the land of Punt and the rather skinny king.

Hatshepsut was full of praise for her painters and sculptors who had to obey such very strict rules. Everything must be drawn in the right proportions and show people in certain poses. This because, as all knew, the picture in a tomb would come alive in the next world, when the priests said the right prayers and spells.

'Place a likeness of the beloved Senenmut in my temple,' the queen ordered. 'I will have him there.'

Trembling, the sculptor obeyed, but knew he was damned. Senenmut was not of royal blood. He had no claim to live with the queen in the hereafter. If it was discovered what he had done, the sky would fall in.

Hatshepsut went often to the small secret alcove where Senenmut's statue stood. It showed him how My Majesty wanted him to be for ever—young, handsome and strong. And the fearful rumour of her sacrilege grew. It was now a growing speculation among those who lived in the royal house that perhaps My Majesty was going mad.

But the ordinary people of Egypt saw only a gracious queen. She who watched over them and saw to it that their bellies were full. They sang praises to her. They rejoiced that her workmen were paid so handsomely and regularly for their labours in clothing, wine, oil and food. They were happy in Egypt's peaceful, traditional ways.

Thutmose's anger and frustration grew. The queen no longer allowed him in the Audience Hall. He needed something to turn the people against her. He needed to have the power given to him by the people to turn the enemy away. But My Majesty was the law while the population and the priests so willed. He needed something or someone to blacken her name. Someone whom the people would believe.

The prince thought of Ranofru, daughter of the queen, who had sought seclusion in the temple of Amun; and of her friend Nebutu, who was now a priestess in the temple of Bast. There was one other name nudging at his mind. Then it came: Zarah!

'Send for Per Ibsen,' he said. 'And for the Grand Vizier, Rekhmire.'

But Rekhmire, the Grand Vizier, had a better idea. . .

Zarah was happy and at peace. Nefer was a glowing, beautiful child who was already walking and had teeth like pearls. The house in which she lived with Caiphus, Nadia and all their staff was graciousness itself. It was beautifully decorated and furnished, with wooden beds, tables, chairs, stools and storage-chests of all shapes and sizes. There were many fine vessels made of blue faience. The lovely gardens were Caiphus's pride and delight.

It came as a shock to Zarah to learn that the house belonged to Per Ibsen.

'How can this be?' she asked Nadia. 'I do not understand.'

'Our lord master was ill unto death,' Nadia told her. 'He could not get over losing you. As the years went by, matters grew worse. Then the lord Per Ibsen came. He looked after our master and gave him the use of this house. He told us of a young desert woman who was always calling out Caiphus's name. He said that when the time was right, he would bring her to us.'

'He knew!'

'My child, Per Ibsen is a great and wise man.'

'Who sides with Prince Thutmose, Nadia. My lord Ramose stood for the queen.'

'Princes and queens, I care nothing for them,' Nadia said comfortably, and wheezed as she gave her great laugh. 'All I care is that our beloved Eastern Brightness and our baby, who is thrice beautiful, are where they so rightfully belong.'

'O Nadia, how dearly I love you,' Zarah whispered. 'I cried for you before my baby was born.'

'And, light of my life, throughout these years old Nadia has cried out for you!'

Petted and spoilt, Zarah began to laugh and sing again. Caiphus became rich, for his fame grew. So it was that Zarah was able now, quite openly, to kneel and learn at his feet. These days she chose to wear the linen dress of Egypt and did not copy Caiphus's more Persian robes. She wore much jewellery: a wide circlet on her head, earrings, necklaces of many kinds, anklets, bracelets. These were fashioned from gold, silver and semi-precious stones, or glazed beads, shells and polished pebbles of bright pretty colours. But her most precious possession of all was a small gold scarab, one that Thickneck had bought for the price of his fine plumage all that time ago.

'One day Thickneck will come,' Zarah told Nadia. 'He is the finest and most dearly beloved in the world. I do not know what is keeping him, but I am sure he will find me. His duty to my lord husband was completed two years ago. One day he will come. He must, if only to tell me that my daughter should have been called Nefer-Nefer-Nefer, the Thrice Beautiful. He rejected the name his own parents gave him, you know. He—He called me Morning Light.'

'It is about the same, I would say. Eastern Brightness, Dawn, New Day.'

'So Thickneck believed. O, sweet Nadia, why am I not allowed to leave this place? I want to return to my house. Thickneck, whose real name is Napata, might be waiting there for me. If he is not, the servants might be able to tell me where he is.'

'We gave our word to keep you here,' Nadia told her for the hundredth time. 'Would you break that oath and bring disgrace on the lord Caiphus's head?'

Zarah knew she would not. She had always known that Caiphus's word was stronger than chains. Yet she kept seeing visions of Thickneck, and she could not drown the cold voice of reason that was whispering in her head. By his absence, it surely meant that the dearest, most precious Thickneck was dead?

The thought made her reach out blindly for her beautiful child and hold her close.

'O Nefer-Nefer-Nefer, my Thrice Beautiful,' she whispered against a diminutive ear. 'I am so afraid. So very, very afraid. Fate seems determined to bring about the death of everyone I love.'

Tears blinded her eyes and she rocked her little girl in her arms. She wondered desperately if she had had to lose Thickneck in order to find Nadia and Caiphus whom she so dearly adored. But Thickneck was her friend and her guardian. She had to know what had happened to him.

She had an idea: Per Ibsen might help. This was his house. She was his prisoner, she knew. But he was all-powerful. He was high in the land. He was probably in the palace with the prince and the queen. He was where there lived the eyes and the ears of the world. Per Ibsen needed only to snap his strong brown fingers and Thickneck would be found. She must get word to him.

Zarah gave Nefer into Nadia's care and went to search for Caiphus. But he was sitting in the garden speaking to two friends who, as he did, studied many esoteric things. She sat quietly in her lord master's shadow, and waited for the moment when she could speak.

When the two men had gone, Caiphus turned to her.

'You are sad, my child, and I believed that you were happy under this roof. Tell me, are you not showered with love?'

'O my lord Caiphus,' she said quietly. 'What I bear in my heart for you is too deep for words. But now I must speak of some things that you do not know. I wish you to understand why I am begging you to break the oath you made to Per Ibsen, the prince's man. It is all to do with my past.'

And there, kneeling at her old master's feet, she told him of her life in Judas's hands. In this story she kept up her lie, saying that Harad had got away, as he planned. That the boy had died of the fever, peacefully, before he could do anything to save her, or reach the father he loved. But above all else, even over her adoration of her lord husband Ramose, there came out of her story her abiding love for the eunuch, Thickneck, who had always been her mentor and friend.

'He—He regularly risked his life, merely by coming with me, Lord,' she whispered, 'when I travelled round disguised as a wise woman and a teller of tales. I hid my face from all eyes, and at the end of each session I would openly ask for news of you.'

'I did not know, my child,' Caiphus said gently. 'I believed you to be dead, and Harad too. I wandered from place to place, looking for you, for all those years. Then I became mortally ill. Per Ibsen found me and brought me here, to one of his houses, and he said that I must get well and strong. He also promised to bring you back safe to me, one day.' He frowned then, and was clearly puzzled as he asked, 'Tell me, how is it that you were able to be accepted as a wise woman?'

'I remembered all that the Young Master and I learned from you, Lord.' She bent her head at the admission. 'Forgive me for daring to presume, but it was all that I knew.'

'And now, Zarah? What do you wish to do now?'

'To find Thickneck,' she said eagerly. 'To care for him if he needs me, just as he cared for me when I needed him. And I have thought of a way, Master. A way in which I can go looking for my dear Thickneck and yet still not break your word. You gave your oath that Zarah, wife of Ramose, would stay here in this house. You said nothing about holding the desert fortune-teller, she who is also the teller of tales.'

Caiphus put his hand gently on her lowered head and stroked her shining dark hair.

'I will give up my ox, my ass and all that I own, my daughter. But I will not give up you.'

'But Thickneck might be in need of me,' she pleaded, and her tears fell anew. 'He might be ill and helpless somewhere.'

'Your man could be dead.'

'Then, Master, I must find out. Let me go, I beg of you.'

'We will travel together,' he said thoughtfully. 'A wise magus and his wise daughter. We will search for the one who was so good to you. But we will leave Nefer with Nadia so that Per Ibsen can see that we still keep faith.'

She began to tremble at that, and her momentary expression of delight changed to one of distress.

'Leave my daughter, Lord?'

'She will be safe here with Nadia,' said Caiphus sternly. 'Whoever heard of a wise woman with a child? But do not let us speak of Nefer; let us consider this. From this day you must learn all that I can teach you. When I am at one with the dead you must tread in my footsteps, as would have Harad my son. I shall give you an inheritance of great wisdom whether you will it or no. This because as a wise woman and a soothsayer your future will be assured in all lands. All men, and all women too, are afraid of the evil eye. We will spread the words of your magic, thus all will be afraid to bring anger to your heart. You will be safe, Zarah. Thus do I love you.'

And Zarah nuzzled her head in the old man's lap. She was overcome with all that he meant to do. But as to his magic and the power of the evil eye, she had her own thoughts.

Judas the slaver had been a very superstitious man, but this had not stopped him when he decided to steal her, and torture and kill the old magus's son.

Caiphus was excited and pleased at what he was about to do, and began making plans for the journey. What they would take with them, where they would go and what they would do. He was a tent-dweller; the caravan trail was his way of life. His whole mode of living had been one of freedom, his ceiling the sky with its moon and stars.

He had been grateful for Per Ibsen's house because he had been ill and frail. Now he was whole again, and happy, for he had Zarah to live for. There was purpose to his living once again. He set about gathering provisions and decided that they would travel to Thebes by boat, as was the Egyptian way, rather than use camels like the desert-dwellers who journeyed overland.

Zarah went along with it all, her thoughts sad at leaving Nefer, but she felt relief that at last she was going to do something constructive again about finding Thickneck. Her conviction that he needed her grew.

She was holding Nefer's hand, and walking in the garden, telling her a story of a princess named Beautiful who owned a magic green bird, when a servant came running.

'Come quickly! There is something wrong. Caiphus our lord master clasped at his chest, moaned and fell down!'

Zarah ran with Nefer in her arms. She ran as if her feet had grown wings.

She was too late. Caiphus had died.

With a deep heartbroken cry, Zarah knelt on the ground and cradled the fragile old man in her arms. Then she began rocking him backwards and forwards, reverently and gently, just as she rocked Nefer to sleep at night. Tears blurred her eyes and made the world a pain-weary blur. In her mind's eye she saw Caiphus as he had once been, tall and strong and alive. She had loved him as dearly as she would have loved the father who had been murdered on the salt flats all those years ago. And Caiphus had loved her. Dear, wonderful Caiphus, who had steadfastly refused Judas's gold and who had lost his only beloved son for his pains.

She thought of Harad and gasped in her agony and began to sob because she could not bear her memories. She could see Harad now, her boy master, so handsome, so brave, so young! He had walked out to face them, erect and beautiful, showing no fear, and she had wanted to run to him, to do anything to save him, give anything! But she had been bound and helpless, a little girl, her limbs cruelly tied. They had tortured him and, towards the end, he had tried to crawl towards where he knew she was. Then, spent, he had rested his poor head in the dust and tried to close his glazed eyes. All the while she was screaming in her heart and her soul. An awful tormented screaming that had stretched out to eternity, and was only a part of the nightmare of it all.

Far away, Zarah heard a screaming that held all the desolation and tragedy in the world. Dimly she realised that she ought to stop screaming, that it was all wrong, she would frighten Nefer. But the screams just went on. Then in all her loss and despair she heard herself crying out to the gods to help her, and all the gods had the faces of Per Ibsen. Then she called out his name, high and wild with all the agony of a broken heart, but she was too crazed with grief to know.

Per Ibsen had been recalled to the palace. He went joyfully, for the prince and he had been friends since the days of their childhood. It had been Per Ibsen a mere step behind the prince on the day of the Incident. This had been during a procession which had formed behind the statue of Amun. Then, 'O!' the people gasped; 'O, how can this be?' Amun and the priests and the holy procession had left the road they should have taken and gone towards the place where the young prince was standing; then they stopped in front of him, as if the god meant to designate his son.

All of these things Per Ibsen recalled as he hurried to the prince and his supporters. Once in his presence, he crossed his arms at his breast and bowed.

'Life, Health, Strength, Majesty.'

'It is pleasing to see you,' Thutmose replied. 'I have worrying matters on my mind. I have long been aware of Egypt's soft belly. But the queen, obsessed with gold and the pleasures of this world, does not seem to mind that the princes of Djahi and Retjnu are already concentrating their forces at Megiddo.'

'O Great One,' Per Ibsen said. 'They are not directly threatening Egypt.'

'It does not take a prophet to see that they will be dangerous. I will not tolerate this. I for one can never forget that there was a time when a Hyksos king sat on Egypt's throne. It is my plan, therefore, to begin to prepare now. Behind the queen's back if necessary. Our land must and will be ready at all times.'

There was a great deal of discussion after that, and Per Ibsen sat watching and learning, and agreeing with most of what had been said. But his heart was full of thoughts of the exquisite little Zarah. Was he cursed, he wondered, to have to live with her for ever on his mind? Thutmose sent his defenders away, and they were bright-eyed, delighted at the turn of events. Even the old fortune-teller agreed that the signs were right, and all the omens were set fair.

Now they were alone, Thutmose called for wine for himself and his friends, and as they drank, the prince said, 'Your task is to go north, my friend. I want you to gather together all free men willing to be mercenaries. I want only those who are brave enough and clever enough to take up arms in spite of the queen.'

'I bow at your command,' Per Ibsen replied. 'But I would remind the great Thutmose that my true work is not chasing from one end of the earth to the other. I am devoted to you and would lay down my life for your cause, but my true wish is to stay here and continue my work. My fingers itch to fashion and shape granite and stone. My mind is full of pictures of the great temples I wish to build in your name. Buildings that will ensure my lord Thutmose the Third lives for ever.'

'I know,' Thutmose replied, 'and I was in two minds. But reason told me that you are the best man to go. You have always been a leader of men and—' here Thutmose slapped his thigh and laughed aloud '—and, by Set and all devils, I swear there have been times when you have all but led me by the nose! Even so, my mind is made up. You will go. You speak many dialects; you're cool and calm; they'll trust you and come along.'

'Lord, I. . .'

'Enough, friend, I will have my way in this. Carry your duties well and I will think on the matter again. Surely you are willing to do this thing for your Pharaoh and friend?'

Per Ibsen bowed low before the man he had known and revered all the days of his life. There could be no further argument. He would have to go, leave the lush goldenness of Thebes and the sweet waters of the Nile. Yet his proud heart was being cut in two. His choice was to stay near Zarah, to continue to have news of her every day. In his position of power, by his very closeness to the prince, it would have been simple to take Zarah as his own, take her and keep her with him for ever. He could make her bend to his will. He could treat her as captor, servant or slave. He could marry her. But, watching her, feeling for her as he did, he knew that none of that would be any use. He wanted, needed, Zarah's love. To have her without her true love would be like living with a beautiful statue and nothing else.

Now his thoughts were bleak. He admitted to himself that he had a great fear of losing her again. He needed to stay, needed to let her see that he was reliable and on her side. He wanted to. . .

'Your wish is my command, O Prince,' he said, and obediently allowed himself to be dismissed.

CHAPTER NINE

RANOFRU, DAUGHTER of the queen, was told that her mother was mentally ill. She called for a litter and, hidden from all eyes by a fine blue linen curtain, she was carried away from the temple of Amun. She was obeying the orders of Thutmose the prince.

'To the great house,' she ordered and the men ran easily and well to the palace of the queen. Once there, she dismissed the litter-bearers and made her way inside. She entered via a secret passage that was known only to those of royal blood.

Ranofru found Hatshesput sitting in the holy private sanctum. She looked well enough. Her face was an unlined beautiful mask of oil and paint. Her hair was pulled tightly back and hidden under her tall red hat, decorated with fine bands of gold. Rubies were set in the wide collar and in her armbands, bracelets and anklets. Rubies also hung like red tears from the lobes of her ears. And then Ranofru looked, for the first time, into her mother's eyes, and saw such an expression in them that she threw herself down in supplication and in great fear.

'What are you doing here?' the queen asked in a clipped, metallic voice. 'Why does the lover of Thutmose come here?'

'O Great Mother, I. . .'

'Great Queen!' Hatshepsut cut in. 'I am your Great Queen!'

'Hail, O Great One, Most High.'

'Why have you come here!'

'I heard that you had been ill, Majesty.'

'I had a broken heart when my beloved Senenmut died. You did not come to me then.'

'I—I was afraid.'

Hatshepsut's eyes glittered and she began tapping the arms of her chair with her brightly painted nails.

'And—' she asked '—you are not afraid now?'

If possible, Ranofru's face grew more pale.

'I am very afraid, O Queen. But I came just the same.'

'Again, I ask why?'

'It has been said that you stayed alone. That you were going inwards to commune with your spirit instead of living this life. I—I left the temple of Amun in order to bring God's comfort to you.'

'So! You have been cowering in the temple of God! You, who are the lover of my nephew. You, who would see me toppled from the throne in his favour, have dared to hide from my sight in the very temple that I maintain with gold? I whose rightful place is the throne of Horus?'

'Majesty, I. . .'

Hatshepsut looked evil now, and she was in full spate.

'Chnum the Creator modelled me on his wheel and the god Thoth recorded the event. Is that not enough for the lovers of Thutmose?' she asked furiously. 'Is it not sufficient that I have restored the temple of Hathor which the Hyksos destroyed during the last great war? Have I not brought back trade and good relations with Byblos? Are our quays not groaning under the weight of timber from the land of Nega, and have I not reopened Sinai's turquoise-mines?'

'O One Above Us as the Stars,' Ranofru sobbed, 'you have achieved many great and wondrous things. Hail to thy might!'

'I am like all Pharaohs who have sat on Egypt's throne.' The Queen's tone became faintly smug. 'Since I adore all luxury. But I am more exacting than they, for I demand as much for the gods as for myself. Who but Hatshepsut gilds obelisks so that they illuminate the land like the sun? I have given gold to the Temple of God until Egypt bleeds—and what do I get in return?' The queen's voice began to rise in a dangerous way. Her eyes began to dilate. 'In return I get a temple that hides in its heart a traitor to me.'

'No, Majesty. No!'

'Why have you come here? What great attraction has suddenly beckoned you out of the arms of Amun and brought you here?'

'I wish to love and care for My Majesty.'

'As Amun-ra, god of the Sun is my witness, you lie. I Makare, Pharoah of the Two Lands, insist that you deliberately lie! You creep here in hypocrisy. You are trying to spy on me for the sake of Thutmose. Just as once, long ago, I was base enough to want a slave girl to spy on him. But I stepped back. I did not do this dishonourable thing. You are no daughter of mine!'

'O Beloved Majesty, I. . .'

'Zarah! That was the name!' The queen's lips were twisted now and all reason had gone. 'It was Zarah. She whose safety provoked Senenmut to take Thutmose's side!'

'No!' Ranofru panted. 'Senenmut wanted Ramose to work for him. That was all. It was Per Ibsen who worried about Zarah.'

'Do not breathe that name!' the queen shrieked, and leapt at the grovelling Ranofru. She pulled the girl's head back by grasping her hair and in one swift moment she had used her long ceremonial sacrificial knife. The rubies in its hilt matched the colour that spread in a thin line across Ranofru's throat. The girl's eyes were wide open and held an expression of surprise. She made one gasping sound as she expired. As she did so, Hatshepsut smiled, dropped the knife and seemed satisfied. She let go of her daughter's hair and the head slipped back into place. The queen clapped her hands together and the man on guard outside appeared.

He gave nothing of his thoughts away. His face was stony as he touched first his forehead and then his breast and waited silently for the Queen's orders.

'Take this spy away,' Hatshepsut hissed. 'See to it that the remains are fed to the wild dogs. Make sure that neither spirit nor soul can find their way back to any part of this foul body again. Hack it to pieces and feed it to the jackals and to the carrion birds. Dispose of it.'

In that way Hatshepsut ensured that her daughter would for ever rot in the darkness of hell.

As the guard knelt down to grasp the body, the blue linen dress slipped to one side. A long, thin-bladed knife, very lethal, came into view. Ranofru's intentions were now quite plain.

'So!' Hatshepsut said silkily. 'I was the winner of the game! I always felt that Ranofru was a little too slow.'

She was still laughing to herself as they carried her daughter's body away.

'My Majesty is as good as dead,' Thutmose said clearly. 'For her own sake, she must be detained. She will be loved and cared for. She is the living Horus, but until she is well, it is I, Thutmose, who will hold Egypt's reins.'

After that it was Thutmose who went to Divine service in Hatshepsut's place, and, the ceremony over, he was as God himself. He instead of Hatshepsut now had the power to transmit the life-essence to his statues, for now he was the counterpart of Ra. But as yet the priests advised that the people should not know.

Alone, apart from her servants and slaves, Hatshepsut was able to order them at will. She heard from the gossip of maids that a wondrous woman had appeared. One who could tell the future, unravel the past and tell tales. And this wondrous person went daily to the ruined temple and spoke to the people. And they were always swayed by her words.

'O She Whose Word is Law, it is very strange. The storyteller always begins and ends the same way,' the queen's maid said. 'But her tales are as rich and beautiful as wine.'

'And what does she say?'

At the beginning she says, 'My name is Zarah, and I must forever hide my face.'

'Zarah!' Hatshepsut breathed, and her eyes began to glitter feverishly. 'And how does she bring her speech to an end?'

'She asks for the wherabouts of a man called Thickneck. Then she explains that he was given the birthname of Napata, and that he was born in the kingdom of Kush.'

It cannot be the same.' Hatshepsut hissed and narrowed her eyes, seeing through the slits the corpse with a thin line of blood seeping from round its throat. For one terrible moment a thought jigged like a crazy demon in the forefront of her mind. Her daughter was there, with open eyes, jaw dropped. Her daughter Ranofru. 'Zarah is dead,' she said firmly. 'I tell you, Zarah of Anshan has gone from this life!'

But late that night, sleepless and alone, the strange and crazy figures leapt again into the queen's mind. She saw her daughter, who had betrayed her out of love for Thutmose, the would-be usurper. Then she saw the Persian girl who had so correctly forecast the signs.

'She said I would always reign alone, Beloved!' Hatshepsut cried out to her departed love. 'She is a bringer of bad luck, a devil from hell casting her spell upon us. She is magic; how else could she have survived all this time? I will put an end to her once and for all. She will step aboard the Boat of Death, my dearest heart, and we will be revenged!'

The next morning, Bek, the beautiful musician who remained faithful to his queen, was asked to play a favourite tune on the lute. Hatshepsut made much of him and with her own hand, popped grapes into his mouth. When he was too bemused, and almost in tears of joy because of My Majesty's kindness to him, she whispered in his ear.

'My faithful Bek, I want you to take a message for me. It must be a secret between us. I want a certain man to come and see me here. He must arrive and depart unseen. My beloved Bek, do you think this can be arranged?'

'Majesty!' Bek agreed.

And so it was done. Wen-Amun came in secret to the queen's private apartment. His eyes were deep and cold and as empty of expression as a frog of the marsh. As he made his obligatory obeisance, Hatshepsut stripped a small fortune from her fingers and arms. Rings with enormous rubies, emeralds and turquoises. Armbands of great width, worth a ransom in gold. With cool deliberation she dropped all these wondrous things at Wen-Amun's small, narrow feet.

'You will see to it, Wen-Amun, that all those even remotely connected with the House of Ramose will be wiped from the face of the earth. All the family and the servants must go. There is a cousin, I believe. Kill him and everyone belonging to him. Make sure that Zarah of Anshan cannot escape if she is hiding there. Go to the old retainer. His name, so I have been told, is Pemu. He knows all things to do with the family. Make him speak. I will leave the details to you, of how this can be brought about. If necessary, cut him into a million living pieces. Make him tell you where you can find

Zarah of Anshan. Then kill her slowly—in my name.'

Soulless black eyes stared into the queen's fevered gaze. Not a word was spoken, but, almost as though hypnotised, she took from round her neck the thick gold collar given to her by her father. It was a glory with its coloured panels of jewels, its fine workmanship. Wen-Amun was unable to hide his greed then, and his hand shot out to take the collar that was beyond price. With cold deliberation Hatshepsut dropped the treasure on the floor, then turned her back and walked away, slowly and with great dignity. But Wen-Amun was not watching. He was too busy scrabbling on the ground.

Two days later the whole of Egypt was numb with shock at the massacres of the cousin of Ramose, his kin and his staff. Even the babies were not spared, or the horses of which the family were so proud. The assassins had even gone to other homes, rich and poor, to kill any who had carried the banner bearing the Ramose name. Pemu, old, crusty, unafraid of death, had nothing to say. Wen-Amun went to the house of Zarah, but learned the girl had gone. Even so, rivers of blood were spilled, and now even the most fervent supporters of the queen felt that she had gone too far! Yes, it had to be My Majesty. There was no other who would dare to perpetrate such cruelties.

Seeing his chance, Thutmose began openly to gather men together. He promised them great victories. He was generous to his new recruits, offering them plenty of good food, plenty of wine and even small gold rings. It seemed that the coffers of Egypt were never-ending in the service of war.

The news filtered through Hatshepsut. She flew into a rage of hate against Thutmose, whom so many were now openly naming king. She beat at the outer door with her hands until they bled.

'Let me free!' she screamed. 'Let me go to my people and tell them the folly of this thing. I order you to set me free!'

But the people round her melted away and left her hammering until she was exhausted and spent.

Hatshepsut's condition deteriorated after that. Her eyes grew stranger. Always she cried out longingly for Senenmut, not knowing that Thutmose had already destroyed the little statue of her lover that had been so carefully placed in her tomb. Her fear grew, that Senenmut was too happy in heaven. She felt terror, for she felt that he might forget her in his joy of the Elysian fields. She grew weak, yet still she raged against the one who had taken her place. She knew pain, terrible pain in her head, yet she embraced it, begging it to increase so that it might bring about her death.

The royal physician was sent for. He considered carefully, then quietly suggested that it would be best to drill a hole in the bone that covered her brain. Hatshepsut laughed aloud and begged him to continue. He bowed very deeply and sent a message to the prince.

'O Great One, it is my opinion that there grows a lump in My Majesty's brain. As a last resource I would remove a circular section of bone from the Great One's skull. With God on our side, I can make her well.'

Thutmose looked down his nose. 'That cannot be. It is a risk that I am not prepared to take.'

'O Valiant Bull!' The physician accepted without question that he was speaking to the Pharoah. 'Hatshepsut is in great and most terrible pain.'

'Then that,' Thutmose said calmly, 'is the will of Amun.'

'Amun!' his courtiers whispered in awe, 'Amun!'

Thutmose took in a deep breath that expanded his powerful chest. He had a heart loyal to his friends, to whom he sometimes looked for advice. When he had refused to save Queen Hatshepsut's life, he was glad that Per Ibsen was away on an expedition to the north, in order to raise troops. Thutmose felt that Per Ibsen was like the beloved Senenmut, and perhaps a far too forgiving man.

The physician once again visited the queen. She was sitting bolt upright on her golden chair, in agony. Seeing her bravery and her pride made him feel as though his heart were cut in two.

'Majesty,' he told her carefully. 'I have a potion that will take away your pain. I believe that such a mercy will be good in the eyes of Amun.'

She raised her hand, palm facing, in agreement to this, and watched as he poured white powder into a dish of red wine without saying a word.

The physician gave her the potion. Her lips curved faintly as she thanked him for what he had done. He threw himself down, full length, his face hidden so that not even the queen could see his tears.

Hatshepsut's eyes became enlarged, the pupils went black. With a great effort she raised herself, pushing aside the help of a weeping Bek.

Alone, proud, remote from them now, she slowly left the chair. With dignity she walked to where she could look out at the beds of cornflowers that Senenmut had so loved. Then she opened her arms wide and her voice was husky with love, agony and tears.

'Senenmut,' she breathed. 'I leave this earth. I will fly to you and you will hold me in your arms. No matter what they have done to us in life, we will cling together in the next. O Beloved, please—please be there, waiting for me.'

The queen stood there for a very long time and her lips were moving, making no sound, as she pleaded and begged Senenmut to be there when she stepped off the boat and into the Realm of the Dead.

No one dared approach her. There were many who had tears in their eyes. Others who watched and waited began to fear that she would not die. Then the whispering stopped, and My Majesty breathed her last sweet breath of life. She gasped once, then sank, with ineffable grace, to the ground. She, who had held all of Egypt in her hand, had reigned for twenty years.

Then the wailing began and the beating of breasts, and terror mingled with the grief of Hatshepsut's true friends. While she lived, they had been secure. Her death would most certainly mean their end.

In the market place there were whispers that Thutmose had caused the drowning of the physician who had brought about the merciful death of the queen. He most certainly attacked the Queen's monuments. He had her name obliterated from her statues, not only in Thebes but in the provinces. The fragments of her statues were scattered far and wide so that she could not return to her likenesses and so live again. He defaced her tablets with hammers and destroyed the sphinxes that bore her face, such was his loathing and hate.

But it was rumoured that it was out of sheer jealousy that he ripped out Senenmut's shrine. . . He caught the assassin, Wen-Amun. Wen-Amun was tied to a stake in the desert and left to die.

Warm and welcome, the sun lay like thick butter over all. The people of the village of Khepera on the bank of the Nile grouped themselves under the palm trees and watched the desert lady in awe. Her voice was sweet, but as her story unfolded, it held all the expression in the world. She was able to carry her audience along with her and they were entranced by the story of Ra.

Zarah watched their faces. The old and the young, her audiences were always the same. Those who worked, did so all the hours of the day. Even the fishermen, and here in the village of Khepera, the people owed their very existence to the size of the catch.

After many moons in her search, she had heard that it was believed that the lady of the House of Ramose had been kidnapped and killed, and that the majordomo and the giant Napata had been poisoned. The majordomo was old, and had succumbed. The black giant was a different matter. He had been too strong and tough to die.

'Then, tell me,' she had pleaded, 'what happened to him?'

'O!' She had been told in nervous whispers. 'He was taken away and hidden. He was an enemy of the queen, as had been the lord Ramose and his wife. No one knew where Napata of Kush went, not then or now. He is probably dead.'

'Who were his friends?'

'He had one whom he loved above all others: Zarah of Anshan was her name. And after Zarah, there were the fishermen. He had always been found in their company. He enjoyed to laugh and talk with them as he carved away at his models of cats and fishes, cows and little boats.'

Zarah faltered in her story-telling, her eyes filled with tears. He is not dead, she thought desperately. I would know if he was. I would feel it in my bones. If only Per Ibsen were here. I know that he would help me if he could.

She remembered how he had been when Nefer had been born. Her heart began beating at her thoughts, and at his understanding on the journey that they had taken to the safety of Nadia and Caiphus, in Per Ibsen's house. And during that journey they had spoken of Thickneck because the Egyptian had been curious about him. She had to be careful not to tell him the whole truth, but in a small, breathless voice she had said, 'Per Ibsen, there was a time in my life when I found myself alone. I had no parents with me, no brothers or sisters, no one of my own. I did not even have a nice old cat to love. I was very afraid.'

'And you were very small, I remember,' Per Ibsen replied. 'Indeed, in terror of everyone, including Ramose, the first time I saw you on the boat.'

'I was never in terror of Thickneck,' she had replied. 'And I will always adore him and call him dearest friend.'

Zarah came back to the present. Her listeners were clamouring to her to continue the tale. Out of the corner of her eye she saw a tall young fisherman watching her. His hair was long and fringed, his eyes elongated and not painted. But he had used eyedrops of kohl so they looked big and black. Here, where the breezes always raised irritating dust, kohl was a necessary balm, as was the green malachite.

The fisherman was strong and dark, his muscles rippling and shining from the oil in his skin. His gaze was intent.

'Go on,' the audience cried. 'Tell us more of the story of Ra.'

Zarah continued until the tale reached its satisfactory conclusion, and with much delight at the happy ending, gradually the people wandered away. Watching them, she felt despair. She had so hoped and prayed for news of Thickneck. The old man whom she had questioned had said Khepera village. True, he had whispered the name in fear and dread since it was claimed that the Great Queen had a mile-long ear, but she had been so sure that she was on the right track at last.

Before she had begun her story, while eating bread and onions with the villagers and drinking pale honey-beer, she had asked for Napata of Kush, and had all but gone on bended knees for news, any news of her beloved old friend. But, apart from one or two hard and suspicious looks—indeed she had been glad that little Nefer was safe with Nadia in Per Ibsen's house—there had been none, nothing at all.

Teti and her husband Cheops, of slow, honest, peasant stock, Zarah's servants, were waiting for her near the well. A meal would have been prepared for her and a secluded spot where she could rest, but Zarah felt agitated and unsure, whereas she had been so certain before. Again a vision of Per Ibsen came before her eyes, and her heart reached out to her memory. Per Ibsen, who had saved her then, could find Thickneck now if the eunuch still lived. And, deep inside, she was sure that he did.

She forgot her reverie because the fisherman was walking over. He stopped in front of her and smiled in a confident way.

He said, 'You asked a question—before you began your story.'

'Yes.' Her heart began to beat with hope and excitement. 'Yes, I did.'

'And what will you give me if I answer that question?'

'I can give you gold bands, or I can give you a sack of grain. The choice will be yours.' She stepped towards him eagerly. 'I will call my servants,' she said, 'and we will go with you. When I learn all that you know, I will give you all that you ask.'

'We will go alone,' he said firmly. 'And I will see your face and your form. My price will be what it will be.'

'I will not go with you,' she told him, and turned away, her flowing desert robe swirling in the dust.

'See this!' the fisherman said, and held out a small gold scarab bearing Thickneck's name. The very scarab that she had given him in return for the one she wore at her heart, which was, to her, the most precious jewel that she owned. She bit her lower lip, but her need to find Thickneck outweighed her fear. She signalled to Teti and Cheops to stay where they were and wait.

'I am Pepi,' the man said as they walked away in the direction of the river bank. 'And I want you to stay with me in my house for two days and two nights. On the morning of the third day, the one whom you seek will come.'

'He is alive and well? He. . . You are sure?' She was laughing and crying, half wild with disbelief and hope.

'I swear in the name of Amun. I swear by Ra. I swear on my mother's soul! And if you do as I say, I will send word, and on the third day Napata of Kush, who is even now still hiding from the Queen's men, will come. He told me that when he received the scarab, he would know you were here.'

Pepi took Zarah to a mud and wattle house built near the river. It was set near a bed of reeds and stood alone. There was only one room, and the brick cooking-oven was situated outside.

'My house is small and poor,' Pepi said ruefully. 'But it gives shelter against cold nights and from sandstorms.'

'It is a very nice house.'

'It is a verminous hole!' he said, and smiled widely. 'But my own. I do have a chair, and you will sit on my chair. I will sit beside you and we will watch the river together. In a little while we will eat, and perhaps you will tell me a story. Then, when we are both ready, we will go into the house—or lie out here in the rushes, if you prefer.'

He went inside and came out with a wooden folding chair that had a leather seat. He set it down for Zarah and stood for a moment just smiling lazily into her wide eyes. He was a fine figure of a man, but not much taller than she. Then he turned away and squinted across the river before turning back again to Zarah, who was sitting as obediently as a small girl.

'It is the capriciousness of gods that formed the ways of the Nile,' he said in a companionable way, 'which makes the holy river extremely lovable, I would say.'

She remained silent, and he went on.

'Who else but a god would make the wind blow from north to south while the Nile itself flows from south to north? Do you not see how contrary it is, O Teller of Tales? A sailor travelling northwards has the current flowing with him, which makes rowing easier, but there is no wind for the sails. On the return journey, the wind is with him and the sails push out, full-breasted, like a woman in need. If the wind drops, well—rowing against the current has never been an easy task.'

Zarah listened politely as Pepi continued to speak. Clearly he loved the great Nile and spoke with affection about Hapi, the river god. But she was only half listening because she knew that very soon she would have to be honest with the fisherman. He would be far from pleased when he learned that she had no intention of staying with him, in his house, for the time it would take Thickneck to arrive. There was a pulse beating frantically in her throat as she realised how helpless she was, alone with such a charming, roguish man, but she had to try. For the beloved Thickneck, she had to. Then she began to relax a little. Pepi was speaking of other things.

'I loved my mother, for she was noble, quiet and kind. She is buried safe now amid her possessions in the dry sand. One day, when I can, I will place a carved stone above her so that the gods will guard her by both night and day.'

'What of your father?' Zarah asked politely. 'Did you have the good fortune to know him?'

'Ai, and I loved him well. He was a sailor of the best kind, for he left the river and would sail out of its mouth into the Great Green. He worked on a trader that sank in a storm—with all hands.'

'I am sorry,' Zarah said, and her eyes were sad as she thought of the sailor who must have looked very much like Pepi, drowning all alone in the great green sea.

'His going meant that there was only myself to provide for my mother, child though I was at the time. 'However,' he grinned, 'one way or another, I saw to it that she never starved. Neither will she go hungry in the Afterworld. She has dried fish to eat, and a dish of grain, onions and even bread. She has her own small folding chair to sit on and a small jar of scented oil, for which I gave all of two catches. I know that the oil will be her proudest possession.'

'You are a fine and honourable son,' Zarah whispered, and felt her heart ache for a mother and father that she had never known. 'You were blessed by the gods to have been given such parents.'

'I know,' he replied, and followed her gaze to watch an enormous flat-bottomed barge being towed by a great many small boats. It was carrying a stone obelisk, cut from the southern granite quarries.

'That is destined for the harbour at Thebes. All of the world finishes up there at one time or another.' His laughing eyes were suddenly on her. 'Are you afraid?' he challenged. 'Being alone here with me?'

'How can I be afraid of someone who so loved his mother?'

'Are you afraid of showing me your face?'

'I am not afraid—of you.' With a small defiant gesture, she let her linen mask fall away. He stared at her in silence.

Then he said, 'I can see that you could never be a woman of Pepi the fisherman. You belong in a noble house, a temple, to the land of the gods, not in the hut of. . .'

'A friend?' she cut in sweetly. 'Yes, a great friend, Pepi, who is going to help me find someone that I have loved since I was a child. And I will be happy and proud to share your home for the required two days and nights.'

'And I will be as proud to guard you,' he asserted. 'I will position myself so that no one will pass even near to where you lie. I am of common stock and proud of it, and I recognise that you are of a far different species from me. Even so, I. . .' He stepped towards her, looking ready to throw caution to the four winds, but she shook her head.

'Do not even think about it, Pepi. I am not good enough for you, neither am I strong enough to be a fisherman's wife. I know nothing of fish. I cannot help with the catching of them, the cleaning of them, the bartering of them for other useful things, or selling them.' Her lips curved upwards then in a delightfully puckish but deprecating smile. 'Indeed, my good friend, I do not think I would be of any use to you at all.'

'You would be my companion. You would talk to me; tell me tales.'

'Perhaps. But you really need a good woman who will be a joy to you in all things—and who will stay permanently in your house. I cannot stay here with you; I must wait for my beloved Thickneck. When I have found him, I shall spend the days of my life caring for him—just as he cared for me when I was a child.'

'You are still a child,' Pepi told her roughly. 'A child of the gods. I am envious of Thickneck.'

'You are?' Her smile still softened her face, but now it was very sad. 'You would honestly like to be my beloved Thick-neck?'

At that Pepi fell to the ground and knelt before her, his arms outstretched, his face in the dark, beautiful earth of the river edge. When he looked up from the position in which he had given her much honour, he said, 'You are wise beyond your years, kind beyond years, and understanding beyond your years. You have shown me that it is a good thing to be Pepi, a proud and joyous thing to be Pepi, and while you stay, I will show you Pepi's ways.'

The light of the day was ebbing, but the mud wall of the house was still warm with the heat of the afternoon. Beyond the black shapes the palms made against the sky, the swiftly falling sun slashed great rents in the livid backcloth of the sky. The home of Pepi that an hour before had been drab in the full Egyptian glare was now a cut-out of gold and red. It nestled warm and inviting against a backcloth of tall reeds that fanned out like a rustling sea.

'I will gather fresh rushes to spread on the floor for you,' Pepi said. 'They will be thick and sweet-smelling. You will sleep easily in my house, and you will be safe.'

'I know,' she whispered and smiled at him, her expression full of faith and trust.

That night, while she slept, Pepi stretched out before his house and kept guard.

Throughout the next two days and long into the evenings, Zarah was made much of by Pepi and the fisherfolk. She was taken on the river in the swiftly skimming boats and laughed aloud at the feel of the wind in her hair and the sun on her face. She learned a gay little song that praised and placated the old river god. She followed Pepi, and her lilting voice drifted over the water as she called out greetings, using the fishermen's names.

Feeling a sense of freedom that she had never experienced before, Zarah discarded her long robe and splashed in the river, waded through the warm mud, laughing as the rich-ness squelched through her toes. For a small moment of time she and Pepi were children of the river, laughing and singing and holding hands. And during those days they found a bond

of friendship that they knew would remain for the rest of
their days.

Late on the second day, as they sat together, Pepi said
quietly, 'I think that the dawn will see the breaking of Pepi's
heart. Your coming has made me see that in reality I am very
alone.'

'You have never been truly lonely,' she told him gravely.
'You had a mother and many fine and wonderful friends. I
will tell you a story, one that is for your ears alone. A special
story, Pepi, because I believe the time I have spent here with
you has been what childhood is all about. There are some
who never know a happy childhood. Believe me, I know.'

'I have known the pain of losing a fine mother. Had I a
bad childhood, I would not have known that agony.'

'A happy childhood is worth any price that has to be paid.
Love is worth more than gold. To find love is why I go from
city to city, place to place, and do not stay at one cooking-
fire. But I will tell you a story: one just for you.'

And quietly, in the moonlight, with his dark head resting
against her heart, she told him the story of the little princess
who had been brought to Thebes from far-away Anshan.

'And all was strange and terrible to her, Pepi. The whole
wide world was cruel and strange. People were wicked, for
the women smiled with their lips but had evil in their eyes.
And noblemen were busy doing their duty as they saw fit—
and were ready to make a sacrifice on the altar of a great and
fine queen. The little princess was to be sacrificed on that
altar, Pepi, sacrificed in a slow and horrible way! She sensed
it, but she was too young to understand fully. Then, one
morning, when the whole sky glowed like a pink lotus flower,
the little princess heard a strange and wondrous sound. And
she turned to her slave who was the only one she knew, and
he pointed to the waters of the Nile. The little princess had
heard the fishermen! They were singing and laughing, and
as free and as wonderful as you. And with all her heart and
soul, the little princess wished that she could live with the
fisherman. Live with them just as I have lived with you.'

'And did the story end happily, Story-teller?' Pepi asked
softly, and his shining black eyes carefully searched her face.

'The gods were good to the little princess, Pepi,' Zarah said gravely. 'They allowed her two nights and two days.'

He was very still and quiet after that, and Zarah sensed his pain. So she rocked backwards and forwards with him cradled in her arms, and she sang him the lullaby that Nadia had sung to her, and that she in turn had crooned to Nefer.

At last she said quietly, 'Pepi, if it is in my power, I promise that I will send you a wife. One who will love you and spoil you. Who will feed you well, and take your own ripe and wonderful seed into her inside. You will have fine children, Pepi, and bins full of grain. I will send you many presents and make you a rich man. I will. . .'

'You will leave me,' he said flatly. 'And there will be an end.'

'No. A beginning!' she promised. 'I will never forget.'

'There is rumour that the queen is gone for ever,' Pepi murmured. 'If that is so, there is no need for you to hide.'

She did not reply, and his eyes became wet with tears.

At last they both slept.

The next day there came the sound of running feet, and litterbearers came to a halt before the house. Pepi hurried forward as the litter was set down. Almost too afraid to move in case there had been a terrible mistake, Zarah waited. Pepi pushed aside the blue linen and helped Thickneck out. The large man looked thinner, and he was very unsure. Zarah hesitated until she saw who it was. Then she looked into his face, and knew.

'Thickneck, beloved, I am here!' she cried and ran to him, tears streaming down her face. 'O sweet friend of my life, I am here!'

He turned his head in a listening attitude, the scar on his face making him look fiercer than ever before. Then his old crooked grin spread across his features, and for that one moment it did not matter that he was blind.

CHAPTER TEN

LAUGHING AND CRYING, Zarah caught hold of Thickneck's hand.

'Beloved,' she gasped, smiling through her tears. 'I have found you at last! Tell me, what happened to you?'

'Well, Morning Light,' the husky voice remained exactly the same, 'I drank very deeply of poisoned wine the night you were taken away, and now. . .' He faltered a little but his face no longer looked so old, tired and strained. 'Now I can hear your voice and feel your hand in mine—and I am wondering if I am dead and in the Elysian fields!'

'You are alive and I am alive,' she said shakily. 'And you are at the house of Pepi the fisherman.'

'Whom I know very well,' Thickneck replied. 'He and Ay have been very good to me.'

'Who is Ay?'

'A young eunuch who gave his oath to Per Ibsen to stay with me. Per Ibsen gave Ay gold rings to barter for food and medicine and was generosity itself, but he did not expect me to stay long in this world. No matter! Ay, Pepi, and many of the fishermen have cared for me and kept me hidden from the queen's men. Now tell me, Morning Light, what has been happening to you? I thought you were gone from me for ever.'

There were tears in the poor eyes that had been unable to see, even when the poison-induced fever had gone. But tears soon turned to laughter and great joy. There was so much to say, such a great deal to tell, so much water had passed down the river. But the really big news that plump, rosy Ay came to tell them excitedly later on, was that the great queen was now Osiris, and that Thutmose III was the living Horus and sitting safely on the throne.

'O Beloved,' Zarah's eyes filled with tears all over again. 'That means that I can take you back to Per Ibsen's house openly and unafraid! I will love and cherish you, and I will look after you as you looked after me. I will. . .'

'There is Ay,' Thickneck said, and smiled his crooked, scar-pulled smile. 'He has become like a part of me. He is, quite literally, my eyes.'

'Then he will stay with us, for always and for ever. O Thickneck, we will make so many plans. You will adore my little Thrice Beautiful, whom I have named Nefer.' She laughed shakily. 'I would have given the sun and moon and stars to have had the lord Ramose enjoy one moment with her. As it is. . .'

'Your husband went safely to his tomb,' Thickneck said. 'And all that he deemed necessary went with him to use in the Afterlife too. I learned that all he desired and wished for had been carried out as planned.'

'Who—Who was responsible for that kind and marvellous deed?' Zarah asked, but deep down she knew, and was not surprised when Thickneck confirmed this.

'It was the great Per Ibsen who saw to it all.'

A proclamation was made. There were to be great changes in the land. The Pharaoh, Valiant Bull of Thebes, spoke aloud these words: 'The Holy Ureas is about spit fire in the face of my enemies. The holy goddess Hathor will give the milk of human kindness to my friends.'

'O Morning Brightness,' Thickneck said with happiness quivering in his voice. 'You will be reinstated. Blessed is Amun-Ra, God of the Sun.'

But in her moment of relief Zarah found herself thinking of Per Ibsen, and she was picturing the nobility and splendour she saw in his face. Her heart went out to him, and she was wondering where he was. . .

Per Ibsen sat outside his tent. It was night, and the sky was alive with stars. The thorn-fires of the men he had enlisted in the name of the prince were smoking and spluttering and giving out cooking-smells. Spicy bread was being dipped in saucers of oil. There was beer to drink and the juice of the grape. As well as the men, Per Ibsen had acquired many slaves and, feeling that he had done his job well, he should have been content. He was not.

His great love was architecture, and building. His joy and pastime was to sculpt proud and beautiful things. But as well as excelling in all creative things, Per Ibsen had an ear for foreign tongues and was able in turn to make himself understood. It was for this reason that he was so often torn away from the temple of Hathor that he had designed, and where he would have chosen to stay.

Now he was on the return journey and restless. He wanted to hurry, but knew that in these conditions slow and steady was the safest way. Yet he kept thinking of Zarah, the little widow of Ramose, whom he had always loved. He remembered her as she had been after the birth of her child. Delicate, but with a glow about her hard to describe.

'She is mine!' she had said, and her voice had been as soft and mellow as warm scented oil. 'After all these years, I have someone who is utterly and absolutely mine to love. Her name shall be Nefer.'

Zarah had seemed like a statue fashioned from gold. Her straight white dress had been dappled with light and shade as they had reached an oasis of palms. Her body had been half turned and her small firm breasts, thrust roundly against her fine linen, were ready to do their duty of motherhood. He had the same aching hunger for her, the same yearning of his body and mind, and he had known with utter simplicity that he would never change. That he would need and love her until the day he died.

As they drew nearer to Thebes, he found himself thinking more of the home of Hathor that Prince Thumose had allowed him to design. With Amun on his side, Per Ibsen thought, the prince would allow him to stay and continue overseeing this important work.

He stopped with his men at a house that sold beer. It was at the river's edge, and by a well-used pathway. It was a perfect place to catch up on the news.

'O landlord,' he said to the jovial man who served him. 'What is the news? I have been long away from the beauty of Thebes.'

'The Great Queen is dead, Lord, and Thutmose is Pharaoh. Now all of Egypt is preparing for war.'

At that, Per Ibsen drank his beer quickly. He called for an official scribe and had him draw up a document that bore the correct number of heads. Methodically the scribe set down the figures of the new recruits Per Ibsen had brought with him. Then the number of slaves. Men and women had separate lists, and they were all ready to serve the glory of My Majesty too. They were good people, and would serve him well.

All those who had come with Per Ibsen on his long journey were taken to the mud-brick buildings where the other soldiers were. Per Ibsen, carrying his very gratifying papyrus, hurried to the palace and asked audience of Pharaoh Thutmose III. He was granted admission to the Hall of Audience at once. He saw Pharaoh, who was wearing a blue crown, the gold ureas jutting out above his forehead in a fierce and angry way. Beside Thutmose stood his son, the young Prince Amenhotep, a handsome child with his long hair worn in the traditional sidelock, the rest of his head smoothly shaved.

Per Ibsen threw himself down, full length, at Pharaoh's feet.

'Life, Health, Strength, Per Ibsen,' Thutmose said. 'You may rise. Now speak.'

'Majesty, I bring you this.' Per Ibsen held the papyrus, and a courtier came forward to hand it to the king. He unrolled it and, seeing its length and the large amount of figures thereon, he was well pleased.

'You have done well, O friend,' Thutmose said. 'And I have brushed aside all opposition. I will make war! And I will be acclaimed the greatest of all warrior kings. I will extend our empire to its widest limits. In their time the Hyksos brought the outside world forcibly to us. Now it is our turn! We will take Egypt gloriously to foreign fields. I will be greater than my grandfather, whose name I bear.'

'My soul cries out to serve you,' Per Ibsen said to the king with whom he had played in the palace gardens as boys. 'My life is yours from everlasting to everlasting.'

'You are my right hand, Per Ibsen, and you are dear to me, but you must stay here. You must see to it that my funerary temple is far greater than that of Hatshepsut. I need you to work on beautiful monuments that bear my seal. While my title is visible, Thutmose, Valiant Bull of Thebes, will live on through the ages. No man dies while there are those living and breathing aloud his name.'

'Majesty!'

'I will be gracious to you. You shall have vast treasures and be responsible for many hundred cubits of land. Your name will be known as Pharaoh's friend throughout the world. You will be a prince, Per Ibsen, and hold reins of power. And all I ask is that you build great monuments, bearing my name and my message of adoration to the gods. They must give me their blessings, Per Ibsen, and smile on me. Now you may leave this place and have some time for rest and pleasure in your home. When it is the correct moment, I will send for you again.'

Happy that he had done well in the eyes of the king, delighted that he could at last stay at home and get on with his work, Per Ibsen made his way into the privacy of his house. To his shock and dismay Zaráh was no longer there.

The old woman servant, whom Per Ibsen had known all his life, was the only one who dared to tell him the truth. He learned of the death of Caiphus and of Zarah's never-ending search for Thickneck her friend.

'So deeply does she love this man, and so indebted to him does she feel, that she left her own child,' the old woman said, and sniffed disapprovingly. 'Left her with Nadia the nurse.'

'Nefer is here?' The relief showed on Per Ibsen's face. If the little girl was under his roof, he was certain that Zarah would return.

'O no, Lord! The black woman, Nadia, and the little Nefer are safe and sound in the Ramose House. Pharaoh Thutmose has restored with all graciousness the rights and freedoms of those that suffered at Queen Hatshepsut's hands. The lady Ramose is now rich and respected, and more: she is welcome at court.'

'What did you say?'

'It is true, Lord. The lady Ramose is a favourite of Meryetre, Thutmose's Great Royal Lady. The Lady Ramose's friend is Nebutu, priestess of Bast, who is cousin to Thutmose's wife.'

'How can this really be?' Per Ibsen was amazed.

'Ai!' The old woman told Per Ibsen in tones of great awe, 'The fame of Zarah of Anshan grows greater by the day. She told the Great Royal Wife that she would bear yet another son.'

'And did she?' Per Ibsen asked. He had not known that Meryetre carried a second child.

'All the world knows that Amenhotep now has a lord brother,' the old lady said. 'We are indeed doubly blessed.'

'And the name of the child?'

'Ahmose.'

'That is a good name,' Per Ibsen said. 'A king's name. Our Pharaoh is fortunate to have two sons.' But he was not thinking of young male heirs to the throne. He was thinking of a child that he had watched being born, and remembering the tiny creature's first plaintive cry. Nefer, she had been named.

Zarah had said with delight soon afterwards, 'I should have called her Nefer-Nefer-Nefer, for she is indeed thrice beautiful!'

He decided to go to the House of Ramose. He called for a litter and set out, longing to set eyes on Zarah again.

'She was called to the Great House,' Nadia said, and beamed her great jolly smile. 'But, Lord, you should see her child.'

'I would like to see Nefer,' Per Ibsen said, and Nadia took him up on the roof and there was Nefer, the Thrice Beautiful child. The large quiet man looked down at the naked, bejewelled, happy little girl, and thought he saw Zarah on the Theban boat again. Nefer was holding a magnificent cat who was purring and looking content. On the ground, by her feet, was a large square reed basket in which slept five kittens, all grey and tawny and very well fed.

Per Ibsen smiled as Nefer looked up at him. She was not shy of a stranger and her eyes sparkled and reflected the gold light of the necklace she wore.

'Her name is Great Mother,' she said politely. 'And the small ones are called One, Two, Three, Four and Five. Five is the smallest and prettiest of them all.'

'Then I think that I will quite like Five,' Per Ibsen said gravely. 'And I am sure that he is spoiled.'

'He is blessed,' Nefer said, 'because he is loved most. Lady Ramose, my mother, told me that love is the most wonderful gift of all.'

'I am sure she is right.'

'My mother is wise and she is kind, and she is the best story-teller in the whole of the land.'

'I know,' Per Ibsen said, and remembered the small veiled figure sitting on her stone seat, enthralling her audience, spell-binding them while her own aching heart was seeking and yearning to find the old man that she had so loved.

He remembered how he had himself gone in search for Caiphus the Wise, and how the old man had wept with joy when he had quietly mentioned Zarah's name. And, learning of Zarah, how she had been found abandoned in the salt flats and of her life after that, Per Ibsen found himself almost coming to love the fine old man. Now Zarah had lost Caiphus and Ramose, but most of all she had lost the huge and splendid Napata, the Thickneck who had been her mentor and guide.

'My lady mother tells Thickneck many stories,' Nefer went on in a companionable way. 'She can make him laugh and she can make him cry, but best of all he says that she can make him see!'

'Thickneck?' he asked, amazed. 'She tells stories to Thickneck, you say? He is blind?'

'He loves her, and he loves fat merry Ay, who stays at his side. But, most of all, he says that he loves me.'

'I am sure he does,' Per Ibsen agreed.

'The lady Ramose, my mother, loves us all. She is kind and gentle and she prays at the Temple of Bast. Great Mother was born in the temple, you know, and the lady Nebutu gave her, as a very special present, to me. Great Mother is a very important and wondrous cat. Pepi catches her many fine fish.'

'Pepi?' Per Ibsen was bemused with the pretty little girl whose perfect golden figure was so generously decorated with gold armbands and necklaces and small gold hoops at her ears. A few years older, drape the small naked figure in fine blue, hang it with little bells, and Nefer would be her mother all over again—apart from in character, of course.

Zarah had been fragile, afraid and shy. Her eyes had always held the mystery of distant dreams. Only too often they had been shadowed by grief. One needed to protect and adore Zarah, to be gentle and treat her with infinite care. But this little person with large, shining eyes was confidence and joyousness itself. Unlike her mother, Nefer had never known a day of want or true sorrow. Nefer was a lovely, very fortunate, child.

He turned and made as if to go, but Nefer was happy to continue the conversation.

'Pepi is very special and important, too,' she said. 'The lady Ramose, my mother, says that she will always love him, and that he needs a good wife.'

'Oh? And do you like Pepi?' Per Ibsen asked and his eyes went very still. 'What is so special and important about him?'

'He helped to bring Thickneck back to us. He allowed my lady mother to share his house. His old house! That has now gone, and Pepi has a new and noble place in which to live. It stands in a field of rushes, and it is by the river. I am taken to see Pepi sometimes. He is very handsome and strong. He says that, to him, my mother is like the sun and the moon.'

'And does your mother truly love him?'

'I think she must. She is always scolding him and saying that he needs a wife.' Black eyes twinkled roguishly. 'I like Pepi, and would like him to marry me.'

'Then I expect he will,' Per Ibsen said, and smiled wide and slow. 'And if he does not, will I do?'

'Ai!' Nefer said cheerfully. 'That would be very nice.'

Per Ibsen left the little girl and made his way down the stone steps to the main hall of the house. Nadia had called for wine and fruit, and it was set there in readiness for him.

'Who is Pepi?' he asked her.

Nadia chuckled richly and told him what little she knew. Reading between the lines made him coldly angry. Then he felt despair. He had been away when she had needed him. She had turned for comfort to someone named Pepi who had a great new house by the river. Pepi had helped her to find her beloved Thickneck whom he himself had given up for dead a long time ago. No wonder Zarah was looking towards the noble Pepi and telling him that he should take a wife. Who could refuse her? Who could refuse to try to clasp the silver beams of the moon?

Per Ibsen went to his litter-bearers and ordered them to take him home. He did not look back at the House of Ramose. He knew he would never look backwards again. Zarah had set her eyes on a strong handsome man. She had decided that he should take a wife. Pepi would do as he was told. . .

Per Ibsen began spending most of his days and nights in the beautiful temple of Hathor. While the workers slept in their squalid mud huts, exhausted by work and bloated with beer, he would go alone to the tremendous hypostyle hall. Here he felt closest to Hathor. He prayed to God to show him how to reach the heart of his love, but found himself to be cowardly and afraid.

Large, strong and brave in the hunt, a champion whom no one, apart from the king, could beat in any physical field, Per Ibsen was like milk and water where Zarah was concerned. He could take her and crush her and keep her for ever, no matter what she herself felt, simply because he was a favourite of the king, but this he would never do. He still desired the small, nervous little bird to hop willingly into his palm, fold her wings and be happy to stay.

He was thinking of these things as he sat with his broad back against the pillars one night, and he closed his eyes and gave himself up to his dreams. He did not hear the tiptoed approach, or see the small figure step out.

Zarah walked among the giant columns that looked so eerie in the moonlight, so alive. She felt like a pale ghost in the silver and blackness and she thought that the wind-whispers were like faint far-away prayers. And she prayed, too. She prayed that Per Ibsen would accept what she had to give. It was the only payment great enough to thank him for seeing her safely through the time when Nefer had been born. She wanted to give to him in gratitude, for he had found Caiphus for her. It had been Per Ibsen who had seen her beloved

Ramose safe on his journey to the Afterlife. It had been the large, regal, very hawklike man who had left Ay with enough gold to get Thickneck through the worst of the poison-fever that had knocked him out almost as effortlessly as the plague, and left him blind.

Thinking of Thickneck made Zarah frown. He had not been himself lately, and had been bemoaning the swift passing of the years. There was something on his mind. Something he wanted to do—but could not because he was unable to see. Then her heart lurched and she forgot Thickneck as she remembered why she had come and what she was about to do. Deep down she was afraid. Silver light glinted on anxious dark eyes and she wondered about the goddess that the great king, and surely Per Ibsen, so greatly loved. She thought of all the statues she had seen; the black stare of the avenue of sphinxes she had just walked through. They looked as though they had waited and watched throughout aeons of time.

And what of Hathor? The goddess with the pretty smile and the small cow's ears? Hathor the most favoured, for she was the goddess of love. Yes, the goddess of love, wine and music too. Hathor who bestowed all the joys of life and who was the favourite companion of Isis herself.

The moon moved slowly, floating lazily in the sky. The pillars cast long shadows and took on an almost menacing air. There came a movement behind her and she swung round, fear and anxiety on her beautiful young face.

Per Ibsen stepped forward, with the bearing of a long-ago king.

'I have been waiting for you,' he said quietly. 'And yet I feel that this is part of a dream.'

'It is no dream, Lord,' she whispered, and her pale face looking up into his was like a night-lily turning its delicate head to the moon.

'You will not change your mind?'

'I—I do not know what you mean.'

'About coming to me.'

'I am no longer a child, Per Ibsen,' she faltered. 'I wanted to come, and I wish to stay.'

'I am glad,' he said simply, and watched as she looked around her. He was still unsure and remained quiet as she

walked towards the shadows that were deep on fine warm
sand. With ineffable grace she lowered herself to the ground.
Then she turned to him and opened her arms.

- He was trembling as he knelt beside her. She looked almost
luminous in her straight white linen gown. He stared at her
for a long time and in the waiting silence there was only the
gentle cadence of their breathing and the whispering of the
sands. He could smell the heady sweetness of the perfumed
oil that she wore and see the gentle rise and fall of her high
little breasts. Her eyes were deep and dark, like fathomless
pools. Then, as he reached out to touch her, he saw little
glints of moonlight tangling in the shining beauty of her long
hair. Her hair was flowing, he thought breathlessly, flowing
and as marvellous as the holy Nile.

He wanted her with the same angry urgency he had felt
when he had first fallen in love with her all those years ago.
His heart was pounding in his throat, his mouth felt dry. He
reached out, very carefully, and pulled the shoulder-straps
of her dress away, and gasped as her breasts were bared only
for his eyes. He pulled her dress down and she lay there, on
the sand, beautiful, perfect, like a statue cut from the moon.

He leaned over her and could feel her beneath him, ripe
and warm. She was fragile, yet even so he could feel the firm-
ness of her breasts and thighs. He could feel the almost
imperceptible yielding of her body to his.

Slowly and carefully he nudged her legs wide apart. He
went inside cautiously as if he was afraid that she might
break. He was large and she small. She gasped as he filled
her completely so that she fitted round him and was stretched
tight.

He waited, all the time staring down into her flower-pale
face. Then he pressed down and, with infinite care, drew back
again. He felt her quiver beneath him and pushed down
again, a little harder this time.

Per Ibsen took his time, his movements slow and strong.
He could feel her gradually becoming alive and he gloried
in his love for this exquisitely beautiful creature, who had
taken him to the Elysian fields. She was like a harp he was
playing, and her slow, voluptuous rhythm now exactly

matched his. She was a slave, she was impaled, she was his to do with as he willed.

The stars stared down and Zarah thought that they glittered like a million polished stones. She could think of nothing, only feel the strength, the power, the indomitable masculinity of the man. She began to burn, to need him to press home. She wanted to go wild, but he was large and intransigent and made her as helpless as a small fish, one that had been pierced to its full length and was now helplessly writhing on the end of a spear.

'Per Ibsen,' she gasped. 'My sweet lord!'

He began to increase the pace and she cried out in a haze of emotion that she had never experienced before. And Per Ibsen, who had known many women, was able to control passion until the moment was right. Then he let go and took his beloved high into the dizzy clouds of ecstasy. She hung there suspended out of this world, then she began to come down to earth again like a gently descending, twinkling star.

Her eyes were wet with tears as she fell to sleep, cradled like a baby in the big man's arms.

He woke her at dawn and began all over again. Slow and smooth and with infinite power, and she gloried in every moment, for the tables were turned. Now she felt alive and fulfilled as never before. She had come to pay a debt to Per Ibsen, and felt now that she owed more, more more.

'I adore you, Princess,' he said quietly when they were lying still and at peace. 'And I feel that my cup of happiness is filled up to and over the brim. I did not dare to believe that the time would arrive when you would come to me and declare your love.'

'I, declare love, Per Ibsen?' she enquired, puzzled, and smiled warmly into his eyes. 'I came out of gratitude, to thank you for all that you did. I came to pay what I owed you in a way that I hoped you would value more greatly than gold.'

He was sitting upright now, his face more aloof and hawklike than she had ever seen it.

'You came to pay a debt, Zarah of Anshan?' he asked, and his voice was cold. His eyes glittered so that he looked ready to kill. 'You are telling me that you came—you bartered yourself because of something you thought that you owed?'

She was shocked at the bitterness, disbelief and anger she saw in his face. Rather than have such a reaction to her words, she thought wildly, she would have cut out her tongue.

'Per Ibsen,' she stammered. 'My lord?'

He had leapt to his feet and pulled her roughly to hers. He was white-faced and coldly determined to push her away.

'O woman,' he said, 'go quickly. Get out of my sight. If payment is what you had in mind, then you have paid—though I do not know what for. I have done nothing more for you than I would for any other helpless person in need. And as for the other thing. . . Well, I thought that kind of bargain was made with beautiful boys, or pretty girls learning to whore. You have shamed me, Zarah of Anshan, and by your action you have shown me just how little you respect me. You allow me no principles at all. You believe that I expected to be paid for what I did?'

'Per Ibsen!' she said, and felt frightened. 'Forgive me. You do not understand.'

'I understand very well. You were, so you believed, indebted to me. Now you have returned payment in kind. Thus you are now free of any claim I may have on your time.' He drew away from her in revulsion. 'So be it. Now you may go.'

'Let me explain,' she cried. 'Oh please allow me to explain! You do not understand. Per Ibsen, I. . .'

'Go!' His face held cold fury and utter contempt. 'I want no part of you. Your body is as sand in my eyes.' He swung on his heel and strode away, the straightness of his back, the tilt of his head and everything about him showing how furious he was.

For a moment Zarah was too stunned to do anything other than stare after him. She was cold, and her heart felt as if it had shrivelled and died. She could not bear her lord's anger, and the awful thing was that she did not understand. What had she done to warrant such monumental rage and contempt? She saw how every step he took was making a greater chasm between them. This when she had hoped and dreamed such tender things in her mind. But the fire and flowers she had experienced while in his embrace was something she could never have foreseen. She could not, would not, let Per Ibsen go now.

Her feet barely touched the ground as she ran after him, breathlessly calling his name. Stiff and arrogant, he continued to walk on. She ran after him, desperate now. She caught him up at last, and grasped his arm.

'Do not leave me,' she cried. 'You are dear to me. I want to put things right between us. My lord, I came here to you of my own free choice. Out of love. Per Ibsen, please listen to me.'

He stopped then, and stared down coldly at her anxiously pleading face.

'The "love" you have offered,' he said harshly, 'was offensive to me. What you gave to me goes by a very different name.' In sudden harsh fury he took her shoulders and shook her hard. 'After all these years, you still look on me as someone quite apart from your own true living soul. I swear that you love and respect your Kushite more than you ever will me.'

'I came to you because I wanted to,' she cried piteously and wrung her hands in despair. 'I stand before you and swear that I feel for you. How else could I have survived, if you had not come to my rescue time and time again? How could I. . .'

'I cannot bear your gratitude,' he snapped. 'I did for you only what I could have done for any helpless kitten caught up in Amun's great wrath. You owe me nothing. Most certainly you do not owe me gratitude. Now go. It is as I have already said: you gave me payment enough.'

'Have mercy on me,' she stuttered. 'Just allow me to tell you all that is in my heart?'

'I said, enough!' he repeated, and left her without a further glance. Crushed and feeling more alone than she had ever been before, Zarah returned to the litter-bearers who still waited patiently.

CHAPTER ELEVEN

THE SUN WAS creeping down the heavens in a tumult of glittering gold. It was still too hot, and there seemed no air to breathe. Zarah sat in the long room that looked out on the gardens, fanning herself with an enormous spray of dyed ostrich feathers.

Two slaves stood behind her, immobile, expressionless, worried because the lady Ramose was so quiet these days and she rarely, if ever, smiled. At a sign from her, they moved magnificent peacock fans to and fro. Wearily Zarah closed her eyes. She saw the image of Per Ibsen and tried to push the memory of him away. But her lips were trembling, her cheeks burned and she remembered again the ecstasy of being held close in his arms.

The sound of Nefer laughing happily took the tension out of Zarah's face. She heard the bubbling and teasing of the rosy-cheeked Ay, and Thickneck's hoarse voice. Zarah knew that they were sitting by the lotus pool, the two men, as always, making much of Nefer as they kept her amused.

But thoughts of Per Ibsen again intruded. Zarah sighed and felt restless, on edge, and badly wanting to cry. Far out on the river the sun was gilding the sails of the fishing boats as they made for the shore. It was a peaceful, beautiful scene.

Yet Egypt was not at peace. Thutmose had lost no time. He was already fighting fiercely on the borders of Egypt, forcing the enemy back. His great army was organised into divisions complete with units of bowmen, spearmen and those who carried the axe. There was also the crushing power of hundreds of chariots pulled magnificently by My Majesty's steeds. And that was not all. Private chariots had been for a very long time annexed for My Majesty's command.

Great ships were to carry supplies to bases in Palestine and Phoenicia as the Pharaoh marched onward, defeating any who dared to stand in his way. Interlocking garrisons were all set to keep communications sustained. Thutmose III had spent many years in Hatshepsut's shadow and so he had had plenty of time to make plans. He was ready for action now.

So fierce and powerful was Egypt's might that it became clear to the neighbouring peoples that it would be as well to accept, and be aware of, the dominance of the god Amun-Ra. Vast treasures won from fallen enemies began arriving by the shipload at gracious Thebes. It came to the people to acknowledge then that aggression was rather more lucrative than the peace they had enjoyed in Queen Hatshepsut's time.

All the men that could be spared from the fields were packed off to the borders to bear arms, and brick-builders followed, as did slaves. And as the conscripts began to walk away in double file, the people of Thebes poured into the streets to watch them go.

'Faith, Health, Strength!' they called out to the soldiers. 'May the gods give all power to you. May you be like wild bulls and lions.'

There was a fervour in the air, excitement and a great national pride. It was good to be Egyptian, good to drink the sweet waters of the Nile.

Learning that even more men were to march to join Pharaoh's troops and having herself given leave to some of her best servants and slaves, Zarah agreed to Nefer's pleas that they should go to the meeting-place to wish those they knew a fond goodbye. They had set out that morning, with presents of wine and food for their own. Nadia was firmly holding the child's hand.

There had been a great deal of excitement, noise and fuss as Zarah, Nadia and Nefer had joined the crowd and then, standing tall, lonely and proud, Zarah had seen Per Ibsen. She had hurried towards him, her lips curved in a smile. She came to a halt before him and looked beseechingly up into his face, willing him to forgive her, to understand.

Per Ibsen had stared at her coldly, and with great deliberation had turned away. She noticed the lovely woman attending him, following him with devotion in her eyes. Zarah had clenched her hands, shocked at the feeling raging through her like a wild tempest. She wanted to kill the woman. And such a seething emotion was new to her, horrible, and brought with it a feeling of distaste.

'I am Zarah of Anshan,' she whispered furiously to herself, 'not a whimpering slave. I do not need Per Ibsen, or any man. I live my own life and live it to the full. I will do what I must.'

'O Morning Brightness,' Thickneck said at her elbow. 'What did you say?'

Troubled and unhappy, Per Ibsen rode into the desert and made his way to one of the great oases. It had been an honour to be chosen to accomplish work that was divine, and it had been wondrous to draw out the temple plans and mark the lines on the sand, but the work had come to be like sour grapes to him now. He wished to be at Pharaoh's side, fighting with the army. He wished he could fight for his land—and die. Zarah had made him a payment, and the memory would feel like flowers in his mind for ever and a day. He had spoken of love, and her lips had smiled and her eyes had been wide. 'I have paid a debt,' she had said, and she had ignored his talk of the heart. She loved Pepi. A man that even the little Nefer adored. And the day would come when Pepi would take Zarah into his house as his wife.

I will leave Thebes, Per Ibsen thought. I must. It is impossible for me to stay. He stared before him, still praying that the gods would, in some magical manner, point him in the right direction. But he was perturbed by vague, premonitory fears—though not fears for himself. His intuition told him that Zarah's need of him was not yet over and done with. And, too, he felt that, no matter where he went, even to the ends of the earth, having once tasted the sheer perfection of Zarah, without her he could never be happy again.

Per Ibsen's horse started at his master's sudden wild cry of frustration and anger. 'O God, tell me why am I so unsure? O God, tell me the right thing to do!'

But God did not reply. The wilderness stretched away, barren and bare. At last, Per Ibsen walked back the way he had come. He strode beside his horse, and he and the animal were one in the shadowy existence at his feet. And Per Ibsen was remembering the shadow existences of Zarah and himself interwoven, interlocked on the warm sand on the temple ground. It came to him then to want to make enquiries about the noble Pepi, whom Zarah and Nefer so loved. And when Pepi was found, he determined, he would have him sent away to fight for Pharaoh. He, Per Ibsen, had this power! He bore the seal of an omnipotent favourite of the Lord of Two Lands.

It took only two journeys of the sun across the heavens for Per Ibsen to find out all there was about Pepi the fisherman who had helped the lady Ramose to find her beloved friend. Per Ibsen went to see for himself the fine new house that Pepi now owned and the stretch of land that had been cleared to grow vegetables.

Per Ibsen, unseen, watched Pepi come home with his fish. Saw him laughing and whistling as he sold his catch, keeping those that looked best to be dried, or else smoked, for the hard times of the year. But, most of all, Per Ibsen saw how the fisherman gave a basket of small fishes and two loaves of bread to a poor family. Now the nobleman found himself liking the fisherman, and realising how it was that Zarah numbered him among her friends.

Per Ibsen strode forward, his head higher than Pepi's by far, and he made himself known.

'Lord,' Pepi said, and bowed low, his arms stretched sideways, his hands open and wide. 'It is an honour to see you come here, and I will happily go out and catch the priests of the temple of Hathor a great many fish.'

'You do not have to give to the temple,' Per Ibsen said. 'I am quite sure that you pay enough. I have come to get to know you, for I have learned that you are the lady Ramose's dearest friend.'

Pepi stood up and grinned, his eyes now sparkling with great delight.

'The lady Ramose is my sun and my moon, O great lord. She has given me this fine house and an old woman to cook and care for me. She has been too generous and too kind, for all I did was bring to her a very old and dear friend.'

'We will drink beer together,' Per Ibsen said. 'And you and I will speak of the lady Ramose and of other pleasurable things.'

In great awe Pepi again bowed low and stretched out his arms. He was puzzled by the presence of the man who was as above him as the stars. Puzzled, and a little afraid, as he wondered whether he had been breaking any laws. But, most of all, Pepi was feeling a growing relief.

At Per Ibsen's nod he led him to where a chair was set in a shady, pretty spot fringed by tall rushes. Once Per Ibsen was seated, Pepi clapped his hands and called to the old woman to bring out beer, then, at Per Ibsen's permission, he sat himself on the ground at the nobleman's feet. He waited in silence for the great man to speak.

'Tell me how you came to know Zarah, the lady Ramose,' Per Ibsen said at last.

Careful not to tell the whole truth, Pepi explained how Zarah had come in search of Thickneck who, at the beginning of his poison-induced fever, had had a rich and powerful friend who had left gold bands for his care.

'I was that man,' Per Ibsen said. 'Go on.'

'Over the years, old Thickneck, Ay and fishermen like myself have come to be close. We are happy together and often have the same thoughts, and air the same views. Now we all have a friend and a benefactress who loves us well. She is the lady Ramose, whom some call Zarah of Anshan. And it is for Zarah of Anshan that I am so afraid. She has insisted on travelling to eyond   Mendea, which is a long way away. The plan is that, in the beginning, she and Thickneck will journey alone. She has told the eunuch Ay, whom we all like very well, that at the right and proper time he will know what to do.'

'Where is the destination to be? Tell me again,' Per Ibsen asked, and although his voice remained calm his heart was now gnawing with fear.

'I am not very sure, Lord. But what I do know is that the lady Ramose and Thickneck are journeying to a place in order to complete a pact that they both made a very long time ago.'

'Explain more fully,' Per Ibsen said sharply, and felt shaken to the core. 'Let me understand.'

Pepi shrugged expressively and told all that he knew.

'Thickneck has been unsettled lately, and he had been complaining of getting old. But he kept warning us that he could never rest in the Everlasting if he left something undone. Something that he had made a solemn oath to do. The lady Ramose was worried for him and very concerned.'

'And what is this thing that is as yet undone?'

'I am not sure, Lord. I know that the lady Ramose made the oath too. Thickneck did not desire the lady to keep this promise, but he expected full honour for himself. He was always accusing the gods of being wicked and unfeeling to have taken away his sight. That without eyes there was very little that he could do.'

'I thought that Ay was his eyes.'

'Ay had no part of this. Thickneck is fond of Ay, and would not allow him to take part in a venture that could perhaps mean his death.'

'His death? The lady Ramose and Thickneck are about to do something that could mean—death?'

'Ai, Lord,' Pepi said quietly. 'That is what I heard. And it is all the more terrible to me because I also heard that it was to be done to bring joy to my name. *My* name, Lord! I do not understand, and I am confused. I want nothing like this, and I never have.'

Per Ibsen was reaching exasperation point and felt his hands clenching and unclenching with the desire to get hold of Pepi's neck and wring out the truth.

'Tell me,' he said carefully. 'Think! Tell me exactly what was said.'

'Many things. Many plans were made. All I could really understand was that the intention was to go and buy me a very loving and beautiful wife. They travel for me! I do not understand.'

Per Ibsen's confusion grew. 'I can see no danger in their determination to get you a wife.'

'Lord, neither could I. But Ay screamed out in horror; and great tears came out of his eyes when he heard. It was Ay's reaction that made me afraid.'

'And what did Ay cry out?'

'That he would give his own eyes, ears and tongue to stop the lady Ramose and Thickneck taking the journey to the place in the Delta. The great town that lies beyond Mendean swamps.'

'Oh!' It began to make sense now, and Per Ibsen exhaled with relief. 'It is the fear of crocodiles that makes your blood run cold, Pepi, and you a fisherman too.'

'I fear nothing that I can see and fight in the river,' Pepi replied with dignity, 'and it was the horror of Ay that made me filled with unease. Ay was not worried about crocodiles—who are the pets of and considered holy by the Elephantine Priests. Ay was afraid of someone called Judas, and of someone named Neb. It is to Judas that my lady Ramose and Thickneck have gone. And ever since I have known Thickneck, he has wished Judas the slaver dead.'

'Tell me more,' Per Ibsen said fiercely, but Pepi helplessly shook his head.

Then he advised, 'My lady Ramose has one very special and close friend. . .'

'Nadia, her nurse!'

'No. Someone to whom she has confessed all the facts of her life.'

'Nebutu! The priestess in the temple of Bast?'

'Ai!' Pepi said, but he was speaking to thin air. Per Ibsen had gone.

Zarah, swathed in desert robes, her face hidden except for her eyes, sat before the fire that Thickneck had made. She knew that she was suddenly timorous, filled with doubt of her own capability. It had been the self-confidence of being 'my lady Ramose' that had carried her this far. But now she was no longer anyone except the slave child being forced to watch the terrifying torture of the boy-master, Harad.

'Thickneck,' she said quietly. 'We will live together or else die together at the end of all this. Either way, I am happy and grateful to have had you as my friend.'

'And I am content that my Lotus Flower never grew too proud, too high, to notice, love and care for something that can never be a man.'

'Has—Has it mattered so much, Beloved?' she whispered. 'Has it irreversibly blighted your life?'

'A man is fulfilled and made whole no matter what his circumstances, when he is loved,' he replied. 'My existence in Egypt has been rich and full. I have had you, and Ay, and all of my friends. I believed I was finished when I lost the sight of my eyes and could no longer carve, but with the help of Pepi I learned to weave rush baskets instead. There are always compensations of a kind.'

'Yet you cannot forget Judas.'

'Judas could not be what he is if his services were not bought and paid for by those needing slaves. But I cannot and never will forgive Judas's cruelty to those in his power. Judas is to blame—even for the piece of excretion they care to name Neb.'

'You can find it in your heart to forgive Neb?' she asked faintly, and felt sick at the memory of the man's spiteful fingers. 'You can really and truly forgive?'

'Not forgive; understand. Neb is formed as a man, yet he is not a man. Judas knew this, and Judas is cruel. Judas knew exactly how to make Neb physically and mentally squirm.' Thickneck's hoarse voice lowered and became very cold. 'Even so, Beloved, I think that it will be Neb who will be the first one I kill.'

'I—I thought that you were happy and carefree in your new life, Thickneck. For all your terrible physical losses, you had food and shelter, and those who loved you, and

people you could love. I thought that you had forgotten
the pact that we made together all those years ago.'

'It was Nefer,' Thickneck said simply, 'who made me
realise the completeness of my loss. Nefer who in so many
ways reminds me of you. Did you know that you both
share the same breathless little laugh? In Nefer, Zarah of
Anshan lives again. When I am gone, I am gone. Like my
shadow in night time, I will be swallowed in the blackness,
and there will be no son or daughter through whom my
soul can live on. My death will be my end from now to
everlasting. It is as simple as that.'

'Not so simple, Beloved,' she told him gravely. 'While
I live, so shall you. Your name will always be on my lips
and your memory will always be cradled warmly and safely
in my heart.' Her voice caught in a little sob. 'O Beloved,
hold my hand. Let me rest my head against your heart. I
will always look to you, dearest Napata. Yes, always and
for ever. And one day we will walk together, hand in hand,
through the beauty and wonder of the Elysian fields.'

He was holding her now, his crooked face full of grief,
turning sightlessly up towards the sky.

'O Morning Light,' he said after a little while. 'Are you
saying that you will be happy to die with me?'

She clung to his hand and smiled up at him like a trusting child. 'Without you, I have no past,' she said quietly.
'The future belongs to my little Nefer. The present is void,
and I am just very tired and sad.'

And she leaned against Thickneck, remembering the
boyish laughter of the young Harad, how his poor, broken body had tried to reach her towards the end of his trial.
The last time he had mouthed her name, a groaning soul-
cry of agony that would always moan deep in the heart of
the cold night winds.

She was full of the past now, choked with it, filled up
with sorrow and pain. She saw Caiphus the Wise who had
said quietly that he would as soon give up his ox, his ass
and his camels before he would give up her. How gentle
he had been, how kind! He had been her father, and now
her father had gone. Her heart and soul cried out to him,

pleaded with him, begged of him to forgive her for not reaching him in time. And Caiphus's face became mixed up with that of Ramose in her mind. Ramose who, too, had left her and had made his lonely journey to sleep in a granite bath full of brine. And, last of all, there was the large and formidable Per Ibsen who had turned on his heel and walked away. She held on even more tightly to Thickneck and gave way to her heartbreak, desolation and despair. . .

It was still in the slave compound, and the night world was closed round it like a giant cat, the moon being one open eye. Before the tightly shut gates, Zarah felt apprehension. She and Thickneck stood silently side by side mutually going back to the time when they had been considered lower than the low. Zarah began to feel sick and her stomach was churning. She felt horror as she remembered how terrible it had all been before.

'Let us go,' she whispered urgently. 'We will return to that good woman's house and accept her offer of wine, onions and bread. I—I can no longer bear to stay here. But we will most certainly go on with our plan.'

He turned without a word, and Zarah carefully led him away to the mud and wattle house that was like the rest of the buildings standing in lines. There it was warm and safe. It had four rooms of a quite decent size, and the roof space was good. From the street, Zarah led Thickneck through the entrance hall and into the living-room, whose ceiling was supported by a single column. Behind this was the kitchen and the room which Zarah would share with Thickneck, whom, they said was the Desert Lady's pet slave. He slept on the floor, at the foot of her bed.

Once he had been settled, during the day, Thickneck would sit in the lane outside the house, next to the big water-jars, near the manger that held the family cow, donkey or goat. These were of such great value that they were taken into the house at night.

Zarah came to know Tausert, the neat little lady of the house, whose husband worked with others at gathering in tall straight reeds. When Zarah was not sitting on the roof watching the children, she would join Tausert in the kitchen that contained the bread-oven, pots, bowls and a mortar and pestle for the grinding of wheat into flour.

'O Tausert,' she would say. 'It is good to find shelter in your house. It makes a great change from walking in the wilderness, for ever going from place to place. Now I have met you I am glad that my curiosity made me come here. To wait and see if the predictions were right in my dream.'

'O Wise One,' Tausert's eyes were wide with wonder, 'did you really see all of that in your dream? Tell me about it again.'

'Ai! A Theban nobleman will come here,' Zarah said firmly. 'A man who owns all the riches in the world. He will be drawn here by Fate, and he will buy a slave. And this slave will, in time, become favourite of the Pharaoh of the Two Lands. And because Pharaoh will learn that the slave came from this compound, he will shower gifts so great upon the owner that he will be as a king. I saw all of that—and I saw this place. So, now I wait to see this wondrous thing. I will know I have seen correctly if I hear of a great and noble Theban coming this way. But, of course, the man who owns the slave must say the right magical words.'

Outside in the lane Thickneck told the same story, with the addition that the Desert Lady was famous for the truth of her predictions and that she had often been called in by princes and kings to interpret the meanings of dreams. But it was not amazement at all these wondrous things that held the people. It was curiosity.

Curiosity about the one word that Judas the slaver must say. The word that would open up for him the riches of the world. That was, of course, if he knew what it was.

It was not long before Judas heard the wild, impossible story that was going the rounds. He wheezed as he laughed, and his fat belly shook. 'A slave of mine becoming a queen?' he said, and his fat fingers twitched. 'I have never heard of such a ridiculous thing in my life.'

Neb, thinner, older, more cruel by far, went among the young women and taunted them with the story that could never come true. Then he reached out with his spiteful, probing, long-nailed hands.

It was a ragged, raging, heat-hazed day when the news came that a great ship had pulled in at the harbour which lay several days' march away. And on the ship there had been a rich nobleman who was on his way to see Judas, no less.

'How can this be?' the slaver asked when he heard this news. 'And how can this man have heard of my name?'

He shook himself, dismissing the talk. There was some-one mischievous around, he thought, who was spreading rumours and playing strange games. But he went out to the compound and looked long and hard at the women there just the same. Then he ordered that they eat better and be given a little oil for their skins. Of course, just to be on the safe side.

Excitement grew, and now even the noble personages had heard of the veiled Desert Lady. She who had experienced a dream, and who had come to wait and see if it was the truth that had been foretold.

Now there was no mistake about it. None at all. A large caravan was approaching. One that was so confident and rich that it seemed the owner was above even worrying and wondering about the Great War! And there was indeed a nobleman, dressed in fine linen, with gold and rubies at his neck, and he wore gilt sandals on his feet, he was so great. He was small in stature, they said, and he had a round, rosy face. He was most excited and anxious because he needed to find out if his dream would come true.

'His dream? He had a dream?' the bemused population asked. 'Could it be that the Desert Lady was magic after all?'

'What did he dream?' asked the headman of the reed-cutters. 'Tell me, messenger, what did the rich Theban dream?'

'That he had come here, to Mendea, and found the slave merchant who had in his compound the girl of his dreams. He will be here by dawn.'

'O!' gasped the onlookers and felt awe and fear. When Zarah went out later, they flinched from her and averted their eyes.

Judas, sitting in the luxury of his home, gorging himself on the meat of a deer, heard of the advancing nobleman and of his search, and he began to believe the story, even though his senses told him that he should not. And then he began frowning, trying to remember all that he had heard. He had to be ready. The Egyptian was all but at the gates.

He paced outside and examined the slaves. He decided that beauty was in the eye of the beholder, and that no one man could judge whom it would be that the rich Theban would choose as the woman of his dreams. Then there came another, most worrying, thought. If the Desert Woman had spoken truly, he, Judas, best slaver in the world, had to know a special word. One word that would be the key to a fortune. A link with a king in time to come. A way of life to which even he had never aspired.

'What is the word?' Judas asked himself, and then everyone around him. 'What is the word?'

'Ask the Desert Lady,' Neb said silkily. 'Perhaps she who knows everything will tell you the word.'

'Go to her. Ask her.'

So Neb, who had always been the one to carry out Judas's will, hurried towards the house of Tausert, and once there he coldly and furiously ordered everyone away.

'The word is for my ears alone,' he said. 'And I will carry that word to my lord and master.'

'And claim a reward!' they laughed and jeered, and finally went away. But they waited and watched, and Neb did not leave. Finally, curiosity got the better of them, and they went near, and called out to Tausert, 'O Tausert, where is Neb, the slaver's first man? Was he not given the special word?'

'I do not know,' Tausert replied. 'I think that he went into the Desert Lady's room. Her servant is there. As far as I know, Neb of the slave-house still waits.'

At that moment Thickneck came slowly out of the house, and he looked very surprised. His blind eyes did not blink in the sun.

'Neb? Came to see my mistress? How can that be? She is not here. He must have realised this, and he must have been long gone.'

'This was impossible!' they said. No one had seen Neb leave the house of Tausert, so what magic could this be? It was all quite illogical, and also all very strange.

'There is no magic,' Thickneck said blandly. 'You must have had the sun in your eyes.'

'But he came to see the Desert Lady.'

'And I tell you that she is not here.'

Then Zarah herself came walking slowly down the lane, and bewildered, shaking their heads, the people had to believe what Thickneck had told them.

'That is all very unthinkable,' Zarah said to Tausert. 'And all very unwise. But I really believed that Judas the slaver would know the word I saw in my dream. Go and tell him that I will visit him, if that is what he would like. I will tell him, for one band of gold, the word that I saw in my dream. And if he sends me the gold band, O friend, I will give you half of what it is worth.'

As was expected, Tausert began to hurry away from her house, telling everyone what Zarah had said. They all followed her, anxious to know exactly what Judas replied.

Once they were alone, Zarah asked quietly and wretchedly, 'Is it done?'

'Ai!' Thickneck replied in such a voice that her blood ran cold. 'It is done, and quite easily. I waited and listened, and struck home when he came through the arch. He made no sound. It was quick and merciful. He will torture and maim no more. I did not need my eyes. My ears and my instincts were enough.'

'Now it has come to it,' Zarah whispered, 'I do not want to go on. Vengeance is not sweet. It is bitter and stale.'

'Speak for yourself,' Thickneck said hoarsely. 'Remember the terror and the pain they have inflicted on others. Think of all the innocent little boys and girls they have

killed. And then thank God that you are helping his
instrument, his exorciser. That is how I see myself. I am
the one dealing out vengeance in the sight of God. It is I,
Napata of Kush! You remain pure and unsullied because
you are only my ears and my eyes. The blame of this cannot be yours.'

She bit her lip until it bled under her veil. Thickneck's
words helped, but she felt the coldness in the pit of her
stomach. She could not bear the expression on his poor
blind face, as he stared ahead and began sharpening his
dagger.

'Is the lane quite empty, my Morning Light?' the big
man asked at length.

'Yes!' she breathed and looked round in fear.

'Good! Then raise your arm high over your head and
beckon them here. Ay will have remembered everything,
and it is all going to happen exactly as planned.'

And Zarah did as he told her, and stood back as two
strong men appeared. One held a sheet of white linen over
his arm. They ran into the room that Thickneck and Zarah
shared, and wrapped up the corpse that lay on the floor.
Then they carried it out and hurried away.

Tausert came back, holding a gold ring which amounted
to more riches than she had ever seen before and never
would again.

'It is for you,' Zarah told her. 'Keep it, my friend. I wish
you Faith, Health and Strength for ever.'

'O Sweet Love,' Tausert faltered, 'you speak as if you
are going to leave.'

'Perhaps soon,' Zarah replied. 'For my own home is a
long distance from here. But I will never forget your kindness, Tausert, and I will see you in my dreams.'

'Oh no!' Tausert said quickly, and backed away.

Zarah sent a runner to Judas with a message to say that
she and her slave would come soon. It would be a good
thing if he would see to it that the wooden bars of the com-
pounds, both of the men and the women, were dropped,
since it might be a good idea if the 'Interpreter of Dreams'
walked among them at some later date. Thus she could see

if the sight of them reminded her of any other character she had seen in her magical vision of night.

She and Thickneck made their way slowly to the house of Judas, and Zarah kept watch all of the time. When they came within sight of the compound walls, she saw one of her men, who signalled briefly before melting away.

'Ay has done well,' she told Thickneck. 'All has gone exactly as planned. But I still feel terrible, as though my whole body is drained. I am afraid, Beloved, and I am distressed.'

'Do not be, Lotus Flower. Think instead of all those you are about to save.'

They entered the place of Judas together. Out of greed and suspicion he had sent all his servants away. He sat on his tall chair, fat and excited. His hands, heavily ringed, were clasped together and resting on the table before him. His eyes were too bright. His colour too high. He remained in his place as Zarah entered through the square opening, and she felt horror and faint, and pulled her veil even more tightly over her face.

Judas barely took notice of the slave who accompanied the Desert Lady. He was too intent on looking at the Interpreter of Dreams, whom he had heard was so clever, so all-seeing, mysterious and strange.

'My man cannot see,' Zarah said, having ignored the barely begun greeting that Judas had mouthed. 'But he can hear very well. And he too knows the word.'

'A slave? He knows?'

'He knows you, Judas, more than I ever will,' Zarah said quietly. 'Allow him to draw near and perhaps you will remember his face. Say that he may stand in your shadow. Just say that he may. He will move towards you, finding his direction by the sound of your voice.'

'This is not regular,' Judas began, and Thickneck moved towards him, like a giant black cat stalking a mouse. 'All I need of you, Woman, is the one word that I should know.'

'The word is Harad,' Zarah said quietly.

'That is a name!'

'Ai!'

'And the Theban will expect me to know it?'

'*I* expect you to know it, but you do not,' she whispered bitterly. 'I will never forget Harad, and his name should be like the knell of doom on your soul. I will say the name once more, O Judas, so that you carry the sound to the Everlasting. Harad, I say. Harad. Harad!'

Judas was sweating. His eyes blinked rapidly in his face. He half rose from his chair, but the huge figure behind him held him down and a terrible voice said hoarsely, 'My name is the one you gave me, Judas. Carry my name to your grave. It is Thickneck, O Judas. Thickneck, I say!'

As Zarah turned blindly away, she heard Judas's high-pitched scream, then his last gasp. She fell to her knees, weeping and sick, and in that moment she was as blind as Napata of Kush, so thick were her tears.

'Come!' Thickneck said quickly. 'We must get away while we can. We have done away with a rich, very respected man. Lead me, Beloved. Lead me to those in the compound so that I may hear their cries of joy. And among them we will, of course, find Pepi a wondrous wife.'

Zarah held his hand and ran with him to where the slaves were held captive outside. The bars of the great gates were lifted, and a man, led by Ay, who had now discarded his nobleman's clothes, helped to free the dazed and unbelieving slaves. They stood there, unsure.

'Follow us,' Ay said joyfully. 'Come with us and waste not a moment of time. There is a caravan waiting to take us away from this place, to where a great ship is ready for our journey back to Thebes. O glory is the name of Thebes. O great is the name of the Nile!'

And all was rushing, and gasps of disbelief, and great silent joy, and there were also many tears of relief.

Those who had so quickly and carefully followed the orders laid down by Thickneck's men seemed to be far more numerous than Zarah had thought. And, instead of knowing all the faces of her own workmen and slaves, some of the men quietly helping them now were strangers to her.

Suddenly a tall, proud man came away from the rest, and Zarah felt faint. Her mouth went dry. She felt dizzy with joy.

Per Ibsen did not look at Zarah, but he took hold of Thickneck's arm.

'I am Per Ibsen,' he said carefully. 'I know that you cannot see me, but you know me very well. I am your friend. I speak to you in Pepi the fisherman's name. He told me to give you this ring. It is the one that you carved for him from thin pliant wood. And on it you have fashioned a fish, a special fish, and the sign of Pepi's name. It is all very exquisite work, I might say.'

Thickneck took the ring and felt its polished surface and the little scaly fish that was carved round it, complete with fine veined tail and round bulging eyes. He was suspicious, but said grudgingly, 'I carved this when I had eyes to see with—before I had to look and listen with my mind. I gave it to Pepi, and he swore that he would take it off only to be shown as a sign of good faith. Yet I am troubled. You should not be here. You are a nobleman, and this is not your concern.'

'Pepi gave it to me so that I would show it to you. He asks that you treat this ring with very great care, and take it back to him safely. And he asks that you listen to me. He says, "Life, Health and Strength to you, Napata of Kush. I, Pepi, who am your friend, and I who love the lady Ramose more than I love the sun and the moon, ask you to do this. Let the noble Per Ibsen see the lady Ramose safely back home. It will be easier if she does not travel with the large caravan—that will surely be followed by the angry people of Mendea. The noble Per Ibsen will travel far more quickly if he travels alone." That is what Pepi believes.'

Zarah's heart was beating painfully, and she had no word to say. Thickneck's lined face was frowning and uncertain, and then he turned blindly in the direction of Ay, who stated, 'I say that I have travelled with Per Ibsen and he is a lion among men. O my great friend, let the lady Ramose go. Per Ibsen will give her his undivided attention. She will be safe.'

'I will return to Thebes with Per Ibsen,' Zarah said quickly. 'Because we owe him everything—even our lives. You know this, Beloved. Trust him!' Her hands fluttered like small butterflies to cup the scowling, scarred face. 'Get home safely, you who are my rod and my staff. I will see you in Thebes.'

There was time to say no more because Per Ibsen had swung her high into his arms and was running with her outside the slave compound to where a man was waiting patiently between two kneeling camels. It took only seconds to sit on the blankets and order the animals to rise.

'Away!' Per Ibsen said sharply, and his beast went away in its long sloping stride. Zarah's camel followed in line.

Numb, hardly believing that she still lived after all the terrible things that had occurred, Zarah let her body limply jerk to and fro, in unison with the camel's lumbering gait. Ahead she could see the blurred figure of Per Ibsen, whom she hated and loved, and sometimes feared. She was too drained to wonder how he came to be here or why he had made it his concern. She was dependent on him now, and she could let go and leave it all in his hands. At least he knew what they were doing, where they were going, and why.

But she was on the first stage of a journey embarked upon with such impulsiveness and ignorance on her part— and now it was all ending. And she was in the hands of a companion who, ever since she could remember, had loomed at the back of her mind like a giant nemesis who had always been staring at her out of fathomless, handsome, dark eyes.

They journeyed on for many hours and were not following the route that would take them to the Nile. So, Zarah thought wearily, Per Ibsen had chosen the overland way. It would be many days and nights before they saw even the outskirts of Thebes. He did not stop until the moment before dawn the next day. He made his camel kneel, but Zarah sat still, where she was, too weary to move, too aching and sore. Her brain was dulled by fatigue and mental depression. There was grit in her eyes and ears, and her veil had not prevented the sand from going into her mouth.

She watched Per Ibsen moving about purposefully, with hardly a thought. She was in an uneasy world. All around her surged the vast enigmatic spread of the wilderness. It was an atmosphere shadowed now by the approaching dawn, and already she could sense something of the malignity of this awesome and empty place. She was suddenly fearful of the gigantic unknown. Then her fear was dispelled a little as she watched Per Ibsen pulling a wide linen sheet over poles he had set in the sand.

They were prepared, then. There was shelter, and probably drink and food. It would be good to try to hide from Per Ibsen how scared she was, how dependent on him. But she could not pretend. She was too unhappy and too tired.

He came towards her then, and his order to the camel was crisp and sure. The animal lurched to its knees and Per Ibsen lifted her off its back and carried her to the shelter he had made. He knelt down and deposited her on a fine woven blanket, then he smiled briefly into her tiredly blinking eyes.

'You can relax now, Lady Ramose, and rest for as long as you like. We are quite safe. The Mendeans would never find their way here.'

He left her, but returned almost at once with a dish of water. He held it to her lips and she drank thirstily, thanked him, closed her eyes and knew no more.

She did not wake until the day was almost through. She felt clammy and uncomfortable, and her eyes were dull. She saw the flickering of the fire that Per Ibsen had made, and she could smell that he had been cooking some kind of stew. She crawled from under the tent and then got to her feet. Her long desert robe clung to her. It was protection against flying sand, and was also warm. She shivered. Already the night grew cold.

'Come!' he ordered. 'Eat and drink, and then you will feel better. But refresh yourself first. You will find all that you need behind that flat rock.'

She did as he told her and found water there, and a small jar of sweet oil for her skin. She made herself comfortable, taking her time, more easy now that she was away from his view. When she returned to the fire, she was relieved and comfortable, and far more relaxed. She sat down beside him and shared the drink and the food, but barely tasted a thing. She was now only conscious of Per Ibsen, the man.

Night came almost imperceptibly. It was as if a great dark hand had been laid gently across the brooding face of the wilderness. There was no sunset, no twilight, merely a blending of matter into brown into purple. The bulbous sun was momentarily painted with scarlet and then still high in the sky, it dipped quickly and disappeared into a veil of pale dust. In the half-light, the stretching vastness was steeped in shadow.

'This is the hour of the day when you can be really aware of the wilderness,' Per Ibsen said as he leaned back against a rock and folded his arms, seeming very content. 'It seems as if it is alive and has a soul.'

She looked at him quickly, her eyes startled because it was as if he was speaking aloud her own thoughts.

'It—It is all very big—and rather frightening,' she said faintly.

'Because, if you listen, you can hear the heartbeat of the world?'

'It makes me feel lonely—and lost.'

'How can you be lost,' he asked her companionably, 'when you are here with me?'

'I—I am glad you are here,' she whispered uncertainly. 'I would like you to tell me how it is that you came with Ay.'

For a long time he did not answer, then he started to speak to her in his deep, calm voice. She closed her eyes and listened. His voice was softer and without bitterness. It was the voice of a younger, happier man. She could feel her fear and anxiety draining away, the phantoms out there beyond the firelight were no longer evil and mysterious. They were little imps beginning to smile, to dance.

And Per Ibsen spoke on, of the life he had seen Zarah go through. He had watched her weeping, laughing, loving and hating. Had witnessed her with her eyes bright with wonder at new things; her face at the moment of Nefer's birth.

As Per Ibsen talked on, her eyes opened and she looked at him, and was suddenly conscious of the poetry of the man's soul. She was conscious too of his tremendous knowledge of her. And she felt awed and humbled, and trapped, and afraid to be set free. Afraid that he would let her go.

He had been speaking effortlessly, as a man would talk who had long been starved for want of confiding.

He stopped then, and said gruffly, 'I must have been mumbling for a very long time! Forgive me. I know that you must be tired. It is getting late, and you need to retire. And take no notice of the things that I have said. It is the wilderness and the spirits of the night getting to me.'

Dismissed, still a little unsure, she did as she was told.

For a long time she lay there without sleeping, tossing and turning, trying to dismiss the pictures of Judas and Neb in her imagination. She then realised that she must have slept, because outside there was a huge moon, full and swollen, looking down on the shadowed world like Amun's all-seeing eye.

She could see Per Ibsen, his long hair tousled, his head buried in the crook of his arm, as he stretched out by the still-crackling fire. She looked again at the ghostly, brooding landscape and suddenly felt fear—a fear without explanation that gripped hold of her limbs and clawed at her brain.

'Per Ibsen,' she called softly. 'O Per Ibsen, are you asleep?'

He lifted his head questioningly.

'No. Just resting awhile.'

'Would—Would you come over here—with me?'

He remained still, silent.

'Please, O sweet lord,' she urged plaintively.

He moved slowly, and then she felt his body stretching out close against hers. She reached out her hand to push back his long hair, aware of the noble brow, the strength and pride in his face.

'I—I would like,' she said carefully, 'I would like you to stay.'

'For the night—while you are afraid?'

She wanted to cry out that she had meant she wished him to stay with her for ever. She was unable to make her lips form the words. For all he had been there to save her, for all his actions showed that he cared, deep in his mind he felt only contempt for her. She had realised that on the night he had spurned her in anger at the temple of Hathor. Her eyelids fluttered and she tried to sleep, but she began to shiver and feel panic again. She had felt no joy at the revenge, no satisfaction. There had been too much violence in her life. Even Per Ibsen had directed at her all but feelings of hate. Why? she asked herself again. Why?

Her head ached and she began shivering again. Then Per Ibsen's hand was on her forehead. She heard his quiet oath, then the concern in his voice as he said, 'You have a slight fever, nothing more. This has all been too great a strain for you to bear. I have a potion that will take the pain away. You must drink it, for it will have a quick effect. Zarah, now is the time to give me your trust.'

He was going to leave her. No! She tried to cling on to him, frantically fearing that he would leave her for ever. She loved and adored him, and always had. But she was nothing to him except the young woman he had once likened to a whore.

He freed himself, but was back in an instant.

'It will help,' he said. 'Take it for me.'

A cool liquid was forced between her chattering lips, and within a little while she was light-headed and finding herself in a strange, terrible world. She was leaning over the edge of a great precipice and watching her dearest ones fall to their deaths. There was Harad, Caiphus, Ramose, falling, falling, to a dark valley miles below. And she was screaming in her heart and mind for Per Ibsen, then saw with mounting horror that he too was plummeting down. He was diminishing in size, then soundlessly hitting rocks that jutted upwards like teeth in the mouth of a crocodile.

'Per Ibsen.' An agony of grief seared her, and anguish as bitter as gall. She was crying out to Per Ibsen, crying like a lost soul in the wilderness, for without Per Ibsen she wanted to die too.

In her dream the rocks beneath her feet crumbled and slid away. Her hands were clawing at empty air. She had the sensation of falling and the air rushing round her was like a fiery cocoon. As if from a million miles away she thought she heard a dearly beloved voice calling her name. She reached out for the voice and for love, but she was reaching for a myriad of shooting stars. And the stars were being swept away, as Per Ibsen and all those she had loved had been swept away from her life. And in the loneliness of the empty dream-world she was screaming out that the loss of Per Ibsen was the worst loss of all.

Aeons of time passed, or was it no time at all? There was a new sensation against her mouth and it was a wondrous tingling on her lips. It was curiously firm and strong, seeking, determined and yet tender. And in the deep recesses of her mind Zarah knew that a miracle had happened. She was experiencing Per Ibsen's real kiss for the first time. And this kiss held warmth, promise and infinite joy. This kiss held love!

'Zarah?' The firm lips moved over her own. 'Zarah, my dearest dear, can you hear?'

'Lord,' she whispered faintly, then again, 'Lord.'

'You are my heart and soul, my sweet breath of life,' he was saying hoarsely. 'I cannot live without you, my love. Come back to me.'

She opened her eyes and saw his beloved face so near to her own. Her lips curved in a tremulous smile as she said in a small shy voice, 'I want never to leave you. Hold me, Per Ibsen, hold me. Please hold me tight.'

'You will take my name, Princess? You will enter my house as my wife?'

'Lord.' She was quivering with emotion. 'All I know is that I want to stay with you for ever. I have always loved you, always.'

'Always?' He was smiling his proud, sweet smile.

'Yes,' she said plaintively. 'But I did not know.'

Then words were unnecessary. His great arms enfolded her and he held her tight against his heart. Her arms crept up until her hands were cupping his face.

'Love me,' she whispered. 'Please love me, Lord.'

Slowly, with infinite care and tenderness, Per Ibsen began taking her with him into the realms of ecstasy—to the kingdom of the sun.

EPILOGUE

THUTMOSE MADE great haste to undo all that Hatshepsut had achieved. The queen's reign had been characterised by a great expansion of trade and a time of peace in the land.

In no less than seventeen campaigns into Asia, which took him twice across the River Euphrates, Thutmose III annihilated all resistance.

Great fleets of ships carried supplies to bases in Palestine and Phoenicia. Communications were maintained by a system of interlocking garrisons. Thutmose was the greatest of all the warrior kings of the Eighteenth Dynasty, and he extended the Empire to its widest limits. He has been called the Napoleon of Egypt.